"WE'RE GOING TO WRITE A NEW CHAPTER IN YOUR BOOK. THE ONE WHERE TRUVY GETS HER FIRST KISS."

Before she could say anything, he captured her chin in his strong hand and turned her face. All the while he brought his head lower, he stared at her mouth. His closed lips touched hers. Lightly. Wet from snow. Cold. But as the kiss went on, warmer. Much warmer.

She could feel the blood beating in his lips. Feel the cadence in her own. Her lower lip became his sole focus; he alternated between gently suckling the flesh and softly tracing its plumpness.

Breathless, she settled into the kiss. Her first. So unexpected. Beyond her expectations. Every one of her senses was in discord. Her body felt like it was plummeting and soaring at the same time; her lungs felt oxygen-deprived. All that she had wondered about was no longer a mystery. The kiss was what *The Science of Life* had alluded to:

The appetite of sexual emotion pervades every element of our bodies and in every nerve it thrills with pleasure, or grows mad with desire demanding to be fruitful.

Pulses came to life in her that she had never imagined she could feel. So maddening with—the need for more than this. . . .

PRAISE FOR STEF ANN HOLM AND

HONEY

"Stef Ann Holm's *Honey* is a wonderfully rich, heart-warming, deeply romantic novel destined to go straight to the heart. Holm's many fans will be enthralled, and her legions of new readers will feel they have just unwrapped a very special gift."

—Amanda Quick

"Few authors paint as warm and wonderful a portrait of small-town America as Stef Ann Holm. The multi-textured plot and three-dimensional characters combined with that Americana feel create a bit of home-spun perfection."

—*Romantic Times*

"*Honey* is a fabulous historical romance [that] will gain the author an MVW (Most Valuable Writer) award."

—*Painted Rock Reviews*

"You don't have to be a sports aficionado to thoroughly enjoy *Honey*. This is also a really wonderful slice of Victorian Americana and a real winner for Ms. Holm."

—*Romance Communications*

Books by Stef Ann Holm

Hearts
Honey
Hooked
Harmony
Forget Me Not
Portraits
Crossings
Weeping Angel
Snowbird
King of the Pirates
Liberty Rose
Seasons of Gold

Published by POCKET BOOKS

STEF ANN HOLM

Hearts

SONNET BOOKS
New York London Toronto Sydney Singapore

This book is a work of fiction. Names, characters, places, and incidents are
products of the author's imagination or are used fictitiously. Any resem-
blance to actual events or locales or persons, living or dead, is entirely coin-
cidental.

An *Original* Publication of POCKET BOOKS

A Sonnet Book published by
POCKET BOOKS, a division of Simon & Schuster, Inc.
1230 Avenue of the Americas, New York, NY 10020

Copyright © 2001 by Stef Ann Holm

ISBN: 0-671-77548-0

First Sonnet Books printing February 2001

10 9 8 7 6 5 4 3 2 1

SONNET BOOKS and colophon are registered trademarks of
Simon & Schuster, Inc.

Cover design and illustration by Jim Lebbad

Printed in the U.S.A.

For Frank and Gloria Wysocki,
whose generosity enabled me to write this book
without constantly having to press the "save"
button on my old, unreliable computer. You're a
couple of swell parents—not to mention much-
loved grandparents. Thanks for everything.

Hearts

❧Prologue❧

In her many years as headmistress of the St. Francis Academy for Girls, Lucretia Pond had never encountered another teacher like Truvy Valentine. Five years ago, Lucretia had hired the Gillette's Business College graduate as an economics teacher and athletic coach. Wise or waggish, flamboyant or foolhardy, indomitable or insubordinate—no single word characterized Miss Valentine. She lived life on her own terms. And in doing so, she created her own brand of havoc—or, if Lucretia looked at it through rose-colored glasses— her own unique style.

For in truth, there were many qualities about Miss Valentine to admire.

But in reality, those qualities worthy of admiration were the precise things that put Lucretia in a precarious position with the new benefactress of the school.

Mrs. Mumford had arrived for an unannounced visit and inspection of the classrooms to view how her financial aid was being used. There had been no opportunity to take Miss Valentine aside and inform her that her best behavior was imperative. When Lucretia and Mrs. Mumford came upon her economics class, today's lesson hadn't been about social science. It had been strictly science—of the anatomy kind.

Human anatomy.

Miss Valentine had been discovered reading aloud from a nonregulation textbook. Lucretia had been too astounded by the dialogue to stop the lesson; she should have done so immediately. But her impeccable memory was able to summon the exact verbiage, and she now recited the delinquent words to Miss Valentine, who stood in front of her desk.

" 'The reproduction of the human species is not dependent on accident. Nor is it left to the caprice of the individual. It is made secure in a natural instinct which, with irresistible force and power, demands—' " Lucretia didn't know what demands were made on instinct. It was at that point that Mrs. Mumford had fainted in the doorway—as Miss Valentine gasped in surprise—and had cut off her oration. After that, feminine chaos ensued. Young girls rose from their seats with high-pitched screams of "Help!" while Miss Valentine, a vial of ammonia spirits in hand, dashed toward the prostrate dowager.

Removing her half-spectacles, Lucretia gave Miss Valentine a pointed stare.

A dark brown braid fell over one shoulder of her white shirtwaist. She'd tucked a pencil behind her ear and wore a whistle around her neck. In height, she was above average, which made her figure quite striking when she entered a room—although she'd confessed to Lucretia that she didn't think it an asset to be as tall as most men.

In the quiet that filled the office, Miss Valentine uttered a single word: "Fulfillment."

Baffled, Lucretia repeated, " 'Fulfillment'?"

"A natural instinct that demands fulfillment." Miss Valentine gave a further explanation that was so blatantly forthright, it dumbfounded Lucretia into silence. " 'It is not only sensual pleasure that is found in the gratification of this normal impulse. There also exist higher feelings of satisfaction in perpetuating one's own single—' "

"That's quite enough, Miss Valentine." Fending off the heat consuming her cheeks, Lucretia motioned with her chin toward the chair before her desk. "I wasn't aware that St. Francis offered a course on life propagation."

Miss Valentine lowered herself onto the leather cushion and conceded, "We don't."

"Then why were you teaching it? What to expect from marriage and sexual congress is a mother's duty to instruct, not ours."

"Yes, Miss Pond, but too many mothers, because of mock modesty, allow their daughters to enter into marriage in total ignorance."

"While I agree with you that women need an education on morality and modesty, what they learn and when is for their mothers to determine. Our duty is to educate in subject fundamentals." Lucretia delivered her next words in a severe voice. "You shocked Mrs. Mumford. And I daresay you've shocked *me*."

"I'm very sorry. I didn't know Mrs. Mumford was coming."

"Neither did I. But she gives this school financial aid and our doors are always open for her visits. I told you and the other teachers, the benefactress believes in the old ways of deportment and education for young ladies. It was on these terms she agreed to support us." Lucretia knit her fingers together with an air of authority she didn't like to use with Miss Valentine. "A strict classroom environment, appropriate uniforms, and proper conduct must be maintained. That means teaching only St. Francis–approved curriculum."

To say Mrs. Mumford had been offended by the textbook reading was an understatement. After she came around, Lucretia had done her best to calm the dowager, but without much success. This very moment, Mrs. Mumford rested in her private chamber with a sick headache, the tour delayed.

"I feel terrible," Miss Valentine said, straightening. "Honestly I do."

Lucretia refit her glasses over her nose. "As you *should* feel, Miss Valentine. This isn't the first time something like this has happened."

Lucretia had overlooked a broken rule here and there, simply because of Miss Valentine's devotion to her students. In spite of her spirited ways, she had a commanding gentleness. But that favorable disposition was packaged with firebrand feminism and its ideals. Miss Valentine argued that the girls should be allowed to wear modern bust girdles—a type of bosom bindery for women—and knickers while playing sports. These "indelicate items" weren't high on Lucretia's list of things for which she felt like taking Miss Valentine to task.

Bordering on the need for censure was Miss Valentine's credo akin to the Thomas motto: Girls can learn, can reason, can compete with men in the grand fields of literature, science, and conjecture. For the most part, Lucretia didn't see any overt harm in that one. However, a major infraction was today's fiasco.

She simply could not overlook such a grave error in judgment. Sexual discussions were definitely *not* within the perimeters of proper St. Francis curriculum.

To step out of bounds was unacceptable.

To do so in front of the benefactress was intolerable.

"If I spoke with Mrs. Mumford," Miss Valentine offered, "I could make her see my reasoning. Understanding is the first step toward acceptance. I would tell her that should a young woman decide not to marry, the journey in life that she'll take has to be commanded with heroism. She may have to rely chiefly on her intellectual powers, her wit, her imagination, her fancy."

"And yet you spoke of her . . ." Even Lucretia, who considered herself modern, had a difficult time of forming the words. ". . . her natural instincts. Really, Miss Valentine, that insinuates that women enjoy having relations."

"Well, Miss Pond, as unusual as that may sound, that's precisely what the book said."

"What book is this and where did you get it?"

"*The Science of Life,* and I ordered it through the mail. The doctor who wrote the book is a member of the University Medical Society and his list of credentials is impressive." Her brown eyes brightened with enthusiasm. "I've learned quite a lot about human behavior. Women's especially." But at that last thought, Miss Pond observed a puzzled lift to Miss Valentine's brows.

It was that instant of vulnerability that had Lucretia softening her tone. "I understand your heart was in the right place."

"Of course it was. The girls gathered their courage

to ask me about the subject and I couldn't refuse. Both Miss Cooper and Miss Price wouldn't talk about it if their—well, they just wouldn't talk about it. We've just entered a new century, Miss Pond." Her face was full of strength, shining with purpose and lively interest. "We're fighting for the vote. We'd better understand the anatomy of men, because that's who we're up against in getting a chance to cast our ballots. Did you know a man's brain weighs fifty ounces and a woman's is forty-four ounces? Is a mere six ounces any reason to keep us from making our opinions count?"

"In this school, it is."

"I don't see why that has to be the case."

"And that's precisely why you're in serious trouble."

The graveness in Lucretia's statement drained the animated color from Miss Valentine's cheeks. "I'm sorry. I honestly will try not to disappoint you again," she said with firm assurance.

With a heaviness in her chest, Lucretia sighed. In the five years Miss Valentine had been teaching, there had been many trials to weather, all with the same well-intended conviction. Only this time, second chances weren't an option. She was left with little choice in disciplinary measures.

"Miss Valentine, you're a wonderfully devoted teacher, but your way of teaching is broader than what we do here."

"I know I shouldn't have—"

Lucretia held up her hand for silence. The time for explanations was over. "You lived with two elderly aunts, then went to Gillette's Business College. Afterward, you came directly to us. Nearly your entire life has been spent in a school. When you applied at St. Francis and wanted to be a part of our staff, that didn't necessarily mean, however, that you were prepared to provide instruction within the bounds set by the school at which you chose to teach."

"But I *will* try. Harder."

The avowal was spoken with sincerity, but beneath the well-worn gray cashmere of her everyday dress was a zest for living she hadn't been able to tamp down behind the somber stone walls of the Boise school.

Firming her posture, Lucretia said, "I propose you go out into the world to think about what St. Francis expects from you. If you can expect that from yourself, you may return for the next term. If not, then I'm afraid . . ."

"You'd dismiss me, Miss Pond?" Her voice kept a fragile control.

"I would have no other avenue to take, my dear." She kindly spoke the endearment. "If you can fully—*without a single doubt*—accept the rules at St. Francis, I want you back here. Right now, you need to decide what you are capable of. The decision is yours."

"That's kind of you."

"Oh, Miss Valentine." Lucretia tried to keep the sadness from her tone. "I don't want to be kind. I want your energy and enthusiasm at St. Francis. But today you overstepped your authority in the classroom. I'll talk with the financial committee and the benefactress, but the matter is ultimately in your hands." She felt a pang of regret at the way things had to be. "I'm going to insist that you stay in Montana beyond your scheduled plans and spend more time with your college friend, Edwina Wolcott. It will do you good to share the company of a woman closer to your own age."

Miss Valentine's mouth opened, but she remained quiet.

Miss Pond put her unspoken fears at ease. "You needn't worry about what your students will think. I'll tell them that you're taking an extended Christmas holiday."

"But arrangements have been made for only a short-term visit."

"I don't see why they couldn't be extended. You've mentioned that the family you'll be staying with is eager to have you as a guest."

"Yes, but . . ." The words trailed off, and in their place came hesitation and remorse. "As it is, I won't be seeing my aunts this holiday. They understood because of Edwina's condition. She's due to have her baby on the twentieth. Miss Pond, I was only planning on a two-week visit. How can I—"

"Now you can be a comfort to her for longer than that." Lucretia didn't bend her resolve. "New babies need lots of helping hands."

"Yes . . . I suppose . . ." A wistfulness stole into Miss Valentine's eyes. She grew contemplative for a long while, then visibly resigned; the softening of her shoulders was a clear indication that she realized she had no alternative. "Very well, Miss Pond," she said quietly, "I'll take a leave of absence. But I will come back in a manner that's acceptable to you."

She rose, determination in her stance. "And that is a promise."

Chapter

❧ 1 ❧

For generations, the Valentines had married on Valentine's Day—every Valentine except for Truvy, who didn't have a beau, much less a prospective groom.

At the age of twenty-five, she was an old maid and a husband was no longer a shining hope on the horizon. With February the fourteenth mere months away, she resigned herself to the fact that Cupid's arrow would be passing her by. Yet again. And although it was disappointing to think that the tradition would stop with her, there was a part of her that was exhilarated and feeling . . . freed.

As the train began to slow into the Harmony depot, Truvy couldn't quell the wild trip of anticipation in her heartbeat. As much as she hated to admit it, Miss Pond was right. She needed time away from St. Francis to see what it would be like to be out on her own.

Her upset over the benefactress incident had subsided, but she took full blame. She knew she shouldn't

9

have been reading that life science book. She had stretched the boundaries and now was being disciplined for her actions. But that still didn't change her definition of teaching.

Even so, she would prove to Miss Pond she could live by the woman's rules. The girls would have nothing to gain if Truvy were ... terminated. Her position meant everything to her. She *could* teach admirably because she loved her task. And because she had a strong moral sense of obligation to her girls.

On that, she pledged to return. But for a short while, she'd be able to test her fanciful speculations about the outside world, a world that wasn't changing very fast for all the hoopla 1901 had come with—and was nearly gone with as New Year's Eve approached. There were times when Boise seemed isolated—local news, features, and editorials printed in the only paper, the *Idaho Statesman.* A long way from the buzz of the *Chicago Tribune.*

While she attended Gillette's, she really had intended on being a clerk. But Chicago was so big and fascinating that her point of view couldn't help but be affected by her surroundings. She threw herself into a variety of causes that required marching, poster pasting, and lecturing; she managed all this while keeping her academic grades flawless. Throughout college, Edwina had been the one who danced ragtime and smoked cigars and socialized. Not Truvy. She kept her nose stuck in her books, The Aunts' words always in the back of her mind:

You're the first lady Valentine to go to college, Truvy. Yes, the wonderful first. Do make us proud.

So she had. But a month before graduation, she couldn't see herself as an office typist. She wanted to be a teacher. With a business degree in basic economics, she knew she could make a difference by educating young ladies. Men thought they ruled the nation, but women governed its destiny.

And The Aunts had agreed. They'd praised her choice.

Teaching at the girls' academy was far more rewarding than filing paper and folders in cabinet drawers. She was also a sports coach. Not exactly what The Aunts had had in mind when they'd paid her tuition. But for Truvy, she had found joy on the playing field. Quite by accident, she'd discovered she had a talent for tennis.

The train's whistle sounded in a blast of steam. Its brakes screeched.

Truvy looked through the soot-covered window at the platform. She couldn't see Edwina. Or her husband, Tom, whom she'd described in her letters. A dozen or so people milled about, their breath creating misty clouds in the cold air. She scanned the group—men in heavy collared winter coats and women in fur-lined capes, some with children tagging after them.

Although Truvy wished the circumstances surrounding her departure from St. Francis were different, the trip to Harmony had been on her agenda since August and she was going to enjoy her time with Edwina.

After Gillette's, they'd written, but the opportunity to visit hadn't presented itself. Truvy had always admired, perhaps envied, Edwina her full social life in college, her unabashed enjoyment of music and dancing and club gaiety. Truvy had made no time for the amusements of youth in a schedule filled with debates at libraries and lunches celebrating women scholars.

Truvy never liked to use the word *regret*, but looking back, she realized she'd missed a lot of fun.

Fun. She tried to think of something she'd done for the "fun" of it . . . but her mind drew a blank. She could come up with many things she'd done for the zeal, the passion, the emotion—but nothing unequivocally fun.

Just before she'd left Boise, she had gone to buy a new winter cape and ended up purchasing some things on impulse. *For fun.* Her firm resolve caved to an extravagant lure she had never thought would tempt her: high-heeled shoes.

She'd never been comfortable with her height but had eventually decided to accept the fact she stood five feet ten and a quarter inches tall, which meant no heels. But after succumbing to one pair of heels, she'd been so convinced that she'd made the right choice with the shoes that she'd bought five more pairs in various styles. Beaded tan slippers, black patent with French heels, lace-ups, and two that required button-hooks.

But the stiff leather of the ladies' welt button high-tops had given her pinkie toes blisters. Which made walking without flinching difficult. The black Vici kid didn't massage her soles as the shoe salesman had proclaimed. Instead, her insteps ached from being elevated by the two-inch-high heels. It was no wonder she lived in Spalding athletic shoes. The soft kid and flat soles were quite comfortable.

"Harmony!" the porter cried as the train came to a stop.

Truvy stood, then immediately winced. She suffered graciously, smiling at the other passengers as she gathered her handbag and adjusted the angle of her new hat, a hat that was frivolously delicious and totally out of character for her but one she adored just the same. It was stacked high with blue taffetine rosettes and two quills on either side of the knobby crown. She'd never worn such a concoction. But neither had she worn such scandalous underwear.

Blushing pink. Everything. All satin. Her corset, chemise, petticoats, and pantalets. Embroidered in the most risqué little places with white butterflies and ruby-red roses. As soon as she'd put each piece on, her entire body had shivered. Wicked.

Truvy moved into the narrow aisle to exit with the others. Each step she took, she could hear the faint rustle. Could feel the cool fabric gliding between her legs, skimming over her lisle stockings. Very wicked.

Once on the iron platform, she went to grasp the railing in the narrow space with its even narrower steps. Before she could, the station porter sprinted forward and lifted his hand to offer assistance. A moment passed before her surprise evaporated; then she laid her gloved fingers in his. She smiled as he aided her in disembarking.

A porter had never tripped over himself to help her.

She thought about the reflection that had greeted her in the Pullman mirror this morning. She had indeed looked quite unlike herself with her thick brown hair piled in glossy curls, a few dangling here and there, her smart hat and blue velvet cape to match with its black soutache braided and beaded trim. Her students wouldn't recognize her stylish apparel. Oddly, it hadn't been a premeditated effort to change her appearance. She had actually liked picking out the new clothes for her trip.

The chill of the afternoon swirled around her while she took several steps on the depot planks. In spite of the nip to the air, she felt beautiful for the first time in her life. But the lift in her mood sank when she realized there was nobody to greet her.

As the crowd thinned, worry built, then ebbed through her. She hoped nothing had happened to Edwina. Today *was* the day she'd notified her she'd be arriving at two o'clock. The train hadn't been late.

Ten minutes later, she was the only passenger left at the depot. Steam wafted from the bellow of the train's engine stack as it readied to depart for the next town. And still, nobody came to collect Truvy.

"Where would you like your trunks, ma'am?" the porter asked. Both of her suitcases were stacked on a handcart he pushed in her direction.

"Do you know a Mrs. Wolcott, sir?"

"Yes, I do."

"Her husband was supposed to meet me. Is her health all right?"

"Fine as can be, last I saw her. Which was yesterday afternoon."

"Oh ... well ... hmm ..." She looked once more at the town across from the station. Dirty snow banked the boardwalk in places where the sun hadn't melted the shoveled piles. The storefronts were decorated in holly garlands and colorful trimmings for Christmas. A town square was occupied by people who strolled in front of businesses, window gazing and conversing.

A man striding toward the station caught her attention—for the simple fact that he was quite tall and broad-shouldered. Extremely so. He stood out heads above the gentlemen he passed. His legs were long and lean, propelling him forward with an effortless pace—but one that was clearly marked with hurry. Directly toward where she stood.

She swallowed.

This couldn't be Tom Wolcott. Edwina said Tom had light brown hair. And was of sound character and respected in the town. A good businessman. An upstanding citizen. The Goliath descending on her didn't look like any of those things.

Namely, because he was drinking a bottle of beer as he walked.

He crossed the street and she turned away, dread inching up her spine. She pictured Coach Thompson from Ward's—the boys' school adjacent to St. Francis. He had big hands with dark knuckle hair, and even bigger arms and legs. An athlete to the bone. She seemed to attract his type and according to *The Science of Life,* that type wasn't suited to her at all.

The chapter on "Physical Forms" clearly stated that a large partner should seek a small partner. Large-boned people should seek those of small bones. Tall people should seek short people. Beauty should seek homeliness. Nervous people should seek their opposites. Those of strong facial contour should seek those with less decided physiognomies, and so on.

Coach Thompson had proved the theory when she'd let him escort her to one of the joint school functions—the Physics Exposition. His end of the conversation had revolved around pieces of athletic equipment, pulled groins, and the best liniment brands—not the experiments. He was tall; she was tall. He taught sports; she taught sports. He considered himself an intellect; she was an intellect. He had exasperated her. Infuriated her. She had never accepted a social invitation from him again. He'd obviously thought she had no more brains than a medicine ball.

He hadn't been the only one at Ward's who'd neglected to treat her as a smart woman. The academic professors knew that along with being an economics teacher, she was an athletic director—and that was all it had taken to taint their view of her intelligence quotient.

The hair on Truvy's nape prickled. Slowly, she turned back around and there *he* was—still coming at her. And she *knew*. Knew this man had been sent to greet her.

Climbing the depot steps, he drew up to her. He swept his gaze over her in a way most men didn't: with an openly approving appraisal of her height. It discombobulated her. A brief shiver caught her shoulders.

"You've got to be Miss Valentine."

There was no surprise in his voice when he spoke her name. But he didn't sound drunk. To her chagrin, she liked the deep richness of his voice. Warm and liquor smooth.

"Yes." Tilting her chin upward, she met his eyes. They were the color of frosty green leaves. A silvery olive. She'd never seen such a shade before. He gave her a slow once-over with those eyes of his, brows rising.

"I was expecting a dowdy teacher," he said at length.

The comment made her bristle. Before she thought better of a reply, she caught herself remarking, "I was expecting Mr. Wolcott, not a man carrying alcoholic refreshment. On a public street."

He lifted the beer and stared at the amber bottle. The set of his chin suggested a stubborn streak. "I just ordered this at the Blue Flame Saloon when I checked the time. I knew I was late."

"You could have left it behind."

"Could have." And at that, he took a sip. A crescent of foam stayed on his upper lip; he licked it in such a way that she thought that beer had to taste as good as any soda pop—if not better.

She studied her escort. He might have the appearance of a very vigorous man, but to be fair, he could have a very high mental caliber. She didn't want to do to him what others did to her—pass judgment too hastily.

His hair, a rich dark brown, was clipped short and neat. He didn't wear sideburns, as was the rage with men. Nor had he shaved today, either. Dark stubble shadowed his chiseled jaw and somewhat square chin. His shoulders were far too wide; his defined biceps strained against the red plaid flannel sleeves of his shirt—a shirt that wasn't tucked into the trousers that molded his hips.

As he lowered the bottle, she noticed his hand was wide, the fingernails perfectly trimmed.

"Hey, Bruiser," the porter said with a jovial chuckle. "Bust anybody's chops today?"

Bruiser. Naturally. So much for reserving objectivity.

"Naw." Bruiser's smile was disarming.

"I've been thinking about entering the Mr. Physique contest," the porter remarked matter-of-factly. "You think you could help me beef up my muscles and show me how to knock a guy's lights out?"

"The contest isn't about knocking men out, Lou. It's about the maximum artistic development of your entire physique. You need to be strong on body definition."

"I've got strength." The porter strained and made a fist.

Truvy was certain she had more strength in her left

hand than the puny porter. But she wasn't about to debate the fact.

"If you want to enter, Lou," Bruiser said while taking another drink of beer, "come by the gymnasium and I'll sign you up. I'll put you on the rower and that'll build all your major muscles. Then you can pump some ten-pound dumbbells—"

"Mr. Bruiser," Truvy interjected. "Where is Mr. Wolcott?"

He gazed at her evenly. Her heart skipped. She didn't want to think about how it felt to have a man stare *down* at her rather than up at her or on eye level.

"I'm doing Tom a favor. He had to stay with Edwina."

Alarm caught in Truvy's pulse. "The baby's come?"

"Not yet. She wasn't feeling that great today."

"I hope it's nothing serious."

"Are you taking Miss Valentine's trunks, then, Bruiser?" the porter asked as he removed the first one from the handcart. It held her personal belongings: clothing, unmentionables, toiletries, Spalding shoes, and *The Science of Life*.

Lou went to pull the second suitcase by the handle and instantly expelled a whoosh of air. Really, the trophies inside weren't *that* heavy. She probably shouldn't have brought them all the way to Harmony. But she couldn't bear the thought of leaving them behind. They were her pride and joy. Her *fait accompli*.

"I'll take that," she said to Lou.

But before she got within inches of the suitcase's handle, Mr. Bruiser shoved his beer bottle into her grasp.

"Hold that for me, sweetheart."

Sweetheart? Not even Moose Thompson had been so brassy. Truvy made a stern face—the very one she used on her students when they didn't complete their assignments on time. "I really don't think—"

"Good," Mr. Bruiser interjected. "I like a woman who doesn't think too much."

Her jaw fell open at his gall. He'd just proven she hadn't misjudged him at all.

"Let's go." He grabbed the other suitcase in his lean hand and began to walk down the station's steps.

She quickly followed, purse in one hand, Heinrich's Lager beer in the other. "Mr. Bruiser," she called, increasing her stride to keep up with him, "I'd rather not be responsible for your beer. People will get the wrong idea about me."

"My name's Jake. Jake Brewster."

"Pardon?"

"Bruiser's just a nickname. My old boxing name. I'm Jake. Just Jake. No mister."

"I'd like for you to take this beer back."

Turning his head toward her, he gave her a shrug and an easy smile, his broad shoulders lifting. "I don't have any free hands. *And* . . . don't think I won't notice if you take a sip."

Her mouth dropped open once more. Twice within five minutes. She wasn't easily shocked. But he shocked her. She glared at him. The big oaf. Insinuating that she, a teacher and woman who carried herself with dignity and bearing, wanted to sample a drink . . . it was beyond appalling. Beyond gross offense.

She shot his back a penetrating look as she walked. The iced boardwalk crunched beneath her new shoes. Even with gloves on, her fingers grew cold from the chilled beer bottle in her grasp. Across the street, a pair of ladies stood in the doorway of Kennison's Hardware staring at her. They *tsk*ed and turned their noses up.

At first, she didn't understand. Then clarity came at her full force. "Oh ... no." She gave them a dismayed shake of her head.

She should have put up a protest at the depot and taken action sooner, but she'd been caught completely off guard. At a curbside planter, she tipped the bottle upside down. The beer poured out. She left the upended Heinrich's in the snowy dirt, dusting off her hands with a satisfied nod toward the ladies. They probably still thought the beer had been hers, but at least she'd gotten rid of it.

Hopefully, Mr. Bruiser wouldn't notice the absence of his beer until they reached their destination. There was a good chance he wouldn't. With the manners of a vagabond, he walked several feet in front of her.

They walked passed Plunkett's Mercantile and the Brooks House hotel on the corner where Jake turned up the street. Edwina had arranged for her to stay with the Plunketts, the family of her former student. The Plunketts' daughter, Hildegarde, had recently married and left a bedroom free in their home. Truvy would have stayed with the Wolcotts', but their house was under renovation, an addition for the new baby that had gotten off to a late start and wouldn't be completed in time. Truvy hadn't wanted to impose. Two under a roof where things were out of place was inconvenient. Three would have been too much of an imposition. And with Edwina's health being in question today ...

"Does Edwina live far from here?" Truvy asked.

"No. Tom said as soon as you got settled to have Mrs. Plunkett walk you over."

"Bruiser!" called a male voice. "Is the poker game on for tonight?"

Truvy turned her head. Across the street was Bruiser's Gymnasium, in front of which a fellow in athletic togs was standing, jumping up and down in the cold.

"Seven o'clock," Jake said, his deep voice carrying over the road.

"See you there."

Beer. Boxing. Poker. With vices such as those, there could hardly be a virtue to count. Mr. Bruiser fell into the Moose category. In light of that, she couldn't explain her disappointment. Disappointment seldom cured her of her expectations. She knew better. Knew that there was no man out there for her. And yet why did the book have to go and talk about the attraction of a woman to a man? Even if that man was solely unsuited for her? The doctor called it sentimentality, and a lady who felt such a thing was of a weak constitution.

She hated to think of herself as being that.

As they passed a granite-faced office building, her suitcase hinges twanged, as if the springs were under too much pressure. Seconds later, the locks sprang free and a jumble of trophies scattered onto the board-walk.

Jake stopped, as did Truvy. They both stood still and stared at the diecast bronze, silver, and gold pieces shining and glittering under the December sunshine. Some were of the goddess Nike with engravings along their base; others were replicas of softballs and tennis rackets. Several basketballs. A torch and ribbon. They represented every statuette for outstanding sports achievement she'd won for St. Francis or while being enrolled at Gillette's. The trophies signified a lot of hard work and years of practice, and they always graced the top of her dressing bureau.

Jake Brewster gave her a sideways glance as if he didn't know what to make of her all of a sudden. "What kind of a teacher are you?"

"Girls'." There was absolutely no point in explaining the trophies.

A man named Bruiser was the epitome of manhood, defined by his male friends and things deemed manly. He probably scratched himself and would no more think about bringing a lady a box of candy than the man in the moon. If she were looking for a soulmate, it would never be him. Not in a hundred years. She desired a gentleman who wore his masculinity with honor—not muscles.

She swept her gaze over his physique. Perfectly formed, honed with a sinewy grace, and a face that wasn't at all unpleasing to look at. He was brash and flawed in manners. And yet . . . her pulse raced as she met his eyes. Her breath hitched in her throat. She had never thought her body would react to a man nicknamed Bruiser. She knew better than that. She had the advantage of the wisdom in *The Science of Life*.

Jake's eyes filled with admiration she didn't want— because with it, she had learned, came bragging about their own athletic prowess, which men thought impressed sportswomen.

She veiled her discomfort and began to gather the variety of statuettes without a word of explanation. Let him wonder.

When he bent down on one knee to help, she shot him a glare that said she could do it. But he ignored her and picked up her trophy for all-around women's tennis champion, looked at the inscription, then deposited it back into the trunk. Then with quiet precision, he examined her velvet walking shoes. There hadn't been enough room in her other suitcase for the five pairs of new shoes, so they'd ended up with her trophies. She quickly put away her prizes and soon everything was safely stored back in her suitcase, the lock firmly in place. She tested it twice.

Looking at her, he said, "The only athletic sport I mastered was belting a guy and posing in my shorts."

"You don't say." She couldn't keep the sarcasm from her voice.

Because Truvy Valentine knew a courtship disaster when she was staring at one.

Jake Brewster was doing Tom Wolcott a favor by picking up Edwina's schoolmarm friend at the station—even though he knew the favor was more of a ploy to couple him off with yet another woman. From the description he'd been given of Miss Valentine, Jake had envisioned a tall woman with a severe twist in her hair—and one so gangly her flat-chested figure wouldn't fill out a corset.

Although Miss Valentine wasn't a stunner in the way a man would call a woman postcard pretty, she was a standout. The color of her cape, its rich hue of blue contrasting against the pale ivory of her skin, ignited his senses. Her hair was shiny brown, with a hint of burnished red to it when the sun caught one of the curls in just the right way. The brown of her eyes reminded him of toffee. Her nose wasn't straight and pert at the end; it had a lot of character to its shape. And her mouth—those lips with their sugary peach color—was lush and full.

"Yeah, I *do* say," he said, countering her skepticism.

Jake dragged air into his chest, expanding a fullness in his rib cage that showed off maximum pectoral definition and made his upper body look bigger. "I won the National Heavyweight Championship three years running, and at the World's Columbian Exposition in Chicago, I had top billing as 'The Strongest Man on Earth.'" That always impressed the ladies. The usual reply expressed a desire for him to flex his biceps; something he happily obliged.

In a tone that sounded like dull chalk over a slate, she suggested, "Let's not dwell on accomplishments, Mr. Bruiser."

"Jake," he countered with a frown.

"Mr. Brewster."

His eyes narrowed. *To hell with it.*

"If you don't mind," she said in a voice that was coolly impersonal, "I'd like to get to the Plunketts' house. It's freezing out here."

Her aloof manner got under his skin. So much so, he tossed aside civil politeness. "You wanted to carry the trophy suitcase. Go ahead, sweetheart. Just give me my beer."

Her brows raised, a momentary lift of trepidation. She didn't seem the timid kind. "I don't have it."

Now that he gazed at her hands, both were empty. "What do you mean you don't have it?"

Standing taller, with her chin high, she explained, "I dumped it out at the corner by the depot. I'm sure you know the one. You'll need to go back and pick up the bottle. I don't condone littering."

"You did *what?*"

"I poured your Heinrich's into a planter. I believe it was a blue spruce with a cranberry garland around the boughs."

He ripped out his next words. "Are you crazy?"

"I was to walk through the town holding onto the bottle—yes. So I had no choice but to rectify the situation. I told you I didn't want to carry it. A woman of my position—"

But he wasn't listening to her anymore. Without thought, he picked up both suitcases—contrary to what he'd offered—and started walking because if he didn't do *something,* he'd just leave her there to fend for herself.

She caught up with him, but didn't speak. Wise move on her part. She must have seen his gritted teeth, the clench of his jaw. He ought to make her pay for that beer. Not that he needed the money. The whole thing was a matter of principle. You didn't chuck a guy's lager and then have the nerve to tell him to go back and pick up the empty.

But Miss Valentine didn't know that. How could she? She didn't even know how to walk with an even stride. For somebody who obviously could whack a tennis ball and dunk a basketball good enough to win an award for it, her steps were short. As if each one pained her feet. What did she need five more pairs of shoes for? She couldn't walk in the ones she had on.

As they rounded the corner of Elm, Jake cursed himself for wasting his energy on trying to figure out why she found him so distasteful.

He was likable, was not bad looking, and treated women well. His sense of humor was all right. He owned a successful business. And he knew the one thing that all women liked—making them feel protected when they were on his arm. Or in his arms. But when he'd tried to help Miss Valentine organize that trunk of hers, she'd shot him a glance that said she wanted to give him a right hook.

She presented herself like a lady but carted around sports trophies. The pieces didn't fit, but he didn't have the inclination to put the puzzle together.

The house came into view. The scrollwork on the eaves made the place seem like a dollhouse; ridges were decked out with tinsel and the porch had been trimmed with a kind of braided greenery and bunches of red berries. The lightning rod gleamed on the front gable; lashed to it was a large Santa Claus figure, his face transparent with an electric bulb glowing in his head. The Plunketts had tapped into electricity, one of the first homeowners here to do so, and Jake always got a kick out of seeing that lit-up Santa.

Soft snow had been shoveled from the walk in neat piles to either side, the shallow banks melting under the late-afternoon sun.

"This is it." He opened the gate for her, let her pass through, then went up the steps with her and set down the suitcases at her feet.

"Thank you for your assistance, Mr. Brewster."

"Yeah, yeah. No problem." But she had been a problem.

He left, telling himself he was glad to be rid of his responsibility for Miss Valentine.

On his way to get his discarded bottle, he passed cozy homes with the smells of roasted meats and fresh-baked pies wafting from chimneys. Parlor windows were decorated by cheery lights. Children were being called in for supper. Families would be sitting at dining tables, talking about their days, sharing stories.

A stab of yearning formed in his gut, but he shrugged it off. He didn't need any of that kind of company. How could he miss something he'd never experienced? The closest people he had to brothers were Tom and, in a way, the boys over at the gym.

Jake could take care of himself. He knew how to cook a thick steak to just the right rareness. He could sew a button on his shirt. Push a sweeper across his rug if he tracked in dirt.

Yeah, Jake Brewster had everything he wanted. Everything he needed.

The Wolcotts should quit their matchmaking attempts, because they hadn't been successful in getting him to the altar. And they never would.

At thirty-three, Jake had a lot of good bachelor years left in him. He had a great life, abundant women, plenty of money, and a solid business. He wasn't about to mess it up with a wife.

Again.

Chapter
2

The door to the Plunkett house opened and a heavyset woman filled the frame. She took one look at Truvy and burst into tears. Truvy didn't know what to do when the woman put a hankie to her wet eyes and babbled, "My baby, my baby girl."

"Mrs. Plunkett? I'm Truvy Valentine."

"I know. I know." She sobbed. "Do come in. My baby..."

Gathering her trunks, Truvy followed Mrs. Plunkett into a parlor with gilt swag draperies. A heating stove in the corner gave off a glow of inviting warmth from behind the grate. The center table was nearly bare—only a black Edison phonograph.

The rest of the area was encumbered with frivolous ornaments: glass birds, imposing volumes of books with gold engraving stacked on the organ shelf, and yarn—lots of yarn balls everywhere, in quarries of colors. The beginnings of an afghan were evident in the blocks of Roman stripes in various places around the room. Multicolored squares dotted the parlor as if

Mrs. Plunkett had grown distracted while crocheting and left the finished squares wherever they landed.

Mrs. Plunkett stood before her wearing a cap and delicate sacque that she must have tatted. She sniffled, looked Truvy up and down, then blew her nose. At least she was getting past her crying.

"Well, I'm glad you arrived safe and sound. From the size of you, you need a nice hot supper," Mrs. Plunkett said while dabbing her eyes. "You're far too thin. Now my Hildegarde . . ." As soon as the name was spoken, fresh waterworks were turned on.

Edwina had told Truvy about Hildegarde, a late bloomer from her class last year who had finally met the man of her heart. She'd gotten married less than two months ago and moved to New York with her new husband. From the overwrought emotional display, Truvy gathered that Mrs. Plunkett was still sentimental about her only daughter leaving the nest.

"That would be nice." Truvy set her suitcases down, hoping to draw the woman out of her tears. "I was told you're an excellent cook."

A pause. A sniff. "Oh, really?" Her brows pitched upward on her high forehead and dimples appeared in her round cheeks. "I do put out a lovely meal. Ask anyone in the Amateur Ladies Avifauna Ornithologists or the Harmony Garden Club. They can tell you I bake the best chocolate cake. I made one for you. It's my pr-pr-precious's favorite."

At that, the dam burst once more.

Having dealt with young girls and the trials and tribulations of their lives, Truvy went into her teacher's mode, coaxing her voice into the gentlest and most effective of tones. "There, there, Mrs. Plunkett. You haven't lost your daughter. Think of it this way: you've gained a son."

She wrinkled her nose. "A son? Why should I want one of those? Men are such a bother."

Once again, Mrs. Plunkett left her at a loss. But at least the change in topic to men pulled her out of her weeping. A small frown twisted her mouth, and Truvy wondered if she was thinking about Mr. Plunkett.

"Well, have a seat, my dear, and I'll bring you a fat slice of cake," Mrs. Plunkett said, scurrying through the room at a surprising speed in view of her ample size. She disappeared.

Truvy moved aside the afghan squares and sat, hands folded in her lap. The tick of a clock echoed through the parlor. She didn't feel at ease in her temporary surroundings. She was used to the laughter and voices of young ladies in hallways, to the cheers from the St. Francis gymnasium.

"Here we are," Mrs. Plunkett said, bringing in a hefty piece of four layers slathered with chocolate icing. There was no way Truvy could eat it all, but she took the plate with a smile of thanks.

"So," the elder woman said, sitting across from Truvy on the organ bench, "you don't have a gentleman caller back in Boise, do you?"

The question threw Truvy, causing her to halt the progress of the fork in her gloved hand. "Ah . . . no."

"Thank the Lord for that, my dear. Let me tell you about men. They only ruin a woman's life. Yes, indeed, they do. Why, I've been married to Mr. Plunkett for a good many years, and I ask you, what woman in her right mind would put up with a man of his temperament? Honestly, the things I bear."

Then she went into a soliloquy of every year of her marriage while Truvy ate as much cake as she could. Surrounded by the drowsy warmth of the stove and the long speech given by Mrs. Plunkett, Truvy grew tired. She was travel weary but concerned about Edwina. She wanted to deposit her things in her room and visit her school friend right away.

"Would you be so kind as to show me to my room now, Mrs. Plunkett?" Truvy set the cake plate on the side table.

"But you aren't finished eating."

"I am. Thank you, it was delicious."

"Oh ... well, if you want to see your room ... it was my ..."—the tears welled in her eyes—"... daughter's."

Truvy hadn't anticipated being uncomfortable occupying the space. She could see how upset Mrs. Plunkett was, but the woman had been the one to offer the use of the room at no charge while Truvy visited with Edwina. Edwina said Mrs. Plunkett had insisted because she was pining for the company of a young lady. But the elder woman was more than pining.

Now Truvy was glad she'd instinctively withheld asking to stay longer. Clearly this was going to be too hard for Mrs. Plunkett. Truvy hoped Miss Pond would allow her to return to St. Francis in two weeks, as was originally planned.

She went up the stairs behind Mrs. Plunkett and came to a room that was decorated entirely in pink chintz, from the chaise longue by the window to the canopy over the plush bed.

"My darling loved pink."

Truvy couldn't help thinking about her pink petticoats.

"If you don't mind, Mrs. Plunkett, right now I'd like to pay a call on Edwina. Could you—"

"Of course I could unpack for you. My Hildegarde

always let me pack and unpack her things for her. But she didn't go anywhere very often. Just to see my mother in Scranton. And then . . . when she . . ."—the sobs came once more—". . . went to New York with *him*."

"Oh, you needn't bother yourself with my trunks," Truvy replied in a rush. "I don't have much to unpack." She had simply wanted Mrs. Plunkett to take her to Edwina's house—which now seemed out of the question because Mrs. Plunkett was in the throes of a weeping fit once again. But Truvy didn't want to delay her visit. "If you could tell me where Edwina lives, that would be helpful."

"Yes . . . of course." She blew her nose into her handkerchief—a loud honk. "You two haven't seen each other in a while. Her house is around the block and on the left. The pretty one with the decorated porch. I suppose I should show you."

"Please don't trouble yourself. I think you should lie down and rest. It's been a trying afternoon for you talking about your . . . daughter."

"My baby girl," Mrs. Plunkett said with a sniff. "Yes . . . I need to lie down. I'm getting one of my headaches."

As she exited the house, Truvy was never more glad for a gulp of crisp, cold air.

Truvy found out Edwina's condition was nothing serious—a stiff back and swollen feet. She was heartily welcomed into the house by the Wolcotts amid a rush of apologies for their not meeting her at the train depot. Ushered into the parlor, Truvy was served refreshments, and immediately, the three of them fell into conversation.

"I'm so happy you're here, Truvy," Edwina exclaimed. She sat in an upholstered parlor chair beside the fire, a great big dog at her feet. His name was Barkly and he was a bloodhound with so much skin, Truvy was at a loss over how he could even see. A cat called Honey Tiger rested in Edwina's lap.

"Your coming means a lot to Edwina." Tom reclined on the arm of his wife's cushioned chair and absently massaged her neck.

"As it does to me," Truvy replied.

They asked her how her travel arrangements had been on the train and if she'd kept pleasant company during the journey. The subjects turned to the upcoming holiday and New Year and the names Edwina and Tom had decided on for the baby.

The back end of a zebra had been made into a clock that hung above the fireplace mantel. Its striped tail ticked off the seconds, keeping her enthralled while she chatted with Edwina and acquainted herself with her husband.

"Do you recall Miss Totten, the typing teacher?" Edwina asked. "She had an ear trumpet and we always had to yell in it."

Truvy was on the settee and sipped tea from a mismatched china saucer and cup. She took a moment to smile at her surroundings. The way Tom had such affection for his wife. The way the tea service was a mixture of old and new pieces. The way the firelight played over the couple in the chair. The way the home seemed so inviting. And loving.

For the briefest of moments, a longing settled so deeply in Truvy's heart it was a physical ache. But she quickly quelled it, forcing the sudden feeling of melancholy away.

"I do remember her," Truvy remarked. "When we typed, she couldn't hear a word we said over the noise of the keystrokes. Once, Abigail Crane called her a wet goose and she replied, 'Yes, Miss Crane, you have to release the bail for the paper to get loose.'"

Edwina smiled in distant remembrance.

Truvy pondered, taking a taste of her tea. "I wonder whatever happened to Abbie."

Edwina responded matter-of-factly. "She married Professor Rutledge."

That news surprised Truvy. She'd had no idea. "Really?"

"How was the weather in Boise when you left?" Tom asked, drawing his arm over the back of Edwina's chair. "I read in the papers the pronghorns are plenty this season."

"Tom," Edwina chided with a curve to her mouth, "I don't think Truvy wants to talk about antelope."

"Oh, on the contrary," Truvy said, sitting toward the edge of the settee. "President Roosevelt is an avid whitetail hunter and I've heard he's going to Idaho next year to hunt."

"Are you a fan of the president, Miss Valentine?" Tom rose and put another log on the fire. As he poked the embers, sparks shot up the flue with crackles and pops.

"I am. Very much so."

Looking over his broad shoulder, he commented, "It was terrible about President McKinley."

"Horrible," Truvy agreed.

Although her alliance had been with the Democratic Party and she'd had her doubts about President Roosevelt—a Republican—the two months since he'd taken office after President McKinley's death had been filled with economic promise. In his own words, he pledged to govern with the qualities of practical intelligence, of courage and endurance.

And above all, lofty ideal.

The clock chimed eight o'clock. Truvy hadn't meant to stay so late, but once they'd begun to reminisce about their college days, she'd lost track of time.

"I really should be going, Edwina. You need your rest."

"I'm fine." Edwina stood and discreetly arched her spine. "But I'm a bit anxious."

Truvy set her cup and saucer on the tea cart. "I'll come back tomorrow and help you with whatever you need."

"That would be wonderful." She embraced Truvy and she fondly placed a kiss on her cheek.

"I'll be off, then."

Tom walked to the vestibule with them and helped Truvy with her short cape and handed her her hat and gloves. Afterward, he collected his own hat and coat. "I'll see you home, Miss Valentine."

The criterion that a lady shouldn't walk alone on the street after dark required she accept his offer. Either abide by the strict standard or suffer the consequences: gossip. Still, the fact that she had no one but Tom to escort her made her painfully aware of her unmarried status. She hated to be a burden. "I don't want you to trouble yourself, Mr. Wolcott."

"No trouble at all." He settled his hat on, then gazed at Edwina. "The usual?"

"I'm not in the mood for my usual. I'd like two candied cherries on my ice cream. Vanilla, please. Butterscotch on one half and chocolate syrup on the other. No whipping cream. And only a light sprinkling of nuts—on the butterscotch side." She gave his mouth a quick press of her lips. "Thank you, darling." Then addressing Truvy, "Can Tom get you some ice cream, too? He could take you by the café, then to the Plunketts'."

The ritual of a husband attending to his pregnant wife's craving was so personal, Truvy felt awkward accepting ice cream for herself. But for Edwina to include her was utterly thoughtful. Guilt plagued Truvy over her omission of the whole truth about her trip. She hadn't been able to admit she was on a leave of absence from St. Francis. But if Miss Pond were to have a change of heart, then Truvy need never mention it. "That's a lovely offer, but I'm going to decline."

"All right. Good-bye, then, Truvy. I'll see you tomorrow. Come over any time you like. I'm up early."

Truvy and Tom made their way into a night that was illuminated by a quarter moon. Its rays gave off just enough brightness to see the glittering ice crystals that covered the street. Because she wasn't accustomed to wearing high-button shoes, she carefully placed her steps but nearly slipped anyway.

Mr. Wolcott's hand quickly gripped her bent elbow to balance her. His assistance remained as they walked along. Such gallantry was foreign to her, and she didn't know what to say—something rare in her life. She usually made the grievous mistake of speaking her mind on all occasions, oftentimes to the great mortification of others.

Edwina was lucky to be married to such a gentleman, but to state that to Mr. Wolcott would be too brazen—even for Truvy. But she did manage to say, "Thank you."

"I suppose in Boise, you have boardwalks everywhere and they're kept ashed all winter long," Tom said. Mist came out of his mouth when he spoke.

"Yes, we do."

"We don't have that here, but I like it just the same." The expression on his face was one of fondness for the town—that was evident in his profile. "I guess it's a good thing Edwina wasn't in her last month in the summer. I'd end up bringing her something melted."

Hearing such ardent affection, Truvy's inward smile barely surfaced. For some strange reason, she felt an empty void settle inside her. But the odd thing was, Truvy didn't covet Edwina's lifestyle.

Truvy's days were filled with her students—her own children, in a way. She was perfectly happy living within those limits. She had a rich and full environment, and so what if no man had ever put on his coat and hat to brave a frosty night to get her a bowl of ice cream . . . butterscotch on one half and chocolate syrup on the other?

Soon, they were at the Plunkett house. She put her hand on the gate latch, its metal slightly sticking to the wool of her heavily gloved fingers.

"Thanks ever so much, Mr. Wolcott." She slipped her arm free from his hand. "I can manage the rest of the way myself."

"All right." He tipped his hat to her and was off.

Truvy clicked the latch open and proceeded up the walkway. Lamplight and shadows flickered from behind lacy curtains, a telltale sign the occupants of the house were still up. Then, a quite clear tall form—a man—moved to light a pipe. Flame from a match sprang to life, its light etching a fuzzy face. Mr. Plunkett.

She drew in a deep breath. Truvy had to make a nice first impression. She didn't want to do anything to upset Mrs. Plunkett and have Mr. Plunkett think Truvy shouldn't stay with them because it was too distressing for his wife, both because Mrs. Plunkett missed her daughter and because Truvy had inadvertently put herself in disfavor with the townswomen when she'd carried that boxer's beer bottle. Ladies talked. Truvy didn't want Mrs. Plunkett to hear about it from them.

Waiting a moment, she paused midway up the walk. She had to collect herself. To make sure she was focused on presenting her best behavior. No slips of the tongue. No lapses in deportment.

She inhaled air into and exhaled it out of her lungs as a form of mental calisthenics. This method always calmed her. She felt herself relaxing and looking at her surroundings.

Pale snow piled against the front fence, on the brown lawn, and against the veranda lattice. Gelatin stars winked from the trees at the house across the street.

Her thoughts drifted to Christmas and what her girls would be doing on the winter break. Singing rousing carols, drinking hot cider, going ice skating, and returning home to families. Before she had left Boise, Truvy had telephoned The Aunts, who lived in Emporia, Kansas. She'd wished them a merry Christmas.

The Aunts had been married to two brothers, both inventors. Because they lived with men who developed ideas for a better future, it was no surprise The Aunts took up the cause of women's suffrage. Aunt Beatrice and Aunt Gertrude had always been free-thinkers and raised Truvy to be such, but they were sedate in their campaigns. Not a single arrest—a record they prided themselves on.

Truvy had no distinct memories of her uncles aside from bushy hair and big beards. They'd both died in an accident when she was four. For the past twenty-one years, The Aunts had been widows. They lived in the same house, slept in the same bedroom, drank tea and ate jellied toast at the same kitchen table in the morning.

After spending the evening with Tom and Edwina, Truvy wondered if Aunt Beatrice and Aunt Gertrude ever thought about remarrying instead of keeping company only with each other. At least there was the pair of them. In Truvy's case, she was alone.

Well, not truly alone. There were the girls. But in her room at night, in the middle of the midnight hours, there was nobody to talk to about her day, not anyone in whom she could confide.

Truvy shifted her stance, ready to go inside. As she moved forward, a stable scene beneath the elm in the yard caught her attention. A baby Jesus lay in the manger. Beside him huddled Joseph and Mary, several camels, some sheep, two donkeys, and three tall wise men.

My—but they're lifelike.

The master craftsmanship of the figurines was evident with only the defused parlor light fanning across them. They stood about four feet high. She studied the one holding frankincense. The artist had actually sculpted and painted the veins on his hands, drawn the creases at the corners of his eyes, and shaded his skin with a healthy glow, and she was certain the hair on his head wasn't a false piece but was real. So real that she wondered how realistically the rest of him was represented.

The chapter in *The Science of Life* entitled "The Most Complete Male Body—Organs and Structures" came to her. She remembered the text word for word because it hadn't made any sense. She'd been baffled by its adjective-strewn interpretation.

The man's penis is designed for the express purpose of conveying the "pabulum of life." In conception, it is divine; in design, perfect; in architecture, grand; in construction, wonderful; in beauty, lovely; in form, symmetrical; in outline, sublime; in strength, great; in arrangements, marvelous; in mobility, transcendent; in adaptability, unexcelled; in fine, when it is studied in all its parts and their relationship to each other, we are led to exclaim with the psalmist David, that the human male is "fearfully and wonderfully made."

The description had the male anatomy sounding larger than life, but it didn't clarify physical shape . . . and size.

Just how *real* was that figurine?

Truvy bit her lower lip, then looked out at the street. Quiet. Deserted. She gazed back at the realistic wise man. Then left and right. Then at the front door to the Plunketts'. And she made a decision.

She lifted the hem of her dress, hiking it higher as her shoes sank into the soggy snow. Her ankles and black stocking-clad calves disappeared in the fluffy white. As she bent over the wise man, a chilling draft shot up her skirts and caused her to shiver.

The rich velvet robe draping the figurine was partially iced over; his one hand stuck to the folds where moisture had formed and hardened from the night air. She paused, reconsidering. This was ludicrous. Then again, this might be an opportunity to see a man firsthand—if indeed the figurine was all there in forbidden factuality.

Bunching in her skirts, Truvy balanced over the wise man to sneak a peek at his "pabulum of life."

She took hold of the robe's hem. With the cloth in a semifrozen state, it came right off in her grasp—like a stiff shell of armor—and the figurine was left standing naked in a blaze of glory. Abruptly, she let the garment go. The fabric fell to his feet in a contoured blanket of shimmering gold.

Truvy blinked. Then squinted.

With his hand outstretched, now minus the frankincense, the biblical figurine was nothing more than a nondescript porcelain. She didn't see any kind of anatomical parts on him.

Or is that something . . . ?

Just as she leaned forward to double check, a hard ball of snow hit her behind with a dull *splat*. Turning with a start, she barely made out an outline of a man on the sidewalk. His arm rose and he shot off another snowball. She ducked and the missile smacked the tree trunk, bursting into a spray of white flakes.

Practically jumping out of her skin, she could only stare in surprise. Although a cloud had drifted over the moon and cast the night in a veil of dimness, she recognized her assailant from his height.

Jake Bruiser—er, Brewster.

With her fists clenched in yards of blue velvet and pink satin petticoat, she froze, thinking that if she didn't move he'd go away.

"Hey, you—come here," he directed.

Panic gripped her. She wasn't keen on facing him, but she didn't want to be standing next to that naked figurine when the moon came back out.

Truvy watched her step on the icy walkway as she went toward the gate. The last thing she needed was to slip and land on her bottom right in front of him. She felt his gaze on her, and it was disturbing.

"If it isn't Miss Valentine," he intoned in such a way that made it clear he'd known it was her all along.

As soon as the length of iron fence picket was a barrier between them, she dropped her skirts. Had he seen what she'd done? To veer him away from the subject of the wise man, she went at him with full-blown indignance. "I don't appreciate being hit by a snowball. Especially on my buttocks."

She hadn't had the presence of mind to cut herself short; now, she silently winced at the vivid word. But then again, she'd been instructing the girls that they should use the correct vocabulary when speaking about the human body. No snickers or slang. On that conviction, she held her ground and stared at him, waiting for his defense.

It wasn't forthcoming.

Mr. Brewster kept a wicked curve on his mouth for longer than was tasteful given the circumstances. Blast him, but he had fine lips, wide and . . . *sensual.* There was no other description.

With the backdrop of winter white blanketing the ground behind him, and Mr. Brewster in a dark overcoat, his body seemed more powerful—if that were possible. And his voice seemed louder when he remarked as casual as a summer day, "I thought you were a thief trying to make off with one of the Plunketts' wise men."

She remained calm, giving no hint of the turmoil inside her. *Oh, what must you think of me for spying on a biblical statue?* "Really, Mr. Brewster, you couldn't have mistaken me for a hoodlum. You intentionally threw a snowball at me, and I can guess why."

"Why?"

"Because I poured out your beer."

"I wouldn't whack a woman with a snowball for a beer offense." He paused. "Although I thought about it."

She immediately shot back, "I thought you were playing poker."

"We ran out of beer."

Beer. Naturally.

The keen air bit her cheeks and carried steam from her mouth as she lamely remarked, "That's too bad."

His eye narrowed when he smiled, providing a brief flash of white. "I thought so."

Their exchange was hardly fit for parlor-room conversation, much less one held out in the elements on a starlit evening sparkling with frost. The moon peeked out from its cloud cover, its light passing over them.

This was the first time in her life a man had stared at her the way Mr. Brewster was. Intently. Curiously. Hotly. His eyes skimmed over her in a slow perusal. From her face to her feet. Then lingering at her ankles—that not minutes ago had been on display. She let his overly long examination get to her. She felt it melt through her bones.

"You have nice . . . shoes," he remarked, lazing next to the fence.

She knew that wasn't what he was talking about. He was being ignoble. A man who liked that sort of silly risqué thing; a pair of female ankles in a pair of shin-topped shoes. And yet, his thinking her ankles in her new shoes were attractive made her palms grow moist.

Her wits returned and she refused to make much of his comments about her appearance.

But then he had to go and say, "You're a tall woman. Tall women have long legs."

Mortification made her want to hide.

She'd never liked her legs. Or her height. There was too much of both. Tall and long. All her life, she'd hated being tall and long-legged. Trapped in a nonconforming body was a ghastly thing to go through when most other women, small and delicate, better fit the ideal proportions prescribed for womankind.

That Jake Brewster would point out her failing made her feel deflated. So much for her notion that he might find her attractive. It was a ridiculous thing for her to think, much less want.

Jake's gaze moved beyond her shoulder, and he lifted his chin toward the nativity scene. "Were you trying to get a look at that wise man's ho ho ho—"

"I was adjusting his robe," she cut in, her voice shaky yet filled with offense. *"Adjusting his robe,"* she repeated for emphasis. Well—she could have been!

He didn't believe her; that much was clear from the expression on his face: the raised brows, the slight quirk to his mouth. For all the shadows in the night, she wished darkness covered it all so she wouldn't have to see him mocking her. There was nothing worse than being laughed at. She didn't appreciate it.

"If you say so." He shifted his weight and dug his hands deep into the pockets of his boot-length sealskin overcoat. She wanted him gone, moving along, leaving her alone.

Squeaky hinges alerted Truvy that the front door to the Plunkett house had opened. She turned and looked into the thin wedge of light spilling down the verandah steps. Filling the space over the threshold, Mrs. Plunkett gazed down her nose toward the gate.

"Who's out there?"

Truvy called out in a manner she hoped sounded nonguilty. After all, she wasn't doing anything. Not really. Hardly wrong at all aside from . . . "Miss Valentine."

"Oh, Miss Valentine. Who's that with you? Is that a *man?*"

"Jacob Brewster, Mrs. Plunkett."

"What are you doing talking to Miss Valentine?"

From the half smile that lit on his mouth, Truvy feared she was doomed and would be up half the night explaining.

Jake's deep voice carried in the night. "We were discussing the birth of Christ and the manger."

Truvy opened her eyes, not realizing she'd squeezed them tightly closed.

"Really?" Mrs. Plunkett stepped onto the veranda. "While I find that admirable, it's not appropriate to be discussing the Bible at this hour. In the dark. At my gate. I have an upstanding reputation in this town and I won't have it sullied, Miss Valentine."

Her heartbeat drummed. "I wouldn't dream of it, Mrs. Plunkett."

"Well, then, come along inside. Mr. Plunkett is waiting to meet you."

Truvy couldn't do anything but turn away from Jake, glance at the wise man from the corner of her eyes, and proceed up the steps. There was no time or opportunity to fix him. She had to leave him just as he was—moonlight beaming off his pale white torso and legs and that area of undefined . . . um, maleness.

There was no plausible reason she could offer Mrs. Plunkett about the figure's being disrobed; so she'd stick with the explanation she'd given Mr. Brewster.

The figurine's robe had fallen and she was merely adjusting it. But to voice that aloud ... in front of Mr. Plunkett ... it would be better to wait until morning, over breakfast, when it was just herself and Mrs. Plunkett after a good night's rest. She'd clarify everything and there would be no fuss made.

As she walked into the house, Truvy glanced at the street while Mrs. Plunkett closed the door. Jake Brewster still stood at the gate, staring at her. She had difficulty swallowing. The hairs at the nape of her neck prickled, and gooseflesh rose on her arms. Not twenty-four hours in Harmony and she'd ended up in his company twice: holding his beer and exposing her ankles to him.

If she kept this up, she might as well tear up her ticket back to Boise. She was as good as terminated from her position.

Chapter

❧ 3 ❧

Jake Brewster used to pose in the nude.

In New York City, he sat for artists and sculptors. Being painted and assessed without a stitch on was a good way to make extra cash when he was developing his physique as a bodybuilder at the age of nineteen. Standing au naturel—as the teacher in the Art Students League called it—never bothered him. Even if it had, from the talent the artists showed, nothing of their work would become well known. Only a guy named Remington was any good. His art was to the point and unsentimental. After classes, the two of them would go sit in the local tavern and talk art— Jake's definition being that of the body and Remington's being that of canvas and pen. Jake and Remmy had formed a loose friendship, and since those days, they had stayed in touch.

If Jake hadn't run away from home, he never would have developed a talent as a boxer and, later on, the body of a muscleman. His problematic relationship with his father had always been on the edge—volatile, and sometimes violent, if his old man couldn't hold down a job because of temper outbursts. Then J. W. Brewster would take out his frustrations on Jake. His mother left after he was born; to this day, Jake didn't know why. His father didn't want him, and it had wounded Jake to the quick when he'd been little. Each time his old man looked at him, he said he saw *that bitch*.

Jake put up a shell of indifference over his pain as the years went by. He hung around with street pals, mostly Irish boys like himself—although there was no strict Catholic upbringing in the Brewster household. Times were hard and his home life grew worse to an unbearable degree when his father didn't have a job more often than he had one.

When he was fourteen, Jake went to a traveling boxing show in Queens. He was a tall boy—six feet. The heavyweights put on good theatrics, shoving each other around the ring. Jake had done that much on the streets in lower Brooklyn. The company manager offered a fifty-dollar prize for any man who would take on the winner of the match. To Jake, it was money in his hand. He wanted to fight. He lied about his age. Said he was eighteen. Because of his size, they believed him, and he was picked. He won in three rounds and was offered a place with the troupe of boxers, who went around the country taking on amateurs. He jumped on the opportunity. That night, he packed his belongings and said farewell to his father, who waved him off with the premonition he'd be back in Brooklyn within the month.

He was wrong. It took three years, and when he returned, he'd gained a small amount of notoriety and some pocket money.

In two years on the road, Jake developed an interest in lifting through one of the performers, Michael "The Irish Torpedo" McGovern. He was an old-time vaudeville strongman. He was heavyset and had a thick bull neck. He shaved his head and had a curling mustache that was always waxed into place.

Torpedo told Jake that being bulked and muscular was good for boxing but that the true test of a man's strength was what he could jerk in weight. Michael taught him the "tomb of Hercules" position—with his abdomen stretched up in an arc, arms back, legs front—a trick that the Irishman did in the boxing intermission. He had a sheet of lumber laid on his stomach and got somebody to walk a draft horse over him. He never once collapsed, a feat that had awed Jake.

He gave up boxing to be a strongman because he didn't have to have his face smacked anymore. Already, he'd had his ribs cracked, his nose broken at the bridge, and his eyelid cut from punches. The year Jake turned eighteen in truth, he and the Torpedo left the company, creating their own act filled with endurance exploits. Along with displays of pressing weight in one hand, Jake broke a chain from his biceps with a burst of muscle contraction and bent a piece of pipe into a U shape and then made it straight again. He learned how to take two complete playing card packs and, with a turn of his wrist, tear them in half.

In 1893, while performing in New York City, he met Florenz Ziegfeld Sr. and his son. Torpedo had opted to retire that year, so Jake was left without a future engagement. He and Flo struck a partnership to produce an act for the World's Columbian Exposition in Chicago.

The show, "Jake 'The Bruiser' Brewster—The

Strongest Man on Earth," was an instant success and ran the entire fair. Women flocked to the pavilion in the hopes of being introduced to him. After performances, he held private meetings where they could touch his muscles while he talked about them. Crowds of matinee girls sent him wreaths, perfume-scented love letters, and other objects of their affection.

But after a successful run with Flo at the Trocadero in Chicago and traveling from New York to San Francisco in a string of shows, Jake had lost his hunger for professional bodybuilding.

Today, he was still a big man with a rock-hard physique. But beneath the appearance of what was considered a marbled Greek ideal, he knew he wasn't as physically fit as he'd once been. He drank too much, indulged in cigars, and no longer put all his effort into bodybuilding. Maintaining his symmetry, proportion, and detail had gone up in smoke, with nights of playing cards and entertaining women.

Since retiring from competitions, he now gave advice rather than took it. He operated a business that allowed amateurs to exercise their bodies for strength and development.

Bruiser's Gymnasium was good-size, with hardwood floors and a row of windows that looked out onto an alleyway shared by other businesses. Each exercise station was marked with an Axminster rug beneath the equipment. Men could stand or lie on the carpets and work the weights that Jake kept racked on the west-facing wall. The gym provided the latest in equipment: striking bags—both single and double-ended—a rower, Indian clubs, dumbbells and barbells, kettle weights, and pulley exercisers.

He sat in his office, at his desk, with the heels of his

feet propped up on the corner. Leaning his shoulders into the lumpy cushion of a rolling chair, he looked at the pictures in the latest issue of *Sporting Life* magazine.

His schooling had been spotty; the lack of education impeded his ability to read the articles without a dictionary close by. When he'd been a kid, he'd never given a damn about reading, writing, and arithmetic. Older and wiser, he was angry with himself that he hadn't paid attention.

But when frustration grabbed him, he reminded himself he was Jake Brewster, the gentlemen's friend, grand pooh-bah of the Barbell Club—the would-be contenders who frequented his gymnasium, kept his company for poker games, and laughed at his jokes. Not being highbrow didn't cause him to lack good friends.

A knock rapped on the closed door and Jake looked up from the issue of *Sporting Life*. "Hey, Milton."

"Hi, Bruiser."

Milton Burditt sported a double chin, and a gold watch chain stretched across an ample field of his silk vest. He always dressed in expensive clothes and smoked dollar cigars, and he trained at Bruiser's three days a week.

"I had a good workout today," Milton said, drawing out a clipped cigar from the breast pocket of his coat. He took off the band, smelled the length of the cigar with a satisfied grin, then lit up. Puffing a chain of smoke rings, he looked at Jake, then at the cigar, and apologized. "Excuse me, Bruiser. Can I offer you one?"

With a fluid motion, Jake lowered his feet to the

floor and gripped the desk's edge; he propped the soles of his scuffed gymnasium Oxfords on the rails of a worn in chair, then rolled himself forward. "I never turn down a Ybor." He took the cigar, placed it between his lips, and used his thumb to flip open the spring hinge of a silver match safe. He'd won the pocket-size holder for being the victor of his first fight. An American eagle was engraved in the silver as well as the year: 1886.

"I'm lifting one hundreds now," Milton bragged through the smoke that began to cloud the tiny room. "Before you know it, I'll be doing two-fifties. Not in barbells either—dumbbells. Or singles on the kettles. You watch, my friend, my name will live forever. Like the name of a cheese. You'll see folks sitting down at a diner and ordering a ham-and-Milton on pumpernickel. It's going to happen."

Milton's goal in life was to get massive enough to gain wide recognition. A rather ambitious plan for a squat man who tipped the scale at more than the two-hundred-and-fifty-pound weights he wanted to hoist. He had a cousin who was named Napoleon and it rankled him. Milton claimed the man looked more like a puff pastry than a relative.

"You keep at it, Milt, and I'll be thinking of you as cheese," Jake said as he blew a succession of perfect smoke rings.

"That's right. I'm in this for the long haul, Bruiser. I want every bit of the glory. The oiling, psychological warfare, and posing. *I'm*"—he hooked his thumb at his bulging chest—"the next Mr. Physique."

Gig Debolski, wearing baggy gymnasium drawers and a sweat-spotted tunic, interrupted their conversation as he came up to the office doorway. He motioned his head toward the expanse of windows on the building that shared the alleyway with the gym. "Action over at the dance studio, Bruiser."

Jake arched his brows, tucking his hands behind his head. "Is that so?"

"A couple a minutes ago. The curtains were moving like somebody was inside. Thought you'd like to know."

"Thanks, Gig." Jake twirled the ash of his cigar against the side of a cut crystal tray on his desk. Beside it lay an assortment of cabinet cards of him holding a raised-fist stance in his boxing trunks; the novelties originally sold to the public for thirty-five cents apiece. When somebody wrote to him for an autographed keepsake, he sent them one.

"I wonder if Mrs. Wolcott got things lined up." Milton checked the time on his watch. "I've got to get back to the office. Let me know how things are, Bruiser."

"Yeah, sure."

When Milton left, Jake stood and went out into the gymnasium.

A machine that resembled a Liberty Bell one-armed bandit took up a spot on the wall just outside his open office door. The lever measured the force of strength a strongman used when it was pulled down. Out of habit, Jake gave the knobbed handle a go as he walked past. The internal mechanism rang out in a series of bells.

As he walked, Jake nodded to a few of the fellows at the stations. At the end of the large room, an exit door led into the alleyway. He stopped beside it and looked out the window.

All the curtains on the dancing studio were closed. Just as they'd been the past two months when Edwina had temporarily shut the place down owing to her condition. She'd put up a notice on the door that read she was looking for a substitute instructor, and as soon as she found one, Edwina Wolcott's Dancing Academy would reopen.

Jake had signed up every man competing for the Mr. Physique belt. Just because a gent had muscle, it didn't mean he was prize-winning material by determination and brawn. Knowing how to waltz and ragtime to the basics was an asset to being agile in posing. A man serious with his training was open to new ideas, new ways of doing things.

Hopefully, Edwina would hire somebody dowdy, a plain woman—a real crow in black skirts and a nononsense starched white blouse. He didn't need his entrants distracted by long legs with a teasing show of pink petticoats.

Sweet Judas. Where in the hell had that thought come from?

Miss Valentine.

Her name conjured hearts and romance. Expectation. Adoration. None of the things he wanted at this point in his life. And yet, after he'd seen her trim ankles, he'd been preoccupied with what her legs would look like. From her height, he knew they would go on forever. Too bad she hadn't hiked her skirt higher when she'd walked over to the gate. He'd had to satisfy himself with a glimpse of her feet in leather shoes with tiny black buttons.

He thought about flipping each button free of its slot and slowly slipping her feet out of the tight leather. Massaging her toes. Rolling down the thin black stockings to caress her bare feet and legs that would be long and willowy.

He recalled the expression on her face when the snowball made contact with her behind. He knew exactly what she'd been up to. He'd watched her a good few minutes before nailing her. So—she was curious. A virgin would be. And she was definitely that.

Get her out of your head, Brewster. You know plenty of women willing to show you their legs.

He puffed on his cigar, looking into the slant of sunshine that made it in between the buildings. Icicles dripped from the roof of the studio, their ends wet as they melted in the early afternoon.

One of the curtains covering the expansive series of windows flickered with movement. Somebody was inside. The brush of gathered fabric had him imagining other things. A lady's skirt. Blue velvet. And an unconventional woman who carried athletic trophies with her in a suitcase.

Then again, legs like hers would be made for sports. All kinds.

A varlet.
An unscrupulous scoundrel.
Degenerate.
Dirty-minded rascal.

Truvy could barely concentrate on what Edwina was telling her about the dance studio. Her thoughts were on Mrs. Plunkett's endless tirade uttered at the breakfast table that morning in regard to the disrobing of her wise man. As soon as Mrs. Plunkett had lifted the shade to her boudoir, she'd discovered the naked figurine in the white blanket of yard.

It makes me sick to my stomach, that's what it does. To think that in our little town, there is a rake on the loose. I'm going to the police to report the incident.

The window of opportunity to explain had been lowered as soon as the roller shade had been lifted. Truvy couldn't say anything about it now, not after Mrs. Plunkett had called her a vandal, a dirty degenerate to be reported to the police.

"I haven't been in here in weeks," Edwina said, whisking dust from the curtains with the palm of her hand.

With the closed curtains blocking the sunshine out, the interior wasn't well lit. The room was very large, with neat planked floors, polished to perfection—but in need of sweeping and a fresh coat of wax. An oak cabinet housed shelves of recordings in brown paper sleeves, and on its top rested a Victrola with a wide-belled trumpet painted with wildflowers. Various pieces of framed sheet music hung on the walls. Scott Joplin. Eubie Blake. Richard Zimmerman. The music companies must have supplied them, as the elaborate frames were decorated with small gold engraved plates, such as: STARK & SON, SEDALIA, MO—1899.

"This really is an enterprise, Edwina," Truvy said, imagining what the studio would look like, brightly lit from the globe lamps suspended from the ceiling, and with the curtains thrown back. One of the walls was a block of mirrors, side by side, to make a continuous runner of reflection. She could envision the place filled with music, the shy responses from young ladies and exchanges of polite words from maturing young gentlemen as they learned their steps.

"It's not so much," Edwina replied with her hands on her hips, "because I don't have the finishing school anymore." She gazed around the room; then a melancholy and contemplative look came into her eyes. "I had a difficult time making the decision, but as a teacher, I think you know that sometimes a class of students can't be replaced. You know that you've done your best, taught all you can, and you've accomplished what you wanted." She gingerly laid a hand over the extension of her stomach and slightly wrinkled her forehead. "I gave up my side of the building on Old Oak Road to Tom. Remember the one I told you he painted half red to my yellow half? Well, it's all brown now. He expanded the store and built an office for himself and his partner."

"Shay Dufresne," Truvy said. "You mentioned him in your letters. Does Tom still have his stuffed bear?"

Edwina laughed, then winced like she sometimes did when the baby was kicking. She'd been doing that a lot this morning—even making slight gasps, as if the unborn child within her was overly active. When they'd drunk their tea at the dining-room table, she'd excused herself to go to the water closet. A short while later, she came back saying she was fine. But on the walk over, she'd stopped to catch her breath, resting her hand on the awning post in front of an office belonging to Milton Burditt, Esquire. A fine prickle of panic had skittered up Truvy's nape. She suggested they go back home, but Edwina said she'd had her heart set on showing Truvy the dancing studio today. They wouldn't stay long, she assured Truvy.

"Yes," Edwina answered after a soft chuckle, "he still has the big grizzly. Along with all those other little rodents he has stuffed, sitting on the counter and hanging on the walls of his sporting goods store."

"I'd like to see them while I'm here."

"I'm sure Tom would love to show them to you. Every single one."

Truvy walked to the phonograph and scanned the

selections. "I like to listen to ragtime. All those nights when you went out and danced with your friends at the Peacherine Club, I stayed in and worked on my assignments. I should have gone with you. You always had more fun than I did."

"There are a lot of ways to have fun without going to a rag club." She went to Truvy and selected a recording of "Maple Leaf Rag." Cranking the handle on the phonograph, she lowered the needle until the snappy notes drifted out the trumpet. "I certainly can't play tennis like you, and it looks fun."

"I could show you how. It's easy."

"Easy for you to say. Look at me." She held up her arms, turning her body sideways. The full gathers of her toasted butter-colored skirts and overblouse were obvious through the opening part of a Brinkley coat. "I'm rather ungainly at the moment."

Truvy thought she looked beautiful. She'd never considered that a woman who carried a child would be so pretty. But Edwina was. Her cheeks were a dusky rose, her complexion the color of cream. She was stylish in her braided hat and soft white gloves without even trying. Truvy had taken over an hour to fix herself up; almond green bouclé etamine, the light wool fabric keeping the chill at bay. The walking costume had been more money than she should have spent. Ready made, it had to be altered—the hem lengthened, the cap of the sleeves untucked a few inches.

"I think you look lovely."

"Lovely and expectant," she replied warmly. "With three full classes in my books, waiting to be taught waltzes as soon as I find them a teacher." She shuffled lightly, her palms covering her belly. "I did have one hired. She fell on the ice and sprained her ankle. So

I've had to—" She bit off her sentence with an abrupt intake of her breath. "I think . . ."

Truvy's eyes widened. "You think what?"

"I think . . ."—she lowered herself into one of the few plush velvet chairs that sat next to the wall—". . . think you'd better go get Tom for me."

"Why?" Truvy practically screeched, knowing full well why. But she'd never been with a woman whose time was due. Clearly early. By a week. How fast was the delivery? Her insides quaked.

"Because something just happened and I need him and Dr. Porter." She frowned, exhaling shallowly. "You'll have to get Tom at his store. It's on Old Oak Road. Down by the train depot."

"To the right or the left once I'm outside?" Truvy rushed. The streets they'd taken to the studio from the Wolcott house had her sense of direction twisted around.

"Right. A few blocks. There's a tin bald eagle over the door. *Wolcott's Sporting Goods and Excursions* on the sign."

She put a hand over Edwina's, meaning to calm her, but Edwina seemed level-headed. It was Truvy who was coming undone. "All right. Okay. Yes. I can find that." Struggling to capture her composure, she drew her shoulders back and collected herself.

Truvy would have been fine, out the door and on her way at a sensible but urgent pace, but it was Edwina's parting word—uttered so quietly and sounding so fragile—that made her fly out the door, the tiny whisper trailing after her.

"Hurry."

Hurry. Hurry. Hurry. Like a litany, it repeated in Truvy's head, over and over, as she traversed the boardwalk in high-fashion shoes that pinched and hindered her flight. She glanced once at the street pole sign to read if she was on the proper road. Dogwood Place. Edwina hadn't said anything about that. *Old Oak Road.* Just a block down was Sugar Maple Street. That should lead to the train depot. You'd think . . .

Filled with indecision, she skidded but balanced herself by digging her heels into the iced-over snow. *Stuff and fiddlesticks.* The mild oath swam in her mind—words she'd heard Edwina use. If Truvy had had her Spaldings on, she could've made a fast and competent sprint across town.

Quickly approaching Sugar Maple, she looked down the slight incline of street to the south. That had to be the way. Keep going. Run. Then again, she didn't see any depot.

The uncertainty that flashed in that split second caused her to slide at the corner with the grace of a duck landing on a frozen pond. She barely had time to put her hands out when she plowed into a man's back as he seemingly came from nowhere around a building's edge. The force of her assault had no effect on him; he didn't falter an inch. If it hadn't been for the thick fabric of his shirt, which she now gripped, Truvy would have been on the icy ground.

"I'm terribly sorry," she blurted, "but I'm in a hurry."

He lowered his chin and slightly tilted his head. Not enough to see her but enough to cause the bristles of an unshaven jaw to snag in the netting on the crown of her hat.

"This is a new approach on studying my anatomy." When he spoke, she felt a baritone rumble dissolve into the heat of her crushed breasts. "No need to hurry. Take all the time you want."

She knew the voice. Should have recognized the breadth of shoulders in the red plaid blur that filled her vision.

"I don't want to feel your muscles, you big toad." She disengaged her hands from him, shoving him away as she stepped carelessly backwards and nearly slipped once more.

Jake Brewster turned toward her, realizing who'd been molded against his back. A quirk lifted one brow; his smile was intimate.

She ignored the lurch in her thumping heartbeat.

"I've got to find Tom Wolcott," she announced in a shaky voice. "It's a matter of . . ."—against her will, her eyes moistened, hotly tearing from fear, frustration, and urgency—". . . of extreme emergency."

The rakish light in Jake's eyes darkened. "Edwina?"

"Yes. She's at the dancing studio."

"I'll get Tom. You get the doctor."

"Where's his office?"

Putting a large hand on her waist, he propelled her to the corner with a firm arm. The hard contour of his bicep pressed against the boning that ran down the side of her bodice. For an instant, she felt his fingers brush over her spine. Gently. Thoughtfully. She didn't dwell on the notion that he might be comforting her as he pointed the way. "Keep going on this street and turn up Hackberry Way. It's on the right."

He was gone before she could thank him.

Chapter

❧ 4 ❧

The zebra clock tolled the hour. Four strikes.

Stretching the kink in her tired shoulders, Truvy stood at the Wolcotts' kitchen sink with her hands on the enamel rim. A small flame flickered overhead from the lamp. She viewed her reflection in the window glass; her hair was askew, pins not fully in place. Smudges shadowed her eyes, and the color of her complexion seemed dull. She looked through the image of herself and out into the dark yard.

Dawn wouldn't arrive for another three hours.

"You can't make coffee worth a damn."

Unbidden, she smiled. Her eyes focused on the man sitting behind her. She didn't have to turn around to see him. His outline was clearly visible in the pale light bouncing off the mirrorlike window.

Jake leaned over a cup of coffee, his strong hands around its tiny circumference.

Defensively, she explained, "It's because I'm a statistic. The *American Collegiate Journal* claims female college graduates make poor homemakers."

"So do stunningly beautiful women."

Turning, she folded her arms across her breasts and slanted her gaze at him. The hair above his ears was trimmed in a way that she found appealing. A day's growth of beard made his facial features appear less chiseled. He'd removed his heavy red plaid shirt, revealing a long-john shirt with its sleeves cut off just below his shoulders. She should have been offended by the liberty and said so. But the honest truth was, the exposed skin on his arms, bronze and smooth as if made of marble, fascinated her. When he put his elbow on the tabletop, momentarily rubbing his brow, she watched, trancelike, the dance and play of the bands of steel that seemed to occur with every motion he made.

The fire they'd kept going in the cast-iron stove radiated through the room with almost unbearable ripples of heat—a heat she didn't dare admit had more to do with the man sharing the room with her than the actual fire.

She forced herself to stay focused on the chapter called "Adaptation."

The parties must have similar tastes, aspirations, hopes, and desires. One must not be an advocate of temperance and the other of drinking. One must not love tobacco and the other hate it. One must not be highly educated and the other an ignoramus, with no love for knowledge and wisdom.

She wasn't sure she despised smoking and drinking. She'd never tried either. And really, Jake might be rough around the edges, but she didn't think of him as an ignoramus.

It is not necessary that the wedded pair be alike in all things.

That line gave her optimism. Not that she was thinking of wedding Mr. Jacob Brewster. Heavens— that was the last thing on her mind.

And yet, he scrutinized her as if she were a mysterious prize in a raffle basket . . . something he wasn't sure he wanted, but the anticipation of the unknown contents made the basket tempting enough to bid on. When he looked at her like that, her insides turned over.

She'd caught him watching her several times. It unnerved her. Made her feel as if she had a thread loose at her neckline. Once, she lifted her hand to her collar to check that everything was in place. Not a stitch of fabric out of order. Why, then, did he go on so with a lingering perusal that left her senses scattered?

With a blink, Truvy brought her thoughts to the present. "I wouldn't have assumed that. What does a woman's beauty have to do with keeping a house?"

A cynical frown caught on his mouth. "They're too preoccupied with it to do anything but make sure they look good all the time."

She detected bitterness in his tone—and a voice recalling experience. Or perhaps it was the hour and the tension that stretched through the waiting. They'd been keeping vigil in the kitchen, Truvy brewing pots of strong coffee, while Tom and Dr. Porter were upstairs with Edwina. Her labor had been progressing for sixteen hours. The last time Tom came downstairs to get a crockery of lard, a bottle of vinegar, and ice pieces for the doctor, he'd said Edwina was holding her own. She was ready; the baby wasn't.

Truvy couldn't dream of what it would be like to have a husband at her bedside when she delivered their child. Even more so, she couldn't envision being a wife. Or having a home of her own. They were thoughts she never dwelled on. Because her life was full.

She was happy. *Honestly.*

But at the moment, she was beside herself with worry. What was the lard and vinegar for? Were they a telltale sign something was going wrong? She felt helpless and awkward, unequipped to take on the responsibility of friend and helper at a time like this. She didn't know what to do.

So she made coffee.

Terrible coffee. She knew it. The problem was, she didn't know how to brew it. She guessed the measurements of grounds to water. Fumbled at the mill, grinding until the beans were dusty brown flakes.

Because there was nothing to do but wait and stay alert in case she was needed, Truvy poured herself a cup of the awful coffee. She splashed a liberal amount of cream and stirred in a lot of sugar into oily, dark coffee to make it more palatable. She joined Jake at the table, sitting across from him but not meeting his gaze.

"I take it you don't know how to cook." His statement was matter-of-fact. Not condescending, but she took it wrong just the same.

"No, I don't," she responded more harshly than she should, giving him a quick glance.

She knew she had failings. That she wasn't marriage material. That her choices in life had led her to be teacher and substitute mother to students while she had their attention in her classroom. She could nurture a young lady who was in the throes of sorrow over her economics grade. She could comfort her if she injured a limb on the playing courts. She was a good listener. She was a good motivator.

She simply wasn't a good cook. Or any kind of cook. She'd never taken the time to learn. It had never been a priority for her. The Aunts were kitchen-minded—so content to create, they had never asked for help. And she hadn't had the interest in inquiring. When she'd left Emporia for Chicago, the campus had provided her meals. As did St. Francis, fully prepared by the refectory cooks. She simply sat and ate and enjoyed. It wasn't important enough to learn on her own.

"And I suppose you do." A listless energy enveloped her. He'd been up all night, just as she, yet lack of sleep didn't seem to affect him at all.

"I do."

She couldn't keep the surprise from her voice. "You do?"

"Yeah." The depths of his eyes seemed ethereal. That silvery green in the flickering haze of lamplight. She didn't want to tear her attention away from them. "I live alone. I take care of myself."

"Well . . . that's interesting." Blood raced through her at the thought. *He lives alone.* Just like she did in her apartment at St. Francis. They were two independent people. They had nothing in common. That much was evident in the little time she'd spend in his company. It was clear he took life without an iota of seriousness. He talked in innuendoes. Made comments that no decent gentleman would. And yet, she found him . . . likable.

It was honorable of him to stay with his friend, Tom. She shouldn't be such a crab. She didn't know what was wrong with her. This whole business of babies . . . of marriage . . . of zebra clocks . . . and dogs and cats and . . .

. . . domesticity.

She was out of her element in this environment.

"I'm an interesting man, Miss Valentine." He cracked a smile, then ate a few of the Powell's candied walnuts in a canister resting on the table. The way he let them drop into his open mouth mesmerized her. He had nice teeth. Even and white. She studied his jaw. The same scruff-bearded jaw that had abraded the netting of her hat. A shiver coursed through her at the memory. It seemed scandalous to think about. A man's chin tucked into the feminine frills of a lady's hat, his mouth but a few inches from her forehead. It had been as close as she'd ever come to being kissed.

Not that he'd been thinking that.

Clearly, no.

"Are you interesting, Miss Valentine?" he asked, leaning forward and coming nose to nose with her, practically touching her. The sweet candy on his breath aroused her senses. She could almost taste the walnuts herself. She could see a few grains of sugar on his lips; her mind spun with dismay as she wondered what it would be like to have them pressed against hers.

Heat blanketed her skin to a degree that she felt perspiration trickle down the valley of her breasts. She found it difficult to sit still in his presence. She needed something to do, something to distract her. Without regard, she ate a walnut. He stared as she chewed, then swallowed. A lump settled into her stomach. She instantly wished she hadn't eaten the candy. "I don't know what you'd call interesting."

"Sports trophies."

The coffee cup she'd brought to her mouth stilled. "They're nothing."

"They're something." Her eyes leveled on the buttons trailing down the neck of his altered long-john shirt. She could see his pulse beat at the hollow of his throat. The cotton fabric molded over his chest and showed every contour and detail of body definition. He was perfectly comfortable, but she felt as if she would wilt. "How'd you get them? I thought you were a teacher."

"I am a teacher." She didn't want to tell him she was an athletic coach. If he knew, he'd look at her differently, talk to her differently. It was vain to want his gaze on her as if she were pretty. But she did.

Sentimentality. Weak constitution.

She shied away from answering directly. "I teach economics—political, not 'home,' obviously. What do you think of President Roosevelt?"

"I couldn't say. I don't know him."

"Neither do I, but I have an opinion on his policies."

"I couldn't care less."

A surge of invigoration came to life in her fatigued thoughts. "But you live in the United States, Mr. Brewster. Surely you have an opinion on how your government is run."

"Not really."

"I can't believe that. Everyone should have a vested interest in how our White House is operating. Don't you care that the U.S. Congress adopted two amendments this past March to the Army Appropriations Bill providing U.S. intervention abroad?"

"I don't live in any white house, Miss Valentine. I make my stake in a room at the gymnasium, so I wouldn't know about any amendments."

"It was in all the newspapers. Because of Cuba."

"I read *Sporting Life.*"

Truvy fought the urge to bring her hands to her cheeks and stare at him, completely dumbfounded.

Barkly wandered into the kitchen, his toenails clicking across the planks of the floor. He lowered his muzzle on Jake's knee and gazed up through his bloodshot eyes. Jake gave his ear an absent scratch.

"I don't have what you'd call a real educational background," he said in a manner that was defensive. "School wasn't a priority for me."

Quietly, she asked, "Your parents didn't encourage you?"

He smiled with such sarcasm, she was prompted to find out why. "Your mother?"

"Unknown."

"Your father?"

"Unknown whereabouts unless he writes and needs money from me."

That he could be so cold about it saddened and distressed her. What a different childhood he must have had in comparison to hers.

"You?" he said. "Parents?"

He spoke in incomplete sentences. As was her habit with her girls, she wanted to correct him, even though she understood what he was asking. But she refrained. No need to remind them both she was a spinster schoolmarm.

"They passed away. My mother had me late in life. She and my father were in their forties." The admission slipped out, surprising her. She didn't normally divulge she'd been born to a couple past their prime. She was comfortable around elderly people because that's who'd raised her. Although Jake didn't know the actuality, The Aunts were seventy-one and had entered her life when she'd been nine years old.

The pain-filled cry of a woman's voice drifted down the stairs that led to the upper floors through the kitchen.

Truvy quit breathing, looking across the table and holding Jake's gaze.

He was just as scared as she was. She could tell. Creases at the corners of his mouth went white as he clenched his jaw.

"It's nothing," he said. "It's normal."

She wanted to ask him how he knew. Had he been with women as they'd delivered babies?

In a clear effort to bring her mind away from the thump of feet overhead and the whimpers of Edwina, Jake reached over and took her hand, giving her a deliberate squeeze. "For a woman who wins trophies by hurling basketballs, you have soft hands, *Miss Valentine.*"

When he called her Miss Valentine, he uttered the syllables in a slow drawl that had the feel of warm honey. It was one thing to hear Moose Thompson say her name with his beefy inflection— "Miz V'lantine"— and another when Jake spoke it. She doubted he was emphasizing her unmarried status, but she caught herself being oversensitive. She felt like a withered-up crone.

"Don't call me Miss Valentine like that." She pulled her hand free from his, feeling the calluses on his palm as it slid over her knuckles. "If you must use my name, call me Truvy."

"Truvy?"

"Yes."

"And how'd you get a name like that?"

"I was named after the day I was born on. February the fourteenth. I was, as my mother said, a true valentine in every sense. 'True V.' became 'Truvy.' "

"I've never met another Truvy."

"It's not likely you will."

After she replied, she wondered if he'd meant a woman named Truvy, or a woman like *her*. She wasn't skilled in male-female conversation, the subtleties of small talk between the sexes. This was the first time she'd revealed this much about herself to a man. Was his meaning that she was unique? Did she want him to think she was unique? Nobody had ever—she abruptly quit the thought. She'd never learn how he intended the comment, because she'd never ask him to explain it.

A span of silence wore on between them, as neither said anything further. A log in the stove fell, crackling and popping as it burned. The noises upstairs came in intervals; a soft whimper, a drone of undecipherable instruction, a stifled sob, and then Tom's voice of assurance.

Truvy didn't know how much more she could take of the endless hours in which nothing seemed to happen; then immediately, she was sorry. If she was tired and anxious, dear Edwina had to be feeling that way ten times over.

As each minute ticked off the clock, frightened anticipation worked up Truvy's spine. She sat tall and unmoving. The longer the birthing took, the more her mind became congested with doubts and fears.

The coffeepot ran dry once more, and she rose to fill it when the sound of a baby's cry came from above, piercing the tense silence in the hot kitchen.

She looked at Jake. He stood.

Footsteps sounded on the narrow wooden stairs

behind her. She turned and saw Tom stopping halfway down. He wore a grin on his mouth as broad as idealism. Relief softened the corners. His rumpled shirt was marked with perspiration. "Edwina's fine. It's a girl." He laughed heartily. "I have a daughter, Jake!" Then he went back up the stairs.

Truvy let out her breath, unaware she'd been holding it.

A girl.

A baby.

Something I'll never have.

Disappointment came in a twinge that tightened the pressure against her ribs, making her corset feel sizes too small, laced beyond comfort. The squeezing hurt snuck up on her, catching her unaware. This feeling had no place or reason in her heart. It was just there, sudden, surprising.

The words from the book came flooding into her mind: *Sexual emotion is absolutely necessary to conception. The child is made in a moment. The best qualities of mind and body are most desirable.*

She'd never know what that meant.

She bowed her head. To her dismay, she wanted to bury her face in the corded muscles of Jake's chest, have him soothe her—make her feel normal, accepted, without motherhood being a part of her life.

Then, she felt arms around her, pulling her close, fitting her head in the perfect hollow between his shoulder and neck. As if he knew. And yet, how could he know the extraordinary void that welled within her?

His large hands stroked her back, up and down. They rubbed, quieted, comforted—offered a silent message of understanding. She laid her cheek at the collar of his shirt, the fabric pleasantly warmed from his skin. She felt his body, hard and strong beneath her palms as they hesitantly rested on the expanse of his chest. His chin rested on the top of her head; then he inhaled, subtly, slowly, as if pulling her fragrance into his lungs. The gesture made her conscious of the fact she'd washed her hair with lemon verbena that morning.

He encircled her tighter, holding her within a sanctuary of safety. Here, in his tender embrace, she didn't feel like a maiden auntie, a plain, nobody woman that no man wanted.

A woman who thought she was fine on her own, without a man.

He said only one word, his moist breath tickling the shell of her ear as the sound passed through his lips.

"Truvy."

Emotional as she was, she wanted to cry, but she refrained. She wouldn't let herself lose all control. She felt better now, ready to go on with her duty to her friend.

Realizing that, she had to prove she wasn't a sentimental fool. Freeing herself from him, she put on a brave smile. "Well, I'd best see what needs to be done for Edwina . . ."

He lowered his arms to his sides. "Yeah, sure."

She dared not recognize the light of confusion in his eyes. Or was that a trace of regret?

"I'll chop some more wood." He put on his red plaid shirt, fastening the buttons with one hand.

The porch door opened and closed.

Frosty air swirled into the warmth of the kitchen, but that wasn't what caused Truvy to shiver. She still heard the mellow sound of her name coming from his lips: *Truvy.*

Velvety smooth, the lingering notes of it remained suspended in the room.

The heavy iron weight of a barbell brought out the veins on Jake's biceps as he curled the bar up in a wide arc. Sweat glistened on his forehead, trickled between the swells of his pectorals, and dampened the body hair beneath his arms. He brought the bar high, elbows close to his body, his feet shoulder-width apart. Following the same half circle, he lowered the barbell again, resisting the weight all the way down until his arms were fully extended.

He was in the middle of his fourth set, and his muscles were in the beginnings of failing. His biceps screamed in agony. But he didn't stop. He clenched his teeth so hard, his jaw ached. His extensor forearms burned as he brought the barbell up to the sixth and final range of motion.

Following through, he lowered the weight toward the floor. As the globe-shaped ends hit the carpet, a small cloud of white chalk puffed beneath each ball. Straightening, Jake shook out his arms as he gazed at his reflection in the gymnasium's mirror.

Although not in competition shape, he was dense and cut with muscle. No shirt covered his chest; well-defined ridges and valleys contoured the expanse of skin, which was covered with a light amount of chest hair. A pair of gym trunks, cut off high at the thigh, molded tightly over his buttocks. His shoulder breadth had a good deltoid development that increased his front lat spread when he posed. Obliques and abdominals were taut but not thick.

He stood at six feet five inches and weighed two

hundred and fifty-seven pounds. When he'd been in prime form, he weighed two hundred and seventy.

Drawing in a deep breath, he flexed his fingers in the fingerless leather gloves he wore. Then he moved his hands over the barbell with a closed grip, putting extra stress on the outside heads of his biceps. With his intense physical strain and mental concentration, his next set was slower but remained tight. The stretch of muscle went to a full extension, then came all the way back to a position of complete contraction.

Dawn's light shone through the windows, reflecting off the mirror. He was a lone man exercising in Bruiser's Gymnasium on a frigid morning when nobody else was up. Except Truvy Valentine, whom he had left at the Wolcotts' an hour earlier.

He willed his thoughts of her to dissipate, focusing on the movement of weight and his ability to follow through the motion.

Highly oxygenated blood pumped through him, elevating his exhausted mood after a long night of coffee and waiting. He counted out the repetitions in his mind.

Two. The speed with which his lifeblood surged into certain vessels more quickly caused his skin to flush. His heart beat at twice its normal speed.

Three. His sweat became profuse; his breathing became increasingly noisy and difficult.

Four! Engorged with blood, his entire anatomy enlarged.

Five! A feeling of heat and heightened sensitivity charged his body's surface. The sensations were strongly erotic. The "pump" climaxed through him, a point of intensity, of emotional excitement. A warm, prickly sensation made his body feel like liquid fire.

Six! On a groan, he lowered the barbell and backed away, throwing his head back and taking in deep gulps of air. With splayed fingers locked on his hips, he walked a small circle, channeling the euphoria that aroused his body. It beat within his chest, pulsed through his veins, scorched his skin.

He sank onto the padded leather of the preacher's bench and rested his elbows on his knees. Breathing came in a rush as he stared at the gym. He let his mind wander to the woman he'd been trying to put out of his head by working out.

Truvy. The echo of her name brought with it the memory of soft, pliant warmth, of breasts crushed next to his chest. Her hair smelled like lemons or flowers. He couldn't decide. It was an exotic mixture of both. The perfume clinging to her skin was that of coffee because of the grounds that had flown out of the mill every time she dumped them into the blue enamel pot. Between the three, he thought she smelled kissable. The way she rested her cheek on his chest, eyes closed, with her lashes demurely down, he'd imagined delivering the lightest, most tender kiss he could give her. There. On those long lashes.

But that moment hadn't been about him, his wants. It had been about hers.

She'd simply wanted him to hold her. She'd said as much without the words. So he had. And in doing so, he wanted more. She projected an energy and spirit that undeniably attracted him to her.

He recalled her fervent political opinions, the way her lips had parted in surprise. Her confusion at his lack of interest. What would she think of him if she knew the kind of boyhood he'd come from?

Who he'd been. Where he'd been. What he'd done.

Jake combed a hand through his damp hair. His reflections of the past had him looking back on a life lived hard and fast, in the limelight. He closed his eyes. The backs of his lids burned with dryness from lack of sleep.

He'd been twenty-five and had things he'd only dreamed about. Luxury, fame, wealth, and success. And a wife.

Laurette Everleigh. A famous dancer, she was renowned across the country for her beauty. Unmatched in womanly sensuality, she'd come to the exposition to perform. Ziegfeld hooked them up for some publicity photographs, and the next day, the *Chicago Daily News* headlined them as the "most magnificent-looking couple of the century."

A week later, they were married.

At the end of his six-week run in Chicago, they were divorced.

She left for Boston with a five-grand settlement out of him. He went back to New York worth twenty-five thousand dollars. He hadn't seen her since.

He broke his partnership with Ziegfeld, then performed in several theaters in Manhattan. Over the years, his father came to several of his shows, asked for money—which Jake gave him—then disappeared again for months. During the nineties, Jake invested in several ventures. He backed a Klondike mine, only to have it go bust. He lost a lot. But had enough money left to realize that the big city made him reckless, self-indulgent, and free-spending.

So he followed the advice of Tom Wolcott and

came west to Montana to open a gymnasium. Jake and Tom had met in San Francisco some years back. Tom was bartending at the Lucky Nugget, and the two of them found they had a lot in common. Both had wastrel fathers and neither one of them had a mother—although Tom knew his mother had passed away. The two of them were independent and business-minded, and when Jake had settled back in New York, Tom moved on to Washington and finally Harmony. He'd told Jake about the town, his new wife— Edwina—and had been after him to come. Jake finally took him up on it.

He liked Harmony, liked the feeling it gave him. The street blocks were those of your typical small town, named by a theme. In this case, the theme was trees. The citizens seemed chronically short of cash but always took care of their own. Anonymously, Jake donated to the church fund through his bank account. Only the Reverend Stoll and Mr. Fletcher, the manager of Harmony Security Bank, knew about it, and Jake said he'd knock Fletcher into next week if he ever revealed Jake's identity.

When he wanted a woman, he sought them in nearby Waverly or Alder. Nobody in town would put up with womanizing right under their noses. They were a stiff bunch but a good bunch of folks.

Tom and Edwina were the best.

At that thought, Jake rose and grabbed a copy of yesterday's newspaper that had been left in the smoking lounge in the men's dressing room. He brought it to his office and sat down.

From his bottom drawer, beneath a box of striking-bag inflaters, he took out a pair of plain spectacles and a dictionary. Wiping the glass lenses on the fabric of his gym trunks, he held them up for inspection. Clean and clear. He fit the straight temples on his ears.

The papers and brochures and booklets and receipts scattered over his desk took on a clarity and deeper definition of light and dark. The miniature world of fine text print came into sharp focus.

He refused to put on the gold-rimmed peepers if anyone was around. A big guy like him wearing a pair of glasses presented a weak constitution. It wasn't good for business. Strong men had strong eyes.

Jake flipped the newspaper to the front page, leaning closer for a study of the words.

Matthew Gage, the editor of the *Harmony Advocate*, had written up a commentary on the U.S. Supreme Court and Puerto Rico. The headline read: UNITED STATES SUPREME COURT EXHIBITS POWER.

Opening the Webster's, Jake searched for the word *exhibit*. At times, it could be a slow process because his attention veered to the multitude of other words. Other definitions. They came at him in an explosion of black ink. He absorbed as many as he could. He wanted intellectual power. To memorize the whole dictionary in his head. So as his gaze skimmed down the columns, he looked up the other *ex-* words.

excruciate: to inflict severe pains upon; torture.

He didn't know that was how to spell *xcrusheate*.

Dragging his finger down the page, he mumbled letters: "*exc ... excu ... execu ...*"

exercise: to train by use; exert; practice; employ activity.

He knew that one.

exhibit: to present to view; display.

Jake continued with the opinion piece that stated inhabitants of Puerto Rico and other U.S. overseas territories were U.S. nationals, not citizens, and that the Constitution applied only in territories incorporated by the U.S. Congress. Roosevelt had his nose in it.

Overseas territories.

U.S. Nationals.

Constitution.

U.S. Congress.

None of that mattered diddly-squat to Jake. But because Truvy thought the president's policies notable, he found himself thumbing through the entire newspaper, looking for things he could find on Teddy.

He didn't want to confront the logic behind such an effort.

It was better for him to think he'd suddenly grown a taste for politics than had a desire to hunt down facts so he could impress a woman named for her birthday.

Chapter

⚜5⚜

"Well, what do you think?"

Truvy stared at the pair of fancy mittens made of cardinal Saxony wool with yellow bows on the wrists, then at Mrs. Plunkett, who sat on the edge of the parlor chair with her hands pressed together in anticipation.

Momentarily, Truvy's voice eluded her. "I—I think they're quite lovely. You shouldn't have."

"Oh but, my dear, I *wanted* to." Her rosy cheeks blossomed like ripe apples. Her ample bosom swelled with pride. "I made an exact pair for my Hildegarde when she was sixteen."

But I'm twenty-five.

"Try them on." Mrs. Plunkett's cheeriness was a stark contrast to the doldrums she'd been in that morning.

Truvy put one mitten on, then the other. They had no fingers, but the knit was soft; they reminded her of her childhood in Kansas, where she spent many winters building snowmen and being pulled on a sled by her uncles. She held her palms up for Mrs. Plunkett's examination.

"Charming!" she exclaimed. "Now . . ."—she rose—". . . let's have our lunch. I already prepared us cheese sandwiches. They're in the dining room. And I steamed caramel pudding. We can pour lots of apple jelly over it—with ample servings. Hiram isn't here to frown at me." She smiled, as if they shared an intimate secret. "While we eat, you can tell me about Mrs. Wolcott."

Half an hour later, Truvy was still seated across from Mrs. Plunkett at the dining-room table, talking about Edwina's daughter.

"My, but I remember when Mrs. Wolcott came back from that Chicago college. It was a shame her poor mother passed on," Mrs. Plunkett remarked, taking a bite of her pudding. "But she's a very strong woman. She took charge and opened that finishing school and . . ." The teaspoon in her hand paused halfway to her mouth. Dark eyes teared up. Blinking rapidly, she went on. "If I hadn't sent my Hildegarde, she might not have gained so much poise. Men find her irresistible. She's so . . . so . . . pretty."

The finely tatted handkerchief came out from her dress sleeve, and Mrs. Plunkett noisily blew her nose.

"Yes, I can see by her photograph in the parlor," Truvy said, trying to keep the elder woman from crying. "She looks like you."

Dabbing the hankie at her reddish nostrils, Mrs. Plunkett lifted her brows and she cracked a slight smile. "Do you think so?"

"You have the same . . ."—she grappled for the right words—". . . features. I'd know you're mother and daughter just by the way you favor each other."

"Oh . . ." Once more, the pudding became tempting

and she fed herself a large helping. "We have my mother's eyes."

"Hmm—"

"And her hair . . ." Mrs. Plunkett mused while studying Truvy. "You know, you should do something with yours."

Truvy's hand went to her hair. Aside from the one time she spent hours pinning it up on the train, the styles she tried never turned out right, nor did the heavy curls stay put. Teaching in a gymnasium left little time for vanity. She was lucky if she had the same amount of hairpins in her hair in the evening as she had in the morning.

"I think you'd look darling with your hair"—Mrs. Plunkett put down her spoon and gazed sideways at Truvy—"just so. More in a Gibson knot instead of loose curls in a twist. Why, I could use my curl iron on you and make you look just like Hildegarde. My baby is very fashionable. That man she married had better a-appreciate th-that a-a-about h-h-h-her."

Mrs. Plunkett succumbed to her emotions and fat tears rolled down her cheeks.

Awkwardly, Truvy attempted to soothe her. "Now, Mrs. Plunkett, don't get yourself in a state. You've been doing so well. More pudding?"

"No," she mumbled into her handkerchief. "I feel one of my headaches coming on. I'm going to lie down. We'll fix your hair later."

"That's all right. You rest. Don't worry about me. I have some letters to write."

Mrs. Plunkett left the table in sniffles, and as soon as Truvy heard her bedroom door close, she cleared the dishes, then went up to her room as well. She brought the mittens with her and set them on the secretary desk, where she took a seat.

Truvy pensively looked out the window for a while at the winter white world and the gray, bare branches of trees.

She poised the nib of her fountain pen over crisp white paper, then began to write.

December 18, 1901

Dear Miss Pond:

Joyous news from Harmony! Edwina had her baby, a daughter named Elizabeth. She was born on December 15 at 5:23 in the morning. Edwina is doing wonderfully. It's so good to see her.

I've met many friendly people since my arrival, such as Shay Dufresne, Tom's business partner, and his wife, Crescencia. The day after Elizabeth was born, they came to the house to offer their congratulations. They brought with them their three-month-old son.

I hope you are in fine health. Did the girls get off on their holiday all right? The weather here is cold, as I'm sure it is in Boise. We had one inch of snow overnight.

Mr. and Mrs. Plunkett have heartily welcomed me, but I'm looking forward to making St. Francis my life-long home. Please let me know how the matter of the benefactress has been resolved. Let me again reassure you, and the school committee, that my intentions are most honorable. In the future, I will conform to all rules and regulations.

That being the case, I'd like to return as originally planned, on the 27th of December. You may write to me in care of the Plunketts at the general delivery box in Harmony and advise me of your decision.

Respectfully yours,
Truvy Valentine

Truvy reread the informative letter. Two times. Wanting desperately to make a good impression on Miss Pond, Truvy had composed the letter in her head before putting it on paper. The words had to be exactly right—optimistic, enthusiastic, earnest, full of promise and energy—the things she honestly felt in her heart.

Satisfied, she folded the paper into an envelope. She sealed the flap and laid it on top of the letter she'd penned to The Aunts last night. Later today, she'd take both correspondences to the post office.

That letter to Miss Pond had more to do with things other than wanting to return to St. Francis than she had divulged in her neat script. Between the lines, Jake Brewster took up space.

She found that her independent flight—the testing of her wings, so to speak—was snagged with thoughts of him. How could she dare transgress against her convictions? The words she'd emphatically spoken to Miss Pond? She belonged at St. Francis. As a teacher. Inasmuch as she was enjoying her visit with Edwina, she wanted to go home and prove to herself she could be what the school wanted her to be.

But she caught herself allowing Jake in her subconscious.

The way she'd held onto him in Edwina's kitchen ... it was shameful.

It was wonderful.

Beneath those muscles and that rakish personality, *he* might be wonderful.

Her fingers brushed the spine of *The Science of Life.* She'd been reading more last night. Sometimes the book confused her. She'd had an impulse to kiss Jake when he'd breathed in the fragrance of her hair.

A *natural instinct* to do so. How could that be, when he wasn't a "harmony of souls" match for her?

The book couldn't be wrong.

She was building him up in her mind—that's what she was doing. She was going back to Boise where she belonged. There was no sense in making anything of him. Of them.

But he could be so . . . interesting.

If she wanted to make him dull, all she had to do was tell him about her coaching position. She knew that would be the end of her idiotic attraction to him, because he'd pour on all the gymnasium talk.

On a sigh, Truvy wondered how Mrs. Plunkett was feeling.

She didn't mind Mrs. Plunkett's company, but her fussing and hovering could be . . . taxing. She knew she should be polite and gracious—and she had been. But there were those moments when Mrs. Plunkett's hankie sessions were hard to bear. Whenever they talked and Hildegarde's name was mentioned, the elder woman cried about this and that.

Truvy hoped the woman would forget about styling her hair. She didn't want to wear a Gibson knot. Bother it, she didn't want to wear cardinal mittens. She wasn't even fond of cheese sandwiches. With Mrs. Plunkett's present state of mind and behavior, Truvy worried that by staying at the Plunkett house, she was becoming more than a boarder.

She was a replacement Hildegarde for the young woman's lonely, heartbroken mother.

Truvy woke as a brush of dawn sky settled on the horizon.

She put her legs over the side of the bed and shivered as she slipped her feet into felt house slippers. The heating stove had gone out during the night and the room's air had a nip about it. She went to the window and parted the curtains.

Frosty ice blanketed the outdoors and new snow had fallen overnight. Even with the chill in the room, the scene outside made her long to feel a bite of cold air on her cheeks, to feel her feet glide over ice. She hadn't been on her ice skates since last winter. She'd brought them with her in the hope she'd find time to put them on.

Today seemed like the perfect morning.

Truvy gazed at the time on the desk clock: five forty-eight. What she wished to do would be considered inappropriate by small-town standards. But if nobody saw her . . . she could go out and be back in the house before Mr. Plunkett left to open the mercantile at eight. Mrs. Plunkett hadn't been fixing him a breakfast meal. She claimed she was too fragile to rise at that hour and face a table without her precious daughter sitting across from her.

Normally at nine o'clock, Mrs. Plunkett dragged herself out of bed to take on the day; Truvy would again occupy Hildegarde's vacated seat and listen to Mrs. Plunkett's sighs of woe while having more food pushed on her than she'd ever encountered. If Truvy could steal a moment for herself, she'd feel much better, be much better company at that table.

On that thought, she swiftly dressed, then quietly crept down the stairs, through the vestibule, and out the front door without a sound. Her heavy cape enveloped her shoulders. She held onto her ice skates hidden inside the folds. She'd laced on her reliable Spaldings. Their soles fit snugly onto the blades.

Feeling decadent, she dashed across town. Nobody was up yet. She had the snowy streets to herself. She knew exactly where she was going. Edwina had told her about a mill pond beyond Old Oak Road and off the tributary of Evergreen Creek. The frozen surface of the pond was used as a skating rink. It was an easy landmark to find—the top of the mill could be seen from her bedroom window at the Plunketts'.

Snow-dusted evergreens lined a trail that had been packed down by the previous skaters. A birch stand grew tall, the trunks strong white sentinels. Leafless bushes marked the north shore of the pond. An inverted icicle crown glittered like a jewel from the lumbermill's roof eaves.

Truvy reached the clearing and sat on one of the makeshift benches—a split-down-the-middle tree. She buckled on worn russet leather straps; the polished runners were bright steel from toe to heel plates. Once the skates were in place, she stood and removed her cape. An instant bite of frigid air curled around her.

Her attire was sparse. And unconventional. She wore an apricot tunic and willow-green Turkish pantaloons she'd sewn. The sports uniform for St. Francis was broadcloth blouses and bloomers, but Truvy found the fabric stiff and unyielding. When she'd come to the tennis court in the pantaloons, Miss Pond had frowned her objection and told her she wasn't allowed to wear such a thing.

Disappointment weighed on her that she hadn't been able to try out the costume. But there was nobody to stop her from wearing the outlandish garb now. No rules. No one to comment on her behavior.

She rubbed gloved hands together, then tested the ice by extending first her right leg, then her left.

The surface was lumpy in places but overall was smooth.

After a few minutes, she worked across the ice with a fast speed. The wind nipped her cheeks, blew wisps of hair across her cheeks, and pressed her tunic flat against her pelvis.

Invigorated was a word that came to mind. Pure heaven and freedom and bliss. The costume proved itself. Simply delicious.

Toe-kicking herself up into a single rotation, she flew into the air. She'd learned the skating trick while growing up in Emporia. She could still do the acrobatic twirl fifteen years after she'd mastered the airborne revolution when her ankles and knees came together and her body tilted slightly. That instant of suspension in the sky was like nothing else.

When she landed, she raised her face heavenward and shouted her glee, her voice echoing in the din of trees that watched like an audience. The tunic sleeves rippled against her arms; the pantaloons melted next to her skin. Oh, perhaps Miss Pond had been right. The costume was too scandalous for girls. But it felt just right on Truvy.

Scissoring one foot in back of the other, she skated backward, pumping and pushing her legs. She lost all inhibition, all sense of place. The only sound coming to her ears was the *whir* of blades as they cut over ice.

" 'Dashing through the snow,' " Truvy sang, the notes on key, " 'in a one-horse open sleigh, o'er the fields we go, laughing all the way.' "

Impulsively, she pulled the long pin from her hat and let the smart blue taffetine rosettes with the two quills and netting sail away. She held her arms out, skating in a broad circle while cutting up the ice. The combs loosened in her hair and bounced off her shoulders as they fell out. Brown curls came free as her hair spilled in disarray to her waist.

She giggled. " 'Ohhh—jingle bells, jingle bells, jingle all the way,' " she chimed, " 'Oh, what fun it is to ride—' "

Truvy's shin struck something in the middle of the chorus, something wet and big and furry. The something was Barkly.

A pair of bloodshot eyes filled her vision as she tripped and fell, landing with a painful thud on her hind end. The dog trotted off, tail happily wagging, slipping and sliding on the ice as he chased a whistle. A whistle belonging to a man who stood on the bank, eyes curiously drawn to her spread-eagled legs and the pantaloons that bunched halfway up her exposed thighs.

The man was none other than Jake Brewster.

Naturally.

Chapter
❧6❧

Jake's imagination hadn't prepared him for legs like Truvy's.

His gaze lingered, appreciatively, over her lithe legs and supple thighs, shapely knees and straight shins. Soft green silk pooled in the juncture of her lap; black knit stockings hugged every visible inch of legs down to graceful ankles, where a pair of tennis shoes had been converted with ice blades into skates.

She wore a suggestive costume. As he'd watched her gliding across the ice, it seemed as if she wore nothing at all. The fabric clung to her body like a lover's whisper, cupping, curving, billowing over the high swell of her breasts and the definition of her legs. He'd never seen anything like those trousers before. He found them exciting. Stimulating. Downright damn provocative. Just like her unbound hair.

The first rays of sunshine kissed the color, highlighting strands of auburn in the deep-hued brown. She had very long hair. The shiny curls fell past her waist and brushed the curvaceous round of her bottom—a bottom that was no doubt giving her a jolt of pain at the moment. She'd hit the ice hard.

She looked up at him. Her pointed chin was thrust out in an attempt to cover her embarrassment. He was conscious of how her lips parted. How moist they were. Long, dark eyelashes fluttered against her cheeks, much like her heart must be fluttering beneath the jerky rise and fall of her full breasts. A tightening sensation gripped his skin at the thought of those breasts thrust next to the whaleboning of her corset.

He could have made things easy for her, but he didn't. Any woman out in the morning wearing something as sinful-looking as underwear should be up for a little ribbing.

"Hurt your bum, Truvy?"

"What are you doing out here?" she shot back, disregarding his query.

Jake walked toward her, his footing firm on the ice in arctic, fleece-lined boots. "Taking Barkly out for a morning run. Tom asked me if I would."

"You couldn't have done so elsewhere? People use this area to skate, you know."

"I know. But he likes to run around with pinecones in his chops, and this place is loaded with them."

"Not another tree with pinecones to be had in Harmony, is there?"

Her sarcasm tempted him. A devilish quirk touched his lips. "Are your cheeks cold?"

Seconds passed as she comprehended that he wasn't talking about the ones that blushed. She took in a quick, sharp breath. Rather than refusing to deny knowing his meaning, she tossed a lock of hair over her shoulder. "Positively numb."

She attempted to stand but winced when she put

pressure on her right leg. The skate's blade slid, and thin ice shaved off the frozen pond in an even ribbon. "I think I bruised my knee."

"Let me help you up."

She gazed through the part in her hair, studying his face for a moment while deciding whether to let him.

In return, his eyes measured her, falling to the creamy expanse of neck where brownish hair brushed against the slender column. His extended hand remained an invitation. Anticipation leaped to life within him at the prospect of what she would do.

Tentatively, she rested her hand in his. His fingers curled tightly over her slim knuckles. The sensation of intimate contact warmed him. Without expending any effort, he pulled her to her feet.

They stood facing each other. Her mouth was a deep red from the cold. The straight edge of her teeth caught a plump lower lip. His blood seared his veins. A burning sweetness cut through him. Her hand felt warm and gentle in his. He wanted to explore the softness of her luscious mouth.

Instinctively, his body arched toward hers.

She slowly leaned backward. He held more tightly onto her hand.

Color spread over her cheeks and flushed down her neck. "I won't fall," she assured him, then added in a restrained tone, "You can release me now."

The dent in his ego wasn't deep, but it was a dent just the same.

Reluctantly, he let her go.

She tested the weight on her leg by taking small steps. A wayward curl teased her forehead. With a raised hand, she pushing the strand away from her face. The absent gesture caused her breasts to rub next to the silky drape of fabric covering them. Jake's body grew taut while his whole consciousness focused on her.

Lifting his chin, he indicated the diaphanous outfit outlining her curves; when he spoke, his voice sounded raw—even to his own ears. "What's with the shirt and trousers?"

The mood surrounding them changed, as if she suddenly remembered how she was dressed. She looked down at the clinging fabric, then back up, but made no immediate comment.

Once again, her skin glowed a pretty infusion of rose in the right places—sensual places: the small width of collarbone exposed at the square-cut neck of her skating costume, the lobes of her ears, the cleft of her upper lip.

His every nerve ending heated, and a stab of wanting shot through him.

"They're called a tunic and pantaloons." Her reply contained a strong suggestion of daring. "I sewed them myself."

"Really?"

"Yes." Defiance held her head high. "I did."

"I don't think the style will catch on."

"How do you know?" In a schoolmarmish bristle, she said, "A time will come when it will be commonplace for women to wear trousers and shirts." She challenged him with the tilt of her head. "I'm not the only one who wears them. Elizabeth Miller and Amelia Bloomer—owner of *The Lily*."

"The Lily—is that a ladies' underwear store?"

"It most certainly is not," she replied, exasperated. Her blush diminished as she came back to herself: goddess of political lecturers. "*The Lily* is a women's journal for suffragists."

"Well, damn, I should have known that one." He folded his arms across his chest. "You aren't a suffragist, are you?"

"I most certainly am." And that was all the elaborating Truvy did on the subject. "Now, don't you think you should go find Barkly for Mr. Wolcott?"

"The dog knows his way around."

"Yes, but you're responsible for him."

"You're right." He whistled for Barkly.

No bloodhound came loping toward them.

Jake commented, "He probably found his way home."

She held her spine straight, but most of her weight was on her left leg rather than the right. "You'd better go after him—just to make sure."

Discounting her suggestion, he asked, "Are you trying to get rid of me?"

"Well . . . yes."

He inhaled; his nostrils flaring with reluctant admiration.

Her face remained composed as his gaze remained steady on her.

He liked a straightforward woman. But he didn't like Truvy's answer.

"You can skate in front of me." He deliberately put a lazy smile on his mouth. "I already watched you."

She brought a hand to her throat. "For how long?"

"Long enough to see you do that acrobatic twirl in the air. I thought it was great."

She looked at him, outwardly sedate, but her dilated pupils told him she warred with acknowledging she'd been beyond the pale of respectability. He couldn't care less. "I couldn't do another one. My knee—"

"Your knee will be fine. You need to loosen it up."

Jake could have sent her home. He could have gone after Barkly, who, beyond a doubt, was back at Tom's by now chowing down breakfast. But there were certain things a man enjoyed doing for a woman. And being chivalrous was one of them. "Lean on me. I'll walk you around the pond a few times."

Without giving her a say, he hooked her arm through his and began to walk. She had no option but to skate alongside him.

The warmth of her body radiated into the density of his coat sleeve. She might have been tall, but she was slender. Curly hair tumbled over her back in a disarray. "Really, Mr. Brewster—"

"Jake," he said, correcting her, his jaw tight. "After I held you in my arms at Tom's house, I think you can manage 'Jake.' "

Her breath quickened, tiny puffs of misty white air expelled through the part in her lips. He'd hit a nerve. The toe of her skate blade jabbed at the ice rather than skimming over it; he tightened his grip on her arm.

"I meant to thank you for that . . . Jake. I wasn't myself that morning."

"No need to thank me. I'll hold you any time you want." He lowered his voice and found himself adding in a husky whisper, "And kiss you, too, if you've changed your mind."

A blush traveled across her cheekbones. "I don't know what you mean."

He was struck by the way she clung to tea-and-crumpets logic when her mannerisms and declarations generally disowned propriety. In mere minutes, she couldn't have forgotten he'd been about to kiss her. "You know exactly what I mean. Have you ever been kissed before?"

"Of course." But her steps over the ice didn't glide like her swift reply. They were choppy. She squeezed his wrist in an effort to brace herself. The contact shot through him like a bolt of lightning.

"On the mouth?" he pushed, cursing himself for asking.

"Of course," she repeated. Too fast. Her left leg pushed out wider than a smooth step, and she bumped against him. The soft, rounded fullness of her right breast pressed into his bent elbow. He could see the rhythmical rise and fall of both as she breathed. Blood scorched through his veins, throbbed in his temples.

"Of course," he echoed. But he believed her as much as he believed in Santa Claus.

They came around the pond full circle.

Truvy stammered, "M-my leg is much better. I—"

"One more time." On that, he kept walking, leaving her no opportunity to protest. He liked the feel of her next to him.

The fleece in his boots kept his feet warm enough. His coat banked out the chill. Hell, he could have circled the pond a hundred more times.

A quiet settled between them as he walked and she skated. The songs from a branch full of finches floated in the air. The only other sounds were the skim of her blades over the ice and the slight crunch of snow beneath the soles of his boots.

"Why is it you came to Harmony?" she asked, breaking the silence. "If you were so famous—Mr. Strong America, and all."

" 'The Strongest Man on Earth,' " he amended.

She gazed at him askance. "I got my nouns mixed up. But it's still the same thing."

It wasn't the same thing. The earth was bigger than

America. But he'd be a gentleman about it and not point that out. Strange, though—her being an economics teacher, he figured she would have known the difference.

As for coming to Harmony, the timing had been right for him to quit long hours of ambitious training to maintain his title. He'd left on top, a belt holder. He'd done and seen what he'd wanted to in big cities, earning money and fame.

The end of the pond came too soon as he turned her toward the left to continue the circle. "I left my profession a champion and I felt like living in a small town."

"I have to say that I like big cities. I don't get much of a chance to go to them."

"Boise's pretty big."

"Relatively. Have you ever been there?"

"Nope."

They passed the bench where her cape was draped.

"Well, this has been—" she began, but he cut her short.

He didn't stop walking. "One last time around."

She looked at him, her feet moving over the ice. He met her gaze with a slow grin. "Were you this persistent when you were heaving iron bars above your head to be Mr. Earth?"

"Persistence has something to do with competing. Being strongest has everything to do with winning." Sunshine peeked over the boughs of trees in the distance. "And I don't heave iron bars. I lift barbells."

The lumbermill's whistle blew in eight short peals.

Truvy's skates skidded to a halt. A troubled glitter filled her eyes as she stared at him. "What time is it?"

Jake never carried a watch. He knew the time from the mill or from the church chimes. "Eight o'clock."

"Eight!"

She broke free of him and glided effortlessly to the log where her braid-trimmed cape was neatly folded. "I have to get back to the Plunketts' house before they realize I—that is to say ..."

"You snuck out, huh?"

"Yes. I mean no. I have to get back before I disturb anyone."

Jake knew Mrs. Plunkett's temperament. Before her daughter married, she could set a person's teeth on edge. With Hildegarde gone, she'd turned into a professional mourner—excessively crying and not giving a damn where she was when she lost her grip. He'd had the misfortune of being on the end of one of her weep and wail sessions at the mercantile; he hadn't returned in a week. If he had to live under her roof, he would have put the slip on her, too.

Bending down, Jake collected Truvy's hair combs and put them in his coat pocket. Snow compacted beneath his boots as he headed to where Truvy had gone.

She sat on the half log and worked on the buckle of her skate. With a jerky movement, she fumbled with the tiny strip of leather and shining silver metal. The pair of gloves she wore must not have kept out the chill. Pausing, she rubbed her hands together while blowing a ribbon of breath into them.

Now that he thought about it, she had to be cold. The cut of her "tunic and pantaloons" couldn't ward off much weather. Again, he wondered about her choice of style. Well-bred ladies flaunted beaded fascinators they wrapped on their heads, fur muffs, smart coats, and flannel-hemmed skirts.

She tried once more to get the buckle but wasn't successful.

"I'll do it."

To his pleasure, she didn't tell him no. She nodded, her hair falling in a curtain on either side of her face. "Yes. Hurry."

Jake knelt and propped her foot on his knee. He took a few seconds to appreciate her trim ankle, gliding his hand over the shoe leather and upward to where black stockings started at the low instep. He wondered why she was without her high-top fashion shoes. "So how come you're wearing Spaldings? I know my athletic shoes."

"I was involved in a sport, wasn't I? Skating." She smoothed her hair, messing the curls more than taming them. "Now, please hurry." She wiggled into her cape while he finished. "Eight o'clock," she murmured. "I'm in deep trouble. How am I going to get into my bedroom without being noticed, much less get through town wearing this?"

He finished, then rose and stuffed his hands in the cashmere pockets of his trousers. "You're all set. We can go."

Truvy stared at him, wide-eyed. She didn't readily stand up. "I can't walk back to town in something that could be mistaken for underwear."

"You said you weren't wearing underwear."

"I'm not. It's a tunic and pantaloons," she said with emphasis. "But it looks ... inappropriate."

"Yeah, well, you said yourself a time would come—"

She cut him off with an emphatic challenge: "I said a time would come. I didn't mean *today*. When I left the Plunketts', my plan was to go undetected. And I would have if—oh, never mind." Dismayed, Truvy heavily sighed and laid a palm on her cheek as if she had a sore tooth that ached. "Why do these things always happen to me?"

"I don't know. Why do they?"

"Quit being flippant." She lowered her arm and placed it, along with her other one, around herself. Shivering, she nibbled on her lush lower lip.

Using one hand, he unbuttoned his coat and slipped his arms out of the silk-lined sleeves. A shot of cold hit him, going through his shirt.

"What you call a cape is as useful as a window decoration," he observed, offering her the sealskin warmth.

She gazed at him, then accepted the coat. "Thank you."

She fit one arm in, then turned her back a little so that he could help her with the other sleeve. At the collar, her hair met his fingers. He didn't stop to think about it—he simply gathered the fullness of curls in his fist and lifted them from the inside of the coat. The texture was like fine satin, cool from the air but warm from being next to her body. The length fell soft and pretty down her back as he freed the curls from his hold. He felt her shiver; he doubted it was because of the weather.

The coat securely around her, she fastened the buttons. "I've got to think of a plan. Mrs. Plunkett will never let me live this down. If I'm seen, it will be a disgrace." Truvy declared, "This wasn't supposed to happen. I was supposed to be back in my room by now and nobody would be the wiser."

Jake watched her mouth, the way her lip grew pinker from the edge of her straight teeth. A habit, he surmised. He gave her a while to mull it over, and when no great plan of inspiration came from that kissable-looking mouth of hers, he spoke up.

"I have a plan."

She lifted hopeful eyes to his. Obviously the time had expired when she would have brushed off his suggestion. "What?"

"We stick to side streets to get to the Plunketts'. It's still early enough. I don't think anyone is up."

"You're up," she said, contradicting him.

"I'm not just anyone," he countered, giving her a grin, then proceeded to tell her the rest of his idea. "Once we get there, you go around to the back and I'll crank the front bell. As soon as you hear Mrs. Plunkett answer the door, sneak in through the kitchen."

"What are you going to do?"

"Distract her."

"How?"

"Don't you trust me?"

"Well . . . I'd like to."

"You should, Tru. I'm saving your reputation."

She gazed at him. Hard. Then with resignation. "I suppose I don't have another choice, another option to consider." Her nose wrinkled slightly. "Do you really know a back way?"

"Yes."

"All right, then." She took a step, then stopped and put a hand on her bare head. "My hat and hair combs."

He got the hat for her. It rested on the ice, an ornamented thing with a small blue roses anchored on the crown.

"My hair combs?"

He couldn't explain why he was disinclined to give them up. He took the pair of combs from his trouser pocket.

As she pulled and twisted and arranged and failed

to do something with all that long hair, he watched. He waited. Her fingers must have been numb to the bone, because she wasn't having any luck at styling the hair. When her patience was at an end, the curls still cascading between her shoulder blades, he took one of the combs without comment.

He'd never fixed a lady's hair before. And he found himself wanting to do this for her.

She stood still as could be, her breath hitched in her throat as he used the tines on the comb as a way to gently untangle her hair. He worked from the bottom up, slowly taming the heavy, dark locks. When he got them into a manageable state, he made one large twist of it all and brought the hair high onto the top of her head. With care, he lowered first one comb, then the other, into the curls to anchor them in place.

The end result wasn't a masterpiece creation. A little lopsided. A little mussed—as if she'd just stood from a steamy bath of bubbles—but he liked it. Liked the way she looked at him with the frame of dark brown curls at either side of her temples.

She wore his coat, its sleeves swallowing her hands. When she spoke, a quiver of optimism mingled with her words. "This should do, I would say, Mr. Brewster." She set the hat on top of the hair arrangement, but without a pin to firm it up in place, the brim covered her forehead at an angle.

She picked up her skates.

They left the mill pond. If he hadn't shown her the streets home, she would have encountered Mr. Plunkett. They'd caught a glimpse of his hat and gruff stature as he walked briskly to his store. Also, there had been the owner of the feed and seed, throwing open the wide barn doors as the sun crept past the roof line of his building. Jake led them, undetected, across a field, nobody the wiser that Truvy Valentine had been out and about at that hour in a pair of pantaloons and a tunic. Once they reached the backyard and were out of view behind the toolshed, she undid his coat and handed it to him. She gave him a brief smile of gratitude.

He nodded, then left for the front as he put the coat back on. The inside still had her body heat clinging to it. The silk lining smelled like her—lemons and flowers.

The house was dark, its shades down. He rapped on the wreathed door and waited. Inside, footsteps stirred. A dull thunk. Then thump. And finally a heavy tread to the front door. Actually, more like a lumber.

A breath of house-warm air blasted him as the door swung inward and Mrs. Plunkett's wide girth filled the opening.

Jake held onto the surprised smile ready to burst out on his lips; with great restraint, he kept a sober, pokerlike expression.

Mrs. Plunkett's cheeks, forehead, nose, and chin were caked with a white lotion that smelled like harness oil. Dangling curl papers made a network in her hair. A wash-faded chenille robe barely covered the ample figure it wrapped around. Breasts resembling melons strained at the bodice buttons of a plain flannel gown.

He adopted an easygoing tone. "Good morning, Mrs. Plunkett."

"Mr. Brewster!" she gasped, her eyes widening against her face goo to resemble two white dollops of cream with raisin dots in the center. "Is there a problem at the Wolcotts'?"

"Not at all." He pulled off his hat, slicked his hair back with his hand, and twisted his hat brim in his hands as a nervous would-be suitor would do. "I've come to call on Miss Valentine."

Mrs. Plunkett glared at him as if he were a raving lunatic. "*What?* At this hour? Miss Valentine is asleep in her room."

"You could wake her up."

She huffed, "I most certainly will not. You should be aware that morning calls are never made before noon."

"I'm anxious."

"Anxious, my foot." She wagged a pudgy finger at him as she lambasted him. "You take yourself home, Mr. Brewster, and don't come back here again. Miss Valentine has more sense than to involve herself with—*a man.*"

Then the door closed. In his face.

The final word.

He disliked being taken down a peg by Mrs. Plunkett—even if it was as part of an entire gender.

If he'd really come to call, he would have knocked again.

And again. And again. Until she let him in.

There was something about being denied access to something that made him want it. Especially if the something in question had long and sensual legs that, in a pair of stockings and pantaloons, made the gym's wall painting of Venus look shabby.

Chapter

❧7❧

Edwina sat in the parlor rocker, baby Elizabeth cradled in her arms as the infant slept. Using a slow and soothing rhythm, she moved the chair back and forth with the tip of her slipper-clad foot. For having given birth six days ago, she looked serene and content in her Chinese wrapper with her long hair plaited in a loose braid.

Dr. Porter had paid a call an hour earlier, given Edwina an exam, and proclaimed she was doing amazingly well. But he said she should limit her company and get plenty of bed rest for at least twelve days so she could devote all her energies to the task of recovering as speedily as possible—both on her own account and for the sake of Elizabeth.

Yesterday, Truvy had floundered her way through a cookbook's instructions and figured out how to make a vegetable broth for Edwina, although the end result wasn't a chef d'oeuvre. This morning, Truvy washed diapers and hung them on the indoor clothes rack to dry by the kitchen stove. And a little while ago, she and Edwina drew a bath for the baby, then, after she was clean, rubbed nursery powder on her behind and dressed her in a flannel sacque.

Elizabeth was the only baby Truvy had ever held. Her sweet skin was so delicate, it seemed translucent. Truvy touched a fingertip to the baby's arm, the skin there as soft as soft could be. Her facial features consisted of deep blue eyes, a little turned-up nose, a heart-shaped mouth, rosy cheeks, and pale blond hair.

Truvy thought her the most beautiful baby she'd ever seen.

"I'm so glad you came to visit, Truvy." Edwina tucked the pink bundle next to her breast. Elizabeth's plump cheek rested against the swell, her eyes closed, her rosebud mouth tightly pursed.

A genuine satisfaction settled into Truvy. "Me, too."

"Christmas will be extra special this year."

"I think so."

Elizabeth's fist clenched. She slowly lifted her eyelids, then they drifted closed again.

"Is there anything else I can get for you, Edwina?" Truvy stood waiting, having just come back from putting away a dirty plate and cup. She'd served jellied toast and weak tea to Edwina.

"Heavens, no. Please sit down. You've been so helpful." She shifted in the rocker, keeping its rocking in perfect rhythm with her toe. "I want you to tell me about your girls at St. Francis."

Truvy settled into the divan and acquainted Edwina with each student she had. She talked about the term and how her instructions had been going thus far, about the dual job of coaching and teaching economics classes, and her various duties for both. She avoided the benefactress incident. However, the sincere look of interest on Edwina's face did have her admitting, "There was a slight problem last year"—*a rather large problem*—"when the girls gave a performance of the play *The Cherry Blossom*. I took on the roll of Miss Cherry Blossom and had the students dress up like geishas and sing, 'I Am a Little Geisha.' Mind you, I hadn't told the committee what play we would choose, never dreaming it would be a problem. The curtain dropped in the middle of the first act, on the dictum of Miss Pond—who explained to me geisha were women of ill repute. I had no idea."

Edwina's laughter was soft and compassionate. "I've had such problems myself when I taught finishing school. It's all part of our efforts to help our girls develop into women."

Develop into women.

That was exactly Truvy's aim when she'd been reading *The Science of Life* to her students—preparing the girls for many life experiences. "Have you ever heard of a book called *The Science of Life?*"

"No."

Maintaining a serious expression, Truvy confided, "I've been reading it and the advice is very apropos of girls developing into women. Of—well . . . sex in general."

"Truvy." Edwina smiled with a lifted brow. *"Sex?"*

"Nothing vulgar," Truvy hastily replied. "But anatomically enough not to leave things to the imagination. Actually, the doctor delves into some of the technical anatomical names." But Truvy didn't elaborate. "It's quite specific on how to find the right true love. Very scientific, and I've found it to be most helpful. To me. Um, *for* me. For my girls. That is to say . . ."

Oh, she should just confess! Get the whole truth

out in the open. She was fascinated by that book and its words had gotten her into severe trouble with Miss Pond and the benefactress. But revealing her failings always left Truvy feeling . . . like a failure.

Dear Edwina would never think worse of her, and yet the right words of explanation lodged in her throat.

"Really?" Edwina continued to rock in the chair. "Oh well. It's too late for me. I'll never know if Tom is my scientific true love. I'm already madly in love with him, so I wouldn't care what the book said." She cuddled the baby in her arms. "What kind of man is your scientific match?"

Slightly flustered, Truvy toyed with the lace cuff on her sleeve. It really didn't matter. She wasn't seeking a mate.

She wasn't seeking marriage.

Without consideration, she remarked, "I can tell you who he's not. Any man with a liking for athletic sports. Any man who's tall. Any man of strong facial contour." Hearing herself, she left the description at that. To say more, she might as well spell it out: any man named Jake Brewster. "I would have to choose my complete opposite or suffer the consequences."

"Oh, Truvy, you can't believe that."

"I most certainly do. I believe in it so much that that's why I—" She quit in the middle of the sentence, then shook her head. No. She must own up to the fact she'd muddled things. "Oh, Edwina, I may be dismissed from St. Francis because I read a chapter in the book to my students!"

Truvy proceeded to unburden her conscience about her darkest hour at St. Francis, Miss Pond's reprimand, and the conditions for her coming back to the classroom. "Several days ago, I wrote Miss Pond a letter asking to return as planned. On the twenty-seventh. I can only hope she'll say yes. If not, what am I to do? I'll have to make new arrangements. Maybe I should just go home and stay at the Idanha Hotel while Miss Pond and Mrs. Mumford decide my fate. If they could see my sincerity, they—"

"Truvy, this is nothing to fret about," Edwina insisted firmly. "You're a marvelous teacher. That much is apparent in the way you talk about your students. I won't let you put yourself in a position of weakness by waiting around in a hotel for word."

While she shifted Elizabeth's position, the tiny baby whimpered in her sleep. "It's a good thing you've come here. To me. Everything will work out entirely for you." Edwina stood and went to Truvy, Elizabeth still snugly in her arms. She slowly lowered herself onto the divan and took one of Truvy's hands in her own. "You'll stay in Harmony as long as you need to. I'd be happy to speak to Mrs. Plunkett about the arrangements, and if there's any conflict, you'll come here with Tom and me."

"I couldn't possibly."

Truvy would take a room at the Brooks House before she did that. The carpenters had already been notified not to work on the renovation of the baby's room for one week while Edwina recuperated. Truvy wouldn't feel right as a guest in the Wolcotts' home while the upstairs was torn apart.

"Don't be silly," Edwina said. "Of course you could."

Truvy fought back tears while affectionately squeezing Edwina's hand. "I would never impose on you with things such as they are for you and Tom right now."

"It wouldn't be an imposition."

"I wouldn't feel right about it. Please don't worry about me. I can ask Mrs. Plunkett if it would be all right to stay on."

"But I know how she can be. I feel responsible for you. I wish Marvel-Anne had an extra room. She's such a dear."

Marvel-Anne was Edwina's hired woman. Any day now, she'd be returning from a visit to her sisters. The woman was advancing in years, but she'd been employed by the Huntingtons, Edwina's parents, forever, and though she didn't live with Edwina and Tom, she came over and helped out Monday through Friday.

"It would probably be easiest if I speak with Mrs. Plunkett."

"If worst comes to worst—and it doesn't have to because we can work out something here, but it if does—Tom has an apartment with Mr. Hess he doesn't use, but I'd hate for you to have to do that. It wouldn't be ideal."

"Well, the worst may happen after today," Truvy said. "When I left to come over here, Mrs. Plunkett had a houseful of ladies." Women buzzed like worker bees around their queen, Prudence Plunkett. "I hope the Ladies Aid Snowflake Ball committee has adjourned. I felt out of place when they took over the house. Especially after I explained about the beer. I knew I must."

"The beer?"

"That Mr. Bruiser's beer." She gave no thought to inadvertently calling him by his boxing name. It suited him. "He made me carry a bottle of lager beer for him from the depot when he came and got me, and like a ninny, I did it without thinking."

"You did?"

"Yes. And the very same ladies in Mrs. Plunkett's parlor are the ones who saw me on the street with that bottle of Heinrich's. They looked at me as if I were a heathen and I had to tell them it hadn't been my idea. I did rectify the situation when I poured the beer out in a planter. Mr. Bruiser was none to happy about that."

Truvy hadn't expected Edwina's laughter, gay and amused.

Elizabeth squirmed and gave a soft cry. "Mama's sorry, darling." Then to Truvy, she said, "Oh, I can just imagine Jake's reaction."

"He wasn't pleased. And neither are those ladies. I'm not sure if they believed me. They had a collective look of distrust."

Edwina patted the baby's back, quieting and settling her into a lulling sleep. "Those ladies do that. But they really are sweet. And once they get to know you, they'll adore you."

"I'm not sure I want to be cozy with them. I don't think in their same way. They spent an eternity debating which would be best—Chinese bucket-shaped lanterns or Japanese ball-shaped lanterns."

"They do every year. And I'm sure they settled on Japanese. Like they do every year." Edwina put a finger to her lips. "Now, enough of that." Her mouth curved in a half smile. "Tell me more about Jake Brewster. What do you think of him?"

Truvy thought he'd been a gentleman at the ice pond.

Thanks to his ingenuity and knowledge of Harmony's side streets, she'd been saved from a disgraceful predicament.

When Truvy went down for breakfast that morning, Mrs. Plunkett was in a fit of agitation. Seeing Truvy, she immediately went into a tirade against *that man,* Jacob Brewster, and his bad deportment. She listed the faults of men—and of *him* in particular, a man who called on ladies at eight twenty-two in the morning.

"Well?" Edwina's query broke into Truvy's thoughts. "What do you think of him?"

Truvy spoke the first thought that came to her head. "He's tall."

"So are you."

"I'm not fond of athletes."

"He's not an athlete. He's a former boxer."

"In that case, I believe I'd prefer an athlete."

"You goose, now he's a businessman. Very successful. And he's quite handsome, don't you think?"

The nape of Truvy's neck, at the sensitive place where her hair began at the base of her head, tingled in recollection of when the knit of Jake's gloves had brushed her skin. His breath had nearly touched her cheek, warm and misted from the cold air. The leap in her heart had almost been a fast jolt. He'd held onto the thickness of her hair in his hand as if he had a desire to kiss the side of her neck. It had been a most . . . stimulating thing.

"I think *The Science of Life* is correct in its observations," Truvy said as she softly touched Elizabeth's downy hair with her knuckles. "Mr. Bruiser and I have nothing to gain by an association."

And yet, he'd called her Tru.

Nobody had ever called her that before. She had always been Truvy or Miss Valentine. She wasn't the type of woman people gave a nickname to. It must be her demeanor, her appearance. She didn't dress in vogue and wasn't in the know. She had schoolmarm written all over her. A new suit of clothes did not change the person inside—nor her mannerisms.

But when he'd pretended to pay a call on her—she'd heard him as she'd crept up the Plunketts' stairs, mindful of the creaky ones—there had been a flicker of anticipation in her breast, a disarming thrum in her heartbeat. She hadn't been prepared for that. She assumed he would have asked to speak to Mrs. Plunkett on a fabricated personal matter. Although she knew his reasons, the thought of his coming over to ask about her . . . to ask if he could see her . . .

"I think that book is nonsense," Edwina said. "He's a very nice man." As if on cue, Elizabeth smiled in her sleep. "Ah! There you see, my daughter agrees with me."

Gazing at Elizabeth, a foreign tightening welled in Truvy's chest. She wished she could quell the feeling, make it go away. She'd been so content at St. Francis, so used to her routine and her life and her girls. But not even a week in Harmony and here she sat with a melancholy she couldn't put a finger on.

"It really doesn't matter what the book says," Truvy pointed out. "I'm only in Harmony on a vacation trip, not to live here. My life is with my girls at St. Francis. I'm a teacher. I'll always be a teacher. Never a wife."

"Oh, Truvy, don't say such a thing. I never thought I'd marry, and here I am blissfully happy with a husband." Brushing a light kiss over the top of Elizabeth's head, Edwina said, "When she's like this, with her eyes closed, she looks like Tom."

Smiling, Truvy wondered what it would be like to see Jake sleeping. Er, rather, a man. Any man. Not him. *Oh, botheration.* Why had she thought of him in particular? Because the image of Coach Moose Thompson sleeping left her feeling like a cold fish.

Edwina rose and left the tailored sofa with the baby, putting her in the infant basket close to the parlor stove. Elizabeth began to fuss. "There, there, baby," Edwina cooed as she laid her down. "I have to get something for your Auntie Truvy."

Auntie Truvy. An unwelcome flush crept up Truvy's neck. A blanket of heat stole onto her cheeks. She hated the image that the pet name conjured up—an ancient spinster.

Truvy stood, putting aside her ridiculous sensitivity. "What is it?"

Edwina came toward her, a hastily grabbed book in her hand. "I meant to loan this to Jake the other day, but I forgot. He's eager to read it. I'm sure he'd appreciate your bringing the book by the gymnasium."

Without looking at the book, Truvy exclaimed, "Edwina, I don't want to face him! I couldn't possibly." She wrung her hands. "Two days ago, he had to come to my rescue when I was in my athletic costume. I was embarrassed and he . . . he . . . he really was nice about it, but I just can't see him again."

"Truvy, you're not making any sense."

Truvy quickly explained what had happened.

"Why, that's wonderful, what he did to help you. He certainly won't be thinking differently of you because of it." Edwina shrugged in good humor. "I never told you this, but I fell out of a tree and landed right on Tom while I was wearing my underwear. You see, I'd climbed up an oak tree after Honey Tiger and the branch broke and—oh, never mind! I'll tell you the whole story later. Now, really, do be a dear and bring this book to Jake."

Reluctantly, Truvy gazed at the cover, a dark plum leather with a gold-embossed title. She arched a skeptical brow while reading, *"Our Deportment: Manners, Conduct, and Dress for Refined Society."*

"Oh! Oh, dear, not that one." Edwina snatched back *Our Deportment* and returned to the bookcase and selected another edition. "I meant to get this book."

Truvy took the second book, but with as much suspicion. *"Crime and Punishment* by Dostoyevsky. Forgive me, Edwina, but for a man who claims he reads only sporting magazines, and probably reads, if I were to venture a guess, the *Police Gazette,* I believe he'd get more enjoyment out of the deportment book."

Edwina laughed. Nervously. "Truvy, you are too funny." She all but backed her into the vestibule. "Take it over to him right now."

Dread worked through Truvy. "Right now?"

"Absolutely." Truvy's handbag was thrust into her grasp, as was her hat and cape. "Now you hurry along. You do know where Bruiser's is, don't you?"

Truvy didn't have a keen sense of direction, but Bruiser's Gymnasium was the one place in town whose location she'd remembered.

"Yes."

"Good. Thank you, Truvy."

The door clicked into place. Closed.

Truvy walked slowly down the veranda steps with mixed feelings. She knew an obviously fictitious errand when she was handed one. Edwina wanted her to give Jake Brewster another look. She didn't need to see him again. He was a big lug. An empty-headed smart aleck.

Unlatching the gate, she paused.

Then again, he had come up with a very enterprising plan to outsmart Mrs. Plunkett. He'd been quite the gentleman to offer her his coat. And she couldn't forget how kind he'd been, waiting with her when Edwina's time had come. The way he'd held her, comforted her. Oh, she was being ridiculous.

Jake Brewster epitomized everything she didn't want in a man. Surely her instincts about him weren't erroneous. Then again . . . there would be absolutely no harm in being civil to him while she was in town.

Perhaps she'd misjudged him. Maybe he wasn't the brutish muscle clod she thought him to be. Picking up her pace, she decided that it wouldn't hurt to have another look before making her final determination.

Jake flipped through the dictionary, finding the word he wanted—which was no easy thing, given that he couldn't wear his glasses. The exercise room of the gym was crowded with men honing up for the Mr. Physique contest. His office door remained open, leaving him available for training questions and the call for when the contestants had on their posing costumes. He didn't know what they'd ordered through *Muscle Builder,* because Milton Burditt had wanted to be in charge.

Squinting, Jake barely made out the fuzzy letters.

pantaloon: a pair of tight trousers; a buffoon in a pantomime.

"Trousers," he muttered. He'd been close enough.

While on the same page, he looked up the definition of *pantomime.*

Then he turned the tissue-thin pages of the book to another section and looked up a new meaning.

Sweet Judas, he could hardly recognize a syllable. Craning his head, he looked out the door into the gym. All clear. He snuck his glasses out and put them on, keeping hold of the temples in case he had to whip them off.

The dictionary's tiny type was in sharp focus now.

flippant: characterized by thoughtless levity of speech or pertness.

Hell, what did *levity* mean?

He thumbed the pages to the "L" section: *la, le, lev.* He dragged his fingertip down the column.

levity: lightness of disposition, conduct, etc.; trifling.

Jake lifted his head. She thought he was being a smart aleck.

Shrugging, he closed the dictionary.

Flippant. It fit him. That's what he'd been.

"Hey, Bruiser!" Milton's voice sounded through the office.

The spectacles were off Jake's ears in seconds flat and quickly returned to his drawer.

"Come on out here," Milton said. "We're ready to see what you think."

Jake hid his dictionary, then rolled the chair from behind his desk and went into the gym. He stopped cold.

"Holy shit," he said as he took in the Barbell Club. They wore leopard-skin bathing trunks, flesh-tone tights, and Roman sandals and were rubbed up with so much posing oil that their naked chests shined like bacon grease.

"This should get the judges' attention, huh, Bruiser?" Gig Debolski stood with his legs apart and his hands on his hips.

"Yeah, Gig, you fellows will definitely get attention," Jake commented dryly. "The wrong kind."

"What do you mean, Bruiser?" Milton asked. His

chest was puffed and basted like a turkey's. Swirling coarse black hair covered him from his neck to his navel. "I think we look like a bunch of swells."

Lou Bernard concurred. "Yeah." The train porter had come over to the gym and signed up. "Any one of us has a chance at that trophy."

"I wouldn't go that far, Lou." Milton corrected his assumption, making a fist. "I'm going to win the trophy, but you gents can give it a try anyway."

Jake absently cracked his knuckles. "I hate to disappoint you, Milt, but you're wrong. The Mr. Physique contest isn't a"—a swanky word came to him that he would never use, but it was fresh in his mind and the definition applied—"*pantomime.*"

"I told you, Milton, we look like jackasses." August Gray was the only one of the bunch who had a chance if the contest were tomorrow. His muscle development was coming along. All he needed was to add more definition on his upper arms and calves.

"What's wrong with us?" Milton objected. "Sandow wears trunks like these, and tights. All this was listed in *Muscle Builder*—his exact costume. I got a shipping discount for buying a half dozen. You mean to tell me I've been misled by Sandow the Magnificent?"

The reigning belt holder, Eugen Sandow, was the best bodybuilder there ever was. He'd all but invented the sport and still enjoyed phenomenal success. Jake didn't want to discount Sandow's fame and glory, but he refused to wear the popular skins in competitions. He'd tried them once. Fur next to his balls made him antsy; it had felt as if his parts weren't hanging right in the leopard drawers. Instead, he chose cotton for his trunks, a fabric that hugged and gave when he moved in various poses.

"Damn you, Milton, I said you should have ordered fig leaves," Walfred Kudlock remarked. Standing at five feet two inches and with thighs like fire plugs, Walfred resembled an ape man. The depth of the recession of his hairline left half his scalp bald, and a heavily waxed handlebar mustache rode on his upper lip. He held onto of pair of rock maple Indian clubs as props.

"Sandow didn't mislead you, Milton." Jake left for a brief moment to go into his office; then he returned with an amber-tinted jar. "What works for him can't be argued with. I personally don't happen to believe in leopard skin and all that Grecian oil." He held out the jar for them to see the label: HAMMERHEAD'S BODY DEFINITION POWDER. "Here's what you want."

"What is it?" Milton asked, stepping forward for a closer look.

"A trick I learned when I was boxing professionally." Jake wore a union shirt with the sleeves cut out, his biceps and forearms bare. In the last wash, the neckline placket had gotten caught in the ringer, ripping the buttons off. Now the faded cotton hung loosely over his chest, leaving more skin exposed than concealed. "I'll show you how this stuff works."

He unscrewed the jar's lid and dusted his fingers in some of the burnt sienna powder; then he liberally coated his arm.

"What the hell does that do?" Milton asked.

"You'll see." Jake grabbed a towel off one of the benches and buffed powder from his skin in all the smooth places. In the others, where the bulge of his forearm flexors formed, the crease on his inner arm, the middle head of his biceps, and his deltoid and triceps ridges, he left just enough of the dark residue to create a three-dimensional image. When his arm was pumped, the artistry deceived the onlooker into thinking his muscles swelled larger than they actually were.

"I'll be damned." August came forward. "It's like magic. You've put on muscle with no weights."

"This isn't a substitute for training, August." Jake put the lid back on the jar and set it down on the bench. "You still have to lift iron for results."

Lou complained, "We do?"

"Yeah." Milton bent at the knees and grabbed a barbell. The weight wasn't right for his body type, but he strained and groaned to lift it high over his head and hold it there. His arms quivered and his belly jiggled. Then he attempted to lower the barbell but dropped it—marginally missing his toes.

"I've said it before, you don't have to have Herculean powers to win a trophy." Jake racked the weight and selected another one for Milton. Fifty pounds lighter. "Palookas push heavy weights and knock themselves out. Putting up twenty-pound dumbbells isn't smart."

"Yeah, but *you* can put up twenty-pound dumbbells."

"I can also bring you down in one punch, but that doesn't mean it's wise for me to do it."

Milton's face blanched. "You wouldn't slug me, would you, Bruiser?"

"Christ, what do you take me for, Milton? A bonehead?"

"N-no, Bruiser. Not at all. I was just making sure."

"Right now, you need to make sure you can lift weight without dropping it like a woman." Jake motioned to the dumbbells, barbells, and kettle weight irons. "Everybody pick up something fifty pounds lighter than you're used to and give me three sets of fifteen."

The men went into action, hoisting and lifting and grunting and making god-awful faces of agony. Sweaty oil added a high polish to their bodies that made their red skin look like ripe McIntosh apples, and the gnashing of teeth could be heard through the metal clunk and thump of heaving and hefting.

While the men worked through their reps, Jake went to the bag platform to limber up his fists. The single-end striking bag was thirty-three inches around and suspended from the ceiling by a top rope. Because it was anchored to a solid platform, it had a true swing from all sides.

Chalking his hands, Jake didn't bother with his gloves. The skin on his palms and the tops of his hands was leather tough, the joints large and hard from years of abuse. Positioning himself and balancing on the balls of his feet, he began to give the heavy calfskin blow after blow after blow.

From the vigorous physical effort he expended, perspiration formed on his body. His hair grew wet at the scalp; droplets trickled down his forehead. The hollow of his underarms dampened. The gathered waistband of his calf-length sport trousers clung just below his navel.

The intensity with which he concentrated on hitting the striking bag had him unaware his name was being called until the shout sounded through the gymnasium.

"Bruiser!" Milton hollered, getting his attention.

Jake lowered his arms and turned, his breathing coming hard and fast.

"Say, Bruiser, I was just thinking." Milt came up to him, his face ruddy. "What about testicle juice?"

Through the frantic thump of his heartbeat echoing loudly in his ears, Jake thought he hadn't heard Milt correctly. "What was that?"

"Steer testicle juice." Milt's expression was stone sober. "I was reading about it in *Vigorous Male* magazine. It says man is a human animal."

"I don't think of myself as an animal, Milton."

"Sorry, Bruiser, I wasn't referring to you. I was thinking more along the lines of us guys who don't have all that you have"—he slapped a fist against his pasty chest—"here. See, this article said that testicular extract—"

August broke in. "Uh . . . Bruiser . . ."

"Just a minute, August," Jake replied, not glancing toward the men. In the last few seconds, they'd grown extremely quiet, as if wanting to know what kind of edge they could get in the contest. "Milt is telling me about something he thinks could be beneficial to you. I want to hear it."

Milton rubbed the back of his hand across his sweating forehead. "Well, this testicular extract has been known to increase mental and physical vigor."

"And how do you take this . . . *steer extract?*" But the method by which a snake oil bottler got that *extract* out of the bull didn't matter. Jake wouldn't put something like that in his body for anything.

Lifting his shoulders, Milt mumbled, "You drink it in an elixir."

"I'm not drinking no bull gravy," Walfred stated loudly.

"Uh, Bruiser . . ." August said once more.

Jake held a hand up to him. "Now just a minute, August. We're trying to figure out this steer testicle elixir Milt is telling us about."

"I haven't bought any yet." A momentary look of discomfort crossed Milton's face. "But I was thinking about buying some if you thought it was a good idea, Bruiser."

"Um, Bruiser," Lou broke in, "somebody's here to see you. And she's been standing there awhile."

Jake inclined his head in the direction of the business door entry and saw who it was that Lou was talking about.

Truvy Valentine.

Wearing one of those Gibson-collared suit waists and a pleated lilac skirt, she gave the room a ray of cheerful color on a cloudy day. A soft blush had caught on her cheekbones. She held onto a thick book so tightly, he could see the strain in her fingers through her kid gloves. She raised her hand to the brim of her hat as if to shelter her eyes.

Stepping back, he viewed the room through her gaze.

Half-dressed men gawking at her in leopard-skin trunks. Tights. High-leg Roman sandals. Surrounding them: exercise equipment, Indian clubs, dumbbells, barbells, kettle weights. And body oil that enhanced the musky scent of masculine sweat.

This was the last place he'd ever thought of Truvy visiting.

"Miss Valentine," he managed to say, knowing she'd heard everything they'd been saying. He kicked himself in the ass for leading Milt on about that steer juice. "What can I do for you?"

"I . . . I . . . Mr. Brewster. I've"—she thrust her arm out—"brought you a book from Mrs. Wolcott. She said you wanted to read it."

Jake couldn't make out the title, but he figured that by its size and weight, the volume had to be a three-pounder. He'd read so few books, he couldn't guess which one he was supposedly interested in. And if he was, he wouldn't pick a book so thick. It would take him a year to struggle through all those pages. Edwina was up to something. If he wanted the details, he'd have to get Miss Valentine alone.

"I'd like to examine that, Miss Valentine. Step into my office."

"But I—"

Jake put his hand on her elbow and steered her in the direction he wanted. He called out, "Ten minutes on the jump ropes, boys."

Walfred grumbled, "One minute about kills me, Bruiser."

"You need to do it. Jumping builds your stamina and exercises your heart."

Once inside his office, Jake debated closing the door. He kind of figured that if he shut out the noise coming from the gym, she'd get all worked up over his motives, take it like he was trying to pull the fast and light on her. As it was, discomfort and distaste made her body go rigid. And her expression worsened when she was in the middle of the office and saw his Venus.

Remmy had come through Harmony last year and painted her for him. Just like he wanted her. The goddess took up an entire wall in a pallet of lifelike colors. Her facial features—tilted eyes and full pink lips—were seductive. Long golden hair flowed, as if windblown, around her voluptuous figure. A toga swirled in a transparent curtain over her generous bosom and rounded hips.

Venus might as well have been naked.

Truvy transferred her gaze from the painting to him. "I take it this is your idea of femininity. Yet another man looking for the perfect woman."

Arching a brow, Jake remarked with a half smile, "I'm always looking for the perfect woman."

"Then maybe you'd better try drinking some of that elixir so you won't have to dream about a painting on your wall, Mr. Bruiser."

One. Two. A left jab followed by a hard right cross. And an uppercut—calling him Mr. Bruiser.

She didn't pull any punches. She told it like she saw it. Which wasn't the truth, but what the hell. He didn't dream about Venus. Lately, he'd been dreaming about legs—

He looked at Truvy.

Her eyes swept over the large, gilt-framed posters he'd nailed on the other three paneled walls.

Eugen Sandow in a cabinet photograph with a Greek pillar as a prop to draw attention to Sandow's impressive biceps.

George Hackenschmidt, in short trunks, in a strongman pose.

Peter Maher in full boxing regalia—gloves, trunks, and canvas athletic shoes—with his dukes up and ready to wallop.

Tom Sharkey, bare-chested, with his famous star-and-ship tattoo on his chest and a block-shaped head with a cauliflower ear.

Jake rolled his chair away from the desk. "Have a seat, Miss Valentine, and we can talk about the book."

"I couldn't possibly."

"Sure you can."

She assessed the walls once more, as if she felt she were being watched by a bunch of strongarms and a naked lady. "No, I couldn't possibly."

Masking his disappointment, he pushed his chair back in. He wouldn't sit if she wouldn't. "Then you can stand and tell me what you've brought."

"Crime and Punishment."

He'd never heard of it. The title suggested the story was about some bad hombres. He didn't think Edwina kept that kind of reading material.

Snagging a Turkish towel from a bar above the radiator, Jake wiped the perspiration from his face. He shared a gaze with Truvy. He didn't miss her obvious examination; he felt her observant eyes trail over his flesh as distinct as a touch. The memory of her body in his embrace captured him. He could still smell the scent of her hair, feel the texture of her skin. Slowly and seductively, he slid the towel up his neck, then down. She followed his hand.

Her lashes seemed thicker to him. Longer. The brown of her eyes was nearly swallowed by the darkness of her pupils. He lowered his hand to the swell of his chest through the open slash cut in his shirt. He was flattered by her interest and totally entranced by her. His lungs felt tight, his throat dry.

"Want a beer?" he asked, draping the towel behind his neck so the ends hung over his shoulders. He was dying of thirst, but he wasn't a thoughtless bum to drink a Heinrich in front of her without offering her one, too.

It was several seconds before she replied, "*No*, thank you."

"Well, I'm going to grab one." Hell, he shouldn't have, but he didn't go for that self-sacrifice polite society crap.

"I really don't care what you do. I have to be going. Now if you'll—"

"Hold that thought." He was halfway through the connecting door that led from his office and living quarters. Right inside the entry, he had a small kitchen with a stove and icebox. He tugged on the handle to the refrigerator chest and took a Heinrich's lager beer. Using the wooden countertop for leverage as an opener, he whacked the flat of his hand across the bottlecap and sent it flying onto the floor.

While taking a drink, he stepped back into his office. "So tell me, what's the deal with this crime and punishment book? Some outlaws do hard time in the penitentiary?"

The coolness in her tone said she wasn't amused. "From the nickninny expression on your face, I don't believe the book is suited to your tastes. But since Edwina asked me to bring it to you, I have." Extending her arm, Truvy added, "Here you are." She set the brick-thick publication on his desk, smack over the latest issue of the *Sporting Life*. "I don't want to keep you from your ..."— she paused, looking hard at his beer, then at him—"...strapping activities."

She was going to leave, and he should have let her, because Bruiser's wasn't a suitable place for a lady. But all he could think of was how to get her to stay, if only for a few more minutes. "What do you think of Teddy inviting Booker T. Washington to the White House?"

Her astonishment was evident by the way she straightened her posture. "Pardon?"

Jake took pleasure in having thrown her off. *Strapping activities.* The words irritated him like a rock in his shoe. Jesus H.—did she really think he was a dense dumbbell to the core?

In a level voice, he calmly repeated the facts—slow and easy—as if he discussed this kind of news all the time. "Teddy Roosevelt invited Booker T. Washington for dinner at the White House."

"I know that."

He took another drink of his Heinrich, the frosty cold alcohol quenching his parched throat. She pasted a smile of nonchalance on her mouth, but he noticed she licked her lips.

"Well, what do you think about it?" he asked once more.

She lifted her chin and boldly met his gaze like a fighter making ready to take down his opponent. "I thought President Roosevelt quite grand for infuriating Southern politicians by the gesture."

Resting the beer bottle's base on the hard cords of his thigh, he shifted his weight from one leg to the other. "You know what I think?"

"I can't say that I do."

"I think it took some oysters on Teddy's part." And he really did. Just the other day, he'd read the story in the *Advocate*. At the time, he'd thought it a waste of energy, but now he was glad he'd forced his brain to soak up the information.

"I don't recall the menu being listed in the *Idaho Statesman*."

Menu? Who was talking about the menu? He'd been talking balls, as in nuts, cojones, jewels. But she didn't understand that he'd been gentleman enough not to use crudeness a second time in her presence. Then it hit him: She was interested in knowing the specifics of the White House dinner menu. As if he would know—or even care. He'd been damn impressed he'd gotten the two players' names right. Now she wanted a menu. He didn't remember reading anything about that.

"Yeah, I know all about the dinner," Jake returned in words with more stretch in them than the rubber connection of his double-end striking bag. If she wanted a menu, he'd improvise one to sound intellectual. He knew about cooking and elaborated on food he could fix. "It was Hungarian steak, stewed tomatoes, fried potatoes, and apple pudding."

"And oysters."

"Right." He brought the bottle to his mouth for a thoughtful sip, then added, "Silver plates of them on the half shell."

Though she tried to hide her excessive interest by blinking, she studied the beer bottle in his hand as he drank. The wooden floor rumbled beneath them from the jumping efforts of the men as they hopped to the beat of the ropes. While he had her full attention, he tilted his head back and downed long, satisfying swallows; then he lifted the bottle in silent query to get her to reconsider her abstinence.

When she didn't take his cue, he asked, "Are you sure I can't get you a beer?"

"Do you think I'm an immoral woman, Mr. Brewster?"

"No," he said carefully.

"Then why do you keep offering me alcoholic refreshment?"

"Because you keep staring at my beer."

"I may stare at a new hat in the store window, but that doesn't mean I want it."

"A hat wouldn't make you feel nearly as good as a beer."

"How do you know? Have you ever worn a lady's hat?"

"Hell no." But his mind quickly jumped to the time he'd been with that actress and she'd coaxed him into putting on her silk petticoat for all of fifteen seconds. He'd been roaring drunk, so he didn't count the moment as any kind of abnormal tendency.

"Well," she said smartly, "maybe you'd find a lady's hat preferable to beer."

"I know I wouldn't." He finished the drink with a toss of his head, then set the empty on the desk. "How's your knee?"

The photographs of him that lay next to that thick outlaw book pulled her attention as she replied. "Fine."

"I don't think so." His eyes were drawn to the same spot as hers: the promotional portrait of him wearing boxing trunks, his arms bent at the elbows, poised in a fighting position. The Bruiser in his prime, ready to take on the Great Zephyr. "When you walked into the office, you favored your right leg."

"No I didn't. Is that really you?"

"Yeah, it's really me."

To his surprise, she selected one of the carte vistas and examined it. Or, more obviously, examined his body. He saw knots and bunches and layers of muscle that at this moment were coiled in anticipation over her reaction to what *she saw* in the black-and-gray image. He wondered what appealed to her in a man. As he waited for her to say something about the photograph, he felt his pulse pounding throughout his body, even in his fingertips.

She met his gaze. "You were pretty good at boxing?"

"Better than good." Fired off with confidence, his reply filled the room. Then he cursed himself when she made no further comment. He didn't want to come off full of vanity and empty of smarts.

Her attention returned to the photograph. And while she studied his portrait, Jake studied her. The tilt of her chin. The angle of her hat. The color of her lips. The fine way her winter skirt fell over her hips.

Deliberately, he looked away. The sharp noise of jump ropes and a dull rattle of equipment intruded on his thoughts. He knew she wasn't staying in Harmony. He knew she was going back to Boise. He also knew he'd never be involved with her even if she were staying.

Women like her were marriage-inclined. Men like him didn't pay social visits to ladies unless they meant business. Even though he was partial to her height, her hair, the color of her eyes, the sensuous length of her legs, for the time being, he wasn't interested in tying another matrimonial knot.

"I have to say," Truvy's voice came to him, "that the nature of the photograph does make you look formidable and maybe a little ... well, never mind." She set the carte vista down. "Now, I really do need to go."

About to leave, she took a step, but he called out, "Wait, Truvy. I have something for you."

The lift of her brows questioned him.

Jake rifled through the disorganized middle drawer of his desk, grabbed a bottle, then presented Truvy with Duggan's Turpentine Liniment. "For your knee. The ache—and everything. It's the best for a sprain. Now if you'd've torn a ligament, I'd've said go with Bomber's Carbolic Salve. But you didn't, so the liniment's better."

A burst of laughter rippled through the air as she reacted to his know-how in a way he hadn't expected. Light hysteria filtered in her amused voice. "Mr. Brewster—*Jake*," she said, rephrasing, "you couldn't possibly know how much your gesture means to me. Let me emphatically *thank you* for this liniment. For a moment, I thought I'd come to the wrong conclusion about your character, and I can see now that I was mistaken." She deposited the Duggan's into the open mouth of her leather pocketbook. "Good day. I wish you well on your—whatever it is those men are doing out there."

She left before Jake could comprehend exactly what she'd meant.

The second she was gone, he jumped on his dictionary, tearing through the pages while he remembered the word. He cursed. The letters were a blur he could hardly distinguish. Squinting, he brought the book up close to his eyes.

en . . . encounter.

Dammit, he was going backward.

ele . . . elo . . . em . . . emboss . . . embroil . . . emery . . . emmet . . .

emphatic: uttered with emphasis; forcefully significant; impressive.

He slapped the dictionary closed and chucked it in his drawer.

Lowering himself onto the chair, he narrowed his eyes, then scratched the stubble on his chin. To hell with reading newspapers.

He'd *really* impressed her with that liniment.

Chapter

8

Discussions about male privates. *Animal elixirs.*

A naked lady painted on the entire wall. *Perfect women.*

Total ignorance of literature. *Outlaws and hard time.*

Jake Brewster occupied Truvy's daydreams. While she stared at the candle flames flickering from the Plunketts' holiday tree, she ceased to see with clarity. White tapers blended together with ornaments and garlands. For a spinster like her, it was unproductive to think about a virile man like him, a man who could have any woman he desired because of his appearance. And his charm.

He was *very* charming. And flattering.

Looking at that boxing photograph of him, with its edge, that streak of determination set in his shoulders, the pride, the intelligent gleam in the core of his eyes, the ambition in his stance, she'd wondrously thought she made a mistake about his character and personality. But then he had to go and offer her that liniment, shattering her illusion.

She was glad. Glad his brain worked the way it did.

Glad she would no longer be tempted by his physical allure. By his body and smile. Those green eyes of his. That straight lock of hair that seemed to always be at his temple. His suggestion she engage in drinking a beer with him. As if she ever would.

"I wonder if it will snow all day." Mrs. Plunkett's voice invaded her mind.

Mr. Plunkett answered quietly. "The almanac said it was going to be a cold winter. Longer than last year's."

Mr. and Mrs. Plunkett's voices drifted in and out of Truvy's musings as her thoughts wandered from the couple sitting in the parlor with her.

She wouldn't be party to any more of Edwina's transparent errands. Because that day at the gymnasium when those he-men wore outlandish skins and leg tights and had been oiled to a high gloss while talking about bull steer remedies—well, that was enough for her. Any doubts she had about Mr. Jake Brewster were confirmed.

He had to be as dense as a knot in a tree to think drinking a potion of that kind and wearing fur made a man manly.

The snap of the fire in the hearth jolted Truvy.

The Plunketts' Christmas tree came into focus and Truvy sat taller on the divan, squaring her shoulders and putting a smile on her lips. This was Christmas morning, after all.

Mr. Plunkett reclined in a gents' easy chair, a cherry stem pipe clamped between his teeth. A sweet-acrid smoke curled from the English bowl as he puffed and talked at the same time. "Now, Pru, let Miss Valentine be."

Truvy had missed something in the conversation.

"Honestly, Hi, I'm sure she wants to." Mrs. Plunkett's face was round and heightened with a blushing anticipation. "Don't you, dear?"

"Oh . . . well . . ." Although Mrs. Plunkett could be quite overwrought, she'd taken Truvy in without relation by blood or friendship, and for that, Truvy could only concede, "If it makes you happy, then I'd be delighted."

"There—I told you she would." Mrs. Plunkett firmly nodded her head; then to Truvy, she said, "Tomorrow, we'll get you suitably outfitted. We'll spend the entire day at the dressmaker's shop. The dresses you wear now aren't right for your coloring. The blue velvet and almond green wool are well and good, but they're too dark against your hair color."

Suitably outfitted. Tomorrow. My dresses aren't right.

Truvy could only sit quietly. What had she agreed to?

"With your fair complexion," Mrs. Plunkett said, happy to be a tutor, "you should always wear the most delicate tints, such as a lighter blue, mauve, and pea green. You need to learn how to group colors." After sipping spearmint tea from a holly-patterned china cup, she *tsk*ed, then said, "I'm afraid I have to tell you, my dear, but that modiste who sold you the lilac dress did you a disservice. Its color *loses* brilliance by gaslight, whereas pea green *gains* brilliance in a strong artificial light."

Truvy tried to form the right words to graciously back out of going on a shopping trip with Mrs. Plunkett. But they lodged in her throat when the elder woman grinned from ear to ear, beaming happily at her. Grateful.

Mrs. Plunkett reached out, took Truvy's hands in

hers, and applied soft pressure. Moisture glittered in her eyes. "Having you here, Miss Valentine, has helped me cope with the absence of my darling Hildegarde. I would be in a fit of the vapors if I didn't have you as company, my dear." She rapidly blinked. "You are such a comfort to me."

Letting Truvy's hands go, Mrs. Plunkett reached down beneath the tree and selected a red-flocked, paper-wrapped box with gold trimmings. "This is for you."

The present's dressing was far too elaborate. Too generous. Whatever was inside had to be extravagant. An unexpected response welled inside her: guilt. For the Plunketts, Truvy had decorated a wickerwork cornucopia with ribbons and filled it with assorted nuts. She had given the gift to them last evening over Christmas Eve supper. The gesture was simple and reasonable.

"Take it, my dear."

Truvy did so, setting the gift in her lap. She only had one present that came in the mail, and she had opened it that morning in the privacy of her room. The Aunts had sent lemon verbena soap. Every year, it was tradition for her to receive a satin-lined box of a dozen cakes from the dears.

Inasmuch as she adored the soap and its sentimental value, she would have traded it for a letter from Miss Pond. But there had been nothing. No optimistic note. No words of encouragement. In two days' time, Truvy was scheduled to be back in Idaho. The date stamped on her return ticket was December 27. That train ticket was in her bureau drawer upstairs, waiting for her, for the one message of hope that she'd been absolved, welcomed back to St. Francis.

But hope hadn't come. Not yet.

Pulling the ties that kept the paper together, Truvy unwrapped the box and lifted its lid. A sterling silver comb-and-brush set nestled on a bed of red velvet. Her initials had been engraved on the back of the oval brush.

"Mrs. Plunkett," Truvy breathed softly, "this is very nice."

Anxiousness brought out the lines at the corners of Mrs. Plunkett's eyes. With her hands clasped together in front of her bosom, she leaned forward. "Well? Do you like them?"

"Yes." And she did. "But you shouldn't have."

"Nonsense. I was delighted to buy them for you. See there?" She lifted her forefinger to the brush. "I had your initials inscribed."

"That was very thoughtful of you."

"My Hildegarde has an exact set. Just like yours. I only wish . . ." She loudly blew her nose into a snowy white hankie. ". . . that I could have . . ."

The sentence went unfinished, overshadowed by a choking sob. Truvy knew what she wanted to say. Hildegarde had not been able to join her parents on Christmas, but she had sent a card with love and the hope that the package from Buffalo had made it on the train.

It hadn't.

For days, Mrs. Plunkett worked herself into a dither over the missing parcel, lamenting that her one wish would have been for her daughter to be with her for the holiday; her second wish would have been to have some token of love from Hildegarde that she could open on Christmas morning.

"Blast that infernal postal service." Mrs. Plunkett's

bosom swelled with resentment. "Wells Fargo and Company promises reliable deliveries. Hi, I want you to make this effective immediately—we aren't going to give the U.S. government another nickel. As of today, we're using Wells Fargo for all our parcels. That goes for the store, too."

"I don't think that will be necessary."

"Of course it's necessary!"

Resting his pipe in a glass tray, Mr. Plunkett rose from the easy chair and went to the firewood cabinet beside the fireplace. He opened the hinged wrought door and withdrew a brown paper package held together with twine. "Now, Pru, don't be angry with me, but I did this for you. You would have ruined it if I hadn't."

"Wh-what?" Dabbing the corners of her eyes, Mrs. Plunkett stood. The flames wavered from the tree's star candle holders as she took a step closer to see the parcel Mr. Plunkett held out.

"I saved it for today. It's from our Hildegarde and her Joe. It came on Monday and I took it from Mr. Calhoon at the post office, then I hid it so you wouldn't be tempted to sneak a peek."

"Hi, you awful, awful man!" The handkerchief in her hand was stuffed into the bishop sleeve of her black peau de crepe dress. "How could you have put me through such grief and misery by telling me the package didn't arrive? You're a scoundrel and a nincompoop." She stretched out her arm. "Give me that present from my precious!"

Mr. Plunkett obliged and the string and the paper were torn open with a quick pull and rip. Inside the box nestled a bright gold-wrapped present with a large silver bow. Mrs. Plunkett made fast work of ridding it of the trimming until a glass photograph frame was revealed. She held onto its pansy-pattern filigreed edges and sucked in a shuddering gasp. "It's a . . . *picture*. Of them."

Truvy looked over Mrs. Plunkett's wide shoulder to view the couple.

In her assessment, Hildegarde seemed very happy by the twinkle in her eyes. Her husband's smile matched her liveliness of expression. He wore a dark suit coat and trousers; she, a dress with Mousequetaire sleeves.

For a couple who—from what Truvy gathered— lived on limited funds, paying for the photographer and purchasing a frame made for a lavish gift.

Gauging from Mrs. Plunkett's woeful expression and wistful sigh, Truvy could tell Mrs. Plunkett wasn't impressed. "I was hoping for something else." But she didn't say what. She began to cry, an awful fit of shuddering sobs.

Mr. Plunkett put his arm around her middle and tried to placate her by patting the round of her shoulder. "Prudence, there's no call to cry your eyes out. It's a bully present." He lifted his head to Truvy, his gaze pleading for some help. "Isn't it, Miss Valentine?"

"Oh—yes. Quite. I think the photograph will look lovely hanging above your organ."

"I don't want it over my organ!" Mrs. Plunkett wailed. "I don't want to be stared at while I'm playing Stephen Foster." She brought a wrinkled hankie out of her sleeve and rubbed its thin white fabric beneath her running nose. "I couldn't possibly sing 'Oh! Susanna' when they look so . . . *happy*. How can she look like that when I'm suffering so?"

When Mr. Plunkett folded Mrs. Plunkett in his

arms, she allowed him. "I miss her, Hi. Why did they have to move so far away?"

"She'll come home soon, Pru, as soon as Joe can leave Buffalo. I miss her, too."

"I want her here now." She cried with a mother's broken heart.

The doorbell cranked, but the Plunketts, in their shared grief, didn't hear the chimes.

Truvy rose and went to answer the bell.

A young man in a blue uniform stood on the stoop wearing a navy bill cap with pull-down ears. A small Santa Claus head with a flaxen beard was pinned on his lapel.

"Telegram for this address." He held out a steel-clip wooden board and ink pen. "Sign here."

The envelope beneath the clip had her name plainly typed on the front. Anticipation fluttered in her stomach as she read the sender's address. The telegram was from Boise. From Miss Pond.

Truvy hastily put her signature on the correct line. She slipped her hand into the deep pocket of her skirt and gave the boy a few coins. "Thank you."

Closing the door, she walked to the staircase and sat down. Neither one of the Plunketts was aware she'd left the parlor. Just as well. She wanted to be alone when she read Miss Pond's reply.

The envelope's seal tore easily, and Truvy withdrew the message that had been transmitted by telegraph. The paper felt flimsy in her fingers. She began to read beyond today's date:

RECEIVED YOUR LETTER **STOP** THINGS NOT RESOLVED **STOP** SLIGHT PROBLEM **STOP** MRS. MUMFORD TOOK OVER YOUR CLASSES

STOP FEEL CERTAIN SHE WILL LOSE INTER-
EST SOON **STOP** WILL KEEP TRYING TO REC-
TIFY SITUATION **STOP** HAVE FAITH **STOP**
LUCRETIA POND

Truvy read the telegram three times, shocked,
stunned, and filled with a disbelief that left her
shaken. She visibly trembled—her fingers, her knees,
her body. It was a good thing she had the bottom step
as support. Her chance to return to the life she knew
was being pulled out from underneath her. The frank-
ness of the telegram hit her like a sharp thunderclap.

Truvy had known Mrs. Mumford was a former
teacher. She'd boasted about her credentials many
times over. She'd been the head of the English department at Smith College. If Mrs. Mumford wanted to
come out of retirement and teach at St. Francis, how
could the school committee tell her no without risking
her sizable donation?

And yet, Miss Pond felt certain she'd lose interest.
Well and good. But in the meantime . . . Mrs. Mumford
was in Truvy's class. Teaching *her* girls. The very
thought washed over Truvy like a violation; it was the
ultimate injury, a horrible penalty. If she'd been terminated, it would've stung less.

What was she to do now?

She had to leave for the Wolcotts' in half an hour
for dinner. How could she go over there for a holiday
gathering and be gay when she just wanted to bury her
face in her hands and cry?

Truvy lowered the telegram into the pool of fabric in
her lap. Her vision blurred; fear chilled her to the bone.

Heaven help her.

A teacher was like a candle. Without the flame of

her pupils' desire to learn, she would grow dimmer and dimmer until she was alone in the darkness.

The candles on the Wolcotts' Christmas tree made the icicles look like they were dancing while they collected colors from the glow of flames; the reflections shot onto the walls and ceilings, reminding Jake of a shadow boxer.

The house smelled like spices. From the tree came the scent of pine and fruit. Sugared apple and orange ornaments gave off a tart-sweet fragrance. Iced gingerbread cookies hung from the branches. Cranberry and popcorn strings draped in loops over the needles.

Throughout the parlor and on the front entry table were those horn-of-plenty things filled with nuts, raisins, and hard candy. A colorful mix of wide ribbon candy and candy canes was arranged in a glass dish on the center table.

While he stood next to the fireplace mantel, Jake sucked on a length of peppermint, rolling it between his tongue and his back teeth.

The aroma of beef ribs and roasting chestnuts came in from the kitchen. Mrs. Dufresne had done most of the cooking while her husband, Shay, looked after their baby boy. Tom's brother, John, and his wife, Isabel, had come all the way up from California, bringing their fifteen-month-old daughter, Bijou.

Sitting near the pile of presents beneath the tree, the curly-haired Bijou gazed upward; she reached out with her pudgy fingers to grab a gingerbread man. She sampled the man's head, gumming and chewing with contentedness while drool ran down her chin.

She was a damn cute little button. Innocent. Much loved.

A rush of memories came to Jake and he cursed them. Holiday cheer and its symbolism made him confront the truth: he had a childhood that stunk.

Without effort, he could think of all the Christmases he'd missed. The way he'd grown up without a mother. Hard knocks. Tough luck. What kind of parents set out to short their kid? *His.* Or so he'd always felt. He'd always blamed them.

On Christmas Day, the inevitable questions pulled at him.

He wondered about his father. Where he was. What he was doing right now. What the past would have been like if his mother had stayed. He might have had a brother or a sister. Was the woman who gave birth to him alive or dead? He'd never know. There was no way to trace a ghost—he didn't want to, anyway.

He'd forgiven her, he supposed. Hell, he'd forgiven his father, too.

Yes, Jake had missed out on a lot of things growing up, but that was life, for Christ's sake. For a while, bitterness and anger had eaten him up. But he had a clear mind now. You couldn't go on living with regrets. Too many "what ifs." So he wouldn't go down that road. Ever again.

But he did know that if he ever had kids, he'd do it right. And seeing Bijou next to that tree made him think about fatherhood. Made him kind of long for the chance.

Only thing was, he had to get the married part right first.

Music played on the Victrola, cutting through the parlor's blend of voices and conversational laughter. The tune was a Joplin rag, its beat foot-tapping. Jake needed to ask Edwina what was going on with that dance teacher. The Mr. Physique contest was six weeks away and the boys really needed those lessons.

The doorbell cranked and the door was opened by Tom. Truvy moved into the vestibule, which was decorated with fir wreaths and holly-berry garlands.

"Merry Christmas," she greeted Tom, handing him a twig basket with a red cloth over it. "This is for you and Edwina from the Plunketts." She held out a tiny package and added, "And this is from me."

Tom took them both as she removed her gloves and hat and set them on the hall tree. Snowflakes clung to the shoulders of her cape, speckling the dark fabric with white. Tom helped her from it and laid it on the stair risers. "I'll bring your wrap upstairs to the bedroom in a minute. Come on inside where it's warm."

Jake studied the frosty pink color on Truvy's cheeks and her lips. Her hair was twisted high on the back of her head, and there were tendrils at her ears. She wore the blue velvet dress she had had on when she got off the train, only now he could fully appreciate the whole design. Before, all he'd seen was the way the skirt gathered at her flared hips. Without her cape blocking his view, he was able to see the top part was one of those blouses with a lot of stitch folds and lace frills. He once heard Edwina talking about the style. The belt was the kind a lady could hang a purse off of. *Chattle*-something. He couldn't recollect the exact term.

In any case, he liked how Truvy was put together.

Truvy entered the parlor and said her hellos while Jake stayed back in the corner. She hugged Edwina and took hold of Crescencia Dufresne's hand. She politely nodded during an introduction to John and Isabel Wolcott. John bent and picked up Bijou; he held her out for inspection, but Isabel looked disapprovingly at the cookie smeared on Bijou's cheeks. The baby was whisked off to be cleaned up.

Shay poured Truvy some eggnog. She took the cup but didn't taste the creamy drink. She looked into the depths of the cup, then back at Shay while keeping a hospitable expression on her face. Jake couldn't blame her for not downing a sip. He hated eggnog, too.

Jake shoved off from the fireplace and went toward the group. Truvy's eyes met his on his approach, surprise catching on her brows. Apparently she hadn't been informed he'd be at the Wolcotts. He knew she would be. Tom had told him.

In fact, today Tom had told him a few things about Miss Valentine.

She was twenty-five. Had lived with two widowed aunts before going to college. Her life was education. Economics. Politics. Current events. *And* she was a sports coach for young ladies at the school.

Interesting revelations.

With the lid blown off the coaching, he got the distinct impression she'd been screwing with him the other day about that liniment. The why of it was what he wanted to know.

"Miss Valentine, may I have a word with you?" Jake asked, excusing her from Shay. He took her by the elbow and steered her to the crackling fire in the hearth.

"Mr. Brewster, I just arrived," she protested, delicate cup held carefully in her hand so the eggnog inside wouldn't spill. "I really would prefer to converse with the other guests."

"You don't want to talk to me?"

"Not in particular. No."

The spark in her eyes was as hot as the fire's blaze. From its reflection, he noticed that she had a few freckles on the bridge of her nose, that her face had been dusted with a very fine powder. "How's the knee?"

She frowned. Dourly. Those lush lips of hers didn't look nearly as good when used to express displeasure; her smile was a lot better. "I told you, there's nothing wrong with my knee. It was a minor sprain. I'm not troubled by any pain."

Relaxing, he folded his arms over his chest while momentarily keeping his doubt in check. "The liniment worked."

"Yes."

"You didn't use it."

"No."

The tactless cut-and-dried reply elbowed him in the gut. She could have at least tried to snow him. "Why not?"

"Because it wasn't necessary." The cup of eggnog in her hand obviously became a decoy for her attention so she wouldn't have to talk to him. Without apparent regard for her dislike of it, she drank some, then promptly shivered. On a grimace, she licked her lips and said, "Too sweet."

He took her cup from her and set it on the mantel. "Nice recovery. It's not the sugar. It's the rum. Beer drinkers don't drink grog. A whiskey every now and then—but no rum or sherry."

"That's not why I don't care for eggnog." A reluctant laugh came from her throat. "You may think it's because I pine for beer, but the truth is—I'm not partial to nutmeg."

Standing there, she looked both pretty and ready to fracture. The cold flush to her cheeks had faded. Her mouth and cheeks were now drained by a paleness. An unreadable misery clouded her eyes. A look of dejection passed over her features. She had one hell of a black dog on her back.

He figured he had nothing to lose by asking—she was already in a mood. "Why didn't you tell me you taught sports?"

No surprise registered in her voice. No reaction. It was as if she knew he'd find out eventually. "Why should I have?"

"It'd add to our conversations."

"I don't see how conversations about things like pulled groins would. Frankly, that's not a problem I've encountered. Now if you'll excuse me, although I've found your lesson on beer versus rum entertaining, I'm not up for a debate on any athletic topics."

"I'm not one of your students, Tru; you can talk to me."

Pausing, she faced off with him. "I believe I just was."

His steady gaze bore into hers with silent expectation. "What's wrong? You're in a sour mood for Christmas."

"Fa-la-la-la-la, la-la-la-la," she sang in reply, then grabbed her eggnog from the mantel. "I most certainly am not."

But he wasn't blind to the quiver in her voice, to the shimmer in her eyes and the way she swallowed down her upset.

"Let's go into the kitchen and dump that"—he hooked her elbow through his—"and then we'll have a little talk and you can tell me what's biting you."

"I don't want a little talk. I don't want a big talk. I don't want—"

But he was already walking down the hallway that led into the kitchen. He pushed the swinging door in and nearly stopped short before going inside.

The tiny room was filled with women. Crescencia and Edwina sat at the table snapping green beans. Isabel Wolcott had Bijou propped on the counter while she wiped the child's chubby hands off with a dishcloth. Some kind of red stuff covered her fingers, her plump cheeks, and was dribbled down the front of her white dress.

All the ladies looked at him and Truvy.

Seeing Jake, Bijou scrunched her upturned nose and grinned. She had only two teeth—both on the bottom. She pointed at him and snorted.

He'd never had a kid snort at him before.

Isabel shook her head with a smile. "She got into the candied cherries."

"Bawr!" Bijou laughed, still pointing. "Bawr!"

Barkly, who was sitting on his haunches begging for what was left of the cherries in the jar, howled.

"Barkly, hush up." Edwina quieted the hound, then her attention went back to Jake and Truvy. Pleasure sparkled in her voice. "It's nice to see you two together."

"Mr. Brewster was j-just . . ." Truvy stammered, slipping out of his arm, "sh-showing me where to put my cup. My eggnog . . . I'm done."

Jake went with the lame excuse because he'd been the one to use it first. He took the cup from Truvy's fingers and poured the creamy eggnog down the pipes, then set the empty china in the sink.

"Bawr! Bawr! Bawr!" Bijou snorted. Her tiny upper lip curled into her small nostrils, and she systematically sniffed air in and out of her nose.

Jake got a little self-conscious. "What's the matter?"

Isabel apologetically explained, "She's calling you a bear."

Damn. Bears were big and hairy and they smelled.

"Thank you, Mr. Brewster, for your assistance." Truvy placed her hands on her hips and addressed the trio of women, "Ladies, what do you have for me to do? I'd like to help."

Truvy was trying to make a fast escape.

Barkly gave a thunderous *woof* again, wet black nose twitching in on the scent of those cherries.

Edwina tossed snapped green beans into a pot. "We don't need any help in here at all, Truvy. But I could use your assistance with Barkly. He's being a pest after those cherries. Could you please take him outside and let him run around? Mr. Brewster, would you go with Miss Valentine?"

"Sure."

Truvy immediately protested, "I'd have to go upstairs for my cape and I wouldn't want to accidentally wake Elizabeth. You know how that floorboard in the bedroom squeaks."

"Not a concern, because my angel is right here." In a wooden cradle decked out with blankets, the baby slept peacefully at Edwina's feet. "And I have something you can use instead of your cape."

"I'd hate to trouble you—"

"No trouble." Listening to Edwina's persistence, Jake bit his inner lip to keep from smiling. "Hanging on a peg in the storm closet, there's a wool cloak I wear when I pin up clothes."

"I'll get it for her," Jake volunteered while walking Truvy through the mud room off the kitchen. He found the worsted gray cloak and settled it over her shoulders. In the small, closed-off space, he could smell the fragrance coming from the warmth of her skin, sweet, intoxicating. His fingers lingered at the cloak's turned-down collar, lightly grazing her throat as he fastened the single closure. She stared at him, her mouth cinched tighter than corset strings, as she kept her arms stiffly at her sides. To his recollection, he'd never done up a lady's garment before. He'd always performed the opposite service.

"You do know it's snowing," she whispered, backing away from him as far as she could manage within the confines of the walls. "We're going to be cold."

"I don't mind the cold."

"You should. Bears hibernate."

Jake held the door open. "I'll remember that for next winter."

As soon as the door opened, Barkly streaked past them—a loose-skinned tawny bullet—knocking his sloping shoulder into Truvy's leg and putting her balance off kilter. To her chagrin, Jake settled an arm around her to keep her from hitting the door frame; then he steered them around the wraparound porch and toward the side of the house where a small series of painted steps led to a side garden.

She was mindful of the way his wide hand rested on her back; her body seemed to suck the heat from his. Her skin grew hot and flushed at the same time—and the temperature had to be at least as low as thirty. Fire seemed to explode through Truvy's blood. When breathing became an effort, she knew she never should have come outside with him. Her appeal to Edwina hadn't worked, so she was on her own to get out of this.

She couldn't be alone with Jake Brewster. Not tonight of all nights.

Not when her concentration was splintered with thoughts of failure and faults. She could barely form sentences coherently.

"My hands are cold." The complaint had a logical solution. "I need to go inside and get some gloves. So I'll just—"

"I have pockets you can use." And so his tweed coat did.

She couldn't come up with an alternative plan for returning to the kitchen. "That's all right." She'd rather her fingers turn as numb as a snowman's nose than cozily angle her hand inside one of his pockets.

This was the first time she'd seen him wear a formal suit. Its color was a deep blue-black, single-breasted in style, with a white dress shirt partially in view. He'd forgone a celluloid collar, its absence obviously intentional because he'd left the top two buttons on his collarless shirt undone. Had the cuffs not been attached, she guessed he would have left those at home, too. And rather than wear knobby-toed men's evening shoes, he had on a pair of Creedmoors. After buying six new pairs of shoes, she knew her styles. Creedmoors were hideously popular in the West. Made of kangaroo calf and supported by a boot heel, the shoes had an oil grain that was polished to a dull sheen.

On any other man, the fashion mishmash would have been a horror. On him, she caught herself *liking* his overall appearance. It made no sense at all. The pit of her stomach tickled and her leg muscles froze. She halted and attempted to excuse herself from his company once more. "It's pointless for the both of us to stay out here."

"Then you go tell Edwina she's pointless." Jake stepped away.

Truvy's indecision lasted a mere second before she kept walking toward Jake. She couldn't tell Edwina that.

Up next to the house's wood siding, a lawn settee had been covered for the winter by a length of canvas cloth. The settee faced the fallow garden and a yard wearing a counterpane of snow. With a sweep of his hand, he removed the canvas to reveal the green wicker beneath.

"Take a load off and quit thinking up ways to get back inside."

Taken aback, she didn't move, unsure. Not yards from the settee, the parlor's lights shone out the window and onto the weathered, but not warped, porch boards. Although the settee was tucked deep into the shadows of the wraparound porch, anyone could press their face against those window panes and see them. But who would without the whole parlor knowing?

Although it was beastly frigid, the awning above was shelter from the snow drifting from the sky. Disregarding her reservations, Truvy took a seat on the lawn furniture and snuggled deeper into Edwina's cloak, burying her hands in the front folds to keep them somewhat warm.

Jake sat down beside her, the wicker creaking beneath his weight. Two tall people on a short settee didn't leave a tennis ball's width of space between them. Their shoulders touched. Their hips touched. Their knees touched. If one of them crossed his or her legs, their legs would touch. Unable to slide down a fraction, she didn't move lest she touch him someplace she hadn't thought of.

Shadows cast from leafless branches melted into a twilight bright in the cold light of snow. Neither of them spoke. Sitting this close to him, she could smell his cologne, a kind of spicy something that threw her senses into utter chaos; her stomach went from fluttering to forming knots. Moose Thompson smelled like menthol and eucalyptus oil, a combination so overpowering at times that her eyes had watered.

Barkly ran around the yard, stopping every now and then to dig in the snow and send a spray of white between his hind legs. Loping through the barren garden, he knocked over the pole for the scarecrow as he bounded up the porch via one route and leaped off it via another.

"You think he's a little hound crazy from being in the house?" Jake's question broke the silence—along with the icy shot of snow Barkly left in his wake when he ran off again.

Brushing off her skirt, Truvy replied, "I wouldn't know. I've never had a pet."

"No cat?"

"No."

"I figured you to at least have a companion bird."

"What would I do with a companion bird?"

"Watch it hang on a perch and fluff its feathers." Then he added—and to her, it seemed he did so just to nettle her, "You seem the type to enjoy one."

She let her eyes rest on him with deliberate censure. "And what type is that?"

"Since you're overheated about it, I'm not going to answer."

She gave him a scorching glare before replying sardonically, "Yes, I was waiting for this. 'She's a sports coach, so she's *manly.*' A real tomboy type. A woman who would like gamy wildlife—*companion birds.*"

"Uhh . . ." He cleared his throat, putting on a darn good show of innocence when she knew he was only trying to back out of his slip-up. "Uh, I didn't mean it the way you're taking it. I don't know of any sports coaches who keep pet birds. I was going for the compassionate and devoted lady teacher type."

She stifled her censurious thoughts of him and studied his face. He did look sincere; his mouth was parted, his brows were straight, and his jaw wasn't ticking. "Maybe I would get enjoyment from a companion bird—a canary or parakeet. But it's not an indulgence I'd buy for myself."

"Then you ought to ask somebody to get you one real soon. I read that having a parakeet helps nervousness, keeps your blood pure, and treats brain anxiety. You've been exhibiting some symptoms tonight. Bad day?"

"I don't have brain anxiety! And if birds are such a general health help, why don't you have one?"

"I have dumbbells."

"Ah," she rallied back with a fist pumped exaggeratedly in the air, "just the ticket for no blood circulation in the brain."

"Naw. I get a Swedish massage for that."

Truvy could only heave a sigh.

There was no talking to him.

Jake shifted his weight on the settee to lean forward. Doggedly, he laid his hands on his knees. His shoulders seemed wider as he went to face her. He stared. Quietly.

"What's eating you, sweetheart?"

She hated that he could be so persistent. "Nothing you can fix." Her gaze broke away from his.

The sun had set, painting the backyard in variegated hues of gray that blended together. A wink of silver moon appeared above the tree boughs. The very same moon that could be seen from St. Francis. Right now.

Truvy shivered, remembering, longing.

"I shouldn't be out here." In spite of her resolve, a quiver touched her words. "I should be inside helping Edwina and Mrs. Dufresne put dinner on the table."

"Don't go."

Two words. Simple enough. But how could she stay without breaking down, telling him her utmost fears, and ultimately making a fool of herself?

She ran her palms over her thighs in an effort to warm her legs. With a forward-to-backward motion, she rocked her shoes from the heels to the tips in an effort to restore her circulation. The blood in her feet had to be frozen; her new shoes might as well have been made out of newspaper for all the good they did keeping her warm—not to mention that her toes were squished together and her insteps ached. But like the saying went: Suffer for beauty.

Suffer for reading *The Science of Life.*

Jake quietly surveyed her. Her indirect reply to the question he had asked hovered between them. She defiantly refused to give in. Pointing at the fancy beaded shoes, she declared, "It's these shoes. They hurt my feet."

"Then why did you buy them?"

Truvy looked down, blinking, seeing only the fringe of her lashes as her vision clouded. The tanned, butternut brown shoes had beckoned. They were stylish, becoming, extravagant—the things she wasn't.

Why did I buy them?

Because she thought she would be someplace new

and exciting for only a short while. Because she wanted to be different from herself for only a short while. Because . . .

Hot tears formed in her eyes. She tried to hold them off.

Because she wished . . .

She wished she was small-boned, delicate, and slim. She wished that she was shorter or, at the very least, that it would become fashionable for women to wear flat shoes. She wished her hair was a lighter shade. She wished her nose was a different shape. She wished she could play the piano. She wished she was more of a social butterfly.

She wished she would be kissed just once in her lifetime . . .

Lifting her chin, she gazed into Jake's face.

"Because I didn't want being tall to matter," Truvy replied in a colorless way. "I bought the shoes so I could be like other women."

He had no reply.

There. She'd shocked him. She'd been too honest. Not only with him but also with herself. Speaking character weaknesses aloud gave them substance, credence.

"I don't think you're too tall." He scratched the bridge of his nose, then knit his fingers loosely together. "Hell, I once saw a woman built like she was on stilts. She has you by half as much."

Truvy felt a smile threaten to curve her mouth.

She wanted to hug him. In his clumsy way, he'd tried, and succeeded, to make her feel a smidgen better. What would his anecdote be for Miss Pond's telegram? Could he overturn her despair again like a bull walking uphill?

The urge to unburden herself lodged in her chest.

"Yeah, she was definitely a hell of a lot taller than you. Christ, she was taller than any man. But it was good for business because nobody'd ever seen a woman like her in San Francisco before. She worked where the lights were red and the beds were soft and—"

"I'm on a leave of absence from my teaching position," Truvy broke in before she lost her courage, "because I read inappropriate material out of a sexuality book to my students. My knee really is fine—I can't walk very well in high heels because they hurt my feet. I'm wearing pink satin underwear because I never have before and I'm trying to have fun. I far prefer my tunic and pantaloons to skirts because I can move around better in them. And"—she took in a breath—"I'm twenty-five and did fib to you about being kissed before. I haven't been—not because I never had the opportunity, but because I think Coach Thompson is a big ape."

Drawing back, he gazed into her eyes without flinching. "Sweet Judas."

Then nothing further. She'd made him speechless.

Truvy fought against lurching to her feet. The tip of her tongue stuck to the roof of her mouth. She swallowed and tried to force her heart not to ram into her ribs. A faint touch of remorse squeezed her throat, but she wouldn't let it catch in her breath. "There, I don't have a single secret from you. I'm an open book."

"Yeah?" As he leaned toward her, that untamable lock of hair fell into his eyes. "After twenty-five years, your book's got to have more secrets than you just told me. I'd rather read the chapters myself and see what's between the lines." An unbalanced grin kicked up one corner of his well-defined mouth. "Actually, I want to go right to that reading about sex part."

Truvy was morbidly aware of the fire singeing her cheeks. A good thing the parlor lamps didn't illuminate the area any more than they did. Surely she was red-faced. She snapped her attention to the sky while explaining, because she had no choice now but to explain.

"As of today, in spite of my optimism," she began, "my visit to Harmony has been extended. Indefinitely. Because I read excerpts to my students from a book called *The Science of Life.* Some of the terms are forthrightly medical. I used what is considered poor judgment by educating young ladies on human anatomy and its counterparts."

"Do you think it was poor judgment?"

"Obviously not."

"Then don't back the hell down. Stand up for yourself."

She inclined her chin at Jake. "I can't stand up for myself if I'm here and the problem is there."

"You've got a point." A contemplative expression settled on Jake's face as he sagely spoke. "Yeah, I was on a boxing tour in D.C. once, and I got fed up with how this sports writer, Hadley Burns"—he said the name with a contemptuous snort—"for the *New York World* kept writing that I performed as a chorus boy when I wasn't in the ring. Over the telephone wires, Burns didn't think I had a beef. So I had to bring him around. In person. I canceled a fight and took the first train back to Manhattan, went to the newspaper offices and rearranged Burns's desk. I never had any trouble with him after that."

"I can tell you're sincere about your advice, but my teaching at a school for young ladies and your being in a boys' chorus are entirely different things. Although I don't see anything shameful in singing."

"Singing? A chorus boy is a man who dresses up like a—" He severed the rest of the sentence while working two fingertips over his smooth-shaven jaw.

A sudden gust of wind blew snow beneath the awning. The soft, frozen dots pelted her face, stuck to her lashes, and clung to her lips. Still pondering his unfinished sentence, she asked, "Dresses up like a what?"

"Never mind." Jake ducked her question, easing his broad back into the settee and taking her with him by holding onto her shoulder. Nestled into the crook of his arm, her cheek grazed the rough tweed of his coat. The faint odor of his cologne came to her. "We're going to write a new chapter in your book." The baritone of his voice vibrated through her bodice. "The one where Truvy gets her first kiss."

Before she could say anything, he captured her chin in his strong hand and turned her face. All the while he brought his head lower, he stared at her mouth. His closed lips touched hers lightly, wet from snow, cold. But as the kiss went on, warmer. Much warmer.

The hard muscle of his side flattened her breast as he held her close. If she moved even slightly, her hand would fall into his lap—deep into his lap at the place where the fly to his trousers began. As it was, from the intimacy of their position, her palm had ended up high on his thigh. Her arm, crushed by where they joined, was immobile.

She could feel the blood beating in his lips, feel the cadence in her own. Her lower lip became his sole focus; he alternated between gently suckling the flesh and softly tracing its plumpness.

Breathless, she settled into the kiss, her first. So unexpected—beyond her expectations. Every one of her senses was in discord. Her body felt like it was plummeting and soaring at the same time; her lungs felt oxygen-deprived. All that she had wondered about was no longer a mystery. The kiss was what *The Science of Life* had alluded to—

The appetite of sexual emotion pervades every element of our bodies, and in every nerve it thrills with pleasure or grows mad with a desire demanding us to be fruitful.

Pulses came to life in her that she had never imagined could feel so . . . maddening with . . . *the need for more than this*. She breathed in, surrounded by the scent of Jake's skin. The position of his mouth changed to a slant and pressed harder against her moist lips. The teasing friction gave a tenderness to her mouth, an extraordinary sensitivity, evoking the feeling of goose bumps along her spine.

Sounds that were foreign to her filled her ears—the scratch of tweed, a mellow whisper of linen evening shirt, the heavy rhythm of a man's breathing. The faintness of her own moan as it welled up in her throat, only to be caught by Jake's lips.

Lost in the haze of emotions spiraling through her, Truvy didn't readily hear the commotion going on in the house until Edwina screamed.

Abruptly, Truvy's limbs turned to ice. She broke away and bumped her nose against Jake's. He sat up the same time as she did.

Edwina's cry came once more.

Fright drained the blood from Truvy every place its heat had pulsed not seconds before. Jake bolted out of the settee, bringing her with him. They rushed inside the house through the glass parlor door, a burst of cold air rolling in behind them.

There in the middle of the parlor, Edwina didn't look distressed. In fact, she stood beside Tom, laughing. Everyone else laughed, too.

And soon Truvy and Jake found out why.

Crack! Crack!

The pinecones on the Christmas tree were exploding in the warm and cozy room. *Crack!* And then another *pop!* And another. The pops continued, and Tom plucked one of the cones from the tree to show his wife. Heat from the fireplace had caused the scales to open. The pinecones had been closed so tightly that nobody had noticed them amid all the ornaments.

Edwina's laughter rang out once more. "Oh, Tom, we'll have to save the cones for next year. They're special now."

"Bawr!" Bijou giggled, snorting at Jake.

Faces turned toward Truvy and Jake. She grew self-consciously aware that her hand was tucked into his. There hadn't been a moment to sort out her thoughts about that kiss when she'd had to focus fully on the exploding tree. But with all eyes on her and Jake, she wanted to hide out of embarrassment. They knew, or had to surmise, what had gone on out there on that veranda.

In what she hoped appeared to be a nonchalant manner, Truvy slipped her fingers free of Jake's grasp.

It was precisely then that Barkly bounded through the parlor. He wove between the furnishings, his whip-like tail knocking decorations off the tree. He was a bundle of hound dog energy, a dead gopher swaying from his mouth. As he came to a carpet-rippling stop, he proudly dropped the rodent at Truvy's feet.

Right on her beaded tan shoes.

She screeched, shook the gopher from her shoe

with a twist of her ankle, then looked into the drooping eyes of Barkly. His tail wagged. Once. Waiting for her reaction.

Barkly bayed, ears lolling behind his boxy head. "I suppose you should be proud," Truvy said. She bent forward and smoothed her palm over his fur. "Good dog."

Tom said, "At least he didn't eat the gingerbread cookies off the tree again this year."

"No, that's Bijou's job." John Wolcott picked up his daughter, her face smeared with frosting.

"Bawr!" Bijou pointed to Jake, then tucked her face into the lapel of her daddy's coat.

Smiling, Truvy looked in turn at the people in the parlor. A dear friend. A baby in a cradle. New friends. Husbands and wives. Children. And a man who sent her heartbeat leaping. The scene filled her with a true appreciation for togetherness: the piano music from the phonograph; a snapping fire in the hearth; the dining-room table spread with a fine cloth, accented by mismatched silverware and name cards lovingly placed at each setting.

She felt an instant's shame that she hadn't wanted to come to Edwina's tonight and be a part of all this.

Crack! Pop! Crack! Another eruption of opening pinecones sang from the tree like a chorus of "Joy! Joy! Joy!"

For Truvy, this was the most memorable Christmas she'd had since she was a child.

Chapter
❧9❦

"When I think of Mrs. Mumford in my classroom, I just want to get on the next train back to Boise and tell her she can't take my place," Truvy said as she stood in the Wolcotts' kitchen pressing a hot iron back and forth over Elizabeth's freshly laundered infant robe.

"She can't, and won't, take your place. Miss Pond said she was working to fix things. And I believe she will." With a pull of her teeth, Edwina broke a thread from Tom's shirtsleeve. The rest of the gray flannel shirt remained in her lap while she sat at the kitchen table mending.

When Truvy had arrived that morning, she'd told Edwina about yesterday's telegram from Miss Pond. Edwina was supportive, once again welcoming her into her home. Although the Wolcotts had been truly gracious to her, Truvy would never impose on them. Tom and Edwina were so tenderly romantic with each other, Truvy felt like an outsider who didn't belong in their married world.

With heartfelt appreciation, Truvy declined Edwina's generous offer by informing her she'd already spoken to Mrs. Plunkett before coming over and that Mrs. Plunkett was delighted to have her remain as a guest. *Delighted* was putting things mildly. Mrs. Plunkett was overwrought with joy and weeping that Truvy could be with her longer. Oddly, the *good* news gave Mrs. Plunkett a sick headache, causing a postponement of their trip to the dressmaker's that morning.

Quietly thinking about how to get out of any future appointments with the modiste, Truvy let Edwina's observance hover between them.

Edwina spoke up. "Truvy, this isn't so bad. I'm sure Mrs. Mumford will come around. And more time away won't make the reasons why you love teaching so much go away. If anything, the separation should reinforce your convictions, and when you go back, you'll be an even better teacher."

Truvy tried to make light of her situation. "At the very least, I'll return a better ironer."

Edwina laughed.

The train's steam whistle blew in the distance, a reminder to Truvy that she wouldn't be on the outbound train tomorrow. "It's just so hard to accept."

Edwina's lips pressed together in thought. "Then we'll just have to see what we can find to keep you busy."

Truvy switched plates on the sadiron. "There's no questioning what I can do while I'm in Harmony. I'll be spending my days with you helping take care of Elizabeth."

"Oh, good heavens," Edwina said, fingering a pin from the pin cushion, "this is supposed to be a holiday for you. I wouldn't dream of your devoting all your time to me. It's not necessary. I received word from Marvel-Anne. She's on her way home."

"That will be nice for you to have her back. You've missed her." Truvy sprinkled water from a sieve-capped bottle onto wrinkles on a handkerchief of Edwina's.

"Yes, I have." Edwina lowered the shirt, and rested her hands on the table. "Now . . . I wonder if Miss Gimble, the Normal School teacher, needs assistance. I can ask."

Truvy didn't want to be a charity case. "Edwina, that's very thoughtful of you, but I'd feel it my duty to tell Miss Gimble my circumstances. I haven't divulged the truth to anyone else. I didn't give Mrs. Plunkett a reason why I was staying, and she was so elated, she didn't ask for one. Only you . . ."—the iron's handle warmed Truvy's hand, much like Jake's mouth had warmed hers last night—". . . only you know the whole truth." *Only you and Jake Brewster.*

She didn't reveal that last part, not wanting Edwina to make anything of her and Jake. There was nothing to make anything of. So he'd kissed her. So he'd given something to her she would never forget. That wasn't a reason to pair them up.

Edwina's astute gaze leveled on Truvy. "Who else knows about Miss Pond's telegram besides me? You can't fib worth a fable."

Quietly, Truvy bit the inside of her lip.

When she made no immediate reply, Edwina guessed. "Jake Brewster."

"Yes."

"Hah! I knew it." Edwina smiled with a gleam of mischievousness in her eyes. "The way you two came in from the veranda—I saw the blush on your cheeks."

"It was cold outside."

"Uh-huh."

"It was." Truvy clunked the iron down on the stove plate too hard and the burner rattled.

"Well, I think it's wonderful that you've confided in him."

"It was nothing like that. I told him only so he wouldn't keep pestering me." She frowned. "He can behave like a recalcitrant student."

"A student—*Jake?*" Edwina said with a furrow to her brow. "Have you taken a hard look at him? He's not boyish in the slightest."

"I can see that."

The two of them continued with their chores, working in silence. After a while, Edwina mumbled something about a student, then suddenly cried, "I know what you can do!"

Edwina rose, pacing the kitchen, hands on her hips. "I told you, the woman I hired to give dancing lessons twisted her ankle and I haven't been able to get another instructor to replace her. Until now." She pointed at Truvy. "You'll take over my dancing classes. You *can* be a teacher while you're in Harmony."

Truvy was so taken aback by the notion, she couldn't speak. She thought. And the more she thought about it . . . the more the idea blossomed with promise. A dance instructor. Young ladies wearing their best dresses with elastic bracelets on their wrists and gold watches pinned to their bodices. Young men in their binding-trimmed Prince Albert suits. Fresh-faced. Eager to learn.

The picture her mind painted of the dancing studio was wonderful. But there was a slight problem. The fact of the matter was, she'd danced very little in her life. She'd *been* to dances, but mostly as an observer. More often as a chaperone. From the sidelines, her toe tapped to the beat, her heart kept tempo with the music. She had it in her to move to the music, but she'd never learned how to artfully do the steps. The one time Coach Moose Thompson had asked her to waltz, she'd stepped on his toes so badly, they didn't finish the dance. He never asked her again.

"Well? Say yes!" Edwina's cheeks were pink from excitement. "It's the perfect arrangement for both of us."

As much as she hated to, Truvy had to confess, "I've had very little dancing experience"—she also hated to pass up an opportunity—"but if you have tutelage books, I could gain some skills. I'm a fast learner."

"I do have a book. *Dance Fundamentals.* It shows the basic moves for the shuffle, two-step, polka, waltz, and beginning ragtime—step-by-step. You can acquaint yourself with it without much effort. Dancing is easy. Like this. Watch." Edwina stepped forward on her left foot, closed her right to the left, put her weight on the right, and stepped left again. She repeated the moves. "You try."

With her interest captured, Truvy set the iron on the plate and rounded the clothing board to meet Edwina. She hummed a tune as she ran through the steps again. One. Two. One. Two. It didn't appear too difficult. Much easier with Edwina than with Moose.

"Left foot first," Edwina instructed.

Truvy did so. Then the right. She followed Edwina's lead. With each repetition, she embedded the memory of the steps more until she wasn't thinking, she was dancing.

"Quick. Quick. Slow." Edwina closed the space between her feet. "Quick. Quick. Slow."

Determination dazzled Truvy as her legs moved to the rhythm. "I can do it!"

"Of course you can."

Breathless, Truvy hugged Edwina. *"Thank you,"* Truvy said. "Thank you for thinking so much of me." Being a dance instructor would be challenging; just the thing to keep her mind focused on a purpose, and not on Jake Brewster. *Jake Brewster?* He'd barely been in her mind since yesterday. Hardly at all. Perhaps a little. *Constantly.* His mouth, his face, his eyes, his body, his easy-going mannerisms—they'd all intruded in her sleep, and they were the first thing to fill her mind this morning when she woke.

Truvy needed to be giving these lessons more than Edwina knew. Even so, to be fair, she had to state, "But after I begin the lessons, if you don't feel I'm competent enough to stand in for you, please tell me. The academy is a reflection of your name and I wouldn't want to ruin your reputation."

Edwina squeezed her, then leaned back. "Don't worry. The students at Wolcott's Dancing Academy aren't enrolled for competitions. They're there because dancing gives them an activity." Then she added with a laugh, "Or their mothers are making them."

Truvy looked at the stack of ironing in the basket, then back at Edwina with a helpless smile. "When shall I start?"

Edwina's mouth curved, slow and deliberate. "Right away. Because just yesterday, I was queried about the classes from an eager gentleman."

"I'll do my very best with him. Even if he's a reluctant candidate, one whose mother is sending him to dance, I'll induce his desire."

Edwina's laugh was marvelous, undiluted. "Why, Truvy! That's exactly what I had in mind for this special gentleman." She stretched her arm out to touch her shoulder. "Right now, I have classes scheduled for Mondays, Wednesdays, and Fridays. And—"

"—tomorrow's Friday!"

Truvy could barely contain the anticipation that filled her—the first piece of optimism she'd experienced since leaving St. Francis.

"Pass."

"Me, too."

"Check."

"Call."

"I'll take that and raise your bet a Boar's Head Red." Smoke curled into the next words uttered. "What are you going to do, Bruiser?"

Jake leaned back in his chair, tilting on the rear legs. A fat Havana was stuck inside the corner of his mouth. He puffed, looked at the five cards in his hand, then at the men around the table. Milton Burditt, Lou Bernard, August Gray, Gig Debolski, and Walfred Kudlock. Tom Wolcott sat across from Jake, his concentration not on poker as he tossed his cards facedown.

Another Thursday night of cards, beer, cigars, and conversation. Only Walfred and Gig were in the game, upping his opening bet.

Jake held onto a full house. A tight hand. But they were playing deuces wild. Five of a kind were a possibility. Royal flushes were more probable but outranked by the quints. Looking at the stack of chips he had in front of him, he contemplated the risk of losing. He rubbed his fingertips over the abrasive beard on his jaw, doing a mental tally on how much he had.

About fifteen bucks and some change.

The colorful pile of bottle caps heaped in the center of his kitchen table could be worth five dollars. They didn't play for cash. Poker playing was a strategic exercise for the brain—and a damn good excuse to knock back some suds with friends. It had taken about a year of them all drinking beer and saving the bottle caps to collect enough "chips" to make playing worthwhile.

Each bottle cap had been given a denomination. Your Wild Goose, blue with the red goose, was worth a penny. Flying Dog, yellow with the leaping dog, was worth a nickel. St. Andrews Ale, black with a white cross, was worth a dime. Heinrich's Lager, green with a silver gryphon, was worth a quarter. And Boar's Head Red, black with the gold pentacle, was worth a buck.

"I'm in," Jake said, tossing in a Boar's Head Red cap with a flick of his thumbnail. "What do you have?"

Walfred unveiled three tens.

Gig showed a straight in mixed suits.

Jake cracked a smile, then fanned his cards face up on the table. "Full house."

"Dang!"

"Horse apples!"

Tom rose and scooted his chair in. "I'm done for the night."

"You've only been here a half hour, Wolcott," Milton observed.

"A half hour too long." Tom went for his hat and coat. "I never should have left the house."

"Edwina wanted you to come." Jake shuffled the cards.

"I know what she said, but it's not what I wanted. I'm going home to my wife."

Walfred snickered behind his hand while August shrugged with a smile.

Tom shot them both hard stares. "Just you wait, my friends. It will happen to you, too." Then to Jake. "And *you,* too."

"I didn't say anything," Jake said in defense.

Buttoning his coat, Tom said, "G'night, everybody."

"See you around, Wolcott," Milton replied.

Jake called after Tom, "If you need anything, Tom, let me know."

"Will do."

Raking the pot toward him, Jake made an offer to the boys with a lift of his chin: "Go and get yourselves another beer out of the icebox before my block melts down. I'm getting a delivery on Monday. No point in wasting a lager while it's cold."

"Thanks, Bruiser."

"Yeah, thanks."

The clink of caps rolling fused with Jake's next words. "You three go on and get another one, too."

The trio who'd quit the game quickly rose and made a stampede for the zinc-lined Alaska.

While they were gone, Jake slumped, his back against the spindles of his chair. He'd been playing cards, drinking beer, and telling jokes for hours. All to keep his thoughts from wandering to Truvy. It wasn't working. She was in the back of his mind all the time.

He hadn't seen her since Christmas. Not since he'd kissed her.

Bad move on his part. Dangerous. His thoughts hadn't been clear ever since. Knowing he was the only man to kiss her made his blood rush—as it did now at the memory of her mouth beneath his. Warm. Pliant. Sweet and soft. Untried. The fact that she'd confided in him about her personal life—it made him wonder if she could ever view him on her intellectual level. Not that he was as smart as her. But there was more to him than she knew.

He'd started reading *Crime and Punishment*. Raskolnikov was all right as a protagonist, but Jake had one hell of a time pronouncing his name every time he came across the lengthy, foreign spelling. He wasn't all that sure why Raskolnikov wanted to transact business with the pawnbroker when he was so mad, but Jake did get that the man was planning some kind of crime. That's where Jake's interest started picking up. But the wording was heavy for him and a chore to read. Even so, he'd been forcing himself through the pages.

Truvy's statement about his being tasteless, and her all but telling him he wasn't brainy enough to understand the book, had prickled beneath his skin like a thistle stuck to the underside of a coat. Not enough to draw blood, but enough to know something was there, irritating.

And yet, thoughts of her filled his head. They shouldn't. He shouldn't be tempted. Hell, he knew the reason why.

Sex.

He was long overdue to ride over to Alder for a night of enjoyment. The trouble was, he had no inclination to make the effort. Not while Truvy was in Harmony making him envision that pink underwear she talked about. She'd said it was satin. He knew about the petticoat. He'd caught a glimpse that night he caught her in the Plunketts' yard up to no good.

He wanted to kiss her warm mouth again, feel the silkiness of her curls.

Why her? He knew lots of women in Alder who had pliable lips and soft hair.

But none had Truvy's legs. Especially not what Truvy's legs would look like in a pair of pink satin drawers. That was something altogether more—

A knock sounded on the locked gymnasium's door and Jake went to see who it was. Darkness had just fallen, so whoever wanted him didn't want to wait until tomorrow.

Clovis Lester, navy knit cap on his towhead and winter overalls snapped at his scrawny shoulders, thrust out a note for him. "Mrs. Wolcott told me to deliver this to you right away. She's payin' me a whole quarter and I'm going to buy a bunch of candy with it."

With the cigar still caught by his lips, Jake took the envelope, then felt inside his pants pocket for some coins. "Here, kid. Buy yourself a soda pop while you're at it."

"Gee, thanks!"

Clovis ran off into the dim night and Jake closed out the cold. Walking, he tore open the seal while reentering his office. He went through the door to the kitchen of his apartment where he sat back down at the table.

"Bad news, Bruiser?" Gig asked.

"Don't know. It's from Mrs. Wolcott."

Jake hoped the print was large and clear, because he wasn't wearing his glasses. Thankfully, the words popped from the snowy white paper, neat and highly legible.

"What's it say?"

Jake read aloud.

Official Notice

Edwina Wolcott's Dancing Academy will reopen tomorrow morning, December 27th, for lessons beginning at 11 A.M. The following students are enrolled in the 2 P.M. class: Lou Bernard, Milton Burditt, Gig Debolski, August Gray, Walfred Kudlock, and Jacob Brewster.

"Hey, Bruiser, I didn't know you'd be tripping the light fantastic with us," Milt commented, lifting his beer bottle to his mouth.

"I'm not." *Sweet Judas.* He hadn't enrolled. "This is a mistake."

"You say that like dancing is for Willie boys." Walfred's frown cut into his chin.

Lou set his beer on the table. "Yeah, I got that impression myself."

"Well get rid of it," Jake returned belligerently, "because you need the lessons to give you grace and body movement."

"Seems to me," Milton piped in, "what's good enough for us should be good enough for you, Bruiser, if I could say so."

"You just did," August pointed out.

Jake tapped the cherry of his cigar in the ashtray. "I'm not entered in the Mr. Physique contest. If I was, then I'd probably be taking the lessons."

"Probably?" Gig was doubtful.

"All right. No. I wouldn't. Why should I?" Jake came back, his tone stilted. Dammit, Edwina's mistake was costing him.

Jake's jaw took on the same tenseness as his biceps after a hard workout at the punching bag. How in the hell could he get out of this and still get them to go for those lessons? It wasn't as if he was against dancing. In fact, he was a faultless dancer. But being stuck in a dance studio for an hour while a teacher made him two-step wasn't his idea of an hour well spent.

"I'll tell you why you should—because men can still be men, even if they're learning how to dance. And anyone here not willing to prove it *is* a Willie boy, more so than the guy willing to put on the dancing shoes." August's challenging remark hung in the smoky air.

Jake crushed the tip of his Havana, killing the cigar with three stabs. "I already know how to dance."

"Is that so?" Milt propped his elbows on the table. "Where'd you learn how?"

"Brooklyn."

Gig asked, "When's the last time you danced?"

"How in the hell should I remember that?" Jake's annoyance gripped him in his gut; he knew they were leading him into something, and for the life of him, he didn't know a way out.

"If you can't remember," Milt declared, "then it's time for a refresher course."

Walfred harped in with "I second that.

Everyone at the table nodded. Except Jake.

"We'll make a wager, Bruiser," Milton offered up, shuffling the cards. "High card says you don't have to take the lessons. Low card says you're in with us—right, boys?"

"Right," came the collective agreement.

Milton tidied the deck, laid it facedown on the table, tapped the top, and cut the cards. He drew a six of spades.

Jake's fingers tightened on Edwina's stationery. Six. Not hard to beat. Not real easy either. It was all a matter of luck. He laid Edwina's letter down and cut the deck once more.

"Five of diamonds!" Milt said, slapping his hands on the tabletop.

Jake lost the bet.

Cheers rounded the table and beers were raised.

"Yeah, okay," Jake remarked sarcastically. "I lose. Fine." He shoved Edwina's folded note into his shirt pocket, then cracked his knuckles. "Now are we playing or what? Milt, deal the cards."

Chapter
❧ 10 ❧

Merrily humming, Truvy pulled open the curtains in the dance studio. But her cheerfulness quickly was dashed as she stared out the window.

There, on the other side of the alley, stood a building with a long row of windows just like those of the dance studio's. And behind the windows, men punched, lifted, and strained at athletic equipment. They moved about, wearing insufficient shirts and loose-fitting trouser pants.

Truvy couldn't believe what she was seeing: Bruiser's Gymnasium in all its crudeness. How could that be? The gym wasn't near Edwina's dancing studio. Dogwood Place and Birch Avenue couldn't back up to each other like this. The streets would have to be crooked for that to happen. Small towns were built with square block grids. This didn't make sense.

Then, an exceedingly tall figure moved across the room. Jake—as sure as Apollo himself. Good heavens, her poor sense of direction hadn't prepared her for this. Edwina Wolcott's Dancing Academy shared the alleyway with Bruiser's Gymnasium.

Just as the awful reality hit her, Jake came toward the window, flipped the sash lock, and lifted one of the three-on-three panes. As he did so, he stopped, then leaned closer to the glass as he caught her looking.

They measured each other for endless seconds, their gazes colliding, with Truvy pushing down the tension that kept her frozen to the spot. She was helpless to turn away. Her eyes remained on Jake.

A Turkish towel lay over his shoulders, but he wasn't wearing that ripped-up shirt without the sleeves—just a simple blue one, collarless and buttoned halfway down the front. Sunlight glinted off his hair as it poured in through his window. He'd combed his hair back and away from his forehead; the style made his face seem more striking than usual. From the way his jaw moved, he chewed on a stick of gum. He licked his lips, then winked at her.

Her throat closed.

Uh-oh. If she could see all these details about him, he could see her just as plainly. Truvy could do nothing but stare back. Of all the rotten luck. Of all the . . . *Edwina!*

Well, Truvy wasn't going to let geography ruin things for her. She had everything planned out to the letter. She would make a successful go of being a dancing instructor.

With a lift of her hand, she waved to Jake.

He didn't wave back. Instead, he tilted his head as if he'd just thought of something. And whatever it was, he wasn't too happy.

Truvy stepped away from the window as if it were electrically charged, then paused. If she closed the curtains, the implication would be obvious. But if she didn't, Jake could watch her every move. She was nervous enough.

She went forward and hastily closed the curtains. She pulled the chains on the globe lamps, lit them, then raised the fixtures back up to the ceiling.

That done, her heartbeat still raced like crazy, but she willed herself to remain composed. He was there. She was here. There was nothing to get all flustered about. Why, then, did her cheeks burn with embarrassment over the remembrance of the kiss they'd shared?

It was futile to think about it. One kiss—and one only. Nothing more. Ever again. She'd been curious. Now she knew. That was the end of things between them.

On that thought, she reexamined the room. Its circumference was larger than she recalled. She did remember she needed to wax the floor, so she'd brought a canister of polishing compound with her. For now, she'd sweep, but between her eleven o'clock and two o'clock class, she'd start waxing the perimeters and work her way into the center. Before she left at the end of the day, the studio would be in shining order.

Truvy went to the Victrola and selected music by Richard Zimmerman. In her first class, she was going to teach the two-step. Edwina had noted that particular move be taught today. No matter what, Truvy couldn't wear her butterflies on her sleeves. She had to have determination. And with that would come the confidence she needed.

As the notes blared through the trumpet and Truvy acclimated herself to the beat, she read Edwina's schedule book. The members of the Amateur Ladies

Avifauna Ornithologists made up the eleven o'clock class. The two o'clock class was simply entered as the B. Club.

Edwina must have meant the Bee Club. Beekeepers. Probably reserved gentlemen, men who would be more comfortable surrounded by a swarming hive than in a ballroom. They would be as self-conscious around her as she would be around them.

Slowly and deliberately inhaling, Truvy calmed herself with breathing calisthenics. She went through the moves of the two-step many times while putting her frame of mind into one proper for tutelage. And by the time her first pupils entered the classroom, she was ready to face them. Or so she thought.

The ladies were the same ones who argued about paper lanterns at Mrs. Plunkett's house. The very same ladies she explained the beer bottle to. Mrs. Plunkett came, too, chirping about how Truvy was going to be with her for a while longer and how happy she was to have such a fine young woman in her home. Truvy was grateful for the support, because her accolades brought acceptance by Mrs. Treber, Mrs. Calhoon, Mrs. Kennison, Mrs. Elward, and Mrs. Brooks.

The hour-long class went by agonizingly slowly. The brief display of footwork Edwina had shown her wasn't enough to fill the time, so they'd practiced the same left- and right-foot movements over and over. By doing such repetitions, Truvy felt as if she'd horribly botched things.

Oddly, nobody seemed to notice. Or perhaps they didn't care. Most of the time, the women were jovial, talking about other topics aside from dancing and the recording playing on the Victrola. Their conversations went from the birds they watched, to the Snowflake

Ball, to the new hat in Miss Taylor's shop window, to the high price of sugar, to the upcoming spring when they would plant their gardens.

Dancing lessons for the bird watchers were purely social.

After they left, seemingly content with what they'd paid for, Truvy went to work on the floor. She ate a hasty lunch, resting her feet in the high heels she wore, then peeked out the alley window as two o'clock neared. Much to her relief, the gymnasium was empty.

Sighing, she threw back the curtains once more. The studio was rather dark without natural light. If the men returned to the gym, she'd close them out once more. For now, she concentrated on the beekeepers. They would be learning beginning waltz in their hour, so she fanned the pages in *Dance Fundamentals* to the right section and practiced.

Three-quarter meter with an accent on the first beat. She wasn't sure what that meant. The diagram in the book had footprints taking a step to the left, a step to the right, a step to the side with the right, and then a close left-to-right by taking the weight off the left. She only knew how Edwina had shown her and how she'd done the dance with Moose. All these footprints made Truvy's head swim with confusion. She snapped the book closed and hid it in the recording stand. There was no reason to panic.

But within minutes, her interpretation of Edwina's schedule book was redefined and she panicked—just as soon as Jake Brewster entered the studio and his appearance all but knocked the breath right out of her. He had four men with him who wore a mixture of fawn- and charcoal-colored suits with peg-top trousers. The "gentlemen" appeared well dressed—most likely with gold card cases in their breast coat pockets—until she looked at what was on their feet.

Roman sandals.

"Miss Valentine." Jake was first to speak.

The arch of his brows and the relaxed expression on his face hinted at no surprise. She, on the other hand, grew instantly uncomfortable under a wave of stunned disbelief that made her feel faint. He didn't have to say it. She knew why they were here.

Jake smiled at her with lips he knew how to use to his advantage. That lazy lift to the right corner. She knew now how velvety soft this mouth was. And just how arousing.

"Mr. Brewster," Truvy said, greeting him in a stilted tone. Her voice was tight, her lips pressed together. "And . . . gentlemen."

"Good afternoon, Miss Valentine," the men answered in unison.

She initially didn't recognize the four of them from the day she'd gone to the gymnasium to give Jake *Crime and Punishment*. Now their identities became clear. And although no one said it, a picturesque phrase hung suspended in the room, as tangible as if somebody had spoken it aloud: *steer extract*.

Truvy sensed the men were thinking about their last encounter with her, as she was—she with a sense of the unsavory, they with ill ease.

Jake made introductions, reacquainting her with Lou the porter as well as the other three, whose names she'd heard in conversation. After the proper salutations, Mr. Burditt gave an explanation.

"We're the Barbell Club from the gymnasium, and

Bruiser is making us take dancing lessons so we can be light on our feet for the Mr. Physique contest."

When Mr. Burditt spoke, she couldn't help lowering her gaze to his feet, and those of the others with their thin leather-strap shoes. She was expected to instruct men who displayed their bare toes? Did Edwina know this?

Certain cultures had fetishes about exposed toes. And along with that came something else. That one thing came to Truvy's mind with the force of a gale— especially in light of the fact these very same men also favored animal skins. Biting on her inside lip, Truvy remembered the chapter in *The Science of Life* entitled "Primitive Peoples."

Among very primitive people, the satisfaction of the sexual appetite of man seems like that of the animal. Openness of the sexual act is not shunned. Men and women are not ashamed to go naked. Even today, we see savages in this condition with open sexuality being a way of life.

Suddenly, Truvy needed a glass of water.

No doubt about it—these men were definitely *not* beekeepers.

When Jake had seen Truvy in the dance studio window hours before, it had taken him a moment to figure out what she was doing in the building. Then reality had sunk in: Truvy was the new teacher Edwina hired. The discovery had unhinged him, but he'd kept his expression neutral, giving no clue to his feelings. He was too surprised that he'd fallen into one of Edwina's matchmaking schemes. At least in the past, she'd been pretty obvious.

"I've never heard of dancing in a bodybuilding contest." Truvy said, her forehead wrinkled by skepticism. "Then again, I've never been to one. But I'd assume partners would be limited. Unless you prefer to dance amongst yourselves."

"They don't need any dancing partners for Mr. Physique," Jake said, intervening, not caring for her implication. "They're here to learn some grace."

"Yeah," Walfred said. "We have no grace."

"Speak for yourself." Gig took offense.

"No, Gig, I'll speak for all of you—clam up." Jake ran a hand though his hair. He wanted to walk right out of the room, go over to Tom's house, and tell Edwina to quit with her romantic schemes. Instead, he mumbled, "They need to learn some grace by learning how to dance."

For a flicker of an instant, Jake thought he saw a look of self-doubt in her eyes. By outward appearances, she was collected now. She wore a dress the color of ashes. That incredible mass of rich brown hair was pinned up in a reserved twist. All that was missing was her ruler. Put together in shipshape order, a no-nonsense set to her lips, she faced them.

But what about her inner turmoil? Her being at odds with the situation came across in the nervous way she smoothed the cuffs of her sleeves. She did that sometimes. She did it now.

Sunlight reflected off the shining gold chatelaine watch pinned to her bodice. It drew his attention—rather, more than the bodice, the breasts themselves did. He'd spent a good hour looking up the word *chatelaine* in the dictionary. Not easy when he didn't know how to spell it.

"You're stating *they're* here for dancing lessons," Truvy went on, "but what are *you* doing here?"

Gritting his teeth, he looked at the Barbell Club, then at Truvy, and in a resigned tone, answered, "I lost a bet."

"A bet?"

"Low card lost," Milt explained, puffing out his barrel chest like a pigeon. Jake noticed that in the short amount of time he'd been in the room, Milt was gawking and smiling hugely at Truvy. "I got a six," Milt boasted. "Bruiser got a five. And here we all are after one fateful cut of the cards. By the time the hour's over, we'll be sashaying the polka on the floorboards like a bunch of real swells."

"The waltz," Truvy said, correcting him, drawing in a breath. Jake's eyes lowered to her mouth and thoughts of kissing her on Edwina's porch came to him with clarity and a longing desire to do so again. Truvy pretended not to notice that he was staring, but the steadiness of her tone was tested. And it failed. "Y-you'll be learning how to waltz. Mrs. Wolcott designated that particular dance in her schedule book." Her gaze dropped, then snapped upward. "But . . . might I inquire as to the nature of your shoes? They're not . . . regulation."

"I made them wear the sandals," Jake informed her, resting his weight on one leg. He acted casual about Truvy's being in the room, but everything inside him was unsettled. "These men are going to be subjected to a series of compulsory poses designed to display every set of their muscles. When they're up on that stage, they'll be wearing Roman sandals, not shoes. They can't get the right feel for flexibility and coordination by dancing in a pair of Congress oxfords."

"Oh . . . then I suppose they're acceptable," Truvy remarked. This time, her gaze lowered to his feet. "But you're exempt."

"Right."

"He's not competing," August explained. "We are."

"That's right. He's here because he lost a bet. And one that I daresay must have been a gentleman's." Her eyes meeting Jake's, Truvy folded her arms across her breasts. "That's a very noble reason."

"I can be noble," Jake put in.

"I'm sure you have your moments, Mr. Brewster." Straightening her shoulders, she said, "Well, then, let's get started." With reluctant footsteps, she went to the Victrola and selected a recording. After cranking the handle several times, she lowered the heavy needle onto the spinning black disc. A crackling noise came out of the horn. She turned toward them.

"This is the waltz. The music, that is." Her cheeks turned bright pink, and for several seconds, she didn't meet anyone's expectant gaze. Jake didn't take his eyes off her. She blushed once more, high on her cheekbones. Then she raised a hand to her throat as soon as the music came on.

"Now then." She cleared her throat. "Since there aren't female partners for you, you shall have to practice with one another. Pair up and I'll instruct you on what you need to do."

August and Walfred made a slap-happy to-do about it, sidling up to each other, bowing, and clicking their heels together. "May I?" Walfred asked.

"Most certainly," August replied.

Lou came toward Jake, but he backed away. "Solo, Lou. I don't dance with men."

"But we're uneven and Milton has Miss Valentine." So he had.

Milton Burditt had a large "bay window," but his thick-waisted body was considered gentlemanly. His girth meant robust good health as well as sturdy prosperity. Maybe Truvy went for that sort. She wasn't protesting over his asking her to be his partner.

A knife of jealousy ripped through him. Jake didn't like the feeling.

"Now then," Truvy said once more, nervously taking Milton's hands in hers and raising her arms. She paused, looked at Jake and Lou, then said, "Mr. Brewster, you aren't paying your partner any attention. Take him into your arms."

"Oh, sweetheart!" Milton teased.

Milton's grin made Jake's fists tighten into hard knots. He wanted to give him one in the jaw.

Calling the whole dancing lesson thing off was on the tip of his tongue. But he couldn't. If he did, he'd never hear the end of it from the boys. He'd be called a welsher. Plus, Bruiser's Gymnasium was sponsoring these contestants and their placement in the contest would be a reflection on his business know-how, on his influence on Lou, Milt, Gig, August, and Walfred. Men were coming in from as far away as Bozeman and Helena. The Barbell Club had to be prepared to take them on the best they could.

Even if their only fighting chance was August Gray.

If Jake didn't dance, August and the rest of them would walk out.

Lou had a broad smile on his face, one Jake wanted to shove down his throat. "All right, Lou, I'll dance with you. But I'm the man."

"Never said you weren't, Bruiser."

Once in position with Lou's clammy hand clasped in his, Jake fought the lurch in his stomach. Holy shit and for God's sake, this was worse than the time he went fourteen rounds with The Rump Steak Slasher.

A broken arm, cut lip, and bashed ear felt better than the sudden clamp of Lou Bernard's hand on his waist.

"Get your damn hand off of there, Lou," Jake growled, towering over Lou by a good twelve inches. "I said I was the man."

"Sorry, Bruiser." Lou removed his hand and lightly placed it on Jake's shoulder.

"Positions, everyone," Truvy instructed. "We're ready to begin."

She tapped the beat of the music with her foot. The tip of a petite black shoe peeked from the hem of her skirt. "A waltz is danced in a three-quarter meter with the accent on the first beat. Waltzing is a smooth and graceful dance stepped in an even rhythm. When you hear the notes descend, we'll push off with our left foot in this pattern: Step forward on the left, step to the side with the right, close left to right, take weight off the left."

The boys' faces took on bewildered expressions. Nobody understood the mathematics of where their feet should be and when. But before anyone could ask questions, Truvy pushed off in a twirling motion and took Milt with her. She instantly stepped on his toe. "I beg your pardon!" she exclaimed.

"It's all right, Miss Valentine." Milt's smile faltered as he jogged about the room without a clue as to what he was doing. "Perfectly all right."

The thuds of Truvy's shoes on the floorboards echoed in the studio as she nearly tripped over the fullness of her petticoats. Pink petticoats.

Jake propelled Lou in the right direction, yanking him along by the fabric of his coat.

The boys made a good show of footwork.

Barely aware he lugged Lou across the dance floor,

Jake kept his eyes on Truvy. She was no serpentine dancer. She had them waltzing in two-time, not three-quarter. She kept apologizing for skewering Milt's instep with the high heel of her shoe.

"Now," she said breathlessly, trying to keep up with Milt's tug and pull around the room's circumference. "As soon as you master these steps," she panted, out of breath from fighting Milton's tight hold, "you'll learn the box waltz . . . the running waltz . . ." Milt spun her like she was a kid's toy top going out of control. His movements were choppy and clumsy, but he didn't notice his own ineptness. He kept staring at Truvy, his face inching closer to hers. ". . . canter waltz . . . and mazurka."

The recording came to an end and Truvy practically threw herself out of Milt's arms. "Well, then. That was . . . fine—for a first try."

Her forehead was damp; her cheeks were flushed. She lifted a hand to her hair and patted the tendrils that had come free.

Lou still held on to Jake, and Jake warned in an ominously low voice, "Cut me loose, Lou, or I'll crack your ribs."

"Oh, yeah. Sure, Bruiser. Sorry."

Lou let go; his gaze, like that of the other men in the room, landed on the rise and fall of Truvy's breasts as she caught her breath. They looked, then looked away. Glimpsed again, then stared at the ceiling or their toes.

The Barbell Club's unsuppressed libidos put a tightness in Jake's chest. He affected a display of vague indifference, but his leg muscles continued to tense until they burned.

"Now then, we'll do this once more." Truvy

restarted the recording. "I saw some technical difficulties that last time around."

Was she looking at herself? Jake wondered. Did Edwina know Truvy couldn't waltz any better than Barkly?

Milton eagerly held out his arms, a satisfied smile on his mouth. "May I?"

"No, you may not," Jake said, interrupting. "Shove over, Milt, and take a turn with Lou."

"But I don't want—"

Jake gave him a feral glare and said nothing further. He didn't have to. Milt took the cue and paired up with Lou.

The music started. Truvy didn't move. She stood there. He could sense exactly what she was thinking.

How do I dare hold his hand in front of these men?

Did she think about their kiss as much as he did? The sight of her, even in the modestly cut dress, did things to him, evoked feelings he had felt only once in his life before—but those feelings had turned out to be erroneous. That was the exact word for how he characterized marriage to his former wife.

erroneous: characterized by error; incorrect; mistaken; wrong.

As the music played on, Jake coaxed Truvy into taking his lead; he held her fingers in his and lifted them to his shoulder. She reluctantly let him. The lightness of her touch sent a wave of heat up his neck where her slender fingertips accidentally grazed his skin. The shirt he wore had no collar and was cambric. The thin, worn fabric was hardly a barrier against the sensation of her hand resting on his delts as he guided her through the motions of the waltz. Three steps. The right-foot pattern. One, two, three. One, two, three.

His quads melded into the thin volume of her skirts. Awareness of the faint rustle of her petticoat exploded in his mind. Pink. She'd said pink satin. He couldn't release the thought.

He stared at her, watched the pink of embarrassment burn on her cheeks. She held her breath. She moved with the flexibility of a broom handle.

As Jake whirled her in tempo to the music, he wondered what she was feeling. What she was thinking. Did she battle the urge to study him? Did she find him more than "interesting"?

As he leaned toward her, her gaze collided with his and she stepped on his toe. The impact didn't affect him. He wore his Creedmoors; the leather on them was thick enough to ward off any pain Truvy's clumsy feet could inflict.

Her eyelids quivered upward. "Sorry."

"You're trying to lead. Let me."

She looked away rather than face him.

He'd mistaken her confidence earlier. She wasn't confident—not in the least. It was evident in the way she refused to meet his gaze. The tension in her body said she feared him—or maybe it was more like she feared men like him, big and powerful. He didn't know who Moose Thompson was, but he knew *he* was nothing like the man. Jake wasn't a die-hard scholar, but he was no slouch either. He didn't do things like duck and punch the air for sport with other men while they were goofing off in the gymnasium. He wasn't a clown, a comic, a character. He could be damned serious. He was no rough and coarse ass.

He kept trying to think of anything political he knew, but all he could come up with was a quote from Teddy: *Speak softly and carry a big stick.*

The latter part of the quote applied to him—he felt his body responding to Truvy in a way that if he didn't get it under control, he *would* look like an ass. Because they were dancing so close, hip to hip, chest to breast, his groin tightened.

From behind, Lou bumped into Truvy, knocking her against Jake. The high, round breasts Jake was trying hard to put out of his mind bounced into his chest. Truvy's nearness, his head down and hers up, allowed him to feel the silky smoothness of her forehead. Instinctively, his arms tightened around her. Every blood vessel inside him pulsed wildly. He didn't want her to jump back, but he could feel she was ready to by the way her hand moved on his shoulder, by the way she gasped and leaned away from him.

He held her close, and blurted, "I was reading about Teddy's diplomatic affairs the other day. He thinks effective government control can be exercised without the formality of colonial rule."

"Oh?" she breathlessly replied, easing back. Regretfully, he let her. He had to remind himself there were four other men in the room and he couldn't exactly be manhandling the teacher. "What were you reading?"

"The newspaper."

"Twice in one week?"

Jake frowned. "Yes. So what do you think?"

"Well, I think it's admirable you're broadening your reading tastes."

"Not that." Maybe he shouldn't lead her into a political discussion. He could lose ground here. What was he really thinking anyway? He wanted her to be attracted to him, nothing beyond that. But dammit, he wanted to impress the hell of out her while he had the opportunity, so he chanced it and pursued the matter—because he had an ace up his sleeve. He knew something she didn't. "What do you think about Teddy's policy?"

A cynical curve lit on her mouth. "Are you setting me up for anything, Mr. Brewster?"

"Why would I do that?"

"Because I'm not quite sure you weren't involved with this—your taking dance instruction while I'm the teacher. You and Edwina could have cooked this whole thing up together. All she does is tell me how wonderful you are."

Jake's heartbeat snagged. "She does?"

"Yes, but her accolades aren't working on me."

"That's too bad. And for the record, I didn't have anything to do with your giving lessons."

"I suppose I believe you." She stepped on his toe again. "Pardon me." Her apology came fast, and right on its heels, she said, "As for President Roosevelt, he advocates a larger and more efficient army and navy. It's his way of making a better Department of War after what happened with the Spanish-American War."

"I knew that." Here was his opening, and he took it like a bull running through a corral. "He also wanted the army to have better dental hygiene."

"What?" She danced over his foot again. "Pardon."

"See, the thing of it is, you can't have our men going over to foreign countries with their teeth falling out."

Puzzlement lifted her brows a fraction. "That's not one of President Roosevelt's diplomatic affairs."

"You doubt me? Look it up. The U.S. Congress established the U.S. Army Dental Corps to make sure the military had dental hygiene."

The previous month, *Obtaining Strength* magazine

had done an article on teeth. The piece was actually on arnica, a homeopathic herb that helped tooth pain, so he took the idea and ran with it—because Jake put the pieces in place and figured out that you had to have teeth in the military.

"I really don't think—"

Jake cut her short. "You don't have to think with this one, sweetheart, because I have the answer. How can you arm yourself to the teeth if you don't have any?"

"What? That makes no sense at all." She stepped on his foot again, but it was she who winced this time.

Jake lowered his voice, "Why do you keep wearing shoes that hurt your feet? You're going to physically harm yourself. You know, in China, women bind their feet and they become cripples, cutting their lives short." He hadn't read that bit of trivia. He'd heard it in an opium den. It didn't take a reading genius to have knowledge.

"As a woman, my life expectancy is already three years up on yours, so if I shave a couple of years off for vanity's sake, I'll still die after you."

The recording ended and Truvy got in the last word. Or so he let her think. Jake had some of his own. "You don't know how to dance, do you, Tru?"

Shaken, she didn't answer.

Milton came over and patted Jake on the back. "Nice show, Bruiser. I guess me and the boys owe you an apology. You can dance. Really well."

"It helps," Jake said, looking directly into Truvy's eyes, "when the lady I'm dancing with knows what she's doing."

"That she does! A great dancer, Miss Valentine," Milton said, complimenting her.

"Thank you," she mumbled.

"You know, this dancing sure can get a guy out of breath," Walfred said as he joined them.

"I know I am," Lou huffed, making a show of gasping for air. "I feel like I've lifted a bunch of weights."

"I'm sure Bruiser doesn't feel winded," Milton added, then turned his attention on Truvy. "I'll bet you didn't know Bruiser can blow up a hot water bottle with the air from his lungs. To do that, it takes six hundred pounds of pressure."

Jake gritted his teeth. He didn't know how to duck from Milton's verbal punch without coming back with a jab of his own. And at the moment, his mind had gone blank.

Even though he'd told that story to the boys over a game of cards and after a lot of downed beer, it wasn't something he used on women. The feat made him look like a sap, a dunderheaded jock with nothing better to do than blow up a hot water bottle. True, he could do it. Blowing up the rubber apparatus was something he'd done at the World's Columbian Exposition. He and Sandow were the only two men who could perform such a stunt.

"I don't think she's interested in that," Jake said, then looked at his motley group of contenders.

"Oh, but I am," Truvy declared, lifting the needle from the record. "My, my! A hot water bottle? Blown up! With agility like that, it's no wonder you were Mr. America."

"The Strongest Man on Earth," Jake said, correcting her through clenched teeth.

"I didn't know you were Mr. America, Bruiser," Walfred commented.

"I wasn't. There is no Mr. America."

"But if there was, I'm quite certain Mr. Brewster would be the winner!" Truvy's enthusiasm was so cardboard, her words practically bent over Jake's head. They annoyed him, more than he cared to admit. But she started things, and he was going to run with them.

"I can tell you this," Jake said, "if there was a Miss America contest, our Miss Valentine here should enter it, because she'd win. She moves athletically on the dance floor. And she's not even wearing sandals."

That got her. Her face went pale.

He didn't go far enough to thoroughly embarrass her. He wouldn't let her secret out of the bag about being a sports instructor. He had his limits. And more than a little class.

"Wouldn't that be something," Milton mused aloud. "A Miss America competition where available young ladies perform acrobatic feats on a stage."

Lou put in, "Say, now that would be something."

"Forget the idea, fellows. There's never going to be any Miss America competition," August predicted, "because what woman would enter it?"

"Prize money would be an incentive." Lou adjusted the knot in his tie.

Jake took charge of the conversation before it got out of hand. "Maybe. Right now, you boys need to really work on this waltz." Truvy stood at the Victrola with a look on her face that said she wanted to whack him. He pretended not to notice. "Miss Valentine, please put the music on again."

"I'd be delighted." Her sincerity was as phony as a thief's honor. "New partners, please. Mr. Brewster, since you danced so well with Mr. Bernard, I'd like for you to partner up with him once more."

Lou jumped to attention. "I'm the woman. Don't worry, Bruiser, I've got it straight now."

The music started and Jake's eyes iced over as Lou headed toward him.

There was no way out of dancing with the porter. And Truvy knew it.

She'd had the last word after all.

December 29, 1901

Dear Aunt Gertrude and Aunt Beatrice:

I'm writing to inform you that I'll be staying on in Harmony for a while longer, until that matter (the one I told you about in my last letter, which you have not yet received) can be cleared up at St. Francis. Nothing to worry over. Although I'm away from Boise, I have something to be excited about.

I'm a dancing instructor.

Edwina needed a teacher, so I'm taking over her classes—temporarily. My first day was invigorating. I found my first class to be utterly charming. My second . . . well, they were apt pupils who need encouragement. Jake Brewster, the owner of the gymnasium, has students (and himself) enrolled so that they can be more poised on their feet for a Mr. Physique competition.

Although I find this training method to be commendable, I also find Mr. ~~Bruiser~~ *Brewster to be somewhat uncouth. He's the tallest man I have ever encountered. And the most muscular, which he feels is an asset. I do not. His manners can be passable when he tries, but he forgets himself at times and acts his shoe size, which I wouldn't put past a ten. But I shall do my very best with all my classes, the one he's in included. Next week I'll meet more students. I'm to teach Monday, Wednesday, and Friday.*

I miss you both dearly. Please write. I await news from you. How was your Christmas?

Mr. Brewster was at Tom and Edwina's house Christmas Eve and I must say his presence was . . . reassuring. I was having a harrowing day and he told me a joke about a woman who was tall—as if she wore stilts. I've never seen a woman on stilts, but suffice to say that doing so would make my own height seem tolerable.

Until I hear from you, stay well and happy. I read in the local newspaper that there is to be a rally in Washington this summer for the passage of a suffrage bill. We should all go.

*Love,
Truvy*

As Truvy addressed an envelope, a knock sounded on her bedroom door and she bid the visitor enter.

Mrs. Plunkett burst into the room holding onto a dress of old rose nun's veiling, and trimmed and stitched with taffeta piping. "Look, oh my dear, just look! I had the seamstress put a rush on this breathtaking creation. And you didn't even realize I took one of your dresses and had her measure it for your size!"

Truvy could only stare, wordlessly. Her mind floundered for something to say. Horror paralyzed her as she gazed at all that pink.

The dress's partially tucked blouse waist had shaped pieces forming tabs over the tucked sleeves. The front opened over a vest of cream white Oriental lace. Yoke pieces formed a border around the skirt hem—a skirt that didn't come to Truvy's ankles.

It was a costume for a young girl, of eighteen at the most, not a garment for a woman seven years older.

"Stand up, my dear. Let's hold it up to see how it will look on you."

A lump formed in Truvy's throat. Woodenly, she rose to her feet.

"Ah! Let me look at you. Hold it up. There now."

Truvy's arms numbly lifted so she could touch the shoulder seams of the dress and keep it in place as Mrs. Plunkett backed away, hands clasped together in front of her bosom. "I knew it! You're as lovely as my Hildegarde. You'll be pretty as can be next Monday for your dancing lessons. *Madame Teacher!*"

It took every ounce of decorum and the most polite smile Truvy could muster not to gasp in despair.

Chapter

❧ 11 ❧

"For some reason, Miss Valentine wasn't impressed with that hot water bottle story, Bruiser," Milton commented while testing the stretch in a newly purchased jockstrap. The balbriggan cotton cup dangled in the air as Milt expanded the length of elastic, then released it with a snap. "You know *I* was when you told it to us. But I detected she was a tad insincere when she called you a former Mr. America. Anybody ought to know there is no such thing, and I believe she knew it, too."

"Yeah, I noticed that myself," Lou added, unscrewing the lid to a jar of Hammerhead's Body Definition Powder. "I also noticed you got tense about it, Bruiser."

August spun an Indian club with a flick of his wrist. He sat on the floor of the gym, legs out in front of him, a rubber tension band on one ankle as he worked out his calf. "Bruiser never gets tense about anything. He couldn't care less if she doesn't like him. And it's plain to see she doesn't."

"I have to agree on both counts," Gig said, testing

an oiling tonic. He rubbed in a wide circle on his forearm.

Walfred nailed the coffin of verbal remarks closed with, "I hate to go with the crowd, Bruiser, but Miss Valentine definitely finds you resistible."

"Are you boys done?" Jake asked, sitting back on the leather preacher's bench, giving the men an even glare. They'd been pulling his leg about Truvy all morning, hashing over the way she'd told him to dance with Lou again.

"No." Milton held up his jockstrap. "Are you sure these come only in one size fits all?"

Jake's arms were folded across his chest while he puffed on a fat cigar. He normally wouldn't give Milt a shot, but he'd started the conversation and its subsequent commentaries, so Jake felt Milton was fair game. "Sorry, Milt, they don't make a little-man size."

That set the four men off debating who had the biggest apparatus. The issue of jockstraps wouldn't have come up if the Barbell Club hadn't just returned from an early Monday shopping venture to Wolcott's Sporting Goods. It hadn't been Jake's idea to buy jockstraps. That had been Gig's. He'd said, and he'd been right, that they were cheaper by the dozen and that because the contestants were on budgets, it made sense to buy a box instead of one at a time. Along with the jockstraps, the boys had to stock up on bodybuilding accoutrements.

Accoutrements. Jake had recently come across that particular word in the dictionary, and even though he wasn't one hundred percent sure such a mouthful applied for bodybuilding accessories, he used it anyway because he liked the sound of its consonants and vowels together.

The Barbell Club hadn't been checking out their items for five minutes when Milton had started about Truvy, a subject that rubbed Jake the wrong way. Not that he didn't like talking about her. But he kept the majority of his opinions about her to himself.

He'd never had this problem before. He always talked about women he thought were pretty and shapely. But he wasn't a man who was intimate one night and told about it the next day. Even so, he never minded conversations about what men liked in women. And about what women liked in men.

The debate reached a fever pitch.

Lou brought his fingers to his mouth and whistled, a method he used on occasion to announce the arrival of the four o'clock train. "Hold up and listen for a minute," he called. "Who in Hades cares what kind of jockstraps we wear? Nobody's going to see them. And besides, the cotton expands or constricts to accommodate whatever you've got."

Grumbles met his observation and Lou held up his hand to quiet them. "What's going here is that we're getting too carried away with how the dance instructor feels about Jake. Bruiser's one hell of a guy—we all know it. The thing is," he continued, turning toward Jake, "we're all forgetting something. And that is, not even you can win this woman's attention. It's not because you're lacking, Bruiser. In this case, Miss Valentine is just very particular."

"Particular against tall, well-built musclemen who know how to dance the waltz," Milton observed, tossing his jockstrap onto the floor. The white lump landed on August's foot; August kicked it off with irritation. "So this opens up the field for us. The trouble is"—Milt's face fell—"me and Gig and Lou are already married. So that leaves Walfred and August free and clear. Neither of them are professional weightlifters. And they can't dance the waltz worth beans."

Jake gazed at both men, his mouth closed tightly. He said nothing.

Walfred spoke up, "I don't want her—not that she's not an attractive woman. But I've got my sights on Miss Gimble."

"And I've got my mind on this competition," August put in. "Afterward, I could ask Miss Valentine to step out."

"You could take her to the restaurant," Milt advised him. "Women like that sort of thing—a meal prepared for them instead of their preparing it. My wife tells me every Saturday evening it's nice to go to Nannie's Home-Style Restaurant for supper so she doesn't have to start the stove."

Walfred lifted his head. "I've never seen you in the restaurant on a Saturday night, Milt."

"I never said I take her there. I said she tells me it would be nice to go. Do you think I'm made of money? I can't be spending my hard-earned cash on an order of chicken and light-as-a-cloud biscuits when my Mary fixes the best in Harmony."

"I wonder if Miss Valentine can bake a light biscuit?" August mused.

"What do you think, Bruiser?"

He merely shrugged, even though he knew the answer. *Hell no, not if her biscuits are as tasty as her coffee.*

Jake let them carry the topic of Miss Valentine, puffing on the end of his cigar and biting back words he might regret. If he played into their hands, he'd find himself talking about her cooking skills—among the other things he was privy to. Then before he knew it, he'd declare intentions to court her when he really had none at all.

Blowing a series of smoke rings toward the ceiling, he thought, *Not that taking Truvy Valentine out for an afternoon would be a hardship.* He'd enjoy watching her ice skate again. Or escorting her to the Ladies Aid Snowflake Ball. Well, on second thought, maybe not. Only two evenings away, the ball was an event for couples in serious courtship or already married. He would, however, like listening to her talk over a dinner at the restaurant.

He'd never once taken a woman there.

Hell, his undivided attention had never been on any woman in town.

"The way I see it"—Milt bent and picked up his athletic supporter—"is that Miss Valentine has made her feelings clear about Bruiser. I hate to admit it, but I wish I could be in his place."

A few brows lifted, then heads nodded as the rest of them grasped what Milton was getting at even before he provided clarification. "And you know why? Because I'd be up for the challenge of trying to win her over if I were available."

"You're right." Gig stuck the cork back in the bottle of oil.

Walfred shrugged. "If we were you, Bruiser, we'd be wanting to change her mind."

"Yeah," Lou said, continuing the thought, "I'd be wanting to get her to go to the restaurant for a supper."

From Walfred: "Of course, this is how *we* would feel, but it's not going to happen. Not for us or for Bruiser."

"Nope." August's tone held certainty. "Not going to happen."

Milt snorted. "Let's face it, Miss Valentine wouldn't go to the restaurant with Bruiser any more than she'd go with any one of us."

"Right." Lou nodded.

Milt began, "Why, she wouldn't go—"

"Bet me." Jake had spoken the words and couldn't take them back. Deep in his mind, he cursed himself for falling to a gambling lure: the hope of gaining an advantage. But what he proposed wouldn't be for monetary gain. The bet was harmless. Just another gentleman's agreement between friends. Nobody had to win or lose. There would be no cash exchanged.

"Bet you what, Bruiser?" Milton asked.

"Let's not bet," Jake said, rephrasing. "Let's say I could take Miss Valentine out for supper tonight at the restaurant if I wanted to. And I want to."

"You couldn't."

"We'll wager on it that I can." Jake rolled the ash off his cigar into the mouth of an empty beer bottle. "Nothing degrading to Miss Valentine, because what we're talking about stays in the gymnasium. And anyone who takes it outside will take on me—outside. Am I clear?"

Affirming nods met his question.

"As for the ante, how about we say . . ."—Jake gazed at the Heinrich, a bottle he'd emptied last night and was using today as an ash receptacle—". . . we'll say six bottles of beer each. I win, you boys bring over some brews. I lose, I have the icebox stocked with six each of your favorites."

All eyes lit up.

The bet was made.

As Jake instructed the boys on how to use the items they'd just bought from Tom, his stomach twisted into knots. Second thoughts pounded at his temples. He shouldn't have made such a stupid declaration. It was one thing to think about doing things with Truvy. It was another to actually fulfill them.

And quite another to make a wager on the outcome.

What in the hell had he been thinking?

The day was sunny enough so that Truvy could leave the dance studio door open without being too cold. The temperatures were still freezing first thing in the morning, so she kept the corner heater stoked and burning fuel.

With *Dance Fundamentals* in her grasp, she looked at the foot diagram while she practiced the steps for the cakewalk. My goodness, but there were a lot of symbols to memorize. X's and O's signified the moves, and the lines and boxes signified a variety of body parts and where they should be at any given beat in the music—shoulders, elbows, wrists, hands, hips, knees, ankles, feet.

Truvy was beginning to grasp the complicated maneuvers, but she had a hard time concentrating— namely, every time she glanced at her reflection in the row of mirrors and saw the old rose nun's veiling dress. The too-short old rose nun's veiling dress Mrs. Plunkett had bought for her.

The very dress she now wore.

Before she'd left for the studio, Truvy had stood in her room staring at the girl's dress laid out with tender care over the back of her secretary chair. Her shoulders slumped with defeat, and yet she couldn't bring herself to put the dress on. The whole pretense of being a person she wasn't was ridiculous. Truvy wasn't Hildegarde. She didn't *want* to be Hildegarde. And she *never* would be Hildegarde. On that thought, Truvy had gone downstairs intending to put her foot down, intending on making Mrs. Plunkett realize she wasn't her daughter.

Truvy wore her own skirt and blouse. As she neared the vestibule, her steps became slower and slower the more clearly she saw the crestfallen expression on Mrs. Plunkett's round face. It was then that Truvy knew she couldn't speak what was really on her mind. Instead, she offered an excuse, saying she thought the pretty pink dress was just too nice to wear for dancing instruction.

Five minutes later, Truvy came down the stairs again, this time wearing the pink concoction and hating every blessed minute of it. But what else could she do? Mrs. Plunkett had stood there, eyes tearing, lips quivering, as if Truvy had put a knife in her heart.

So now Truvy was stuck in the girlish dress. In the studio. With a class coming for instruction in one hour. Thank goodness they weren't the Barbell Club. Today's students were this year's graduating class from the Harmony Normal School, and they were here to learn how to march to John Philip Sousa's "Stars and Stripes Forever." Thankfully, that was an easy task for Truvy, as she'd taught her girls in basketball to dribble to that very tune.

The previous Friday, Truvy had been ready to concede defeat to Edwina. They'd shared a long conversation after dinner and Truvy had voiced her displeasure over having been duped by the "B. Club." Edwina claimed an honest error, a simple misunderstanding over an abbreviation.

Although Edwina had soothed Truvy's apprehensions and convinced her to carry on, she felt helpless about the whole idea of Jake Brewster in her class—and yet sentimentally giddy when he held her in his arms and danced with her. But that had quickly turned to a deflated feeling when he'd told her that he knew she didn't know what she was doing.

At least it was only twice a week that she had to teach the Barbell Club. Just thinking of having to go another round with Jake and his cronies made her palms sweat. He might have saved her from embarrassment over further botching the waltz, but he'd teased her afterward with that athletic comment.

Truvy whirled around once more, book outstretched in her hand as she both read and moved her feet at the same time. She'd rolled the waistband of her petticoat so the bottom wouldn't show beneath the high hem of the pink dress.

During a quick right pivot, then a sharp step left, *Dance Fundamentals* flew from her grasp and sailed through the open rear door of the studio. She sucked in her breath, went to the door, and saw that the alleyway was empty. No book to be seen. It was then that she noticed that the rear door to the gymnasium was open—just like that of the studio. Within seconds, Jake filled its frame, her copy of *Dance Fundamentals* in his hand.

She gazed at him with deliberate censure. He was a virile man—a fact he obviously knew—and it bothered her that he could be so at ease about his masculinity. He needed to use a razor and put some sleeves on his faded shirt, but she doubted he would take her advice if she were to offer it. In spite of the weather, he wore loose-legged boxing trunks that showed every inch of his powerful thighs and calves. She'd never thought a man's calves could be attractive, but his were. With only a light amount of dark hair on them, his skin had a caramel color to it that hers never took on—even in the summer if she went without her hat. He was naturally dark. Naturally good-looking.

"If you were trying to get my attention, it worked," he said with a pull to the corner of his mouth.

Naturally confident, too.

"I was trying no such thing. That book slipped out of my hand."

"And you criticize my reading habits." A thick lock of hair fell over his forehead as he leaned out the doorway. "You read as ineptly as you dance."

Truvy hid her ire. She refused to let him know he disturbed her. In a gamut of ways. "May I have my book back?"

His eyes narrowed. "What's that you've got on?"

She instantly remembered what she was wearing. Mortified, she looked down at the exposed line of her risqué petticoat. The pretty embroidered hem with its white butterflies and ruby-red roses had slipped below that of the dress. A wave of humiliation warmed her. When she'd bought the suggestive underwear, she'd never intended anyone to see it. She viewed herself as she was sure Jake would: a twenty-five-year-old woman, grossly tall, apparently too clumsy to hold a book, and with a demimondaine petticoat contradicting a dress sewn for a much younger woman.

She wanted to die.

She wanted to cry.

"A dress," she woodenly replied.

"What kind?"

"Pink, obviously."

"Like the color of your petticoat and underwear."

"Yes," she whispered. "I believe we have covered that topic."

"Well, it's uncovered now, so I thought I'd bring it up again."

"That's a good idea." On that, she brought up the hem of her petticoat by rerolling the waistband, not easy to do through the piping and stitching that made her bodice rather thick at the waist. She felt Jake's eyes on her every move, disconcerting her and making her feel even more inelegant than he could ever think. She felt every tight stay of her corset and she wished she could be free of it, free of Jake's watchful gaze, free of the dress . . . of having to be polite and gracious to Mrs. Plunkett. It was a terrible thought, but she couldn't help herself.

Once she lined up her underwear into the proper position, she extended her hand. "My book, please." Dignity laced her words and her chin lifted high with pride. She wouldn't let him know how embarrassed she was. She just wouldn't.

He didn't pass over *Dance Fundamentals*. Instead, he questioned her. "You aren't going to wear that for a class, are you?"

In a last-ditch effort to save what remained of her tattered dignity, she decided to fib. "I most certainly am. My next student is a . . . very eccentric man and I'll be teaching him the . . . dance of the geisha. Yes, that's what he wants—to learn the steps of the Cherry Blossom Dance, and only I know how to teach it. In modern Japan, geisha wear dresses just like this one, so there's nothing out of the ordinary about me. And since the Cherry Blossom Dance is very secretive, I don't need that book you're holding because only geisha teach other geisha and I had instruction when I was in . . . college. So . . . so that's all I have to say. Good-bye."

Not waiting for him to comment, she turned and went back inside. To make sure Jake couldn't follow, she twisted the lock on the door. She gulped in three long breaths. *Calm yourself.* More breaths. She felt her limbs grow relaxed, more at ease. She was in control once more.

Satisfied, she proceeded with her tasks as if nothing had happened.

Marching to Sousa didn't require reading from *Dance Fundamentals,* and when her next class was over, she'd sic Tom Wolcott on Jake and get that book back. In the meantime, she'd have to close the curtains so he wouldn't see that her mystery man was really a group of youths instead.

She raised a hand to the curtains and swept them shut—just as the lock on the door clicked and the panel opened. Jake appeared in the alleyway door, a key in one hand and the book in the other.

He explained, "Edwina gave me a key to the place so I could keep an eye on it when she wasn't here."

Exasperated, Truvy could only stare as he pocketed the skeleton key in the breast pocket of his shabby shirt.

"But *I'm* here, so you don't have anything to check on," she informed him.

"Maybe I'm checking on you." His voice was disarmingly low and filled with an implication that made her heartbeat speed.

She couldn't speak.

"I'll give the book back to you," Jake went on, "because it says *Edwina Huntington* in the front. It's hers."

"Of course it is."

"What do you need a book for anyway?" He came farther into the room, and Truvy had to try to quell the leap to her pulse. She refused to move the closer he got to her. "I thought you were a great dancer."

"I am. You said so yourself."

Mere inches separated them now; she had to remind herself to breathe. The color of his eyes reminded Truvy of the hue of frost-touched leaves, a green-and-silver combination. "What's this geisha dance and how come you know it?"

She liked that she'd made him curious. A quiver of a smile touched her mouth. His wonderment gave her confidence. She played up the situation oh-so-nonchalantly and walked to the Victrola.

Keeping her tone breezy, she said, "I told you, it's a dance I learned in college." Little had she known at the time that her big failure with Miss Pond would one day help her. "Its elements are extremely guarded among geisha."

"Geisha are women of ill repute, you know."

His knowledge threw her off kilter. How did he know that? "Not the geisha in this dance. They're tea servers and fan—fanners."

Jake came to stand beside her, and she stiffened. The lingering scent of shaving lotion on his skin, along with the saltiness of sweat, came to her nose. She looked up, only briefly, and noticed his hair was a little damp; the collar of his shirt was rimmed by moisture. He must have been pummeling that punching bag of his when *Dance Fundamentals* shot through his open doorway. He had a stubborn, arrogant face. Why was it he could look so rough and unruly and be so . . . so handsome?

Clearly, she couldn't think straight when he stood this close.

Truvy picked up her schedule book and pen, pretending she had to write some notes. She pulled the cap off the fountain pen and began to scribble on a clean page, not letting Jake see over her shoulder.

"Who do you have written in that book?" Jake's face loomed over her as he tried to sneak a look. She held the open binding close to her breasts. "Tell me the name of the man who wants to know this geisha dance. Is it Milton Burditt? Because if it is, you should know he's married."

Truvy had to cut off a laugh. *Milton Burditt?!*

"Oh, it's not him," she remarked slowly, actually enjoying that she was putting Jake in a place few—if any—women had ever done. "The gentleman doesn't live in town. He's a city man and travels a lot."

Jake practically pressed his body against hers. She gripped the schedule book tighter. "Let me see that."

"Really, Mr. Brewster, you most certainly cannot." For good measure, she made another false notation. "This is private."

"I don't believe you have a man coming."

"I do."

"Then I'll wait and meet him."

"You will not!"

"Then let me see that book."

Suddenly, they both had their hands on the book and were engaged in a tug of war—and then an explosion of blue ink shot from the tip of the fountain pen. Truvy instantly quit struggling, a horrified scream welling up in her throat. It didn't leave her mouth; she was too stunned to shriek.

She let Jake have the scheduling book. Apprehensively, she cast her gaze down, and she saw what she feared most—a large blotch of blue ink. Right on the center front of the dress. The bodice carried an irregular blob, too. The gathers of the skirt were splattered. And already, the midnight blue seeped into the combined seams of bodice and skirt.

The dress was ruined, utterly ruined.

"Oh . . . no . . ." was all she could manage in a choked voice. Thoughts of Mrs. Plunkett flashed in her head. The woman was going to be beyond distraught; she'd be offended to the highest order. And after that morning's events, Mrs. Plunkett would be hard pressed to believe Truvy had had a mishap with her pen.

"I'm sorry. Really sorry." Jake set the scheduling book on top of the Victrola, the page she'd tried so hard to hide now exposed.

"What am I going to tell Mrs. Plunkett?" she asked. "She's going to be terribly upset. She'll think I did it on purpose."

"Mrs. Plunkett?"

"Yes! Mrs. Plunkett!" Truvy shouted, no longer attempting to cover the fact she'd been cajoled into wearing a juvenile dress just to satisfy an elder woman's fancy. "She bought this for me, and it meant a lot to her that I wear it. Now what am I going to do?"

Jake raked a hand through his hair, then scratched his jaw. "I'll explain it was an accident."

"Don't you dare," Truvy said levelly. She expelled a weak breath of frustration. "You'd only make things worse. A man in my studio, alone with me? It would be scandalous."

His brows pitching together, Jake contradicted her. "But you said you had a man coming for your lesson."

Truvy's lips clamped shut.

Right then, Jake's gaze shot to the open scheduling book. Directly onto one of the Katzenjammer Kids she'd poorly drawn to throw Jake off the truth. She was a good teacher. She was a bad artist when it came to funny-paper characters.

Jake grew thoughtfully quiet.

After a moment, he softly said, "Ah, Truvy, you don't have to make up things for me. I know you're pretty enough to have men want to spend time with you. And you're a decent woman, too, for wearing a dress that's—" He stopped.

A dress that's degrading.

She didn't dare meet his eyes. She felt her own betraying her, growing hot and moist at the most inopportune time.

"Truvy." His utterance of her name was a caress.

She kept her chin down.

Then he gently coaxed her by saying, "Tru. Look at me." She found herself staring into his sensual eyes. "Would you come to dinner tonight at the restaurant?"

A heartfelt sincerity marked his words, but fearfulness seeped into her consciousness. No. She couldn't go. Because she couldn't trust herself to be with him. Even in a public place. He tempted her. He teased her. He wittingly, and unwittingly, toyed with her emotions.

Using every ounce of willpower she possessed, she untangled her gaze from Jake's. "No."

Knowing Jake's compelling face remained above hers riveted her to the spot. His nearness was overwhelming. The vitality radiating from his body captivated the pulse point at her throat. Her instinctive response was to tilt her head higher so his lips could touch hers.

What was she doing? This was crazy.

Slowly, she lifted her chin. Then his mouth covered her mouth. Briefly. Hypnotically. Nothing like the kiss at Tom and Edwina's house. This was a whisper of mouth over mouth. Just a light touch. A testing of responses. An igniting of senses. "Say yes."

The vibration of his words went to her soul.

"No," she replied, even though her heart lurched.

Jake pulled back, the posture of his shoulders hard and set. "Are you a member of the Idaho Women Suffrage Association?"

His question was as unexpected as a snowstorm on an August day. She felt as if she'd been doused with a chilling brace of ice water. "Am I a *what?*"

"A member of the Idaho—"

"Yes, I heard you," she replied, angry with herself that she'd been swept into his kiss, only to be deprived of it as quickly. Confusion made her heartbeat settle down to its normal cadence. "And no, I'm not."

"Then you aren't—excuse the expression—all piss and swagger."

"I beg your pardon." Agitation worked up her spine as she held herself straight and unyielding, giving him The Aunts' famous oration: "A woman can be whatever a woman wants to be in this day and age. I don't need to belong to any club to validate my modern views—so long as I'm getting a fair chance."

"Good. Then give *me* a fair chance."

Her mouth dropped open. She'd walked right into the trap he'd set for her.

Right into another kiss.

Jake's mouth covered hers once more, opening her lips and touching her with his tongue. She hesitated, blinking, then opening her eyes wide. She wasn't prepared, didn't know what to expect. Certainly not this. The smooth stroke of his tongue felt like an artful dance step.

She knew Jake could execute a flawless waltz, so she let herself dissolve into his kiss while his tongue slid over the soft interior of her mouth. She stopped breathing. In the quiet, she heard the thump of Jake's heartbeat. Could feel it against her palm where she'd raised both hands and laid them on the solid wall of his chest—to keep him away. No, to keep herself away from him.

She let him explore and probe. And boldly, brazenly, she returned what he gave—she kissed him back in the same manner. A secret thrill tingled over her skin as she matched the sweep of his tongue through her mouth. At first, her strokes were tentative, curious—then enraptured.

This kind of kissing wasn't mentioned in *The Science of Life.*

In fact, kissing had gone unnamed, as had—pretty much—women's needs: *A well-bred woman's sexual desire is small. If this were not so, the whole world would become a brothel and marriage and family impossible.*

If that were true, then how could she be doing this? And enjoying it?

Finally, she remembered to breathe through her nose. Her knees grew weaker. She could barely comprehend what she was feeling. The juncture of their mouths was so sensual, so intimate, and so expressive that she uttered an inarticulate cry.

Jake stopped kissing her momentarily, and then his voice rumbled through her fingertips where they lay on his rock-hard muscles. "Say you'll have dinner with me."

"I . . ." She was lost in a haze clouding her mind.

"Say yes."

She should say no. She should remain firm. She should—

"What time?"

Chapter
❧ 12 ❧

Cold air absorbed the warmth from Jake's cheeks and numbed his nose. Leaning a shoulder against the trunk of an elm tree at the Plunketts' curb, he thought about lighting a smoke but refrained. Even the smallest flame in the dark would carry. He didn't want to be seen by anyone in the house

Truvy wouldn't let him collect her at the door. She told him she'd meet him at the restaurant at six o'clock. She needed time to soothe Mrs. Plunkett after she confessed about the dress, and it was better not to have a caller at the house the same evening. Truvy didn't come right out and say it, but he knew how Prudence Plunkett felt about him. She didn't like him. Hell, she disliked men in general. Truvy reasoned that by her entering the restaurant a few minutes after him, their dinner together wouldn't appear pre-arranged.

The whole "chance encounter" thing rubbed Jake the wrong way.

But it didn't much matter because they weren't

going to Nannie's after all. Only Truvy didn't know that yet. That's why Jake was standing outside instead of staying warm in the heated eatery. He planned on ambushing her when she left the porch.

That afternoon, as soon he'd seen Truvy searching for her dance book wearing that girlish dress, he'd abandoned any thoughts he'd entertained about satisfying a recklessly made bet. When he'd asked her to dinner, the wager had been a distant memory in his mind. If he'd had lingering ulterior motives, every last one vanished during their kiss. The touch of Truvy's lips, the feel of her body, the pressure of her hands on his chest, the silkiness of her tongue in his mouth—the combination had rendered him incapable of logic and made him impulsive.

Impulsively stupid.

He could just see Milton or Lou smashing a face next to the window of Nannie's to spy on him and Truvy to see if Jake had won the bet. But where else could he take her? The place would have to be respectable yet discreet enough so the boys wouldn't find out he and Truvy had gone out together. He didn't have many options.

Durbin's ice cream parlor was a worthy choice. Too bad it was in plain view of the town square and always had customers at the soda counter. Tom and Edwina's would be a good solution. But Jake didn't want to make social talk and vie for Truvy's attention. The only two other places he could think of were the Blue Flame Saloon and Dutch's Poolroom.

Neither would fly with a lady.

He'd already done enough to cause her resentment with that fountain pen. Earlier, he'd gone to Edwina's and borrowed a dress from her for Truvy to wear during her dance class, a class that didn't include Milton Burditt—or any men. It was a group of Miss Gimble's schoolkids.

After her class had let out, he'd returned to the studio and been insistent on walking her home, but she wouldn't bend. He'd wanted to tell Mrs. Plunkett how the ink spot on the pink dress happened. Truvy emphatically—a word he now knew the strength behind—refused.

Worse yet, that was when she'd insisted on meeting him at the restaurant or else she wouldn't go. She didn't want him to corroborate her explanation and further complicate matters.

corroborate: confirm; strengthen; establish; verify.

Hell, he was going to make something up. He'd say he'd been watching Truvy through the window and saw her trip while holding the fountain pen. Ink came out of the nub and the front of her dress got the short end of the stick.

Maybe that wasn't the best story, but because Truvy didn't want to go for what really happened, at least his lie had some credence. Mrs. Plunkett was enrolled in the academy and had firsthand experience with Truvy's footwork expertise.

A cold wind gusted, shaking the bare branches of trees lining either side of Elm Street. Jake ran his pocket-warm fingers over the neatly blocked brim of his hat, making sure the stiff black derby stayed on his head.

He glanced at the house once more. Lights were on inside. From what he could tell, they were in the parlor. Because the night was cold and threatened snow, he wore his long sealskin coat, Levi's, and low-ankle storm boots. It had taken him a while to figure out which shirt to put on and whether he should add a string tie.

After fifteen minutes debating with himself, he decided to forget the tie. He hated any kind of neckwear. But he did pick out a dark gray flannel shirt, iron the sleeves and collar to an A-1 grade, and give himself a close shave.

Shadows created by evergreens and scalloped canvas window awnings played over the street. Jake regretted not carrying a watch. What time was it? He began to wonder if Truvy was ever going to step outside.

Maybe she'd changed her mind—

"Bruiser," came a hoarse whisper. "Hey, Bruiser!"

Jake was a big man, and anybody with half a brain would never consider putting the jump on him. He swung his body around, hands raised and ready, but then he saw who'd called him. Lowering his arms, he swore. "Dammit, Milt! I could have knocked your lights out."

Milton lurked behind a lodgepole electric line post across the street from the Plunketts'. With Jake's attention on him, he skulked forward and asked in a whisper, "Where's Miss Valentine?"

Jake wasn't expecting a cutoff at the pass. He'd figured the boys would stake out only the restaurant, not where Truvy was staying. He had to think fast. "Well, Milt, you caught me." Inflecting heavy disappointment in his voice, he stated, "She won't come to the door to talk to me, so I guess you boys win the bet and I'll be eating my own cooking tonight."

"I knew it! Beers for us. And you know the brand I like."

"I do, Milt." *You slice of cheese.*

Milt rubbed his hands together, steaming breath escaping his mouth. "I told them we'd win."

"And you were right."

"Indeed I was." Milton shoved his hands into the pocket lining of his business coat. "Cold night."

"Sure is."

"I reckon I'll go home now that I know the outcome."

"Me, too."

"Yeah."

Neither of them moved.

Jake held onto an oath. He cocked the angle of his hat, then pushed off into the night pretending to be on his way. Looking over his shoulder, he saw Milton had turned around and headed in the opposite direction for his house on Sycamore Drive. Slowing his steps, Jake kept watch; then within seconds, he ducked behind the snow-dusted hedges of the Higginses' house. The flare of gaslights illuminated the front room. From behind the frothy parlor-window curtains, a hairy face stared at him.

An Airedale terrier.

The Higginses had an ankle biter that peed on every hydrant in Harmony when he busted out of his yard. Jake liked dogs, but not this one. Especially now, because the Airedale began to yap at him and scratch on the curtains and glass. Higgins appeared in the window, fisted the sheer panel, and yanked it to the side so he could see out.

"Jesus," Jake mumbled, then took off in a sprint through the bushes as he cut across the yard into the Elward property. He clipped the corner to the Brookses', then ended up back at the Plunketts' in their side yard just as the front door opened and closed.

Jake held back to see who walked to the gate. From the decorated hat, he knew the person was a woman. From the height, there was no mistaking Truvy Valentine. She'd barely raised a gloved hand when he drew up to her and disengaged the latch.

A startled cry escaped her as she turned and recognized him. "Jake."

"Come on." He took her by the elbow and practically dragged her into the night—away from the street where the restaurant was located.

"What are you doing?"

"Change of plans."

"Wh-what?" she stammered with distress. The uneasy tone of her voice didn't escape his attention.

Just around Birch Avenue and a short distance from the Plunketts' was the law office of Alastair Stykem. Jake stopped at the indented entrance to the granite-fronted building and took Truvy into the niche.

Even in the dim night, he could see the whites of her eyes, the sweep of her lashes as she blinked in confusion—in ire. He was gripping her shoulders and softened his hold. "Sorry."

"I told you I'd meet you at the restaurant." She frowned. "Why are we standing here?"

He had to tell her about the bet. She'd probably slap him. He wouldn't blame her. But he owed her the truth about why they weren't going to Nannie's for a nice supper. "The thing of it is—" He quit the thought.

While regarding him, she didn't disguise her blatant annoyance. For a woman who suffered in high-heeled shoes for the sake of fashion, she didn't hold back her rebellious feelings for the sake of Victorian decorum. And he hadn't even confessed anything yet.

"She won't speak to me." Truvy's burst of words filled the small space, and he figured out that he wasn't the only one giving her thunder some roar. "Everything went wrong. She said her Hildegarde would never have been so careless. I've done nothing to give that woman the impression I'm ungrateful or insensitive. I wore the dress even though I nearly died of shame."

Tears glittered in her eyes, but she forced them away before Jake could offer comfort. "Because of the disastrous way my evening has gone so far, I convinced myself you wouldn't be at the restaurant and I'd have to sit there alone. Then all my expectations of integrity would be doused."

Ah, hell. Why did she have to go and say that? He felt like the lowest of all louses.

"Our having dinner . . . your asking me to go with you . . ." Her voice dropped in volume as if she were having a hard time expressing her feelings. "Well . . . this is the only saving grace of my day."

Then she looked at him, her eyes welling with moisture again. Desolation came to mind when he gazed at her. Jake's throat ached and he couldn't get out the words he needed to. "Ah, what else happened with Mrs. Plunkett?"

"I told you—she won't speak to me." Truvy's arm rose and she touched the corner of her eye with a fingertip so no tear would roll down her cheek. A part of him wanted to enfold her in his arms and tell her that the old baggage was a pain in the ass and she shouldn't take any crap from her. But what was he doing? Making that bet had been cheap on his part—and held its own kind of crap. "That is," Truvy went on, with a soft sniff and a rub on the underside of her nose, "she *did* speak to me before she *wasn't* speaking to me, and that was to tell me I showed a lack of consideration for her generosity."

"I think—"

She groaned. "It doesn't matter what you think. What's done is done and . . . oh . . . I don't know. I probably shouldn't have left her alone with Mr. Plunkett after she took to her bed with a headache— her worst one since the day her Hildegarde walked down the aisle and married that man. I feel badly I didn't stay with her." A soft frown caught the smoothness of her forehead. Just at the spot where the netting of her hat rested.

Conflict tore through Jake's chest. "I could take you back."

"No, I'm not feeling that bad." She pushed herself taller, determination crossing her face. "Talking about what happened makes me feel justified in my actions. I apologized. It's not my fault if she doesn't want to accept it. She judged me unfairly. Now that I'm out of the house, I'm actually looking forward to ordering a hot supper and having a slice of apple pie to end my evening on a sweet note." Her eyes rested on his. "Why can't we go to the restaurant?"

He couldn't tell her the truth, even with the liberal dose of guilt eating at his conscience. At least he couldn't tell her right now. Not like this. Not after what she'd been through. "Kitchen fire. It's closed."

The straightness to her shoulders slumped. "Oh . . . no."

"We can go someplace else," he countered, hoping she wouldn't tell him to take her home after all.

"Where?"

"The ice cream parlor." But he knew damn well

they couldn't go there. "But I think it's closed. The ice-box is . . . out of ice."

"Oh."

"There isn't much in a small town. Nannie's is the only restaurant."

She grew very quiet. Very disappointed from the way her chin fell lower as the seconds ticked off. "Then I should go home—"

"There's the Blue Flame Saloon," Jake said. "If you take away the beer, scotch, and all the other liquor and the naked-lady pictures and the clientele at the bar, it's not offensive to ladies."

Demurely, she replied, "I don't think so."

"Yeah." Jake let out a breath of air. "I figured."

The night seemed to close in around them. The distant sound of sleigh bells carried in the brisk air, followed by the nicker of horses.

"I'm going home," Truvy said resignedly, moving past him.

"Dutch's Poolroom," Jake blurted out; it was his last suggestion.

Truvy stopped and turned to face him. "A poolroom?"

"Sure. Dutch's is closed tonight to decorate the joint for New Year's Eve tomorrow. I saw Dutch in there on my way to your place." Jake spoke matter-of-factly. "You know, if Dutch Vermeer was a woman, he'd be an acceptable chaperone."

"Really?" Truvy's sarcasm dripped from each letter, elongating the word enough to make Jake smile in the face of adversity.

"He's sixty-three, never been married, and he doesn't curse or spit. He keeps a bar stocked—not with liquor. Never touches it. All he serves is soda water and sarsaparilla. And he's always got stuff to make sandwiches." Jake was talking fast, trying to entice her by building the place up. And now that he thought about it, there really wasn't a problem with Dutch's. It was true—Dutch *was* putting up streamers, paper balloons, and the whole shebang. The door had been ajar when Jake passed by. "So what do you think?"

Truvy didn't say anything for a while. "The reason I'm on a leave of absence is because the benefactress of my school found me reading material that was educational, *not* meant to be provocative. Even Miss Pond sided with her. I felt utterly unworthy of my position when she was finished speaking to me. And yet, I held my chin up and vowed to return."

He knew that already. So what was she getting at? He hesitated, not commenting, figuring she thought aloud—rationalizing something or other.

"On my arrival to this town, I was spotted with your bottle of beer and then mistaken for having been drinking it myself. On a public street, no less. Although I cleared that matter up, I've gotten myself into another predicament, this time with Mrs. Plunkett, who will be less, if at all, forgiving." She sighed forlornly. "She doesn't even know I accidentally disrobed the wise man in her front yard. I never told her, although I meant to. The police have an open report on the incident but no suspect. I might as well turn myself in. I seem to cause people to form opinions of me from my actions, not my intentions. In the most innocent incidents, I'm highly misunderstood. So why do I bother to try to keep a flawless reputation?"

He waited for her to say something further. She didn't.

Because she didn't give him a definitive answer about going to the billiard parlor, he tossed out, "Dutch has entertainment, too. A player piano. I heard music coming from the upright. Dutch could probably use some help tacking stuff to the walls in exchange for a roast beef sand—"

"Do you think he has roast beef?"

"He almost always does. Pickles and peanuts, without a doubt."

"All right."

"All right?"

"All right, I'll go to this poolroom with you." She wagged a prim finger at him and added in warning, "But I will say this: it had better be closed and you had better not be embellishing about the man who operates it. If I find he looks like a rowdy sort and there's liquor in there, I'm leaving."

"I swear it'll be like I said."

And it was when they arrived.

Dutch Vermeer ran a first-rate operation. The poolroom was spacious, the walls covered with dark wallpaper, revolving cue racks, time clocks, and slate scoreboards. Dutch had five Brunswick tables: beautiful quarter-sawn oak with a hand-rubbed satin finish, iron pockets with nickel plates. The rail-top tables were massive beasts—boat-framed with turned legs and crocheted baskets dangling red fringe. Above each one, four-arm gaslights with Italian glass shades hung just low enough not to leave a single shadow on the table.

A short bar occupied space along the back wall. That's where Dutch served seltzer—no booze, being as Dutch was reformed. He might not have had Old Walker, but he always had something to eat. Meats, dilled cukes, crusty bread, peanuts, pickled eggs, olives. Real man fare.

As Jake let Truvy step inside ahead of him, Dutch looked up from the bar where he wove tinsel garlands through a wire-back billiard chair.

"Hello, Bruiser," Dutch said.

"Hey, Dutch." Jake laid a hand on the small of Truvy's back and guided her toward Dutch. "Dutch, this is a friend of mine—Miss Valentine."

Sporting a full beard and mustache and a thick head of red hair, Dutch came across larger than his body frame. He held out his hand to Truvy and she reluctantly accepted it, as if she'd never shaken a man's hand before. "It's a pleasure to meet you, Miss Valentine."

"Thank you." The smile on her lips was one of approval. Dutch passed muster. "Likewise." Her arm went back to her side and she gazed about the room with wide eyes.

"Got a proposition for you, Dutch," Jake said, nudging the brim of his bowler back with the pad of his thumb. "What do you say to me and Miss Valentine helping you out in exchange for a bite to eat?"

Dutch waved off his offer. "Help yourself to anything you want. I don't have much left to do except inflate some paper balloons. Got a new kind. You ignite the attachment and they blow up without alcohol. I never heard of such a thing."

Nodding, Jake took Truvy's cape off her shoulders. "If you want me to ignite some, I can."

"You two enjoy a sandwich," Dutch returned with a broad smile aimed at Truvy. "It's not every day—in fact, it's been never—that Bruiser's brought a pretty lady to visit."

Truvy blushed.

Dutch continued on, "I've got corned beef in the icebox. Just don't eat at the bar, because I haven't buffed the wax yet." He went behind the length of rosewood with its murky surface and brought out green wool yardage. "I tell you what"—he snapped the billiard cloth open—"lay this down on one of the tables and have yourselves a picnic."

"Will do." Jake took the length of green and selected the pool table closest to the slightly ajar entry door. There were no windows in Dutch's on account of his theory that if a man had to keep track of the time by where the sun was in the sky, he wouldn't be able to concentrate on his game.

"Are you sure we should?" Truvy whispered, standing next to Jake and alternately glancing at the plane of green table before her. Its edges hip high, the Brunswick was enormous and grand.

"Sure." Jake laid her cape aside, slipped out of his coat, then fanned the cloth and let it fall without a wrinkle. "I'll help you up."

She flashed him a lift of her brows. "I could climb up."

"Not in that dress."

She wore the same curve-hugging dress she had on the day Edwina had had her baby and he'd held Truvy in the Wolcotts' kitchen. The dress was a soft green woven out of an even softer-looking wool. When he placed his hands under her arms to boost her onto the table, he reacquainted himself with just how soft, how feminine she felt. The contact shot through his body with a lightning heat that held him in its grip. The round edges of her breasts were inches from his thumbs. He could splay his fingers and catch the tips, feel the shape of her nipples beneath his touch.

He didn't. Not with Dutch in the room. And not with Truvy's words about integrity still swimming in his head.

Truvy let out a low gasp as he effortlessly propped her behind onto the rail of the pool table. The gaslights hissed overhead, casting her in a buttery haze. While he looked into her oval face, he felt a knot of emotions. The one at the forefront of his mind: caution. He hoped he hadn't made a mistake bringing her here. No woman had ever studied him like this. With open curiosity, unbending attention, and God help him, pure trust.

Slowly, he withdrew his hands and backed away. "Sit tight. I'll make the sandwiches."

"You will?"

"I told you I could cook," he called over his shoulder.

"Slicing corned beef isn't cooking. Even I can do that."

"But you don't *like* doing it. *I* do."

Jake went to the bar, took out what he needed from the icebox and bar shelf, and fixed a plate they could share. Dutch moved a crate from the top of the piano and set it on the floor. The inside was filled with varnished animal masks, comic paper noses and strap-on beards, fool's caps, and costume bells. All trappings for one hell of a New Year's Eve party.

"Tomorrow night's going to be a humdinger," Dutch said, fumbling for another piano roll from the upright's bench. "You ought to come on by if you're not stepping out with your lady," he added with a wink. "You want to hear anything special, Bruiser?"

He held up several curled papers with tabbed holes in them. "I got 'Dixie Flyer,' 'The Ragtime Dance,' 'Rubber Neck Jim,' and 'Salina Sassafras.' "

"Never can pass up 'Dixie,' " Jake replied.

"You got it." Dutch fit the paper roll on the piano's drum cylinder, then shut the case. The ebony and ivory keys plunked out the notes of the song.

Jake brought the plate to Truvy, hopped up onto the pool table, and sat down Indian style. She sat more demurely, legs pressed together, both out at her side with barely the tips of her shoes in view. The quills on her hat wavered as she leaned forward and took in what he offered. "Mmm. Looks good."

She removed her gloves and set them aside. Her fingers were slender and pale, the nails neatly filed. Knowing her academic background, he found that imagining the woman before him on a playing court was hard to do. She appeared too graceful, too ethereal, to be anything other than a proper lady.

He had a desire to see the gaslight shining off her hair.

"Take your hat off, Truvy."

"All right." She reached up and withdrew the long hat pin, then slipped the hat from her head. The strands of her hair shimmered in hues of browns and with some red. He knew from experience that day she'd been ice skating with her hair down that the texture was superfine. The curls were put up in neat twists around her crown, some dangling at her neck. He hadn't seen her wear her hair like this since she'd arrived in town and he'd been sent to get her.

Likewise, he removed his bowler and angled it beside her fancy hat. He couldn't explain why, but the pair of hats looked right together. Kind of like what it would be with a husband and his wife's slippers on the floor at the foot of their bed.

That the notion had occurred to him perplexed him. He'd never once thought about Laurette's slippers beside his. Could be because neither had owned a pair. But even if they had, Laurette Everleigh wasn't the kind of woman to find a quiet bliss in something like one pair of slippers beside another.

"Dig in," Jake said, sliding the plate toward Truvy. "Pick out whatever you like."

Selectively, she chose a wedge of bread with a pint-size stack of corned beef inside. He'd purposefully made the sandwiches on the skimpy side. He was no goon when it came to knowing a lady's needs—both in and out of the bedroom. He had the manners to keep the portions lean but plentiful enough. Ladies liked small things. They favored tiny china cups with even tinier patterns on them, thin pieces of bread, and those petit fours they served at parties.

After taking a bite, Truvy delicately chewed. Jake ate his sandwich in three bites but waited for her before he went for something else. He'd take whatever she took.

She went for a mouse-size piece of cheese.

He picked cheese, too.

With lively music playing in the background and Dutch rubbing in the wax on the bar, Truvy asked, "Why aren't you a boxer anymore?"

"Well," Jake responded, after swallowing, "I got tired of having my face busted."

Tilting her head sideways, she gazed at him as if assessing where he'd taken his hits. He knew his nose was a little crooked. And he had a few scars. His eyebrows weren't perfect, but his smile was all right. He'd never had any teeth knocked out.

For the fun of it, he gave her a wide, toothy grin, then said teasingly, "All mine."

He was glad when she laughed at his joke.

An olive found its way into her hand next.

He took a half dozen to her one.

"I've never known a man," she said, blushing as if implying she hadn't known any men—*period*—aside from that Moose character, "who was keen on being the strongest. I wouldn't be able to differentiate between the vigors of boxing and weight training. And I myself am," she added softly, "an athlete."

He knew her admission was difficult. Since he'd met her, she'd played down her coaching position. That she invited him to share his views on boxing and weight training strangely made him feel good.

No woman had ever talked to him about this. All they cared about were his muscles. They wanted to feel them, have him flex them, make them grow taut and hard, have him show off his stamina. Truvy's affirmation that she was, in some way, like him made him feel closer to her than he'd ever felt to a woman— even his wife. "Boxing is a sport. Bodybuilding is an art. Boxing depends on muscular and cardiovascular endurance. Bodybuilding depends on discipline and control." He popped another olive into his mouth. "Aren't you studying anatomy in that science book?"

"They don't go into that much detail on this topic. They do have a section on gym equipment." Her hand paused, tiny olive between her fingers. "And—oh, I read that men who lift weights were sickly as children."

The ego that she'd been building in him fell flat.

"I never was sickly."

"No . . ."—her gaze went slowly over him and he

felt her stare, innocently seductive, at every inch of his body—"... you don't look sickly."

She took another sandwich but, before sampling it, commented, "Your childhood must have been hard. You said you don't speak with your parents. How awful."

"Not really."

"Yes, it is. I can't imagine not talking with my aunts. They're the only relatives I have. They're a bit bohemian."

He could only guess what she was getting at. "Rebels?"

"Of course." She smiled, giving him a glimpse of her even, white teeth, then confided, "They sleep in flannel union suits."

Suggestively, Jake countered, "I don't sleep in anything."

"I sleep in a blue Mother Hubbard." The intimacy was out before she caught herself with a clap of her hand over her mouth. "That is to say—"

Jake cut off her explanation with a deep laugh. "You don't need to say anything, sweetheart. I'm already seeing yards of blue."

"I shouldn't have disclosed that." She brought fingers to her lips, as if on the brink of asking something, but she stopped herself.

Resting his arms on his knees, he leaned forward. "What?"

A seriousness overtook her features. "How old are you?"

"Thirty-three," he replied without hesitation. He wasn't one to give a good goddamn about age. He felt virile enough not to care what the number was.

"You don't appear to be thirty-three."

"You don't appear to be twenty-five."

Her chin lifted with surprise and she met his eyes. "My being twenty-five doesn't put you off?"

He shrugged. "Should it?"

"It would any other man."

"I'm not any other man."

The song ended and the paper flapped inside the piano. Dutch changed the roll and fed the cylinder, and music sounded once more.

"For you, Bruiser," Dutch called over the piano's snappy melody, "'The Fig Leaf Rag.'"

Truvy bit her lower lip and looked at Dutch, then at Jake, and dropped her voice to a near whisper. "I've wondered . . . just recently . . . how do you get those fig leaves to stay on? I mean . . . I saw the photographs in your office of those men . . . and . . . do you use glue?"

The laughter that rumbled from his chest all but shook the table. "I'll be damned, Tru," he drawled, "you just surprised the hell out of me. I didn't think even you would ask that."

Self-consciously, she cleared her throat. "For purely scientific reasons, I can assure you. As you pointed out, I'm reading *The Science of Life,* and there are some matters that, as an educator, I need to expound upon. My subject matter must be broadened and—"

"Would I be a gentleman if I told you how a fig leaf stays on?"

"I suppose not." In an obvious move to distract him from her bold-as-brass question, she rearranged her long legs; they had to be cramped in the awkward position she'd had them in. Her shoes disappeared into the volume of her green skirt. But not before he could see the patent leather was a network of scuffs.

He asked, "Why not wear your Spaldings?"

"Not on your life," she replied. "I have enough idio-syncrasies, like my height."

Id-eo-sin-crass-ees.

He'd never heard of them. What were they? But he wouldn't show his ignorance for all the cigars in Farley's Tobacco Shop. So he let the comment slide, but he damn well intended on looking that word up when he got home.

Truvy picked up another sandwich. "How is it that you knew about the Chinese women's feet?"

He followed her lead, wishing he had a sandwich with more meat in the middle. His stomach threatened to growl, but he didn't want to come across as a wolfish pig. "I learned about it in an opium den."

"Really?" He heard the quick intake of her breath. "What were you doing in an opium den?"

"Getting a tattoo."

"A tattoo!" she exclaimed as if they were something sinfully secretive. Because her voice rose, she glanced at Dutch once more to see if he'd heard her. Dutch had moved on from polishing the bar and was going through the crate of masks.

Turning back to Jake, Truvy wickedly asked, "Where is it?"

"Around my ankle." He grinned. "Disappointed?"

"No. I'd like to see it."

Sweet Judas. Fig leaves and tattoos. Tonight's Truvy Valentine wasn't holding back curiosity for the sake of stuffy propriety. The longer they talked, the more he realized he'd underestimated her. She wasn't all class-room and political essayist. She was skilled in conver-sation, an intriguing and intelligent woman. He admired and respected that.

Stretching out his leg, he pushed his sock down to

the edge of his boot and showed her the ink-drawn Chinese symbols.

"What are they?"

"Words. A proverb."

"What does it say?"

He dragged his fingertip along the circumference of his ankle as he read aloud: " 'A man without determination is but an untempered sword.' "

A deeply thoughtful expression captured her face as she repeated. " 'A man without determination is but an untempered sword.' Why, that's very profound. And quite apt for your profession. I can see why you chose it."

She didn't shrink away or sneer at the marking that would forever stay on his body. The tattoo's ancient wisdom influenced his mind, in the way he thought and the way he molded his body, but others might find it something easy to scoff at. In fact, women had done so before when they'd seen the tattoo. He hadn't cared. But he did care that Truvy wasn't one of them.

"You smoked opium."

Her words didn't fully register, then he had to admit, "While I got the tattoo, yes I did. But I stick to cigars now. Opium was something foolish I did in my younger days."

Cautiously, she glanced up while sighing. "I have a confession."

He braced himself.

"I thought tonight would be full of bland conversation," she divulged. "I never dreamed I would . . . that is . . ." A moment of strained silence lapsed, but her face didn't lose its sincerity. "I've had a very good time . . . Jake. You really are more than . . . muscles. I apologize for ever thinking you weren't bright because of them."

A bolt of remorseful awareness turned inside him, twisting, nagging, tightening. He hadn't expected her to say something like this. He'd figured she had a lot of opinions about him, none of them high. But he was dumbfounded by her admission. Recovering from his surprise, he knew he had to tell her about the bet. Right now.

"Truvy . . . I have to tell you something." He plunged in with his story, getting it all out in one breath, before she could say anything. "Me and the boys were at the gym last night and they were talking about how you snubbed me in the dance class and they said I couldn't get you to favor me no matter what I did and they went on so much about it I found myself betting I could get you to come to dinner with me at the restaurant."

He watched her eyes grow larger and larger with each piece of the story that he revealed.

"I know what you're thinking," he said as her breathing increased to an even, angry tempo. "That I'm an ass for making a bet about it. I won't argue with you there. And that's why I couldn't go through with it. I—"

"Couldn't go through with it?" she said accusingly, the deep brown of her eyes darkened with pique. "What am I doing sitting here with you for if you don't have a stake in my being with you?"

"But we aren't at the restaurant."

"It's closed. Kitchen fire."

"Ah—no. I made that up."

"You made that up?" She brought a hand to her eyebrow and pressed fingertips on the spot as if she'd developed a sudden headache.

"When I asked you to Nannie's, I wasn't thinking

about a bet. All that was on my mind was you. Kissing you. Holding you. And wanting to be with you over a supper. I swear." He reached out and caught her hand, lowering it from her forehead so she'd look at him. His eyes locked into hers. "Truvy, *I swear*. This is why we're here and not at the restaurant. I couldn't take you anywhere near there and give the boys the wrong idea. Can you believe me?"

Music from the piano played over his question while she sized him up pensively. Contemplating. Thinking. Wondering whether he was telling the truth. "What am I going to cost you for losing?"

He swore but had to come clean. "Six cans of beer for each guy."

She folded her arms across her breasts, inhaled, and admonished him. "You dolt, I'm worth at least twelve."

Jake's chin dropped to his chest; then he slowly lifted his head.

If they were alone, he'd kiss her, hard and quick, on the mouth. Any woman who after being told she was part of a ludicrous bet could up the ante was one of a kind.

"I'm sorry, Truvy. I really am."

"You should be."

The song came to an end, a prelude to the end of the evening.

Jake didn't want to take her home, didn't want to have to enter a dark apartment, drink a cold beer by himself, and read *Crime and Punishment* with nobody around to discuss the meaning of the chapter.

"I'm going to close up now, Bruiser," Dutch called as he turned off the gaslights over the bar.

"Okay, Dutch," Jake said, reluctantly hopping down

from the pool table. He helped Truvy climb off, then took the plate to the washtub behind the bar.

A moment later, they exited the poolroom door just ahead of Dutch, who turned and locked up. The night smelled like hearth fires, damp snow—which quietly fell—and the pines that banked Evergreen Creek.

"Maybe I'll see you tomorrow night, huh, Bruiser?" Dutch said. "Good evening, Miss Valentine." Buttoning up his coat, he walked into the night.

"Come on." Jake took Truvy's arm. "I'll walk you home."

It didn't take long to reach Elm Street. Just around the corner of Birch, Truvy stopped. "I need to go the rest of the way by myself."

He wished she didn't. But he understood why.

"I'm sorry, Truvy," he reiterated. "But I'm not sorry you came out with me."

"At least you told me the truth. I appreciate that."

"Yeah, g'night."

Turning, she quickly walked to the Plunketts' house, alone, while Jake stood and watched her go.

His heart expanded and caught in his throat. He fought the compulsion to ignore the emotions behind its pounding. But the strange pumping continued, pulling him from reserves of indifference.

A tightness gripped his chest and a feeling of uncertainty claimed him. On its heels came a thought he'd not anticipated:

When Truvy Valentine left town, he was going to miss her.

Chapter
❦ 13 ❧

"Miss Valentine," Mrs. Plunkett announced sourly from her perch on the divan, "I'm *so* disappointed."

Truvy stood in the archway to the parlor, any thoughts of breakfast gone. She held herself erect, not showing the restlessness that crept up her spine. She put on a sober face and gazed directly into Mrs. Plunkett's eyes.

The elder woman's disappointment couldn't be traced to the pink dress, which had mysteriously disappeared from Truvy's room last night while she'd been out with Jake Brewster. It bothered her that Mrs. Plunkett had been in her room. Mrs. Plunkett's speaking to her this morning in such an agitated tone was more bothersome. Her stiff voice meant some other horrible thing had happened and Truvy was the cause.

"About what, Mrs. Plunkett?"

With her arms over her full bosom, Mrs. Plunkett lifted her chin so that the loose folds of skin were no longer doubled. "Mr. Higgins informed me his Airedale was barking last night."

Truvy didn't see any connection between her and the dog. She hadn't heard a sound from the Airedale. "Yes?"

"Baron alerted Mr. Higgins to a man in his yard skulking through the shrubs in a deviant manner. Mr. Higgins couldn't tell who. It was dark and the scoundrel ran away." She picked up a coffee cup and took a sip, then gazed over the floral rim as she continued, "Mr. Higgins sat in the armchair in front of his window for the rest of the evening, looking to see if the miscreant would return. Ever since my wise men were vandalized, we have all been keeping watch for hoodlums. Some two hours later, Baron spotted an approaching figure on Elm Street and barked. This time Mr. Higgins got a good look. It wasn't his prowler but Jacob Brewster. And he wasn't alone."

At that moment, the pendulum in the foyer grandfather clock gonged the hour, deep, heavy notes that seemed to symbolize the mood. There was no reason to let Mrs. Plunkett say anything further.

"Yes, I know he wasn't alone. He was with me." Truvy walked into the parlor.

"That is precisely why I'm disappointed." Mrs. Plunkett set her cup on the tea cart beside her chair. "I thought I made it clear that men were not to be tolerated."

Truvy stared at the ceiling, wishing she were any place but here. Then, on a resigned sigh, she lowered her head and faced Mrs. Plunkett. "You never told me I couldn't be friends with people."

"Men are not people. They are . . . *men*." Mrs. Plunkett all but shivered with annoyance. "I warned you about Mr. Brewster's ill-bred behavior. He calls on ladies at an ungodly hour of the morning. He operates a gymnasium, a place to convene and *sweat*. A gentleman does not sweat. He perspires. But I have seen firsthand the men who depart Bruiser's with their collars wet and their hairlines damp. It's indecent."

Using a fork, Mrs. Plunkett took a bite of sweet cake, then replaced the utensil on the side of her breakfast plate. The lump of food in her mouth was discreetly chewed, then swallowed, while Truvy's propensity to be comforting and accommodating was chipped away, piece by piece, as the seconds on the clock ticked by. Just seeing Mrs. Plunkett with that cake, hearing her tone, having had a horrible night's sleep for worrying over the other woman's feelings, only to be set upon like this—as if she were an immoral woman—brought Truvy's patience to an end.

"And inasmuch as I find that offensive," Mrs. Plunkett said in a voice chocked with authority, "what I find even more atrocious is that you went out to socialize with Mr. Brewster last night—without telling me—when I was under the weather."

You weren't speaking to me! Truvy screamed the words in her head, tensing.

"Where were you, Miss Valentine?" She sampled the cake once more, then scorched Truvy with an expectant gaze. "I have a reputation in this community and cannot have it sullied by an indiscretion on your part."

"I met him for dinner."

"At the very least, that man should have rung our bell to collect you so that Hiram could slam the door in his face and tell him we don't condone the practice of callers for our boarders."

To Truvy's knowledge, she was the first boarder the Plunketts had ever had. And as far as she could tell,

Mr. Hiram Plunkett wasn't averse to Truvy's having dinner with a man.

"But that's not the point." Mrs. Plunkett took another sip of coffee and then wiped her fingertips with her silky handkerchief. "After what transpired yesterday, you should have stayed here. With me. I needed you. I was upset and distraught."

I was upset.

"I had such high hopes for you," she pouted. "When Mrs. Wolcott told me you were a teacher, I thought you had more sense than to involve yourself with trouble. You were my shining star, the young miss I could count on to fill my days now that my precious is gone. I've been so lonely without her. She had to go and marry that dreadful man and leave me." Her eyes misted. "It's been awful. I'm disappointed. I'm so very disappointed in you, Hildegarde."

Hildegarde.

The name unhinged Truvy and she could no longer hold back what had been bottled inside since she'd walked into the parlor. "I'm *not* Hildegarde. I'm Truvy Valentine."

Startled red splotches roughed Mrs. Plunkett's cheeks. "I meant *Miss Valentine.*"

"No, you didn't."

Mrs. Plunkett gasped.

The previous night, Truvy had lain awake fretting how to make amends. But all was for naught because there wasn't—and never would be—any pleasing Mrs. Plunkett. And it was time to put an end to this.

"I'm sorry your daughter got married and left you alone," Truvy said. "But at least she got married. I'm not going to get married. So if a gentleman asks to take me out to dinner and I find that gentleman to my liking, I'm not going to say no. You have Mr. Plunkett, so you have no idea what it's like to have thoughts and not have anyone to share them with at the end of a day." The admission was just as much of a surprise to Truvy as it was to Mrs. Plunkett. But she had started this quest for freedom and there was no stopping her.

"I find Mr. Brewster's company enjoyable," Truvy decreed, the pulse at her throat beating against the buttons of her bodice. "I don't care that he's a gymnasium owner. I'm an athletic coach—as you well know from snooping in my room. My trophies are on clear display, although if they weren't, I'm sure you would have found them."

Another gasp, this one so loud its force all but sucked the air from the room.

"Miss Valentine!" Mrs. Plunkett warned. "That's quite enough. Saying anything more—you're jeopardizing your place in this house."

But she'd never had a place in the Plunketts' home. Because her name was Truvy, not Hildegarde. The brush-and-comb set, the lunches for two, the dress— everything was meant for a beloved daughter.

Truvy wondered if Hildegarde had ever felt like this, as if she were trapped and had no place to turn, yet in desperate need of getting away. It was a strange and uncomfortable farce, this trying to be somebody you weren't, just to please Mrs. Plunkett.

"I'm not going to impose on you any longer, Mrs. Plunkett. I'll pack my bags and be gone within the hour." The statement was uttered before Truvy thought a plan through. She'd figure something out.

"You can't leave me," Mrs. Plunkett said with sudden worry in her voice. For all the bluster in her reprimand, a single fear held her. And that was being the only woman in the house where she'd raised a daughter, a daughter who was now gone.

Even knowing this was a chance to undo what she'd just declared, Truvy stood firm. "I have to leave, Mrs. Plunkett. This isn't working out."

The woman's round face reddened in shock; her full lips pursed. The cake sitting beside her was forgotten and her coffee grew cold. "Y-you can't leave. Because I know good and well Mrs. Wolcott doesn't have room for you. And the hotel is filled up because of a hardware convention. There are no other choices for you, Miss Valentine. I'm all you have. You must stay here. With me." Panic and despair gripped her face. "Now, my dear," she said, laughing nervously. "I've forgotten all about the dress. It was an accident. We'll get you another one."

"No, thank you."

"But—"

"No, thank you. You've been very generous with me and I won't accept anything further from you."

She quit the parlor, then went to her room to pack. Her hands trembled with the locks on the suitcases as she opened them, then threw her things into the yawning spaces without regard for neatness or order.

Repercussions began to sink in. Putting herself in Mrs. Plunkett's disfavor would surely have an effect on Edwina and the dancing academy. But the situation was beyond mending.

There was no alternative but to leave.

Less than an hour later, Truvy thumped up the front steps to Edwina's house on Sycamore Drive. She'd barely managed to cart the two suitcases. Her ankles were bruised from being banged and she'd walked the whole block with an ungainly balance. But she'd made it, clothing, shoes, books, trophies, and all.

She hated to impose herself on the Wolcotts, but Edwina had offered to put her up. Truvy could sleep on the settee, and she'd make herself so useful that it wouldn't be a problem.

As she raised her hand to knock on the front door, she heard the cries of a baby. They were long and shuddering, high-pitched and unhappy. Mingled with Elizabeth's cries were the sounds of Edwina's uncontrollable sobs. In between breaths, she spoke to Tom.

Truvy's heart squeezed; she felt Edwina's anguish. She left her trunks on the veranda and approached the parlor door at the side of the house. She pressed herself next to the door's frame. She didn't want to eavesdrop, but from the distress in Edwina's voice, this wasn't a good time to ring the bell.

"I—I just want her to stop," Edwina cried. "Wh-why can't she stop? I've done e-everything."

"Ed, it's okay. I'll walk her. You go back to bed. You haven't slept all night."

"I-I c-can't s-sleep. Not when she's crying. It breaks my heart."

This was the first time Truvy had heard Edwina not perfectly in control, not a happy, content new mother. From the sound of things, she was a mess.

"But I want you to go back to bed, Ed. I'll take care of the baby."

"She wants her m-mother. I have to f-feed her. You can't do that!"

Elizabeth's screams increased.

"Oh, Tom . . . I'm sorry. I didn't mean it. I'm just s-so tired."

Edwina cried harder.

Distress seared Truvy's heart. A helpless yearning assaulted her, but she knew there was nothing she could do. This was a matter between a wife and her husband. It was fragile. And private.

Silently, Truvy turned around and went back to the front of the house. She lifted her suitcases and walked down the steps without Tom and Edwina knowing she'd been there.

As it turned out, Mr. Hess owned the livery and the apartment.

When Truvy had left the Wolcotts' two weeks earlier, one thought had surfaced in her mind: *Tom has an apartment with Mr. Hess he doesn't use.*

The conversation she'd shared with Edwina about her leave of absence from St. Francis seemed eons ago, but Edwina's saying that Tom's apartment would be at her disposal if necessary had found its way back into her consciousness, so Truvy acted on the information.

Truvy had purposely neglected to dwell on Edwina's decree that it wouldn't be ideal.

She now knew why.

She hadn't been prepared to find her temporary residence above a livery stable. It had taken tactful convincing on her part to get Mr. Hess to give her the extra key. Tom had the other one. And because he wasn't with her to tell Mr. Hess she could tenant the apartment, she had to assure Mr. Hess that Tom would be agreeable to her being a short-term resident. Contrary to what Truvy assumed, Tom didn't own the apartment. After having lived there as a tenant, he continued to rent the space from Mr. Hess as overflow storage for his sporting goods store.

The cramped area wasn't a true apartment—like one would envision a cozy studio to be. It was more of a loft, an enclosure with its own front door, privacy, and faded cotton curtains on the dirty window, but those were luxuries in a place that was dark, dusty, mannish, and smelled like harness leather. Boxes of super-raspy duck calls, Flightmaster clay pigeons, and field dressing kits were stacked against one of the walls with a taxidermist's mallard sitting on top of it all. The furnishings consisted of a narrow bed with a brown coverlet, a bearskin rug, a combination heater-stove, and a table and spindle chair.

No pink chintz. No pink wallpaper. No pink beds.

In all honesty, Truvy felt the livery room was peaceful and perfect.

Especially after Tom gave her his okay to occupy it. Truvy had gone to the Wolcotts' the evening of the day she'd overheard Edwina crying. All signs of tears had been erased. Edwina had been gracious and warm. Marvel-Anne attended Elizabeth, who slept content-edly in her baby basket. Truvy informed them of her departure from the Plunketts' and of her hope of staying at the livery, if that was all right with Tom.

There had been that moment of uncertainty, but in the end, Truvy saw that there was relief, too. It was the right thing. Tom and Edwina needed to have each other, not a houseguest. Everything was for the best this way, and to Truvy's unexpected delight, she was glad.

She'd never lived on her own and found the every-day things unfamiliar yet exciting. Relying on her own means was a new experience. The rent was taken care of, but she had to feed herself, which meant eating food requiring no oven, because all she had was one stove plate. If she opted not to cook, she had to dine at the restaurant. Which translated into an expense. And became a problem because she only had so much in her pocketbook.

Frugality was the key word.

As for the rest of her life, she'd traded her freedom for inevitable gossip.

Mrs. Plunkett had her own take on the circumstances surrounding her departure from the home. Her story was that she'd asked Truvy to leave because of Miss Valentine's choice in acquaintances. Mrs. Plunkett didn't come to class anymore for dancing lessons, but she hadn't turned the other ladies against her. Truvy continued with her other classes, including that with the Barbell Club.

In all of them, Truvy also continued to flounder with the dance steps. So her priority was practicing on getting them right.

She sat at the table, her bare feet on the fur rug beneath her. She read from *Dance Fundamentals* while absently rubbing her toes in the plush fur of the bearskin. It felt deliciously wicked to lounge in her housecoat, without shoes on and wearing her hair down, all at one o'clock in the afternoon. She didn't have a dance class today. And she wasn't going to see Edwina until later this evening.

Flipping through the pages, Truvy ate a chocolate from a heart-shaped box filled with them. Valentine candy. Her birthday was a month away, but The Aunts had sent the gift early. A pick-me-up for having Mrs. Mumford take her place in her classroom.

While she chewed, Truvy took in the patterns of foot movements, but her mind wandered to another image beyond those in the book—that of an extremely tall man. A very handsome man . . . one who held her too closely when they danced. One to whom she hadn't spoken other than to trade polite niceties during his hour at Edwina Wolcott's Dancing Academy. Not since that night on the pool table had they discussed anything remotely personal.

There were times when Truvy wondered if she'd imagined their picnic. That those hours on a cloth of green, with a piano playing ragtime, had never happened.

That maybe—

A knock on the door broke her reverie.

Truvy glanced down her wrapper's front where the folds overlapped. Beneath it, she wore her old shimmy and plain linen petticoat because both were soft and good for flopping, on a cold winter day, with the hiss of a heater in the corner, a book on the table, and a box of chocolates within arm's reach.

The knock came once more, insistent.

Slowly, she inched back the curtain to peer out the window. Perhaps Edwina was paying a call—

The sight that met her stilled her hand.

Jake Brewster.

On her outside porch—if you could call a wooden landing atop a steep incline of rickety steps a porch.

Truvy pulled back from the window.

"Truvy, I know you're in there," he said through the front door. "I saw the curtain moving. Open up. I have something for you."

The first thought to come to her was that it would be scandalous to let him in. But the second thought was that it would be scandalous not to and allow any passersby to see him standing out there. The chances that the latter would happen were slim because the livery was set apart from the main businesses in town. Still, the log building was located on Main Street.

Brushing unseen wrinkles from her pale floral wrapper, Truvy drew in a breath and turned the bolted lock. Allowing only a small wedge of daylight to spill inside, she peered through the crack and tried to hide her appearance as best as she could.

"Yes?" she asked through the slit. "What is it?"

His face filled her view as he leaned forward, first with his upper body, then with the toe of his boot, which widened the conservative crack in the door to a huge gap. She was no match for the power in his leg as he kneed the door open. "I told you I have something for you."

"Well, yes; you could just give it to me without—"

With a fluid and impatient stride, he moved right on past her, bringing with him a draft of freezing air. She vacillated between closing the door and leaving it open. It had taken her most of the morning to fuel the heater with enough wood to make the room warm. Now the cozy heat drifted out by the seconds.

She quickly closed the door, turned around, and crossed her arms over her breasts, severely self-conscious over her state of undress.

Reluctantly, she admitted she had thought about Jake Brewster coming to call on her, to ask her to supper once more, to collect her for an afternoon or evening walk; but even in her most dreamy fantasies, she'd been wearing her best dress.

"This really isn't proper at all. I'm going to have to ask you to leave until I can—" Her gaze fell onto the blanketed, bell-shaped cage he held on to by its handle. "What's that?"

Using the flat of his hand, he slid her open book

and chocolates aside to set the cage on the table. "I brought you a parakeet."

"A parakeet?" she choked.

"Yeah . . ." The word dragged out once Jake viewed her from head to toe. "A companion bird."

"Oh."

The silvery green of his eyes roamed across her body, slowly, moving down, then upward. He seemed to get hung up on the neckline of her robe where bare skin at her throat was displayed. The fine hair at her nape rose and she foolishly let her breath catch. His pupils darkened, dilating as his gaze lingered an overly long time, especially on the sight of her hair, which was unbound and fell past the nip of her waist in loose curls. She tried to remain composed, to ward off the heat of a blush that tried to cover her cheeks, but it was difficult.

His presence swallowed up what little space was in the room. The wide set of his shoulders in his sealskin coat and his sturdy legs made him appear taller than he actually stood. He looked lean and strong and overdressed next to her near-nothing. The short-trimmed ends of his hair rested on the turned-up collar of his coat, and snow had fallen over the crown of his bowler hat.

Truvy crept forward, arms hugging herself, as Jake lifted the blanket to reveal a brass birdcage. Inside the wired confines flapped a green bird with a yellow head and blue tail. It flitted from perch to swing, anxious, bobbing up and down when it alighted.

Leaning closer, Truvy looked through the brass wires to inspect the tiny creature. The bird was rather pretty. It had beady eyes that blinked so fast it was hard to tell what color they were. Black, maybe.

"Why are you giving me a bird?" she asked while straightening, making sure she kept a modest distance between them. She was so transfixed by him, by his sudden appearance, that she could hardly think straight.

"You said you'd never buy one for yourself."

"I know, but I'm not staying in town. How am I supposed to get it home?"

"Take him on the train."

"It's a boy?" she questioned, curious. "How can you tell?"

"The guy in Waverly told me."

She knew Waverly was a distance from Harmony. The thought that he had gone to such trouble to get her a bird . . . well, it was quite touching. She just didn't know what to do with a parakeet. She'd never taken care of a pet before. Strange, as most unmarried women had, at the very least, one cat.

She had no experience in the cat department. Nor the dog. Or bird.

"Well . . . this is incredibly nice of you, but I . . . that is, how do I—what do I do with it?"

"I got you all the stuff you'll need." From his deep coat pockets, Jake produced items and informed her of their importance as he laid them out. "Cage hook with wrought-iron screw. Tell me where you want the birdcage to hang and I'll install the wall screw for you." Next, and with an explanation, was, "Glass birdseed bottle with wire loops." Indeed, the item looked like just that. Then came a type of shallow saucer, which he held up for her inspection. "Combination birdbath and water dish." From his left pocket appeared a tall canister and a spear-shaped object. "Your package of mixed birdseed and your cuttlebone."

Looking at all the things on the table, she thought it seemed like a lot for one small bird. Helplessly glancing toward Jake, then at the parakeet, she asked, "Does he come with an instruction book?"

Jake's laughter rang out. "Don't take this the wrong way, sweetheart, but from the improvement you've shown in your dance steps, I think an instruction book isn't going to do you any good."

She feared he could read the message in her eyes: *You're right.*

"Well, then what am I supposed to do with all this?"

"I'll set it up for you." He took the glass bottle, poured birdseed into the mouth, then hung the bottle in the cage. "Where's your water?"

She kept a full pitcher and washbowl on top of the rudimentary dresser. Alongside her trophies. "There."

He brought the dish with him and filled it. "Maynard needs fresh water every day."

Her brows lifted. "Maynard?"

"That's his name." Jake eased open the cage door and carefully set the dish on the bottom without spilling the water. Maynard flew around in a tight circle, wings fanning, then landed on Jake's forefinger. He promptly clamped his beak into the calloused flesh. Jake didn't flinch. Maynard jumped off in favor of his swing, leaving a red, horseshoe-shaped beak mark on the side of Jake's finger.

"He seems a bit aggressive," Truvy commented, hands on her robe sash to make sure it remained tightly around her waist.

"Naw. You just have to get to know his temperament." Jake attached the cuttlebone, tied a bell to the perch, and closed the cage door. "On a four-feather scale, four being the best, the man in Waverly who sold him to me gave Maynard four feathers."

A finger-biter got four feathers. Truvy wondered what it was that a one-feather bird did.

"Now, all you do is hang up the cage. Where do you want it? He likes a warm spot. I'd suggest by your heater pipe."

"All right."

Jack positioned the cage hook on the span of wall between the stovepipe and the window frame. With a twist of his wrist, he screwed the hook in without any tools—just the firm grip and turn of his hand. As soon as it was in place, he took Maynard's cage and hung it up at eye level.

Walking up to it, Truvy looked inside. Tentatively, she addressed the bird. "Hello, Maynard."

"You can train him to talk," Jake offered, standing beside her.

He was close. Close enough that she could smell his aftershave, and the snow that had melted onto his coat. The day had been blustery, with the promise of worse weather all week. A hot cup of coffee would be just the thing to give him before sending him on his way, a thank-you for his trouble. But it wasn't a situation that lent itself to such a gesture.

His shoulder nearly brushed hers as she leaned away from the cage and adjusted the lid on her candy box. Why was it that she kept remembering the way his mouth had felt on hers? That intimate kiss . . . the dancing of their tongues in that deep and thoroughly ravishing kiss?

She wished he didn't smell so good. Didn't look so tall and broad. Didn't make her stomach tingly.

She felt she had to say something. Putting some distance between them, she said, "I should offer you coffee—only I don't have any and I don't think you should stay and chat while I'm—"

"In your skivvies?"

"Something like that."

An awkward pause stretched out.

The minute his eyes lowered to her bare toes, she sank them into the fur rug, trying to hide them. She didn't have ugly feet. But she did have a blister on her right big toe from those dreaded high-heeled shoes.

"Tru," Jake said softly, "the bird's a peace offering. Tom told me you moved out of the Plunketts' and I can only guess why, with the way Mrs. Plunkett feels about me. I could have talked to her for you."

"It's all right." She didn't want him to feel bad about something that wasn't his fault. "It was time for me to find someplace else to live."

He gazed at her book. At the box of candy. At her trophies. Her little touches that made the room her own: dresses hanging on hooks, her hat on the wall peg, her shoes lined up in front of the Flightmaster boxes. "So are you staying for a while?"

She'd recently heard from Miss Pond, this time in the form of a letter. Mrs. Mumford wasn't tiring of her classroom position. In fact, she was going at teaching quite enthusiastically. There were no athletic classes, tennis or basketball. She'd put an end to them. In their place had come bridge. To Truvy, bridge was an old-lady card game. And a boring one at that.

"For now, I'm taking each day as it comes. But I fully intend to return to my school as soon as . . ." The sentence trailed; it was so painfully embarrassing to concede temporary defeat. "Soon."

Miss Pond had assumed that Mrs. Mumford would

tire of teaching Truvy's economics class, but it had been three weeks now, and no change of heart. If Truvy thought on it for too long, she grew discouraged. Thank goodness the dancing lessons kept her busy.

Jake absently ran a finger over the page of *Dance Fundamentals* where she'd been reading about the sugar cane—a new fad dance that was growing in popularity and that Edwina had asked her to teach. The complexity of the boxes and squares—denoting right and left feet—wasn't helping Truvy grasp the moves. It was so difficult to figure out a dance when she didn't have anyone to practice with.

"Sugar cane, huh?"

"Yes. Edwina says it's fun."

"It can be." Jake's voice dropped in volume. "With the right partner."

The richness of his voice sluiced through her; she fought off a shiver of wanting more than just his voice to caress her.

She hadn't made Jake pair up with Lou Bernard these last few sessions. It became an unspoken tradition that he be her partner, which put Truvy out of sorts on many occasions.

"I was thinking, Truvy." Jake tipped the brim of his bowler back with a thumb, then slipped his hands inside his pockets. "How about we meet in the studio an hour before each class, and I show you how it's done?"

The offer was beyond generous, one she shouldn't refuse. But how could she possibly accept? Being alone with Jake Brewster was like leaving Eve in the garden with Adam. And everyone knew how that had turned out.

"What do you say?" Jake's eyes held hers, dark and fathomless.

She tried to disregard her awareness of him. But it was too easy to get lost in the way he looked at her. An unwelcome surge of anticipation caught in her heartbeat. She couldn't deny the spark of excitement at the prospect of dancing with him without watchful eyes observing their every move.

Then she berated herself for thinking such a thought.

This would be purely for instructional purposes. It would be perilous to make anything more of their being together.

"All right," she replied.

"We can start tomorrow at ten o'clock." He went toward the door, then stopped. "Oh—there's a condition."

"A condition?"

"You have to wear your Spaldings."

Flat-soled athletic shoes. "I don't think—"

"No Spaldings, no dancing. I want you to be able to move, Tru." He glanced over his shoulder. "The fancy getups you've got lined against your wall aren't worth the boxes they came in."

"But I like them."

"But you can't dance in them." Firmly, he stated, "Spaldings or forget it."

The corner of her mouth lifted in exasperation. "Fine."

Chapter
❧ 14 ❧

"It's *veerrry* interesting," Truvy observed while cranking the Victrola's handle. She set the needle on the recording and scratchy notes came out of the trumpet. She spoke over the softly playing piano. "I do something that's considered shady—moving into an apartment above a livery—and nobody comments about it to me." She paused, her brows lowering. "Have you heard anything?"

"It hasn't come up during poker," Jake replied. "And nobody's talking about it at the Blue Flame Saloon. Or Dutch's. Those are the few places I go. Maybe you ought to be asking Edwina and not me."

She and Jake stood in the dancing studio on Wednesday morning, the heater in the corner emitting a cheery glow while snow fell outside.

"I have asked Edwina." They talked about the apartment last week and how Truvy was settling into it. Truvy did ask about the townspeople. "She claims there's been nothing. Not a single utterance. I believe she's put in a good word for me. I'd venture a guess and say she's explained the situation I was in—delicately—to her circle of lady friends. That my intentions were not to offend Mrs. Plunkett."

There was gross irony here. For all of Truvy's past good intentions that had turned into debacles, this was the one time she'd knowingly gone against convention and nobody was taking her to task over it. She was waiting for something terrible to happen. Like it always did.

"You sound disappointed nobody's talking."

"I'm not. I'm relieved." She rested her hands on her hips. "I just can't help wondering if there's going to be a surprise attack. Mrs. Plunkett hasn't been seen in days."

"That's because she left town two days ago." Jake made a quick-footed step to the beat. Right step. Left hop. And a diagonal something-or-other. "Her husband sent her to Buffalo to visit her daughter."

"I didn't know."

The music filtered around her as Truvy's thoughts went to Mrs. Plunkett. It was for the best she spend some days with her daughter. Truvy was glad Mr. Plunkett booked her a train trip to Buffalo. The scene between herself and Mrs. Plunkett had played out in Truvy's mind several times, and each time it did, she felt bad. But the situation couldn't be helped. Perhaps if Mrs. Plunkett saw how happy her daughter was, she'd be happy for her in return.

There was no denying marital bliss. Surely married life put a glow on a woman's face because it gave a wife undeniable happiness. It certainly did that for Edwina.

Thinking of weddings, Truvy grew distracted, the recording and Jake Brewster fading into her musings.

She shouldn't expend time on such thoughts of grooms and the Valentine family heirloom wedding cake topper with its two entwined hearts just because that historic day was less than a month away. She knew, as she remembered every year, that the Valentines in past generations had married on Valentine's Day. Even The Aunts had recited their double vows with their husbands on February the fourteenth. She was happy for them and for all the Valentines before her. There was no point in getting melancholy over that date as if she were eighteen again.

That particular birthday had been very difficult for her. Eighteen years old was on the cusp of lifelong spinsterhood. But she'd taken it like a dose of medicine—with steadfast resolve to swallow but a shivering aftermath. Nineteen had come and gone, and she'd been in college so she'd been too busy to think about marriage. Then twenty came and went. Twenty-one. Twenty-two. Twenty-three. She was a schoolteacher by then and so involved with her students and the school that a birthday hadn't mattered. Twenty-five. That had been a bit hard. She'd had some doubts about living the rest of her life alone, but she'd shoved them aside, thinking she was so very lucky to have St. Francis and the girls.

Her twenty-sixth birthday approached. And oddly . . . as of late, she'd begun to dread the date. Twenty-six was so sobering. Twenty-two or twenty-three—she'd felt young and energetic. There had been a last chance, a hazy ray of hope, for a husband. *If* she wanted one. Twenty-four and twenty-five, the hope had all but died. Turning twenty-six meant chances were gone. A future as a missus was done, finished. She never would get married. It was a simple as that.

Oh, why had her thoughts turned to such nonsense?

Because watching Jake Brewster, with his wide shoulders defined in a faded blue flannel shirt, his hair nicely trimmed at the back of his neck, and the easy way he occupied the hardwood floor, dancing alone and completely at ease with himself ... made her wonder. Wonder if she was ready to commit to a life of solitary confinement.

And like it.

But why him? Why was he the one to make her question her life's path, the journey she'd been prepared to make? He wasn't marriage-minded. Not in the least. He'd made that clear. Besides, he wasn't scholarly or bookish, the things she would choose for herself if she were choosing.

And yet, as he raised an arm to beckon her to join him in the sugar cane, a part of her yearned. A part of her hoped, for precious seconds, that there could be something more ... romantic between them.

"Dance with me, Truvy."

She tried not to, but her breath caught. She took a step forward.

"Wait," he instructed, holding up his hand.

She stopped.

"Let me see 'em, Tru."

Biting her lower lip, she notched the hem of her skirt up to reveal a pair of Spaldings on her feet.

"Excellent." A broad smile curved his mouth.

His gaze lingered before she dropped her skirt. She didn't know why he'd think athletic shoes were anything interesting to look at. Scuffed and well worn, the leather served her well in agility. As for her ankles, they were covered by stockings, and she'd barely showed a hint of petticoat. Still, the whole idea of showing him a part of her she shouldn't rose goose-flesh on her skin.

"Come here."

She went to him and laid a hand in his. His gaze was so galvanizing, it was hard to resist throwing herself into his arms.

"Good choice in music," he murmured, seemingly not affected by their closeness at all.

She'd selected "The Sugar Cane" when she'd wanted to pick "The Fig Leaf Rag." Weeks after Dutch's poolroom, she'd been humming the song's melody; she'd bought the recording three days earlier.

As if he could read her mind, Jake squeezed her fingers. "We could have danced the sugar cane to 'Fig Leaf.' Same beat."

"Yes . . . well, I did think of that because I thought you favored it," she said quickly. "But then I wasn't sure if the song would work or not." When he made no immediate remark, she hastened to add, "I shouldn't have asked you about the fig leaf and the . . . glue."

She wished she'd never made the inquiry, but she had and there was no taking it back. Since then, the incident had weighed on her like a dark cloud she couldn't shake. She felt clarification was necessary so he wouldn't think her curiosity was distorted. "Sometimes I speak without thinking. It was just that the fig leaves were on my mind—not that I'm preoccu-pied with fig leaves—but I saw them in the pictures in your office and I was wondering. That's all."

The pad of his thumb rubbed across her knuckles, and a wave of ecstasy throbbed through her. Pure heaven. His caress was so lazily methodical, she could easily drown in the sensation, a sensation of wondrous headiness that wasn't remotely described in *The Science of Life.*

Jake's voice dropped in pitch when he spoke. "Sweetheart, at any time, if something's on your mind—you go ahead and spill it."

She inhaled sharply.

His fingers warm in hers, Jake turned her around and manipulated her into a position in which he stood behind her. He grasped her other hand as he lowered his face next to her ear.

Her heartbeat thundered. "Th-this isn't the sugar cane."

"No," he said, then gave a low laugh. Warmth from his breath caressed her earlobe. "This is just sugar."

She cleared her throat, pretending not to understand. "Is this how you start the dance?"

His voice was deep and held an edge of seriousness to it when he asked, "You really want to know how the fig leaf stays on?"

"Um, not necessarily." The lie was as bold as this morning's sunrise had been when Maynard's chirping had awakened her. She *did* want to know. But she didn't want him to know just *how* much. The fig leaves intrigued her; it was more that she was interested in the *pabulum of life* beneath the leaf. She would rather die a thousand deaths than confess such a thing.

"Okay. Then I won't tell you."

Then he let the subject drop. Just like that.

He drew her to his chest by bringing her arms in. Her shoulder blades pressed next to the bands of muscles that spread out between the buttons of his shirt. The contact kindled a fire in her pulse. "You stand in front and I'll show you how to move your feet. Do like I do."

She could barely think, much less do what he did.

Truvy shook off her idle musings about those fig leaves and tried to focus on their lesson.

Although he hadn't shaved this morning—in fact, he was put together rather coarsely—his appearance in the studio earlier had riveted her to the spot. At precisely ten o'clock, he'd shown up for their private tutelage.

There he'd been—unshaven, with a few wrinkles in his shirttail and his untrimmed hair combed back with water. Why was it he could clean up so wonderfully and then look equally as attractive to her when he was ruggedly ragtag? Coach Thompson militantly groomed himself and her pulse had never skittered out of control when she was beside him.

Jake raised her arms, her fingers still interlocked with his. Standing in such a way, she felt as if her breasts were thrust out in front of her like a pair of carriage headlights. She felt vulnerable, on display. Coach Thompson's gaze sometimes lowered during their conversations. And Jake's eyes, well . . . he made no bones about what he found interesting on her. He might be standing behind her, but she felt the effect of their position as he shuffled his feet and brought himself closer to her backside. As soon as he did, her nipples beaded into tight knots. It felt as if the room had suddenly grown extremely cold, when the opposite was quite true. She was hot and perspiring on her upper lip.

She blamed her flushed state on the blasted heater. It had been stoked and burning for hours. To her surprise, when she'd arrived this morning, the Acme had been lit; the air that greeted her had been quite toasty. And the room had smelled like cigar smoke. Not that she minded the aroma of a good Havana. They reminded her of her uncles' humidor, pleasing and nostalgic.

The lingering hint of smoke made her realize that it hadn't been Tom Wolcott who'd come by so early to see that the studio was comfortable and not freezing. Tom didn't smoke cigars. But Jake did. And he had a key.

Even now, she could smell the tobacco clinging to his shirt as they practically stood on top of each other.

"I wanted to thank you," she said, over the thudding of her heart, "for lighting the heater. That was thoughtful of you."

"I can be thoughtful sometimes."

He needed to give himself more credit, so she helped him along and said, "Maynard was a thoughtful thing to do."

"How's your parakeet getting along?" Jake's chin all but rested on the top of her head as they spoke. "Did you change his water dish this morning?"

She combated the delicious tingles at the nape of her neck. "Yes. He's doing all right. He got up early this morning."

"Companion birds'll do that."

"I didn't know."

They talked without the ability to look into each other's eyes. But when she turned her head to the right, she could see them standing in the mirror, a couple who fit perfectly together because of their unique heights. She'd never thought being tall was an asset, but now she was happy about it. Happy that she molded next to Jake and felt compatible with him. The unexpected thought comforted her.

"You'll get used to him." Jake's eyes met hers in the mirror's reflection.

"Yes . . ." She watched the rise and fall of her breasts.

So did Jake.

He made a low noise in his throat, then faced forward.

So did Truvy.

"Okay, what you're going to do is"—he firmed his grasp on her fingers, the calluses on his palms imprinting on the backs of her hands—"crossover step on the left foot in back of the right."

His direction was completely befuddling.

"I don't understand."

"I'll show you."

On a two-count beat, he made a three-stepped maneuver that she had to watch by keeping her head down and by feeling the motion of his body.

"I . . . don't understand." She was loath to admit it a second time. He must think her an imbecile.

"It's okay. We'll try it a different way." He loosened their fingers and snugly put his arms around her waist. The touch sent the pit of her stomach into a spiral. His keeping her so close to him was like they were one instead of two. She couldn't think clearly with the flat of his hands securely on her, with the underside of her breasts aching against her corset stays. With his thumbs fractions away from her nipples.

When Jake rocked left, he took her with him. She felt the line of his jaw resting on the side of her head, teasing the strands that had come loose from her upswept hair in its two combs.

"Weight"—the rich timbre of his voice wasn't as assured as it had been—"on the right foot now." His instructions came out in a husky whisper, as if she had invaded his awareness to an intimate degree.

Jake moved once more. She had to lean to the right and forget that his thighs all but burned through the fabric of her skirt and scorched her pantalets.

"Step left side, right foot cross over in front." The huskiness in his tone intensified.

Truvy let him lead her into the steps, thoroughly confused. It was a wonder she'd managed to get through her dance classes this far without the students standing off to the side in sheer puzzlement. And even laughter.

"Step diagonally right back on your right foot."

"I think I've got it now." She so wanted him to find her a worthy dance partner, but his nearness was overwhelming.

"Right foot." Jake lightly patted the side of her right leg with a strong hand. The jolt of consciousness that swept through her left her sucking in a gasp.

She thought she'd used her right foot! In her haste to reassure him she was catching on, she must have stepped the opposite of what he told her.

"Stop," he all but grated in an impersonal tone as the music continued to float out of the Victrola. "Hold this position for four beats. Then we're going to start over from the top."

She could barely breathe for four beats, much less hold the position for that long. Why did he have to flatten himself so intimately next to her? Was that his fig leaf—without the fig leaf—pressing against her bottom? She lost all focus. All concentration. This was hardly what she'd call a dancing lesson. Not when she was torn inside . . . wanting to turn around in his arms and kiss him.

I want to kiss him.

She'd never been inclined to kiss a man. Not once in her life. But right now, she caught herself wanting to kiss Jake in the worst way. Wanting him to kiss her. Everything inside her body ached, longing for more than just this superficial touch. She wanted his mouth over hers, hot and moist, his chest crushing her breasts. She wanted to feel total and fiery passion. She wanted that kiss again where they used their tongues.

"Shift your weight." Jake's voice intruded on her fantasies and she all but shuddered her reaction. He went on, "Small step forward on the left foot. Step on your right foot, bend your knee slightly. Crossover step on your left foot."

He might as well have been tutoring her in Latin verse. She couldn't comprehend a word. As he tried to run through the movements, she fought following through. He moved left; she stayed still. He stopped.

"What's the matter? I said to cross over on your left foot."

She turned herself around in his arms, barely looked into his eyes, then pressed her open lips over his. Soundly. Without thought. Without justification other than one simple thing: she wanted to.

Jake's muscular arms rose and gathered her in tightly. Breath mingled with breath. Lips touched lips. Currents of desire shot through her while her knees weakened.

She started the kiss, but Jake took it over. He nibbled on her lower lip; she nuzzled her nose next to his, losing herself in the dreamy intimacy. His hand lifted to gently massage the skin on the back of her neck as he kept his mouth on hers.

The rhythm of the music gave their unpredictable

kiss syncopation. As the tune crescendoed, so did the sweep of their tongues. Truvy might not have been able to dance to the music, but she felt compelled to kiss to it. The notes swam inside her head. She danced the dance of kisses.

Her hands lay on Jake's shoulders and she lifted her fingers into the soft hair at his collar. So silky. So cool. So . . . wonderful.

At the base of her throat, her pulse beat. Jake found the spot with his fingertips. Then his fingers drifted lower, between them, grazing downward. She waited, her pulse quickening. The hot ache in her breasts made them feel full and heavy.

The side of Jake's thumb brushed her tight nipple. The touch caused a shudder to pass through her. She let out a sigh, her wildly beating heart the only other audible sound. His hand cupped her, the full globe of her breast. He softly massaged, fondled.

They kissed for an eternity.

She reveled in the velvet warmth of his mouth over hers, devouring and burning with fire. His hand on her breast singed. She wound her fingers into his hair, fisting the locks. She lightly held the back of his head so he couldn't break the kiss.

This was truly and utterly insane.

But she didn't care.

She was twenty-five and she was never going to get married and she was never going to make love to her husband and she was never going to learn the secrets in that book she was reading unless she figured them out for herself.

She curled into the curve of his body, her hands moving down the length of his back. He was so taut. So hard and muscular. So—

The music stopped. The room became stone quiet.

Except for their gasps and pants, the soft sounds of mouth against mouth. Slowly, Truvy grew aware of her surroundings but didn't do anything to pull away. *Please don't stop kissing me.*

But Jake's hold on her loosened. The moment was slipping away.

"Christ, Truvy." The rumble of Jake's voice reverberated through her breasts, to her heart. "I was trying damn hard to be a gentleman about these lessons. I didn't want to grope you like a big toad."

"You're not a big toad." She kissed his open mouth, then gazed at his face.

The green of his eyes darkened. "You called me one before."

"I apologize. Truly." She leaned into him. "Now kiss me again."

He did. But not the kind of kiss she needed. It was swift and placating. He gripped her shoulders and put her at arm's length.

"If I keep kissing you," he said, the vein at the side of his neck pumping blood furiously as he attempted to keep his breathing normal, "I'm going to want to do more than just kissing. I don't think you know what you're getting into. I didn't offer to give you the dance lessons so you'd have sex with me."

His words were blunt, and she hated that he felt he had to say them. "I never thought that."

"Yeah, well . . ."—he ran a hand through his hair— ". . . it did cross my mind." He walked to the window and stared out to the alleyway and the falling snow.

"As it did mine," she returned, quietly. "It was me. I kissed you."

"Not with any resistance on my part." The broad width of his shoulders heaved a sigh.

Truvy remained still. She feared he'd walk out the door, leave, never come back. She'd never see him again, never watch the smile play over his mouth, see the light dance in his eyes, hear the quips he could make with a joking grin or shrug. He might not have thought he was anything special.

But she thought he was . . .

Truvy didn't dare finish the thought. Instead, she composed herself and asked very judiciously, "If I promise not to kiss you, will you still teach me the sugar cane?"

For what seemed a long while, he didn't move. Didn't comment. Didn't face her. Then with the feathery white snow drifting as a backdrop behind him, he turned around. His steady gaze regarded her, then he presented her with a familiar display of rakishness. "No."

"No . . . ?" The word practically wedged in her throat, and she flushed. Miserably.

His grin flashed briefly, dazzling against his bronze skin. "I'll teach you the dance without your promise."

Chapter
❦15❦

"I'll pay for it, Bruiser," Milton said as he stood over Jake, who knelt beside a jagged hole in the gymnasium's floor. "I didn't mean to . . . I'll cover all the repair damages. Every last penny."

The wide hole gaped and Jake looked through it to the ground about a foot beneath the elevation of the building. He could make out an object down below—an iron bar and two round balls on either end. Drafts of cold air blew up in a gust from the dark pit. On the surface, the highly varnished planked wood was splintered and spanned a circumference of a good forty-eight inches.

Milton Burditt had really done it when he dropped a two-hundred-and-fifty-pound barbell from hip height. The floor hadn't been able to withstand the sudden, forceful blow and had collapsed.

Jake gazed up at Milt through the fringe of hair resting in his eyes. He shook the hair back but didn't temper his glare at Milt.

Milton's complexion went white. His double chin

seemed to triple. And the sag in his gymnasium drawers appeared like he'd lost a little something out of fear of Jake's reaction.

"Now Bruiser, I know what you said—that we shouldn't try to lift more than we can handle. But I swear to you, I thought I was ready for it. With the Mr. Physique contest two weeks away, I have to be in prime condition if I'm going to walk off with that first-place win."

"We *all* have to be in prime condition," Walfred grumbled.

Walfred, Gig, August, and Lou, along with other gym members, crowded in to observe Jake's reaction.

Jake had been in his office during the destruction. There had been a loud crash, then the sound of ripping wood and the leaden thud of metal against frozen earth.

Gig's brows arched. "I'm not ready for the two-fifty. I'll do what you tell me to, Bruiser."

"Quit trying to get on his good side, Gig," Milt groused.

At this moment, Jake didn't have a good side. But he kept his temper in check, although it was hard not to let that tick at his jaw go a little wild. He reminded himself it was an accident. Hell, he knew about accidents. Shooting Truvy's dress with ink came to mind.

"It's all right, Milt," Jake said carefully, trying not to ground the words out. "I understand."

"Do you, Bruiser?" He all but blanched his relief. "You're a swell guy."

Jake rose from his crouch. In everyday situations, he rarely—if ever—used his full six-foot-five height to an advantage, but he rather liked towering high over Milton Burditt. And worrying him.

Milt took another step backward. So did the crowd.

"I'm going to have to close for a few days, gentlemen, while I wait to have this repaired," Jake said while pushing back the leg frame of the rower. He didn't need anybody tripping on the equipment and falling into the hole. "My building insurance won't let me operate with a hazard in the room—I can be held liable if somebody hurts himself."

"I . . . sorry, Bruiser." Milton's face had fallen as low as his oxford shoe heels. "I'll buy you a case of beer."

"I don't need your beer, Milt."

"Bruiser, you always need beer," August pointed out.

"Not when it comes as a pity party." And not lately. He'd been cutting back on the beer and spending more time working out. The physical vigor had done him good, fed his body and fueled his mind. His mental outlook wasn't clouded by liquor and poker. And he was feeling good about that. He hated to examine why the change in routine. Because deep down, he knew the answer smelled like lemon verbena.

"Then let's not call it pity beer. Let's call it something else." Lou didn't spell out the gist of his suggestion, and Jake didn't ask.

"I have to close up." He was going to have to talk to Alex Cordova, a carpenter who had a shop out on Elm, and see when Alex could come by and install replacement planks of wood. With the hole being the way it was, Alex would have to cut it back to the floor joists and replace an even bigger section than the actual hole. "Everybody collect their gear and head out."

"But, Bruiser—" Milton called.

"It's okay, Milt. Let it go."

Jake walked away, not really interested in what the fellows were going to propose. There was a time, not long ago, when he would have been up for whatever they had in mind.

He went toward his office, forgoing giving the handle of his Liberty machine a pull. He wasn't in the mood to measure his strength today. He already knew he could break a guy's leg without any effort. But he wouldn't do that to Milton. He kidded around about trouncing them, but that was just gym talk.

Hell, he wouldn't do that to anybody.

The only person who gave him any credit these days was . . .

Truvy Valentine.

She thought he was thoughtful.

He was getting in deep here with feelings for her. Big mistake. But they'd started and he didn't know how to stop them.

The day he'd brought her Maynard, he hadn't been prepared for her to be wearing next to nothing. After he entered her apartment, his entire body had tightened when he saw her in full view. He knew she had a voluptuous figure. He hadn't realized just how voluptuous tall women could be.

He'd had to call on all the stamina and control he possessed not to kiss her senseless and lay her down over the bed. He knew going to her house was bucking trouble. The townspeople wouldn't look the other way if he visited a single woman underneath their noses. He knew it was a crossing-the-line kind of thing. But it hadn't stopped him.

Hell, buying her that parakeet meant he was taking their relationship from impersonal to personal. A man didn't give a woman a companion bird unless he caught himself always anticipating when he could see her. And a man didn't kiss a woman with his entire mouth and walk away unaffected.

Sweet Judas—who was he fooling? He did that kind of thing in Waverly and Alder and walking away had never bothered him. Women came and went in his life. He enjoyed them, the feel of their skin, the smell of their hair, the taste of their lips. He took them to bed. That's all they wanted. That's all he needed.

Why the hell, then, hadn't he visited any of his lady friends since Truvy Valentine had come to town? He'd always been meaning to. But he kept telling himself he couldn't get away. The business. Mr. Physique. Paperwork. There was always something standing in the way.

Another lie.

Jake moved behind his desk and sat down, no longer in the mood to look at the pictures in *Sporting Life* magazine. He leaned his upper body back in his chair and thought about what was going on in *Crime and Punishment*. He'd made it to part one, chapter three. The story wasn't really picking up in the way he'd hoped, but he was forcing himself to read the anvil-weighted book. Luzhin had revealed himself as a selfish ass. And Raskolnikov—whose name Jake couldn't get beyond pronouncing as *Rash-Nickel*—thought his crime was discovered.

For the most part, the plot confused Jake. And frustrated him. Getting through the pages had become a struggle because of his lack of education. He was going to prove to himself he could read the whole thing.

Even if it put him to sleep.

The five members of the Barbell Club intruded on Jake's thoughts as they filed into the office.

Jake hoisted his feet onto the corner of his desk, boots hitting hard, as he knit his fingers together and rested them on his chest.

"Me and the boys," Milt began, "we—"

Lou finished. "We want to smooth things over—all of us."

"Yeah," August said. "We feel bad, Bruiser. We want to make up for Milton's putting a hole in your floor."

"Don't remind him, you nitwit," Milton scoffed.

Walfred put in, "We want to propose another bet. A sure winner for you, Bruiser. That way you won't feel like the beer is pity beer."

"Exactly." Lou expanded his chest. "So we propose you can't make five consecutive smoke rings from one puff of your cigar."

Even Reverend Stoll from the church knew Jake could do that.

Jake gazed at Lou and dryly commented, "That's not a bet. It's a sure thing."

"Well . . ." Milton began, ". . . that's the point here. We wanted to give you something we knew you could do so you could win and then get the beer."

"I don't need to bet you boys anything." Jake inverted the mesh of his fingers and cracked his finger joints, eight at once.

"But we want to do this, on account of your being behind us in the Mr. Physique contest." August looked genuinely sincere, his unruly hair combed in place by a rake of his fingers.

"I told you Bruiser needed a challenge. That's why my idea about Miss Valentine was a good one," Gig said.

The mention of Truvy's name made Jake swallow

hard and put his guard up. Clenching his teeth, he kept the curses from flowing out of his mouth.

Walfred came back with, "But that bet is too much of a sure loss. He couldn't get her to go to dinner with him at the restaurant and he's had plenty of time to change her mind."

"Walfred's right about that, Gig." Lou shook his head. "Any bets about Bruiser taking Miss Valentine to the Valentine's Day dance are as good as lost, and then Bruiser can't get his beer."

Milton mumbled, "I hate to agree with you boys, but Bruiser would have more of a chance escorting Walter Zurick's mule. And with a ribbon around its neck."

Gig spoke up. "Now wait a minute—let's give Bruiser some credit. I think he can do it. So what do you say, Bruiser?"

Jake's pulse slowed to near nothing; he felt as if his blood had thickened to the consistency of heavy machine oil. And he swore the taste of it filled his mouth—metallic, bitter. He stared in turn at the faces above him, waiting expectantly, wanting him to take the challenge.

He should take them on. Laugh some laughs. Joke around. Talk about winning. Offer them all cigars to seal the deal.

Instead, he wanted to kick their asses out of his office. But he couldn't send them packing because he'd developed a conscience in the past few weeks. Conscience or not, though, he was still a businessman who had to make a living, to eat and pay his bills.

But he didn't have to take on a bet. And he didn't have to explain why he wouldn't.

"No." The single word cut like a dull knife.

"No, Bruiser?" Milton's expression grew confused.

"No."

The air in the room closed in. Jake did everything he could to keep both his facial expression and body language impartial.

After a long moment, Milton spoke up. "You think it over, Bruiser. You can change your mind. You don't have to agree to anything. Just bring her to the dance and we'll know why."

Shifting his weight in the seat of the chair, Jake rubbed a hand over his jaw. "I have to lock up now."

"Sure."

"Okay, Bruiser."

"Right."

As soon as they were gone, Jake picked up a set of dumbbells. With iron in each hand, he contracted his biceps and curled both arms as far as possible, then extended them downward under full control. He felt contractions peak in his muscles over and over. He continued until sweat ran from every pore and he couldn't do another set without his knees buckling from exhaustion.

Truvy picked up Edwina's mail from the general delivery grate on the way to Wolcott's Dance Academy. As she closed the studio door, anxiety drummed in her thoughts. There were two letters— one from Miss Pond, the other from her students. The return address on the latter included the words: *Your Economics Class.*

Without delay, she deposited her handbag and schedule book on the oak Victrola cabinet and tore open the envelope of the girls' correspondence.

She recognized the penmanship. Myra Jepsen. Of

all the students in her class, Myra had the most elegant handwriting. But each girl signed her name individually at the bottom of the stationery.

January 9, 1902

To our dear Miss Valentine:

Please forgive us for not writing sooner. We have all thought about it scads of times. But with winter break and us going home to our families—and then Mrs. Mumford—our good manners were neglected. We regret the lapse in deportment.

But now that we have gathered together, we're all agog to tell you what has transpired at St. Francis in your absence.

Clara Jane received a marriage proposal from her Harvard beau. (I told him I'd have to think it over, but of course I'll say yes.) Essie accepted a social engagement from a boy at Ward's. (Parlor games, but Miss Pond doesn't know it.) Verda Mae has decided never to wear flounces again because they make her look plump. (I would consider lace ruffles.) Impi stuffed her shirtwaist with her pillow case. (I did not!) Laura said she kissed a man who called her snookums. (I'm not telling who.) Essie learned 'Oh Promise Me!' on the organ so she can play it at Clara Jane's wedding. (If my parents will let me travel to Vermont for the ceremony.) Our Annabelle tried a switch from the Sears and Roebuck catalog. (The length of golden hair is four feet and looks real when pinned the right way.) And myself, I am planning on taking a governess position in Atlanta at the end of our term. (She'll get paid thirty-five dollars a month!)

As for Mrs. Mumford . . . she is tolerable. But she's not

*you. We wanted you to know how sorry we are that you
got into trouble for reading that book to us. Laura discreetly looked for a copy at the Boise library, but naturally they didn't have one. Could you explain what it
meant when you read "gratification of normal
impulses"? Until then—*

Your very devoted students,

*Miss Myra Jepsen, Miss Clara Jane Hill, Miss Impi
Tretheway, Miss Annabelle Gardner, Miss Carolee
Weaver, Miss Verda Mae Johnson, Miss Essie Kerwin,
Miss Laura Case*

The words in the letter filled Truvy's head as she
lowered her arm, the stationery firmly in her hand.
She hadn't expected the painful squeeze to her heart
from having read their news. Not since the day she'd
left St. Francis did such a strong sense of loss assail
her. The result of her departure was clearly not as
traumatic for them as it had been for her. The girls
were getting along as if nothing had happened. They
had not written *Mrs. Mumford is an ogre. You must try
and return at once.* They had not written *Miss
Valentine, you are irreplaceable.* Just: *She's not you.*

Begrudging them their focus on their own lives
would be unforgivable on her part. They were young
ladies, on the brink of womanhood, facing marriage and
opportunities. They were eager to venture out of St.
Francis, to learn more about life. Of that, she was proud.
But she could no more give them a detailed definition of
what *The Science of Life* meant about "gratification of
normal impulses" than she could stand five feet two
inches. Doing so would mean her sure termination.

She was now faced with how to reply and remain true to her standards and to her students' inquisitiveness—and to the promise she had made Miss Pond.

Miss Pond.

Truvy opened the second letter. The sentences were concise, and she read them in a rush.

> *The financial committee has voted on disciplinary measures and has agreed that no further action is needed. Your leave of absence has hereby been lifted. There remains one problem: Mrs. Mumford is still in your classroom. But I see signs of her interest waning. Her affiliation with the Boise Belles is overshadowing her duties. They're putting on a production of Ye Ancient Dames and she has her heart set on playing the lead. Should she land the part, which I'm quite certain she will do, you'll regain your position. I hope this news pleases you. I'll send a telegram as soon as the outcome is final.*

Truvy folded the letter and slowly returned it to the envelope. She had assumed that when she received notification of Miss Pond's decision, her trunks would be halfway packed before she read the signature in closing. Instead, she stood in the large studio with her emotions in a whirl of uncertainty. The steadfast determination she'd felt less than two weeks ago had begun to trickle away.

For the first time since leaving Idaho, Truvy questioned returning to the school. And not for reasons she could have ever foreseen.

Her gaze went to the closed curtains and she walked to the long row of windows. Opening the curtains, she looked out the windowpanes, searching for a glimpse of Jake in the gymnasium. The reflection of wedged sky in the square of glass didn't reveal signs the building was occupied. Jake's business had been closed for several days. He'd told her he'd sustained some damage to his floor. Yesterday, a carpenter had come by and repaired it. She assumed Jake would reopen today.

The fact that he wasn't there made her feel empty.

It was an inconvenient moment to recognize she was falling in love with Jake Brewster.

Under the spell of that admittance, she felt the heat that was radiating from the Acme warm the back of her neck. She still wore her cape. Turning, she went to the heater and paused.

Next to the pipe collar lay Jake's cigar.

She brought the tightly rolled cylinder of fine tobacco to her nostrils and sniffed. She closed her eyes as a cynical inner voice questioned the choice to be made between conformity and rebellion.

At this moment, the answer was easy.

There was a fire in the dance studio.

From the gymnasium, Jake saw a billow of white smoke clouding up the window. Moses Zipp, whose barbershop backed the alley two doors down, could see it, too. Standing in the narrow alleyway, Moses turned and ran toward Birch Avenue—a man whose mission was to get the fire department.

Jake, on the other hand, had his own alarm that went off.

He had left his cigar over there that morning, and he hoped to God it wasn't what was torching the place.

Flinging the back door open and fumbling with the

key to Edwina's place, Jake unlocked the studio door and slammed it open so hard, the hinges groaned. His sharp gaze cut through the hazy smoke and went straight to the heater.

But there was no fire. No smoldering cigar.

The choking coughs to his left made him frantically look down. Sitting on the floor, with her back propped up against the wall and her bent knees pulled up next to her breasts, Truvy held a cigar between her fingers and thumb.

His Ybor.

"J-Jake." His name was mingled with smoke that she exhaled, and her voice wavered as if her stomach was turning upside down.

Relief, irritation, and surprise clashed inside him. "What in the hell are you doing?"

"Smoking." She drew in another puff, then promptly coughed so hard it was like the sound Barkly made when he treed a squirrel—a deep and throaty bark.

"I swear, Truvy, you're going to puke if you draw that smoke into your lungs one more time."

"But . . . I wanted . . ." she wheezed, ". . . to give cigars a try . . . while I had the opportunity." Disregarding his advice, she took hearty puffs on the cigar, emitting tufts of smoke that rolled out the open door into the alleyway.

Jake remembered Moses Zipp.

And the fire department.

He reached down, grabbed Truvy's hand, and yanked her to her feet.

"*Ahhh*—you're making me dizzy!" she protested when he pulled her out the door, shut it in place, and dragged her into the gymnasium. He let her go only to lock the gym door; then he took her by the upper arm and hauled her into his office. After he released her, she wobbled, face on the greenish side. She made a valiant effort to keep the cigar clamped between her lips, but it began to sag, ready to drop and scorch the papers on his desk.

Raising his arm, he ordered, "Give me that."

She parted her lips and the Ybor dropped into his open palm.

He crushed the burning cigar end in the bottom of his ashtray.

The color on Truvy's cheeks would have fit in just fine at a St. Patrick's Day celebration. Her eyelids were heavy. She kept swallowing, licking her lips. He knew the signs. She was going to upchuck on his floor.

"For God's sake, don't do it here!" he ordered, then pushed her through his kitchen and beyond, into first his bedroom and then the lavatory.

Two seconds later, she vomited into his water closet.

He held onto her shoulders until she lost whatever she'd eaten that day. Then, on a whimper, she slumped against the wall on her feet. He kept a hold on her while one-handing the cold-water spigot on his sink faucet. After dunking a towel into the basin, he squeezed most of the water out and pressed the cloth to her forehead.

"I'm feeling under the weather," she mumbled, her eyes closed and water trickling down her cheeks. "I believe I have one foot in the grave." Her melodramatic declaration was out of character. Something must have set her off into the doldrums.

"You'll live." On that, he pulled the chain to the W.C.

Keeping the towel on her face, he aimed her out of the lavatory and into the bedroom. The room was dark, the shade on the only window lowered. Its wall colors and decor were on the earthy side, the hues of tanned leather. He owned walnut furniture, its heaviness making for a sturdy and masculine den. Everything fit together in a way he appreciated—the narrow wardrobe with its swing frame mirror, chest on chest, secretary desk, brass globe lamp he used for reading. He liked burnt umber and deep red together, so those were the two colors that made up his draperies and bed quilt.

Once he maneuvered Truvy beside his bed, he ordered, "Lie down until your stomach settles."

To his surprise, she didn't protest about the lack of propriety in the situation. She must have really felt like crap.

As soon as she lay on the bed, ankles together and skirt properly in place, she took off the towel. She gazed at him, narrowing her eyes and then lifting her brows. Her lips parted as she gave him a long, drawn-out stare in silence. Sudden surprise flitted across her features as she said, "Now I know what it is. You're wearing spectacles."

Jake bit down on an oath. He'd forgotten he had his glasses on.

When he'd noticed the smoke in the dance studio, he'd been applying a coat of varnish on the new floor planks, a job that required keen eyes, so he'd put on his gold-rimmed peepers.

Without a word, he unhooked the curved earpieces from behind his ears and slipped the glasses into the breast pocket of his shirt.

Standing over her, he said, "I'll get you something to drink."

"A brandy?"

He shot her a look and clarified his statement: "A bicarbonate."

"Oh . . ." The disappointment in her tone was as obvious as the clang of bells and clatter of shod hooves growing louder across Dogwood Place.

"What's that?"

"Fire wagons."

"Oh no . . ." With a loose curl teasing her earlobe, she struggled to sit up, then groaned and fell back. "A fire. It was me. The cigar. I have to go explain."

"Forget about it, Tru. The fire department will see there isn't a fire at the studio and they'll leave."

Clamping the towel back on her brow, she looked at him from beneath the fringed edge. She spoke in a weak whisper. "If the fire department found me—instead of you—smoking that cigar . . . I would have died."

"Forget about it," he said again, then left for the kitchen. He mixed up a glass of soda and water, then brought it to her.

He stopped shy of the doorway and stared at the bed, one thought freezing him: Truvy was the only woman he'd ever brought to his bedroom.

Some of her curls were out of place. She scratched her nose, then gave a long, shuddering sigh and turned her head. With luminous eyes, she looked at her surroundings as if suddenly realizing where she was.

"This is your bedroom," she commented.

"Right." He walked into the room.

"I—I shouldn't be here."

"No. But you are." He sat on the side of the bed, dipping the mattress beneath his weight. "And you're staying until you get blushing pink back on your cheeks."

Absently, she lifted a hand to the side of her face.

"Drink this."

"Thank you." She took the glass. He reached behind her and plumped up the tapestry pillows so she could partially sit up.

She took a sip of the cloudy mixture, grimaced, then blinked. Her lashes fluttered next to her pale complexion as she added in a low tone, "And Maynard thanks you for rescuing his mother."

Jake had never considered parenting a pet, but if that's how she wanted to look at it, who was he to say otherwise? Seeing what she'd been through, he wanted to cheer her up and offer the right thing. "I'm sure you're treating him like a son."

"A . . . son." Moisture glittered in her eyes. Her lower lip grew plump and pouty. "Yes. Maynard's the only child I'll ever have."

Sweet Judas. He'd said something wrong.

"Truvy, I didn't mean—"

"What's that smell?" she asked, then rubbed her nose again with her free hand. "It's strong."

"Varnish," he supplied. "I was painting the floor."

She drank more of the bicarbonate, then leaned back on the pillow and held the glass out for him to hold for her. "Why is it you've never worn your glasses before?"

"I do. You just never saw me."

"You do in front of people?"

"No."

"Why not?"

He was uncomfortable with the line of conversation they were drawing, but after she'd done something as intimate as throwing up in his W.C., he figured he owed an honest answer. You couldn't get much more personal than puking in front of a person. "I don't think glasses suit my business."

"I don't understand."

"Strong men have to have strong eyes."

"President Roosevelt wears glasses and he's a very powerful man." Her gaze drifted to the bedside table where Jake kept Edwina's book. He used his carte vista as a page marker. It wasn't in the text very deep, a clear sign he hadn't progressed far. "You're reading *Crime and Punishment*."

"When I get the chance."

"I couldn't read beyond the first chapter. It bored me."

Jake felt his mouth curve, and his pulse quickened. "It did?"

"Completely." She reached for the glass again.

He asked out of curiosity, "What do you like to read?"

She sipped the baking soda elixir, then lowered the volume of her voice when replying, "*Madame Bovary*. I've read it four times."

"Who is she?"

"A French doctor's wife ..."

The subject matter didn't sound compelling to Jake.

"... who finds herself," Truvy added, "ruled by her passions. The natural instinct in a woman that demands fulfillment."

There must have been sex in the book. Or a damn good hint of it. Soft pink touched her cheeks. She was recovering from her ordeal; he was discovering he was glad she'd smoked his Ybor. If she hadn't, she wouldn't be here. With him. In his room. Talking. As if it were the most natural place for her to be.

He didn't want her to leave.

He stared at her, pensive and fascinated. The fine brown hair of her right eyebrow was ruffled from the towel, which had fallen off. He watched how the beat of her pulse lightly drummed at her temple. The skin of her forehead looked like silk. He found himself pleasantly aroused—not to a sexual degree, but by her voice, her presence.

"The ending is tragic. After she's lost everything, she realizes that Dr. Bovary was the one true constant in her life. The one man who . . ." Truvy's eyes met his and her words drifted to nothing.

Jake's body felt heavy and warm. Her gaze melted into his; he fought a compulsion to cover her lips. But it was the tender contemplation in her eyes that stopped him. That, and the quiet confusion that gripped his chest. There were a hundred definable things about her that attracted him. And a hundred undefinable ones beckoning him to discover.

"Would you be . . . that is . . ." She fought with words, then came right out and asked, "Is there a chance you're marriage-inclined?"

The question threw him. It seemed to come from nowhere, and without thought, he gave his stock answer. "Not hardly."

"I didn't think so." She struggled to pull in a breath, and he wished he hadn't said what he had.

Only . . . he didn't tell Truvy his response was reflexive and questionable in light of the fact it was *her* asking him if there was a chance he'd ever propose. He'd never asked a woman to marry him before. He and Laurette had fallen into bed one night and gone over to the justice of the peace the next morning. He'd been convinced he loved her like crazy. It wasn't until his divorce that he'd realized he'd been in lust with his wife, not in love.

Up until this point, he'd thought love made fools out of men.

Now he wasn't so sure he wasn't the biggest fool of them all.

Chapter
❦16❦

The apartment came with an oil stove that had only one burner three inches wide. A griddle fit over the iron plate and could be heated to a sufficient cooking temperature, as Truvy found out while attempting to fix herself a scrambled egg and cut of ham. She'd watched Mrs. Plunkett several times to know the pan required a fair amount of lard.

Using a spoon, she scooped a large portion of the white fat and whacked it into the griddle. The fat sizzled and splattered as she cracked her egg.

Maynard chirped from his cage and she glanced at the green-and-blue bird. In a short amount of time, she'd gotten used to him—but not to his sleeping schedule.

He flew from his perch to his seed bottle, making a mess with the hulls of feed. They sprayed out of the cage and littered the table. He was messy, but he was a companion.

The only companion she hoped to have in spinsterhood.

She hating feeling sorry for herself. As she wiped a tear from the corner of her eye with her knuckle, she vowed she *wouldn't* feel sorry for herself.

Quit being foolish.

But she hadn't been able to forget what she'd asked Jake Brewster. Nor the reply he'd given her. She'd known he was a man who'd say he'd never get married.

Why did the confirmation have to hurt so much?

She scrambled her egg with a fork, barely aware of her efforts. It would have been another thing if he'd been marriage-inclined—but toward someone else.

"That's something to feel better about. Isn't it, Maynard?"

The parakeet dug into his seed, flinging hulls as he ate.

Truvy watched as the lard melted into a hot and smoky puddle. Mrs. Plunkett's lard had never smoked, but she was an expert and Truvy was a novice. She made an adjustment to the flame. Two biscuits she'd bought from the restaurant yesterday warmed on top of the heater. She'd wrapped them in a gingham cloth.

"I can do for myself, can't I, Maynard?" Truvy said to the parakeet.

This hot meal was a testing ground. It was the first meal she'd ever made for herself—entirely on her own.

Ever since she'd moved into the apartment, she'd brought in goods from the mercantile that didn't require cooking on the burner. Sometimes she had splurged and eaten at Nannie's. The other times, she took her meals at Tom and Edwina's house.

The lard smoke grew odious, and she fanned her hand over the griddle. If she put the ham in, that should cool down the pan. So she did. The meat seared and spit as soon as it touched the heavy cast iron black bottom.

Maynard flapped and flew from the feeder to the swing, bobbing his head and squawking.

"Yes, I know it smells smoky in here. But there's no help for it."

Truvy was rushing a bit because she had to be at the studio to teach an early class, and then she'd be off to meet Edwina at the Harmony church to go over instructions for Elizabeth's baptism. Crescencia Dufresne was sponsoring the baby and Truvy was the second-in-line godmother. Then later today, she was supposed to have a dancing lesson of her own.

The schottische. With Jake.

She didn't know how she'd get through it. How could she face him after yesterday? He'd saved her from sure and complete mortification with the fire department—only for her to show Jake sure and complete mortification when she disgraced herself in his water closet. She'd been ridiculously naïve to think she could smoke that dreaded cigar without it affecting her. Women weren't made to endure such things. Their sensibilities were too—well, sensitive.

Poking the ham with her fork, she found it wouldn't move. The bottom was stuck to the pan. She had to grasp the pan's handle with a towel to get the needed leverage for another try. This time, she was met with success.

And a charcoal-covered side of meat.

Smoke swirled up from beneath the ham, the lard sizzling away.

Maynard screeched.

"I know!" she snapped while giving the egg one last

stir in its bowl before spilling it in over the ham. The moisture from the egg should ease the burning of the meat.

The odor of smoke reminded Truvy to put the fire department's note in her handbag. They'd pinned a call letter on the door of the studio, notifying Edwina of a potential fire problem the source of which they were uncertain.

Truvy knew. And she had to confess to Edwina today.

Jake had been kind enough to walk her over to the dance academy after the fire wagons left. He'd helped her lift the windows and air the room out. A short while later, her students had begun to arrive and he left discreetly out the back door—the same door through which he'd come to save her.

She hadn't slept last night for thinking about him. About his bedroom and its deep, dark colors. And about lying on his bed, which was soft and large with plenty of pillows. He'd taken care of her, brought her something to settle her stomach. They'd talked about books. She'd never thought he'd really read that stale old tome of Edwina's. And she'd certainly never thought she'd reveal she had an affinity for a story based on immorality. For surely Madame Bovary was immoral with her many love affairs, and yet, Flaubert painted Emma in a way that drew Truvy to the story in wistful longing.

What would it be like to know a lover's touch?

With a hand that slightly trembled, Truvy folded the fire note and put it in her purse, then closed the clasp. She stuck a forefinger in Maynard's cage. He didn't come anywhere near her offering of a perch. He merely stared—two beady black eyes. Then after a long moment, he preened his feathers as if she weren't there.

Sighing, Truvy turned back to her ham and egg.

She stabbed at them with her fork. They were inedible. Why bother to try to fix things when she could never eat such a mess? So she took the griddle off the burner, careful of the lard still hissing, and went toward the heater and her biscuits. The thought of butter and jam on them, a small salvation, made her mouth water.

Only . . . when she glanced at the heater, she saw the gingham napkin on fire.

"Oh my!" she screamed.

Maynard screamed with her.

With nothing to use for picking up the flaming cloth, she quickly went for her wash pitcher to douse the fire. The water put out the napkin and biscuits, but it also trickled down the heater collar sleeves and into the embers of wood. A mighty burst of blue-gray smoke erupted and Truvy flailed her arms as if she could dissipate its potency. But there was no help for the rolling cloud. It grew larger and stronger until the smell was all but overpowering.

There was no fire, but the smoke was enough to choke and make her gasp for air. Fumbling her way toward the window, she unlocked the latch and lifted the sash all the way up. A sharp gust of cold hit her, sucking the warm smoke outside.

Flying around in his birdcage by the window, Maynard grew more and more excited.

"Don't worry, Maynard. I'm not making the same mistake twice."

This time, she'd keep the window open to get rid of the smoke. If she'd done that in the studio, the fire department wouldn't have been called. She picked up the towel and fanned the grayish haze out the open window in large drafts. Maynard continued his hollering, spraying seeds and tinkling his bell with the tip of his beak.

"Yes, I know."

The apartment smelled horribly.

She ventilated the room as much as possible. Maynard began to quiet down, but the odor remained heavy. Truvy took a quick glance at her watch. She had to leave right now or she'd be late.

Lowering the window, she stopped the bottom sill four inches up so that Maynard would have fresh air in her absence.

"There you go, Maynard." She put her forefinger in the cage once more to reassure him. This time, the most amazing thing happened.

He lit on her finger.

"Why . . . Maynard." She put her nose up to the cage and looked at him. "You do like me."

Smiling, Truvy stood there and enjoyed the feeling of being wanted by a tiny creature. She vowed she would always take care of him and see him live a long and happy life.

Maynard flew off and Truvy collected her cape and handbag.

"I'll be back, Maynard."

Then she opened the door and took a last glance over her shoulder. The room was a disaster, but she'd just have to clean it up later when she returned.

Jake stood in Wolcott's Sporting Goods and Excursions talking with Tom and pitching rubber balls at Buttkiss, a humpty-dumpty target with hat, ears,

mouth, and tongue. Points were given for each direct
shot to the clownlike face, the hat coming in highest at
twenty. But it was better to strike Buttkiss's teeth
down; they were held in place by hinges, and as soon
as a ball knocked them all in, a tongue shot out.

Taking a turn, Tom coiled back his arm and let the
ball fly. He clipped the target on the nose.

"Nice," Jake commented, standing in the aisle of
camouflage gear. "Bet Cordova would knock Buttkiss
off the wall."

Tom shrugged. "Hell, I don't let Alex Cordova anywhere near Buttkiss. He'd blast a hole *through* my
wall." Handing over a ball to Jake, he went on to add,
"Alex said he was over at your place the other day fixing your floor."

"Yeah, he was over. Damn talented on many
accounts. You can't even see where the damage was."

Not only was Alex a woodworker and carpenter
but he was also the star pitcher on the Harmony
Keystones' baseball team. Recently married, he'd spoken a lot about his wife while he'd been working on
Jake's floor. Tom talked a lot about his wife, too. Come
to think of it, Shay Dufresne always had a word or two
about Crescencia to share. None of these men had
been running away from marriage. They seemed to
have walked into it with eyes wide open. And the end
results were obvious.

Happiness.

Jake rolled the ball in his hand a minute, looking at
Tom and then about the store for a few seconds. It was
a nice place to come when a man felt like being
around nothing soft or frilly or remotely reminding
him of women. Except for the long since dried bouquet of flowers in the stuffed grizzly bear's grasp, Tom

ran a purely masculine place. A retreat. Every time he came by, it made Jake think about taking up duck hunting. And he didn't much care for duck.

"What's on your mind, Jake?" Tom's question invaded Jake's thoughts. "You've been quiet since you got here and you keep drifting off on me. I know it's not because you like the look of my deer scent display," Tom joked.

Reeling his arm back, Jake released the ball and whacked the target in the mouth, knocking teeth down and making Buttkiss's tongue appear. "I've been wondering about something."

"What?"

"How do you like being married to Edwina?"

"No complaints." The answer was quick and forthright.

"Not a one?"

"Not a one," Tom replied.

Jake nodded, walking behind the counter to sit on a stool. This kind of domestic conversation was one he'd never had with a man before. Flo Ziegfeld had doled out two words over his wedding to Laurette Everleigh: *big mistake*. But they'd come after the certificate of marriage had been signed by the judge. Jake had married Laurette without a plan.

From the childhood he'd had, Jake didn't know how he would feel about being a father. His father had been a piss-poor parent, and even now, Jake hadn't heard from him in over ten months. His mother— gone. How could Jake ever be a parent when he had nobody to show him the way of it?

"How do you like being a father?" Jake asked, gazing at a box of colorful fishing lures.

"I love my daughter more than anything," Tom said,

joining Jake at the counter. It was nearing time to close the store and the place was void of customers. "There've been rough spots. Edwina's emotional right now, but she's a strong woman. When you own your own business, you have to be running it. We're damn lucky to have Marvel-Anne and Truvy for the times I can't be with Edwina. I take care of the baby when I'm home."

"How do you know what to do? You didn't have a father around."

"You just know, Jake. I can't explain it." Tom fiddled with a pencil and tablet. "When I first held Elizabeth in my arms, I became her daddy. There's no describing that feeling."

Jake rested his elbows on the counter. "You had a brother, growing up, so I imagine that's part of where the feeling comes from."

"Maybe. But we weren't close. We patched things up only recently. It was good to have him up here for Christmas." Tom opened a can of Powell's candied nuts and passed them over to Jake. "You hear anything from your dad lately?"

"Naw."

They ate walnuts, each in thought. Then after a while, Tom turned to Jake. "Are you thinking about getting married again?"

Jake didn't have an immediate answer. He'd spoken too quickly with Truvy. He wouldn't do that again—even though his feelings hadn't changed to make him say otherwise. "I wonder about it, that's all."

"I think you ought to wonder hard," Tom advised, dropping several nuts into his mouth; chewing around them, he added, "And if my wife has anything to do with it, you'll be wondering about it over Miss Valentine."

* * *

Truvy didn't show up for her lesson.

Dusk fell and Jake waited an hour for her. He gave up and went to the gymnasium, thinking she must have been detained with Edwina. After being in the gym five minutes, he disregarded that thought, locked up, and walked to Truvy's apartment.

The night was pleasantly cold—not frigid, not snowing. But snow was on the ground, banked and soft from the afternoon brilliance of sun melting into the mounds. The steps to Truvy's place were cleared of ice. He glanced at the window upstairs; the interior was dark. She probably wasn't there, but he'd try anyway.

He kept his disappointment from showing. He'd watched the clock all day, waiting to see her, anticipating when he could enfold her in his arms, if only to show her how to dance. That she hadn't shown up had caused loneliness to seep into his soul, only confirming that he was feeling more for her than he'd previously acknowledged.

He climbed the stairs, knocked on the door, and waited.

No answer.

He hadn't thought there would be. But something compelled him to twist the knob and see if the door was locked. It wasn't. The brass doorknob turned in his grasp and he pushed the door inward.

The first thing he noticed was the stale odor of smoke.

"Truvy?"

The inside of the apartment was so dark, he couldn't adjust his eyes enough to see a shape or form that was recognizable. Barely discernible in the corner was a glow from the heater. The coals had long gone beyond being ignited. His foot hit an object—the leg of the table, if recollection served him.

Swearing, he reached into his coat pocket and brought his match case out. He fumbled for a stick, then struck the tip; a tiny flame erupted into a wavering light. Extending his arm, he dragged the illumination from the bed to the table. The table was a mess. Eggshells, greasy fork, and griddle with charred remains. He moved forward and passed the match by the heater to the other corner by the window. There on the floor, Truvy sat with a blank expression on her face.

"Truvy . . ." Jake searched quickly for the lamp and lit it. Then he went toward her and dropped to his knees.

"Jake . . . ?" she uttered.

Her hair had come down from its pins and she shivered from the cold in the room. How long had her heater been out? Had somebody been here? Had somebody—

"What happened?" he all but growled. If anyone had dared touch her, he would be going to prison for murder, because the culprit wouldn't be alive in the morning. "Truvy? Did somebody come here?"

She didn't answer.

"Truvy?"

"No . . ." she whispered, a tear rolling down her cheek.

"You have to tell me what happened so I can help you." He touched her arm and she winced. "Are you hurt?"

No reply.

He looked her over, quickly. She sat with her knees bent and her hands in her lap—with something else. A floral-embroidered handkerchief with lace edges. Wrapped around a tiny lump in a neat little circle, the tails tied evenly, carefully, with a gentle hand.

"Truvy?" Jake reached out, wanting to take whatever it was she had.

She wouldn't let him. Staring up through the fringe of tear-dampened lashes, she said in sheer despair, "I killed Maynard."

On that, shuddering sobs shook her shoulders. She slumped forward, dropped her forehead to her knees, and cried like there was no tomorrow.

The news of her admission hit Jake and he didn't know how to react to it. She'd killed the parakeet? Not on purpose. Not Truvy. She wouldn't kill Maynard. Whatever misfortune had befallen the bird, it hadn't been at Truvy's hand.

Damn that salesman in Waverly! He'd sworn the bird was healthy.

"Ah, Truvy, don't cry. It's not your fault." Jake laid a soothing hand on her shoulder, wanting to take Maynard from her. She didn't need to be holding onto a dead bird. But the way she was hunched over and clinging to her legs, he couldn't reach the hankie.

"I—it is my fault," she cried. "All my fault . . . my M-Maynard!"

"Truvy, give him to me."

"N-no."

"You're not thinking clearly. You're upset. I'll take him and get rid of him."

"No!"

Sweet Judas! He didn't mean it to sound like that. "I mean I'll make sure he's resting comfortably."

She looked up, searched his eyes, then asked, "Where?"

"I'll—I'll bury him for you."

"You will?"

"Yes, Truvy, I will."

"In a pretty little box?"

"Ah ... okay. A nice box."

"With his bell and his cuttlebone?"

"Yes."

"And a colorful flower to keep him company?"

It was winter, there were no flowers in bloom. Jake racked his brain for a substitute. "How about a cigar band?" The band on his Ybor was red and gold with blue writing. And it was convenient. Right in his breast pocket.

"No."

No. "All right. We don't have to use that."

"I want a flower. Use one from my hat. It's hanging on the wall by the door."

"I'll get it. You give me Maynard first."

"No."

Jake gritted his teeth. The right words didn't come to him; he fought to be tactful but gently persuasive. "Sweetheart, he's diseased and it's not good for you to be holding him."

"He's not diseased," she replied sharply. "How can you say that?" A fat tear plopped onto her bodice front. "He was a charming little bird and I've ... I've treated him deplorably. I should be arrested!"

A fresh crying jag started anew as she cradled the handkerchief next to her breasts.

He didn't want to get forceful with her, but that bird had been doomed by a health malady and it was going to have to go. "Truvy—"

That was all he was able to say.

"I killed Maynard by leaving the window open!

He froze to death and it's my fault! I didn't know. I didn't know. I just didn't . . . know. I've never had a bird before. I didn't know!" The words came freely now, just as freely as the tears splashing the dark fabric covering her breasts. "I burned my breakfast and I thought I was doing the right thing for Maynard by leaving the window open four inches while I was out. I feared the smoke would harm him. Dammit," she swore, her language taking him aback, "why can't I cook without a fiasco?" She sucked in a shaky breath. "When I came back from the church, expecting my fluffy little green-and-blue sunshine to greet me, he wasn't on his perch. He was on the bottom of his cage, his tiny feet stiff and his eyes . . . o-o-o-o-o-open."

She did do the parakeet in. He might have had a chance if Jake hadn't hung his cage next to the window. Although Jake wasn't a bird expert, he felt irresponsible in not spelling out to Truvy that Maynard had to keep quite warm.

"I'm guilty! It was me. I'm the horrible mother."

Jake gripped her shoulder. "Tru, look at me."

She slowly faced him.

"You didn't do it on purpose. It'd be one thing if you did. Hell, I knew a kid back in Brooklyn when I was growing up who used to set cats' tails on fire with turpentine." He put pressure on her muscles as emphasis. "The little shit knew it was wrong and didn't care. You cared about Maynard. This was an accident."

"I loved Maynard."

"Yeah . . . okay. You loved him. That's good."

"Just like I love—" She hiccuped and cut off the thought. "I want to come with you when you bury him. We have to pick out a nice spot. I don't want a cat to dig Maynard up. Not even Edwina's cat—and I *like* Honey Tiger."

"We can do that—find Maynard a nice resting spot."

Truvy moved to stand up but wouldn't hand over the bird. "We have to do it now."

Outside, it was dark as pitch without a moon to give off vague light. To wander around the outskirts of town at night would be like searching on fog-covered banks for the perfect place to fish—a person could only see what was in front of him unless he moved on. And Jake had never been one to fish, because he didn't have the patience.

"Tomorrow we could do a better job for him, Tru—"

Stubbornly, she replied, "Then I'll do it by myself."

Grinding his teeth, Jake helped her to her feet. "All right, sweetheart, we'll do it right now. I'll get a shovel and lantern from the livery."

Chapter

17

They buried Maynard in the woods by Evergreen Creek, beneath a blue spruce with a pretty flouring of snow on its needles. Truvy had asked Jake to dig the hole two feet deep, and he had, without complaint. No cats would be able to get her little Maynard. Once the frozen earth was poured over his tiny box, Truvy had cried a final good-bye to her pet, and she and Jake had walked back home.

With a detour to the Blue Flame Saloon.

Truvy waited outside while Jake disappeared inside. If she could have, she would have gone in with him. But a lady should never feel compelled to sample the forbidden drink; unfortunately, Truvy apparently wasn't a lady. She *did* wonder what alcohol tasted like, as she had wondered about the taste of that cigar. And about the looks of the "fearfully and wonderfully made male anatomy" described in *The Science of Life.*

After a short moment, Jake came out of the saloon and they continued back to her apartment. The lantern light waved over the side steps leading up from the livery. She didn't know what time it was. But she dreaded going into the small room. It was an awful mess and everything reminded her that she'd failed poor Maynard.

Jake hung the lantern on a peg, turned down the flame, and opened the door for her. She stepped inside but didn't move further than the threshold.

"Tru." Jake's hand laid softly on her shoulder. "Wash your face, put your nightgown on, and crawl into bed. I'll clean up."

The very last thing he said barely registered. *Put your nightgown on.* Her thoughts converged on undressing in the same room as Jake. "But I . . ."

"You wash up and I'll take care of something else."

Without another word, he went to Maynard's cage and unhooked it from the wall. After gathering the birdseed and items that had been the parakeet's, Jake stored the things in the cage while Truvy sat on the bed and loosened the laces on her high-heeled black shoes. As she slipped them off, Jake cleaned the birdseed hulls from the table, then wiped off the surface.

Truvy rose and went to the washbasin; the pitcher wasn't there. It was by the heater where she'd left it after dumping the water on the biscuit fire.

"I'll get more water," Jake said. "And I'll leave you alone for a minute." Quietly, he opened the door and took everything of Maynard's outside.

The pump was downstairs and it didn't take long to get water. In his absence, Truvy unbuttoned the front of her dress, removed it, and then took off her undergarments. She moved quickly and efficiently, not wanting to be caught in such a state. Once she was free of her stiff corset and chemise and stockings, she fit her flannel nightgown over her head and made fast work of the pearl buttons in front.

Tossing her hair over her shoulder, she stood there. Waiting. For Jake to come back. When he did, he had the water pitcher in his hand and was without any signs of her parakeet. Thoughtfully, he poured the water into the basin.

"It's ice cold."

"That's all right."

She washed her face while Jake continued to clean up—eggshells into the waste bin, the griddle and plates set aside. Before they'd left, he'd stocked the heater with wood to warm the room on their return. It still felt cold to Truvy. Her feet sank into the bearskin rug beside the bed and she folded her arms across her breasts. Even though she wore a nightgown, she felt naked.

"Into bed, sweetheart." Jake's words seared her, but he meant no untoward implication.

"It's all right . . . I can help you."

"Done."

And he was. The room was cleaned and tidied in no time. "You're very handy," was all Truvy could think to say.

"Cleaning is only one of my many charms," Jake teased, clearly trying to lighten the mood. It was awfully sweet of him. She appreciated it. "Now into bed."

There was an awkwardness, a moment of hesitation. But Truvy did eventually move and pull down the covers on the narrow bed. She felt awfully self-conscious as she slid beneath the sheets and blankets. She couldn't bring herself to lie down. There was something about being flat on her back, in her nightie, with Jake towering over her that made her nervous. So she scooted as far as she could with the two pillows propped up behind her head. She tugged the coverlet all the way up to her chin.

Jake's back was toward her and he stood in front of the table. When he turned around, he handed her a glass barely full.

"Drink this."

She took the glass, their fingers brushing in the transfer. It was like an electric shock of heat surging through her. "I-is it a bicarbonate?"

"No. Brandy."

"Really?"

"That's what I got at the Blue Flame. You needed it, Tru. I don't think I've ever seen a woman cry as hard as you did." He pulled up the chair from the table and straddled it, backward. Arms over the chair's back, he stacked the fists of his hands and rested his chin on them. "You scared me. I thought I'd have to get the doc. Go ahead and drink it. There's not enough in there to get an ant drunk."

"Then perhaps I'll want a second."

Jake's mouth curved. "You do seem to surprise me at the oddest times."

Truvy brought the glass to her lips and sipped. She swallowed, silently choking back the river of flames that poured into her stomach. After throwing up from that cigar, she wouldn't choke on this liquor for anything.

Raising the glass to Jake, she said through watery eyes, "Delish."

Jake merely laughed.

Truvy drank another small amount. Then another, until the glass was empty. There had been only a half-inch's worth of the brandy to begin with.

"Things'll look better in the morning." Jake reached for the glass. She didn't let go.

"Another small splash. Please."

Once she'd burned out her esophagus, the brandy wasn't half bad. She could already feel a lull sweeping over her. A calmness. An ease to her joints and muscles. A languid warmth seeping through her bones, flushing across her skin.

Leaning on the chair, Jake reached for the bottle on the table and gave the glass just a slight bit more.

She drank it while Jake watched. The fire in the heater snapped, a low and dull noise that was soothing, cozy.

"Thank you for helping me with Maynard," Truvy whispered. "I appreciate it."

"It's all right."

She gave him a bittersweet smile, then sipped the brandy, letting herself be relaxed by its effect. Thoughts swirled in her head, much like the liquor in her glass. "I've been thinking," she said after a spell of silence. "And I think you should wear your glasses in public."

His brows rose as he rested his chin on the flat of his hands. "I don't think so."

"But I do. Because they make you look distinguished."

"I don't want to look distinguished."

"Why not?"

"I'm not the distinguished type."

The green of his eyes bore into hers. With his hair combed back and his hands wide and fingernails neatly trimmed, the way his collar lay next to his neck, and the firm set of his mouth, he was breathtakingly handsome. And refined-looking.

"That's debatable."

"Maybe for you." His voice washed through the room, as smooth as the liquor warming her stomach.

Feeling a heated flush on her cheeks, she replied, "No. I think for the many women you know."

"And how many women do you think I know?"

"Scads." Was that seductive tone coming from her? It seemed so far off, as if the throatiness belonged to somebody else.

Jake watched her. Intensely. She didn't move, didn't breathe—merely looked into his eyes and wanted nothing more than to drown in the wonderful golden green of his gaze.

She brought the glass to her mouth and drank the remainder of the brandy. Its intoxicating effect sluiced over her skin, prickling and tingling. She really hadn't drunk enough to become inebriated. It was Jake's presence doing it to her, Jake who made her blood slow. Made it become like thick syrup through her veins, sluggish, drowsy. Made the heat pool inside her body, converge to the place between her legs. Make her breasts feel heavy.

Jake reached out and touched a long, loose curl that had fallen over her shoulder. He rubbed the hair between his fingers, thoughtfully, silently. Her hand rose to his, and she grabbed his fingers, squeezing softly.

The emotional waves she'd been up and down the past few days came out in a flood tide of vulnerable honesty. "Jake . . . I don't want to be an old maid. I know I have my girls, but they're just girls. And they have their own lives to lead and they're going about it quite splendidly. With no help from me."

Her movements were fragile as she lifted her hand

to the opening of his heavy winter shirt. The blue-gray plaid material was warm and rough. With uncertainty, she felt one of the gray buttons near his throat; its round texture was smooth and hard. He didn't move. But he sucked in his breath, deeply and steadily.

"So where does that leave my life five or ten years from now?" She mused aloud, rambling on in the hazy warmth of the room. "I'll have taught young ladies who've moved on to wifehood and motherhood. And there I will sit in my room at St. Francis. With Miss Pond—a very dear but unmarried woman who doesn't even have a cat. Maynard was my ray of hope. At least I would have him to keep me company. And now I have nothing." Surprise closed her eyes; she couldn't believe she just confessed such a private fear of loneliness. Flickering her eyelids open, she clunked the bottom of her empty glass on the bedside table. "Don't listen to me."

Jake smiled. "You're drunk."

"I'm fractured." With her right hand, she still touched the short bridge of thread that kept his shirt button in place. "That's what college students call it. When I went to Gillette's, it seemed like everybody got 'fractured' but me."

A muscle worked at the back of Jake's jaw. Short bristly beard from one day's growth darkened his chin and throat. "Sweetheart, you don't have to be like everybody."

"Sometimes . . . I don't want to be a teacher. I want . . ."

Unabashedly, her hand slid up his chest. Her eyes never left his. He sat still as she touched the skin at the base of his throat, taut and hot and sleek, his pulse visibly thumping in the hollow. She'd never figured that a man could be so tempting.

"Tru . . ." He spoke her name in a ragged whisper. "I should leave."

"No . . ."

He caught her slender wrist within his strong fingers, his gaze melding into hers. "Then if I stay, I'm staying all night."

"Yes . . ."

She realized she'd made the decision days ago. Because she would never marry, she wanted to know what it would be like to be with a man. To know what *The Science of Life* meant by: *Our very soul pervades every element of our bodies, and in every nerve it thrills with pleasure or grows mad with pain.*

Jake was the only one who made her want to find out. She could never give herself to anyone else. Only him.

"Do you know exactly what you're saying?" His deep voice clung to control by a thin thread.

"I know exactly what I'm saying. And wanting." She dared ask, fearing that perhaps he didn't feel the same way, "Do you want to?"

"I've wanted to since Christmas Day, but you aren't the kind of woman a man has a casual encounter with."

The admission of Christmas Day astonished, and reassured, her. "My wits are fully about me. I'm not innocent about human anatomy and what happens."

Slowly, he let her hand go. She left the weave of his shirt and fingered the area of exposed hair on his chest. She observed, "You're not wearing an undershirt."

"Don't need one," he replied huskily, "with you. You keep me warm, Truvy."

"That time I came to the gym to give you the book.

You stood there in a shirt that was torn and its sleeves missing. I saw only parts of your arms and chest. I'd like to see everything." She swallowed. "Please."

In a sensual whisper, he commanded, "Then unbutton my shirt."

Slowly, she moved her hands over the fabric. One by one, she fingered each button free of its tiny slit. Her knuckles grazed his burning hot skin and he jerked with what she knew was "mad pain"—something good. The notion that she could do that to him sent excitement through her. Once the last button was undone, she parted the shirt off his broad shoulders. Shrugging free of the sleeves, he let the plaid cloth fall to the floor.

Truvy leaned back in the bed, wordlessly staring but unable to fully see every contour of his upper body. The spindles of the chair blocked a full view of him. "Sit the other way."

He stood, pulled the chair away, but didn't sit back on it. Instead, he remained standing. In front of her. As if he liked her watching, studying.

"You do that well—stand still," she observed.

"I used to pose in the nude."

"Indeed?"

"For artists. In New York."

"Is your likeness hanging anywhere in a gallery?"

"Not that I know of."

"Hmmm."

Jake's chest was expansive and perfectly sculpted, like a marble statue, an Adonis. She'd always thought him chiseled when he was fully clothed; to see him like this made her imaginings pale.

His skin was in a shade of golden tones; the dark brown whorl of hair on his chest appealed to her. It tapered, a faint line of hair disappearing into his trouser waistband. Behind the fly placket, the carrier of his . . . *pabulum*—no, his penis—was defined in a thick ridge.

The book's poetic description in reference to man's contribution to "life" meant nothing. It said nothing. It was flowery prose written for a Victorian need for tact in the treatment of delicate subjects. *Pabulum of life* was silly, ridiculous. *Say the correct anatomical name. Even in your mind.*

Penis.

But even thinking the word made saliva grow thick against her tongue. A man's appendage was something she couldn't fully envision. A fair idea was nothing in comparison to reality.

Jake moved forward so that his thighs bumped the side of the bed. She had the urge to stand up, to meet him, but she couldn't quite move. It was difficult to think. Gingerly, she lifted her hands and slid them over his bare torso. Nothing had prepared her for the pleasure of touching him like this. She'd always felt wonderful when he kissed her. But this was giving to him, and she knew he liked it.

He dragged in his breath once more; this time, his hands captured her face and brought her lips to his for a kiss. She rose to her knees and pressed her body firmly against his. Her nipples came to hard and aching points the instant his mouth covered hers in a fusion of heat. Between them, her hands were pressed flat. She managed to move them lower. And lower yet, over his abdomen, feeling the washboard definition of muscle that covered his ribs.

She was jolted by the moist warmth of his tongue. She lifted herself up into his full embrace, kissing him, fighting the urge to rub her breasts next to him, needing to feel friction across their tips. He deepened the kiss, stroking her, his hands traveling across her back and pushing her into his groin. She wrapped her arms around him, tracing the bones of his spine, daring to move lower and lower until her palms lay on his buttocks ... cupping.

Beneath her nightgown, her skin tingled. His tongue traced her lips as she wove her fingers into the silky tangle of his hair. She'd always loved his hair, so thick and satiny. The hair covering the hard muscles of his chest abraded her nipples, which strained against the flannel of her nightgown. In one quick tug, Jake had the fabric bunched in his hands and she was free of the gown.

She knelt there, on the bed, before him ... completely naked.

The room's air suddenly felt degrees colder.

Nobody had ever seen her without her clothes on.

With her nipples in tight buds and her skin flushed with gooseflesh, she was assaulted with a sudden and unwanted shyness. A feeling of insecurity about her body overwhelmed her. It took everything she possessed to remain absolutely still, to not cover her breasts and the private place between her legs. She was tall. Too tall. Not slender at all.

It was agonizing to let him stare at her, his gaze roving up and down her body. She couldn't watch him looking at her.

"You're beautiful, Truvy."

The awe in his voice was real.

Even so, she couldn't help herself. "I'm tall," she whispered thickly.

"You're just right. For me."

He brought her to him and kissed her tenderly, mouth touching mouth. Nothing else. It wasn't enough. She fell into him, into the warmth he offered. She clutched him, bringing her fingernails down his naked back. Everything was so untried. So new. Each thing about them, about touching, was like a myriad of foreign sensations.

His hands rose to fondle her breasts, fingering her nipples, teasing and arousing. He had light calluses on his fingertips, the harder skin against her soft and sensitive flesh bringing forth an eruption of dizzying bliss. It seemed as if she were spiraling down into an abyss of raw pleasure.

Truvy moved her hands along the sides of his neck, feeling the strength in the tendons. Their lips broke apart when she began to pant, their foreheads touching. She marveled at the softness to his brows where they blended with hers. His nose met hers, tip to tip. They gasped, their breath spent.

She lifted her face, holding his between her hands, searching his eyes. They were hooded and filled with passion she hadn't anticipated. Everything in his gaze was for her—desire, wanting. She marveled at his need for her. She ran her fingertips over his mouth. His teeth nipped at her while he unfastened his trousers, then kicked them off.

She knew he was naked, but she hadn't looked when he'd undressed, hadn't dared watch him shed the last piece of clothing between them.

Now, her eyes lowered, slowly, toward the part of him she'd wondered about.

Once her eyes were there, she stared in amazement. He was larger than she'd thought possible, extended and thick, a long shaft of smooth skin with a rounded end and cleft. At its base, dark hair curled. Like hers.

"Is . . ."—she cleared her throat—". . . are you average?"

"Not hardly."

Not hardly. He'd said that about marriage. And he'd meant it. He had to mean this. He was larger than most men. Of course he would be. He was taller than any man in town, broader and wider, thicker. *My goodness* . . . how would they manage this?

The question was broken in her mind as his body loomed over her, then came down on top of hers in a pleasant weight. She felt his penis next to her leg—between her legs, brushing her hotly. With both of them lying on the bed, the mattress sank. Springs creaked.

Jake rested on his elbows, his hair falling over his brow. She touched a corner of his mouth. He briefly kissed her fingertip. Every one of her senses was heightened, making her ecstatically radiant.

Natural impulses.

This felt natural, right.

"I have to tell you something," he said, very seriously.

She grew fearful and bit her lower lip. "You've changed your mind."

"No." He shook his head, keeping his arms straight and his upper body off of her. She felt his lower body stir. "If I don't take myself from you," he said, his chin lowered so that he drew her full attention, "at the most sensitive part of our making love, I could get you pregnant."

"Oh . . ." Truvy knew about that detail. The chapter entitled "The Marital State" was quite clear on conception. "You don't have to worry," she said, surprising him. "It's not a time for me to . . ."—the words were difficult for her to speak—". . . get into a situation. The book I told you about that I was reading—"

"The science book."

"Yes, that's the one. I figured out the pattern of a woman's time—not for myself but in general—from the 'Table of Conception and Barren Periods.' " Unable to keep a warm blush at bay, she revealed, "It's not my time."

"You're sure?"

She couldn't go as far as telling him the date of her last menses. It was mortifying enough that she'd said what she had. "Quite."

A log in the heater fell, causing an eruption of fiery sparks and snaps to fill the room.

Truvy's passion-swollen lips longed for his kiss, some signal that what she'd said hadn't shocked him.

Jake lowered his face toward hers; the ends of his hair brushed across her collarbone. Then he did the most exquisite thing. He pulled her nipple into his mouth; his free hand teased the other into a peak. The newfound discovery of intense pleasure brought a deeper longing to her. He suckled her for a long moment, and she felt as if she were being pulled toward a heady direction of complete surrender. It was a sweet pain, not a mad pain.

There was no thought of consequence or tomorrow.

Truvy wanted today and this moment to last forever.

She let herself be lost in Jake, his mouth, his hands, his body.

He trailed kisses between the valley of her breasts and took her nipple inside his hot mouth. Her hands kneaded his back, the sinewy cords of pure muscle.

In the middle of this bliss, there came a moment when Truvy realized where they were going. She instinctively parted her thighs for him. As he broke away from her breast and captured her mouth, he slid a finger inside her. Shock left her lips, but he caught it in a searing kiss. The length of him pressed against her. She felt as if everything converged to that one spot in her, a pulsing knot begging for release, for something to fill its emptiness.

As Jake stroked her, harder and faster, she cried out. A torrent of pleasure skimmed her skin. She trembled.

He moved his knee between her already parted legs, wanting her wider and ready for him. Slowly, he probed her slick entrance. Then lifting his face so that he could look into her eyes, he inched himself inside her. For a split second, Truvy braced herself against the sharp pain that knifed through her womb. She'd wanted this, to know him like this. She hadn't known the sweet ecstasy would dissipate for the actual act.

She clutched his shoulders, holding tight, as he began to move deeper. Each time he pushed a little farther, the pain eased. When he had buried the entire length of himself and stopped, the discomfort ebbed to nothing.

His eyes fastened to hers.

Truvy stared, confused. "This is it?"

The crisp hairs of his chest rubbed against her as his chest vibrated with gentle laughter. "Not if I can help it."

"Oh . . . do we rest now?"

"Maybe later. After the first time. Not now."

Then he began to move within her, a methodic rhythm, the friction of his smooth penis against her innermost private place. The steady and driving rock of his hips puckered her nipples and made all her earlier desires come flooding back. The emptiness was gone—filled by Jake.

Her heartbeat thrummed beneath her soft breasts, which jiggled gently from the motions he made with his lower body. Raising her arms, she clenched his hips, feeling an urgency for . . . something more.

Without modesty, she matched his tempo, the rhythmic labors of his lovemaking. A drop of perspiration dropped from his brow, splashing her cheek. His breath came out in choppy waves. She held onto him, bending her legs so that her knees bumped the sides of his torso. In this position, when he drove into her, he went much deeper. The sensation enveloped her, causing her to suck in her breath.

The entire moment was an awakening the likes of which she'd never experienced. She needed to release tension she wasn't aware she'd had. With Jake's every thrust, the tension built and built, until she was sure she couldn't stand the coil growing tighter and tighter any longer.

Then everything released deep, deep inside her. He groaned, and her body let go of the tension, a whirlwind of heat flooding her as Jake plunged one last time, harder than he had before. She felt the muscles on his back tighten like ropes, and she clutched his damp skin.

She held onto him, eyes closed, lost in the sexual desire she'd repressed for weeks. Fulfillment claimed her in every way.

Jake's ragged breath hotly caressed her ear as he nipped her lobe and his body shuddered on top of hers. They lay there, entwined, the place where they were joined still throbbing, pulsing and wet.

And as for Truvy, she now knew what it felt like for every nerve inside her to be thrilled.

Truvy buried her face in the crook of Jake's shoulder. Her soft, sweet breath touched his neck. He tried to regain control of his senses. The fragrance of lemony flowers came to his nose. His breathing was labored. He pressed his mouth to her ear, kissing her. Still deep inside her, he rose on his forearm, needing to see her face, to search her eyes and see how she felt.

The cloud of her hair fanned about her head, cushioned on the softness of the pillow. Her lips were parted; her breasts rose and fell beneath his chest.

There were no dictionary words for Jake that could describe what had just happened. He'd never been with a woman before and felt like this, total and complete. A quiet peace filled him.

He was in love with Truvy Valentine.

More than he'd thought possible. It had crept up on him, taken him by surprise, and roped him in. There were so many things he wanted to tell her, so many things she didn't know about him. Hundreds of questions plagued his mind. A future between them would mean digging into the past; namely, it meant telling her that he'd had a wife before. If they were to consider marrying, Truvy had to know.

Marriage.

The idea came at him in a rush. But if he asked her now, she'd think he felt obligated to. He did need to reassure Truvy of one absolute truth: he had no regrets and he hoped she didn't either.

"Truvy, I—" That's all he was able to say.

The length of fingertip placed to his mouth stopped him. Seriousness overtook her face. "Jake, there's no reason to say anything. I don't want you to feel like you have to. We had a nice time." Slowly lowering her hand, she almost begged, "Please, let's leave it at that."

Jake's muscles tensed. Her implication didn't go unnoticed. With her meaning as crystal as the glass on the bedside table, she might as well have said: *It was just sex. Nothing more.*

How many times had he just "had sex" and he hadn't cared? When he finally did care beyond his imagination, the woman he was with gave him *his* stock answer.

Jesus. Anyway . . . what did he think she would say? Do? Throw away her teaching position for him? She'd never given any indication she wanted to. Or would. Yes, she'd questioned being at that school of hers a while ago, but she'd been feeling the brandy.

Nobody just walked because of good sex.

"All right, Tru." Jake nodded. "We'll leave it at that."

But his words belied the ache in the pit of his belly.

Chapter
❧18❧

The following Tuesday, Edwina went to the dance studio to meet Truvy for a late-afternoon tea at Rosemarie's Tearoom. Baby Elizabeth remained at home with Marvel-Anne.

The baptism had been the previous day. Jake was at the church and sat in the front pew beside Tom and Shay, with Truvy, Edwina, and Crescencia at the other end. Before and during the minister's sermon, there had been no opportunity to speak with Jake; Truvy had given him a glance here and there, trying to keep the butterflies from fluttering in her stomach. Afterward, he'd been asked to the Wolcotts' house for refreshments and cake, but he'd passed on the invitation. Truvy's pride concealed her inner turmoil at his decision.

Four days had passed since Truvy and Jake had been together, and each day went by more slowly. Her spirits fell and longing, mixed with doubt, swirled through her head.

She had pushed him away, and he had allowed her to.

330

Yesterday, out of fear Jake wouldn't appear at the studio, Truvy hadn't arrived early for their private dance instruction. Nor had she stayed late. He hadn't been in one of her classes, so she hadn't seen him the entire day. She threw her energies into the lessons, having made great improvement on her technique ... thanks to Jake. She was somewhat successful during daylight hours at keeping him out of her thoughts. But at nighttime, it was more difficult not to think about him while lying in her bed, unable to sleep.

His scent lingered on the cotton sheets—the spicy smell of his shaving cologne, the woodsy shampoo for his hair. She told herself that she'd just had her linens washed the day he'd spent the night; they didn't need to be brought to the laundry. But she'd been deluding herself. Lying in bedclothes that reminded her senses of Jake Brewster wasn't something easy to give up to the harshness of borax soap.

Out of concern for his being discovered in her room at an inappropriate hour, Jake had left well before dawn last week. Throughout the night before he'd left, they'd made love. And each time, she'd enjoyed the coupling more than the last. He was better than brandy, the sensations he evoked moving through her slower than the torrid liquor, fanning hotly through her body.

Longing for him was foolish. By telling him that their encounter had no emotional attachments, she made it easy for him, knowing he would feel bad for taking her virginity and afterward offer some sort of apology or condolence. She couldn't hear it. It would make her crazy if he pitied her or felt sorry for her in any way.

She would have to face him tomorrow, talk with

him, dance with him—force herself to remain unaffected in his arms. The men of the Barbell Club were coming for their final lesson before the Mr. Physique contest. She had to try desperately to pretend nothing had changed between them.

"It's dark in here," Edwina commented, putting recordings away.

"I drew the curtains so I could lock up."

But that was a lie. She'd kept them closed for most of the day, unable to bear knowing Jake was right across the alleyway, available to her . . . but not available.

"I'm ready to go." Edwina brushed off the front of her coat, then gave the angle of her hat a check. Appearing stunningly beautiful, she'd blossomed into motherhood like a rare rose.

"Me, too."

Truvy locked the studio and she and Edwina made their way over to Main Street.

The sun was high in the late afternoon sky, the temperatures in the low fifties. Unusual for January, but Harmony enjoyed the unexpected warmth, and most everyone was on the streets walking and socializing.

A commotion rose from the train depot a block away. Men's voices came up Sycamore Drive. Truvy recognized Lou Bernard, the porter, as he fired off a disclaimer about railroad policy. Several men argued his point—loudly, undeniably excited.

Within minutes, approximately a dozen men appeared at the top of Old Oak Road with Lou in the front of this makeshift procession. Behind him, the fire department's draft horses pulled a low-bed wagon. Sitting on the bed was a towering wooden crate—one full story in height and at least six feet wide on all sides. The massive box had writing burned into its cedar siding and caused quiet an instant attraction.

Businesses emptied as Lou Bernard led the entourage toward the town square.

"Good heavens! I wonder what that is." Edwina rose on the balls of her feet to get a better look over the group of teetering young ladies who'd just departed Rosemarie's Tearoom. Their hats were high and trimmed, but Truvy had no problem seeing.

That crate was the largest she'd seen. And had to be heavy as sin. The draft horses strained and pulled, their shod hooves pounding over the bricked street.

"Come on," Edwina said, gleefully curious. "Let's go see what it is."

Truvy snuggled into her cape and walked swiftly behind Edwina to the town square, where it seemed as if the entire town gathered to wait and find out what would happen. The wagon made its way through the east pathway and stopped dead center in front of the white gazebo.

"All right! Stop!" Lou shouted with a raise of his hand. "Where's Jake Brewster?"

"Here he comes!"

Voices rumbled through the crowd, while a surge of anticipation fired through Truvy's pulse. She quickly craned her head with the others. She couldn't miss him as he walked forward. The crowd parted in a rush. Faces anxiously peering up at him, children yanked on their fathers' coattails and their mothers' skirts with wonderment. Nobody knew what the crate meant to Jake, least of all Truvy, who drank in every inch of him as he came to the wagon.

He took her breath away, made her heartbeat sing. There was nothing like the feeling of looking at him, of knowing she'd been with him in the way a woman is with a man. She'd seen him naked, had him inside her, intimate and sated. Of that, she was glad. She knew him in ways that were private. It seemed as if the town expected him to be larger than life, and he was. And he also seemed as if he liked living the legend. But for all his notoriety, Jake had made her feel special for one night.

And as their eyes finally caught and held for mere seconds, she fell even more deeply in love with him than she'd thought possible.

Jake looked away first, his gaze lingering just an instant. He went straight to Lou and bracketed his wide hands on his hips. "Milton said you wanted me." Jake looked at the crowd. "Looks like you all wanted me. What's going on?"

Lou took out a folded piece of paper from the breast pocket of his navy uniform. "It took sixteen men to get this crate off the inbound Number 101 and I cannot legally let anyone open it but you, Bruiser. It's for you."

Sidling his gaze over the crate, Jake stood back. "What's it doing here?"

"Instructions." Reading a docket, Lou said, " 'Shipped from New York City' "—an impressed gasp rose—" 'for Jacob Brewster of Harmony, Montana.' Here's the good part—'Special terms of the Railroad Code of Ethics to be followed.' " Then he read: " 'This crate is to be brought to, and opened, at the eastern location of Harmony's town square and displayed for public view.' "

Jake rubbed his hand across the back of his head. "Who's this from?"

Lou skimmed the paper. "Mr. Frederic Remington. And there's a letter here for you, too."

"Remmy." Jake's mouth curved in a smile and he gave a shrug as he took the envelope and tore it open.

"What's it say, Bruiser?" Milt asked. "Read it out loud."

Jake held the paper at arm's length while he read the handwriting. " 'Both of us were wrong. Art is physical *and* emotional. Your body is the inspiration, but my mind brings the idea to life. This is for all the hours of conversation in New York.' " Looking up, Jake said, "You have a crowbar, Lou?"

"I got one, Bruiser!" Milton stepped forward, along with other members of the Barbell Club, all armed with crowbars and hammers.

The men set to work, wrenching out nails and hammering the crate's sides apart. They had to stand on the wagon and hoist several men to the top of the crate to pry the lid loose. The noise reverberated through the tightly knit circle of onlookers.

"I wonder what it is." Edwina clutched Truvy's shoulder. "This is so exciting. Where's Tom?" She looked around the crowd. "He's missing this. The whole town is here."

Perhaps not quite, but the majority of citizens.

Truvy was as excited about the contents of that crate as the rest of them. Who in the world was Frederic Remington from New York? It became increasingly difficult to remain outwardly calm, but Truvy affected a demure air.

Then all at once, the men backed away and the crate's sides fell down in unison. Truvy's demureness was instantly flattened—like the cedar boards strewn on the ground.

Edwina's fingers gripped into her flesh, and both ladies gasped audibly—as did everyone in the crowd.

Shock zipped through the mass, and in its wake came total and deafening silence. All eyes converged on one thing: a life-size likeness of Jake Brewster astride a life-size rearing stallion. The artistic details were flawless and represented undeniable talent. But it wasn't the horse's wild mane and long tail or the bulky leg muscles and veins popping out all over his hide that drew the crowd into stunned quiet.

It was the fact the man on that horse was stark naked.

Every sinewy muscle on him was depicted in perfect detail. The swell of his chest, the width of his shoulders and the definition of his upper body and lean legs, his feet in the stirrups. Reins were wrapped around one hand, and his other arm flailed out to help him keep his balance on the bucking bronco. The swell of the saddle met him at the crotch, his private area nondescript in the formed bronze. The artist had had some modesty. But not much.

"Oh . . . my . . ." Edwina whispered. "Oh . . . my."

Shock reverberated inside Truvy like the electric impulses of telegraph transmissions. She had no words.

The police had plenty.

With swagger to their steps, Chief Officer Algie Conlin and Deputy Pike Faragher blustered their way through the mob.

"What's going on here?" Conlin hollered, the badge on his coat winking silver beneath the sun.

Pike Faragher pointed to the statue, his mouth dropping open.

Closely viewing the artwork, Conlin gave it a thorough exam, and then let out a low whistle. Facing Jake, he declared, "Brewster, I'm going to have to arrest you for public indecency."

Murmurs went up in the crowd.

Folding his arms across his chest, Jake stared down at the chief officer. "What's indecent on me?"

"Your body."

Jake reported, "Nothing's missing off it."

"I'll say," Pike commented, staring hard at Jake's saddle horn—or rather, the area thereabouts.

Snickers erupted from the younger boys. Members of the Barbell Club jabbed each other in the ribs.

"Shut up, Pike," Conlin dictated. "Brewster, you have a point about not personally being indecent—but this fellow on his horse is as buck as they get."

"Not buck and a horse," the deputy said in correction. " '*Strongman On A Horse*, by Frederic Remington.' That's what's spelled out on the plaque on the bottom." He read the rest of the large print engraved in the brass sheet at the statue's wide base. " 'For the population of Harmony, Montana, in honor of Jacob Brewster, a man of epic strength.' " He ran the tip of his index finger over the letters and enunciated clearly. " 'Work in bronze. Completed November 1901 in New York City.' "

"Who's Frederic Remington?" Conlin asked, scratching his ear.

"He's an artist. And a very good one." The reply came from Prudence Plunkett, who must have been on the No. 101 train herself.

Truvy turned and watched as she entered the crowd wearing a fur muff and matching ermine stole.

Reaching the center of the square, Mrs. Plunkett informed the officers, "Many of Mr. Remington's paintings are exhibited in the National Academy of Design on Fifth Avenue in New York."

"How do you know?" the chief officer snorted.

"Because I've just returned from a visit to my daughter in Buffalo and we traveled to Manhattan for a mother-and-daughter excursion. Where," she added, while giving the statue a brief going-over, "we toured city museums and galleries." If she were appalled by the blatant sexuality of Jake's likeness, she didn't show it. "Mr. Remington's dynamic revelations of our American West awe those people who have no concept of the beauty and savage nature we are privy to for living in Montana." She stared at the ladies gathered in a huddle, their mouths open. "Mrs. Elward, Mrs. Calhoon, and Mrs. Brooks, I suggest you accept the placement of this statue without a fuss. We must learn to accept the things we cannot change, and embrace them—or else we will lose them entirely."

The only utterance to follow Mrs. Plunkett's oration—which had less to do with Jake Brewster's statue and more to do with her relationship with her daughter—was that of her husband's voice.

"Pru, you're back."

"Yes, Hiram, I am."

"You didn't tell me."

"I wanted to surprise you."

The pair met and gave each other a short hug, then drifted outside the crowd. In their departure, the chief officer's tone lifted in annoyance.

"All this highfalutin talk about Frederic Remington of New York City is well and good, but it doesn't change the fact we've got us a naked statue in the middle of our town square. It's got to go."

Algie Conlin pushed the long lapel of his coat behind his service revolver as if the display meant his word was law. Jake leaned forward and Algie took a step back. The stare-down lasted all of five seconds.

"Now, Bruiser, I think we can work something out. I'll give you twelve hours to get this heap—"

"It's called art," Mrs. Kennison said, her hat and gloves in perfect harmony with her attire. She was one of the most beautiful and respected women in town. "What we have is a work of art from a well-known artist. I have heard of Mr. Remington, and Mrs. Plunkett is right. We should embrace this statue and be honored Mr. Remington thought of us."

"Well, he didn't think to put Bruiser's clothes on," Conlin shot back. "It is a disgrace."

"Only if it were you on that horse," the deputy mumbled, "without your clothes on. I don't want to see you naked, Algie. But Bruiser's got a far better build, and I kind of think this bronze does him justice. Makes me want to join up at that gymnasium of his so I can look like this."

"Pike, I'm going to remind you of your place." The chief officer sneered at Pike Faragher.

"Remind me all you want, but there really isn't a law against statues in the town square if the citizens pass a vote to put one in."

"But no vote has been taken."

"We could vote right now."

"Wait a doggone minute!" Conlin raised both hands, aimed a pointed finger at Jake, and blasted, "Brewster, aren't you opposed to having yourself made a spectacle of in public view?"

Jake unfolded his arms and shrugged. "No. I like the horse."

"Vote!" came a call.

New murmurs sounded from the crowd. "I'll second that," shouted a voice from the back.

"Call a vote," Pike stated, and quickly went on. "All

in favor of Jake Brewster posing on a horse in the town square say, 'Aye.' "

Hearty ayes arose.

"Those opposed say, 'Nay.' "

Several nays sounded.

"Ayes have it," the deputy said with a firm nod of his head. "This vote is closed! We've got us a Frederic Remington statue."

"Pike!" Algie Conlin fumed. "You're filling out all the permits."

The crowd began to disband, many people walking in for a closer inspection. It wasn't something Truvy would do. There was no reason. She'd already seen the real thing—flesh and blood, genuine man.

"Well," Edwina remarked. "*This* was something."

Truvy had no opportunity to reply. Mrs. Plunkett walked forward and stopped in front of them. Her eyes were sincere, her mouth set in remorse.

"I'm so very sorry, Miss Valentine," she said with a quiver in her voice. "I hope you can accept my apologies. It was unfair of me to treat you the way I did. I was missing my Hildegarde so much that I neglected to think of your feelings. It was disgraceful of me."

There was no reason not to put Mrs. Plunkett at ease with a warm smile of acceptance. "Did you have a nice visit with Hildegarde?"

"Wonderful. I should have gone much sooner."

"I'm so glad you did."

"Well, my dear . . ." From the pocket of her coat, she brought forth a tatted handkerchief and dabbed her eyes. Truvy could tell the glisten in them wasn't caused by loneliness for a faraway married daughter but rather by relief that the situation had been mended. "I hope you're getting along all right in your new surroundings."

"I'm fine."

"If it's agreeable to you, I'd like to return for dance lessons."

"I'll expect you in the next class."

Then Mr. Plunkett took her by the elbow and they went to toward the mercantile.

Jake walked up to them on the heels of the Plunketts' departure. "Mrs. Wolcott." Then to Truvy, with a deliberately deeper tone, he said, "Miss Valentine."

"Hello," she automatically replied, but her breathing came too fast. His formal address to the both of them felt stilted.

"*Hello, Jake*—you rascal," Edwina exclaimed. "My goodness, but how did you manage to do something so grand?"

"I never posed for this. Remmy had to have used sketches from a long ways back. I used to sit *au naturel* for the art school when he was enrolled."

"I'm impressed. The detail he put into the work is incredible. Don't you think, Truvy?"

She didn't immediately answer. She thought the detail accurate to the letter, but she wouldn't admit that. "Yes. Very nice."

"He got your face perfect. Wouldn't you agree, Truvy?"

"Yes."

"And the chest looks about right." She gave Jake a glance, then one to Truvy. "Wouldn't you say so, Truvy?"

Truvy knew one thing. She had to get out of there or she'd no longer be able to disguise her feelings. She was shattering, piece by piece, being so close to Jake and pretending she didn't know what he looked like in the nude. "I'm afraid I'm developing a headache, Edwina," she fibbed. "I can't make it to tea after all. I'm going to go lie down."

"Is there anything I can do?" Edwina touched her gloved hand.

"Not a thing. I'll be all right."

"I'll walk you home, Miss Valentine."

"That's not necessary."

"Thank you, Jake," Edwina replied for her. "That's thoughtful of you."

"I can be thoughtful."

Truvy headed toward the livery, Jake beside her, helpless but to let him accompany her across Main Street. "You don't have to go out of your way."

"I'm not. I wanted to talk to you."

"Yes?" She didn't miss a step.

"You've been avoiding me."

Truvy almost stopped. But didn't. "I thought I was making it easier for you."

"Easier for what?"

"So you wouldn't feel obligated."

Jake took her elbow and her arm knocked against his. Truvy steeled herself against the contact, refusing to let her heartbeat clog her throat. "I never do anything I don't want to. And being with you isn't an obligation." He pulled in a deep draft of breath, then exhaled with the comment, "You weren't at the dance studio the other morning. I waited for you."

"I was detained."

"The hell you were."

"I wasn't feeling well."

"You were fine by eleven o'clock. Mrs. Treber

looked out the dancing academy's window, so I know you were in there with those ladies."

"I was."

"Of course you were. I know exactly when you're in there, especially on the days those bird watchers are supposed to be dancing. They peek through the curtains to watch the men in the gymnasium."

Truvy honestly hadn't realized that. "They do?"

"Yep."

"Oh . . . well, I'll talk to them."

"Don't bother. Talk to *me.*"

"I thought that's what we were doing."

They neared Dogwood Place; rather than letting Truvy continue on, Jake veered her off in the direction of Bruiser's.

"Wait! What are you doing?" she exclaimed.

"I want to show you my Ping-Pong game."

"Your what?"

"Table tennis. The table arrived the other day. Shipped from Chicago. You're the only woman I know who could appreciate it."

Truvy had no inkling what a Ping-Pong game was. She'd never heard of one. "I don't want to see it." Dubiously, she added, "If indeed there is such a thing."

"There is. I haven't had anybody to try it out with. Give me a run for my money, Tru. Play me."

"I will not. I have a headache."

They were at the door of the gym.

His gaze bore into hers, capturing her pulse and making her stand stock still. "You have as much of a headache as the guy riding the horse in the town square does."

"That's you on that horse."

"And don't you know it, sweetheart." The low-voiced sexual implication wasn't offensive to Truvy. In fact, she reveled in the intimacy of his words as they wrapped around her in a heated caress.

On that statement, he unlocked the door and nudged her inside.

"This is outrageous," she protested.

"This is my Ping-Pong table," he declared, the hand on the small of her back as he steered her toward an extra-long table with a short net dividing its center. The dimensions of the table had to be at least nine feet by five feet. Two paddles lay on the table's wood surface, along with one tiny white celluloid ball.

Truvy observed, "It looks like regular tennis, only in miniature."

"Pretty much."

She went forward to have a better look. "Why did you buy it?"

"The manufacturer says it's supposed to be good for stamina. And a lot of fun." Jake picked up a round paddle and bounced the ball against it, using his wrist to keep the paddle steady and to keep the ball from dropping to the floor. "Play me and we'll see."

Truvy removed her gloves, set her pocketbook aside, and took the other paddle. With the paddle, Jake tossed her the ball. She caught it in her hand. The ball was very lightweight without the bounce to it that a tennis ball had. "Interesting."

"What we do is whack the ball back and forth over the table. You ping and I pong."

"What?"

"Ping-Pong. That's the name of the game. Serve by holding the ball on the flat of your palm, then throw it up and strike the ball when it falls."

"I can do that."

Guiding her wrist to propel the paddle, she hit the tiny ball and sent it over the net. Jake struck it to return. The white flash went sailing back to her. She whacked it to Jake. He missed. They tried it once more—and within a few minutes, they'd gotten the rhythm of the motions.

Back and forth.

Ping. Pong.

An apt title for the game.

"How did you learn how to play lawn tennis?" Jake asked, balanced on the balls of his feet so he could cover edge balls at his end of the table.

"By accident," she remarked, hitting the ball back to him. "I wanted to make a donation to the Daughters of Liberty campaign, but I didn't have any money. So I entered a tennis tournament, hoping to get the third prize of ten dollars."

This time Truvy missed the return ball.

She bent, picked it up from where it had rolled to the rowing machine, then went back to the table. Serving, she shot the ball over the short net as she got back into the proper playing position.

"You won the ten bucks?"

Ping.

"No. One hundred. I took first. I had a knack for tennis I didn't know about."

Pong.

"And you forked over the one hundred to the Daughters?"

Ping.

"What do you think?"

Pong.

"Every last Abraham Lincoln."

Ping.

"Yes—who, by the way, was the most powerful president of any party we have ever had in office."

Pong.

"He was a Republican. Right?"

Ping.

"Right."

Pong.

They played five complete games. Truvy won all five by scoring twenty-one points first. After the last, she set her paddle down and accused, "You let me win five times."

"No. You beat me five times."

"Fair and square?"

"Truvy, I play to win. Never to lose." A succession of emotions crossed his chiseled face: honesty, desire, and reverence. In the seconds that followed, he uttered three words that went straight to her heart. "I've missed you."

Her throat felt constricted and she was unable to reply. She looked at the planks on the floor, then at Jake, who came around the table to stand in front of her. "I want to show you something in my office."

She let him lead her to his panel-walled domain with its vague odor of cigars. The desk wasn't organized, papers here and there, those photographic souvenir cards of Jake wearing boxing trunks in the midst of everything.

He rounded the desk's corner, opened the top middle drawer, and rifled through the mess. When he found what he was looking for, he grasped it and withdrew a modest-sized photograph. Without a word, he handed it to her.

Truvy looked at the woman in the picture. She was so beautiful, not even the black-and-white shadows creating her image dulled her appearance. She was dressed in a rich gown and stood beside a pillar with a fern on its top. Her hair was curled to perfection; her eyes were large. Her figure was perfect—delicate and shapely, the epitome of womanhood. She wasn't tall—average to more on the dainty side.

The woman in the photograph was everything a man desired.

"Who is she?" Truvy asked, lifting her eyes.

"My wife."

Truvy dropped the photograph. The thick paper fell onto the desk and she took a step backward. "Your . . ."

"My *former* wife. Laurette Everleigh."

Shaken, she knew the blood had siphoned from her face. "She's the stunningly beautiful woman who made a poor homemaker."

"You have to understand why I married her. Hear me out." His eyes probed hers with a silent query. "Please, Truvy."

Jake told her about his career with Florenz Ziegfeld's touring show at the World's Columbian Exposition and how he met Laurette Everleigh, billed as "Every Gentleman's Dream." Truvy's gaze lowered to the picture; she could see why men would dream about Laurette.

Truvy didn't want to look at that photograph, but she was helpless not to as Jake explained everything, from the reasons—the wrong ones—he'd married Laurette to how quickly they'd divorced.

"You're divorced," Truvy murmured.

"It was a mistake to marry her," Jake said, taking the photograph and putting it away in his drawer. "I wasn't thinking about what I wanted for the future. Just the moment."

"Like you and me the last time we were together," Truvy whispered.

Jake put his hands on her shoulders and willed her to look at him. "No, Tru. Not like you and me. Never like that. Don't you see—I didn't have to tell you about Laurette. You would have never known."

So true. But did she feel better for knowing? Perhaps. Not because of the truth itself, but because of the honesty behind it.

"I wanted to tell you that night we were together, but I couldn't. And it's been eating my guts ever since."

"Well . . . don't let it anymore." Disconcerted, Truvy pointedly crossed her arms and looked away. "It's done."

"No—my marriage is *un*done."

Lowering her gaze in confusion, she wanted to hurt him and make him want her at the same time. Her mind spun; her pride had been driven into the ground. Even after what he'd told her, she still loved him. But with his admission of a former wife, nothing had changed in *their* relationship.

She waited to go back to Boise, to teaching and her students.

He had his life, and the groove of bachelorhood, here.

Because he hadn't spoken a single word about rethinking marriage. He wasn't interested. And she'd all but told him that neither was she.

So where did that leave them now? Here standing in his office . . . her longing for him. Him coming closer to her, and without words, enfolding her in his arms.

"Just for a few minutes, Tru. Let me hold you."

Truvy had no time to fortify her resolve, to put up

barriers against his arms as they came around her shoulders, cradling her next to the width of his chest. He smelled of freshly laundered linen, exotic cologne, and just a hint of cigar. Everything about him was warm. Unbidden, she rested her cheek on the part of his shirt where it opened at his throat. Breathing in, she identified every facet of his scent, growing content and mesmerized by how wonderful he could feel. He spread his hands across her back, keeping her close.

Her nose nuzzled the base of his neck, as her arms lifted to encircle his waist. "Why do you have to feel so good?"

"You're the one who feels good, sweetheart."

Sweetheart.

"Oh . . . Jake . . ." She sighed, knowing she should leave but unable to tear herself away.

His heartbeat hammered next to hers. It felt natural to stand like this, breast to chest, thigh to thigh, feet between each other's—as close as they could get. The strength of his arms wrapped tighter. Then he pulled back to see her face and cradled the back of her head in his hands.

He kissed her.

She let him.

She kissed him back with everything she felt in her heart. They stood together, mouth to mouth, tongue teasing tongue. She moved her fingers to his neck, feeling as if she'd been lifted by a gauzy cloud of heat. She wanted his mouth on her body—everywhere—on her naked skin. The sensations he created in her made her knees weak, radiated in a warm torrent from the tips of her toes in her new shoes to the top of her head. That warmth swirled and centered on the place between her legs, making her moist and wanting, needing him to touch her there.

Their kiss grew to an intensity that Truvy could neither deny nor stop.

"Tru, I can let you go—"

"No . . ." The denial was lost on his lips as he reclaimed hers for a hot and searing kiss that went on forever.

When she was breathless, her legs barely able to support her, she felt herself bumped next to the edge of his desk. Paper fell to the floor. The hard edge of wood caught her bottom and she leaned against it.

Jake backed away from her. The loss she felt was indescribable, and she even whimpered her disappointment. Reassuring her, Jake brushed a chaste kiss on her bruised lips, then fumbled with the buttons on his shirt, cursing his unsteady hands. He slipped out of the sleeves and Truvy slid her hands over his chest, feeling the smooth skin that covered the taut muscles.

"You're better than the statue," she said, bringing her fingers across the fine flesh that jolted beneath her touch. He felt hard and tight. He was so male, so perfectly sculpted and honed—he was the epitome of perfect male anatomy. It was right that his likeness had been captured in a piece of bronze. Never had there been a better subject. Jake Brewster's honed and hewn body put Michelangelo's *David* to shame.

As Truvy fingered the line of coarse hair across Jake's chest, she slowly outlined his nipples. They were the color of dark pennies, flat and wide. In a lazy, circular motion, she traced them. His breath caught low in his throat, and the discovery that she could pleasure him in such a way brought a quiver to her already weak legs. She liked knowing she could drive him mad, make him want her beyond anything else—because that's what he did to her.

Jake ground his mouth over hers while moving his hands up her waist. He cupped her breast, reshaping it from beneath and stroking her nipple. She was fully aroused, needing him to make love to her and unwilling to hide her desire.

"Jake . . ."

With one swoop of his arms, he lifted her into them and carried her out the office door and into that of the apartment off the gymnasium. They went through the kitchen and into the bedroom, where he laid her on the bed and quickly removed his clothes.

As he stood nude before her, she marveled at his physique.

"Take my shoes off," she whispered.

Jake unlaced a shoe with slow precision. "I told you not to wear these anymore." He threw first one, then the other. Then his hands stroked her calf and higher, toward her thigh. He stopped at the apex between her legs and rubbed the mound that ached for him.

Her pantalets came down, then each stocking with an exquisite roll off her leg and toes. Truvy unbuttoned her dress, frantically and efficiently. As soon as she was in her chemise and corset cover, she made fast work of getting rid of them.

When she was naked, she held her arms open to Jake and he came down on top of her. Their open-mouth kissing moved from lips and earlobes to shoulders and nipples.

Truvy discovered Jake got pleasure from the same things as she did, and she explored him with her hands. Dropping her hand lower, beyond his belly, she held him. The shaft was long and smooth and hard. Its tip was moist and ready. He was jolted by her boldness and ground his lips over her passion-swollen mouth. Her nipples had sprung to tight buds; her body had stirred and longed for him beyond imagining.

A well-bred woman's sexual desire is small.

The book was wrong, so very wrong.

The velvet hardness of his penis lengthened and she guided him toward her innermost place, taking all of him in one slow entry. Her hands lifted and felt the contours of his back and buttocks as he moved within her.

This time there was an urgency to their lovemaking. She wanted him to move faster and harder. She met his tempo with her own, lifting her hips to him, driving him quicker.

She felt herself nearing that place of utter release, and then came a shudder that rocked her to fulfillment. Jake buried himself deep, one last time, and groaned in ecstasy, kissing her fully on the mouth as he sought his gratification.

They lay there, perspiration covering their bodies. Their mingled breathing was labored, their hair damp, their mouths tasting of salt and sweetness.

It was a long while before Truvy spoke. Or moved.

When Jake rolled to his side and took her with him, she gasped and held onto his shoulder. They settled in with their heads on the pillow, their legs in between each other's. Gazing down, she saw the tattoo around his ankle.

" 'A man without determination is but an untempered sword,' " Truvy recited, remembering what the tattoo meant. Turning back to face him, she nestled into the coverlet. "Tell me everything about you. Right now. In this moment. I want to know it all."

Stroking her hair from her brow, he tucked a strand behind her ear; the tender touch evoked shivers across her bare skin. "I can't fit a lifetime into a moment. Tell me where to start."

"Where have you been? What have you seen?"

"Hmm . . ." He brought the end of her hair to his lips, pressing the curl next to his mouth. "Well, I was born in Brooklyn. Grew up spending a lot of time in Queens. I did some traveling to Chicago. San Francisco. The Klondike."

"You were at the Klondike? Was there gold everywhere?"

Jake laughed, reaching out to tease the tip of her nose with the end of her curl. "For some. My investment didn't strike it rich."

She burrowed deeper into the warmth of his arms.

"Cold?" he asked.

She shook her head.

Bending his knee between her legs, he held her closer. "Tell me about you. Something I don't know. Has anyone else in your family been born on Valentine's Day?"

"Just me." She touched the side of his shoulder, feeling the silkiness of his skin. "There is something. It's a tradition with the Valentines. We have a family wedding cake topper with two entwined porcelain hearts. For many generations, I believe going back to the mid-eighteen hundreds, that topper has been on every wedding cake of every Valentine who marries on Valentine's Day. My aunts have it. They're keeping it for . . ."

She didn't complete the thought.

Jake finished the sentence: "You."

"I won't need it."

Jake gathered her tight, bringing his face to the curve of her shoulder and breathing in.

"Are you sleepy?" she asked in a dreamy murmur.

"Why?"

"Because I want to watch you sleeping . . ."

His voice rumbled next to her breasts when he whispered, "Let's keep what's happening between us, sweetheart. For as long as you're in Harmony. We don't have to define it if you don't want to."

She faltered in the silence that engulfed the room as he waited for her answer. She was more shaken than she wanted to admit, more in love with him than her heart could possibly hold. "I—I don't want to define it."

Because if she did, she couldn't bear to ever leave him.

Chapter ❧ 19 ❧

Backstage at the Elm Street theater, members of the Barbell Club prepared for the Mr. Physique competition to take place at seven o'clock that evening. The house was packed, each red velvet chair occupied by a resident of Harmony or the surrounding communities. Behind the curtain, competitors had their own area in which to get ready, to warm up their bodies, to strike poses, and, for the Barbell Club, to get last-minute advice from Jake.

Jake's heart pumped double time as the strings of the orchestra began to tune; he felt as if it were him getting ready to go out there on that stage.

"Look, fellows," Jake said, calling them to attention, "it isn't just your physique that's going to be evaluated out there. It's how you present your physique to the judges."

Wearing warming togs, Gig Debolski, Milton Burditt, Walfred Kudlock, Lou Bernard, and August Gray stood ready to hear Jake out. They hadn't gotten to the oiling-up and body-powdering part—Jake had told them to wait until the last minute so their sweat wouldn't dilute or cake those enhancements. He could see Milton was sweating faster than he could dab his brow. His expression was one of a deer that had been caught in a hunter's sight and knew it was history.

"Facial expressions." Jake looked pointedly at Milt. *"Facial expressions."*

Milt's expression soured. "Yeah, Lou—don't screw up your face on the lifts like you're sitting on the closet wrestling with a—"

"Milton, that was uncalled for," Lou shot back. "I never do that."

"Listen up," Jake broke in, not in the mood for joking around. "When you're out on that stage, you are not only an athlete but also a performer. You keep your facial expression true to the art. Don't fake it. You really have to believe in yourself and show that belief to the audience."

August Gray diligently listened, his body in the best shape it could have been in for tonight.

"August, I want you to focus on posing with your arms overhead."

"Sure, Bruiser."

"Milton and Lou—back poses."

"Right," they said together.

"Gig and Walfred—side delts."

They nodded.

Jake sternly went on, pacing as he spoke. "Your mind needs to be sharp for all three categories. You can do it." Clapping once, he meshed his fingers together and called, "It's time to oil, get the hair combed back, put your heads in the right places."

Rather than move into action, the four of them

stared hard at Milton, as if waiting for him to confess something.

"What's the matter?" Jake asked.

"We want to see if Milton went through with it," Lou said.

"Through with what?"

"The bet."

A bet. That's just what they needed.

Tamping down his raw anger, Jake ground out, "You boys don't seem to understand; this isn't a situation for betting. This is damn serious. There are thirty-eight other men around you—in case you haven't noticed—who want to win this title. Get rid of the clothes and get on with the oil."

The boys began removing their cotton tunics and loose-fitting trousers, giving Milton furtive glances. Milton took his sweet time about it, to a degree that Jake urged him to speed it up.

As soon as Milton stood there in his leopard-skin trunks, flesh-toned tights, and Roman sandals, Jake saw what the drama had been about.

Milton Burditt had shaved his chest as smooth as the bottom of a beer bottle. Not a single shadow of curling hair. Just wide chest, a pooch of a pot belly, and a navel.

Looking embarrassed at first, he then pulled his barrel-shoulders back and sucked in his belly as far as he could get it. Proudly, he declared, "I told you I was going to win the Mr. Physique belt."

Jake wasn't shocked by the shaved chest. Hell, he'd seen all sorts of tactics at events. Despite his opinion of Milton Burditt as a piece of cheese between two slices of pumpernickel bread, you had to admire the man's nerve. "Milt, you go out there and win 'em over."

"Yes sir, Bruiser!"

"I never figured you'd go through with it, Milt," Gig said in admiration.

"I told you I would. And it wasn't for any bet, either."

The boys passed around the Hammerhead's Body Definition Powder, then oiled up in other places where the reddish powder wouldn't give a body its full effect. As they readied, they talked about the competition. And about the bet they'd made with Milton.

"I guess we owe you big, Milt," Lou said, buffing the powder from his upper arms.

"Really big," August remarked.

Gig put in, "How much was that? A five spot each?"

"Geez, Milt," Walfred mumbled while calculating beneath his breath, "you just made out with twenty dollars."

"And that twenty is going to buy me a Winchester twenty-five- to thirty-five-caliber 'Take-Down' rifle at Wolcott's Sporting Goods. And a lot of beer at the Blue Flame with the change." Milton greased up his chest. His pomaded hair was parted down the middle, with two curls at his forehead that looked like commas. "Bruiser, I think you should take the boys on for that Miss Valentine bet and up the ante from beer to cash. These fellows are on a losing streak, and that dance is only a week away."

Jake's jaw clenched down so hard, his teeth ached. "I told you all to drop that. I'm not betting on her."

Milton attempted to argue. "Yeah, Bruiser, but—"

"Milt, if you don't shut your mouth, you'll never see your name on a sandwich marquis because it'll be on your tombstone instead."

Milton blanched.

"Wrong facial expression, Milt," Jake noted while walking toward the curtain to look out. "Never show your fear in front of your opponent."

Jake gave each man final instructions; then he took his place in the audience to wait for the event to begin. Walking to his seat, he looked for Truvy. She was coming to the competition with Tom and Edwina. He would have asked her to come with him, but as a sponsor, he was too wrapped up in the night's events to be of much company to her. And afterward, there was going to be a party at Bruiser's Gymnasium for all the competitors, losers *and* the winner—beer, cigars, sandwiches from the restaurant, and lots of gym talk.

Spying a feather from a hat, and the familiar shade of blue cape, Jake found Truvy toward the rear of the large theater. She saw him at almost the same time. She smiled at him and waved. He did likewise, then sat down in the second row.

Looking at the floodlights beaming on the stage and its curtain, seeing the master of ceremony in his fine suit-tails, Jake was brought back to other places, other times. And in spite of the speed of his pulse, it seemed to him that it was all right that history was left behind. He wasn't that man anymore.

The other sponsors who sat beside him conversed with one another, going on about the sport in loud voices, reliving past competitions and arguing who was the best strongman. They all knew who he was, of course. Everyone had met at the Brooks House hotel last night and had a good time reminiscing. It was a new era for strongmen, and Jake had no desire to chase it.

For now, Jake lost himself in thought.

About a special woman.

Never in his days had he let himself be pulled in by a woman on the day of a contest. Not once. Not when he was married to Laurette. Now, he slowly turned his head, looked up in the theater seats once more, and caught a glance of Truvy Valentine.

Her head was close to Edwina's and they were talking.

God, Truvy was beautiful—her face, her hair, her eyes, her body, and those long legs that wrapped around him when they made love. Everything about her made him want her for the rest of her life. The trouble was, she didn't see things the same way as he did.

For the past week and several days, they'd spent every night together at her apartment. He arrived at an hour of the evening when the street traffic had ceased and he left well before dawn. Protecting her was uppermost in his mind. He would never let her be talked about.

In these past days, he'd taught her parts of his world. The Irish jig, for one, a dance he'd learned in Queens. She'd caught on much better than she had the waltz. He'd had her to his apartment last Wednesday when the gym closed for the evening; he'd cooked her dinner—steak and salad and even an apple cake for dessert. He never minded cooking. In fact, he liked it.

He'd done everything he could to make Truvy fall in love with him, but she hadn't changed her mind about their relationship. But neither did she go on about returning to St. Francis. He sensed she had doubts of a future there as a teacher—and they were of her own accord, not because some benefactress was teaching her class. If Truvy was questioning her future . . .

So Jake was going to take matters into his own hands.

And it did have to do with that Valentine's Day dance. He'd already put the ball in motion when he'd written to Truvy's aunts. He'd gotten the address from Edwina.

Now all he could do was wait.

And hope two militant suffragists from Emporia, Kansas, had romantic hearts.

FEBRUARY 12, 1902
GOOD NEWS **STOP** ISSUE OF MRS. MUMFORD'S PRESENCE HAS BEEN RESOLVED **STOP** RETURN TO ST. FRANCIS IMMEDIATELY **STOP** YOUR GIRLS ARE WAITING FOR YOU **STOP** WELCOME BACK **STOP** LUCRETIA POND

The telegram from Miss Pond arrived yesterday. Truvy had read it a half dozen times. She'd just come back from the train depot after getting her ticket reprinted for Boise. She'd leave the day after the Valentine's Day dance, on February 15, in three days' time. She'd spend the night of her birthday packing for a place she never thought she'd reluctantly be going back to . . . because of Jake Brewster.

In her waking hours, she welcomed the renewal of their togetherness.

Last week, at the Mr. Physique competition, her gaze had strayed to him more often than it remained on the stage. He occupied a seat in one of the front rows, critically observing and cheering on the members of Barbell Club to compete with other bodybuilders. Harmony's hometown man, August Gray, won, and there had been rousing applause. The night had been a triumph for Jake, and he'd spent it with his friends and colleagues at the gymnasium.

Truvy wished she could have congratulated him then, given him a hug and a kiss firmly on the mouth. She'd saved it for the following evening when he'd come to her apartment. They'd lain awake most of the night, touching and holding each other, talking about the event. She listened to Jake, letting him go on about this and that with enthusiasm in his voice. Then she'd given herself to him, exploring, learning, searing him into her memory for when she had to leave.

These past days had been heaven. They'd played Ping-Pong; he'd made her a wonderful dinner and taught her lively dances. He'd also convinced her to get rid of her high-heeled shoes and go back to her Spaldings. She hadn't laced or buttoned or slipped on stiff leather shoes in ages. Now she wore her athletic shoes all the time. And with a confidence she'd never had before when she'd worn them in public. Jake had given her that, done that for her. She would take him with her in her mind, keeping him close to her heart, and move on with her life in a way that would be forever changed.

She'd been expecting Miss Pond's telegram. But when it arrived, she'd been devastated to receive it. The words were short and to the point, filled with an unwritten eagerness to have Truvy come back to the academy, to take charge, once more, of her girls.

Days ago, she'd finally penned her students a letter. It had taken many tries, and many drafts, to get the wording just right. They'd wanted to know about natural impulses. About the book, *The Science of Life,* and its deeper meanings. Well, for Truvy, the book now seemed ludicrous, a waste of her time and energies. If she hadn't been worried about starting a fire, she would have burned the tome in her heater—and good riddance.

Natural instinct. Normal impulse. Sexual emotion. Fruitful desire.

Rubbish. The only thing that mattered was love itself and how it made a person feel. And none of those overly poetic words used in the book could adequately describe the feeling.

Truvy had taken hours to write down her thoughts, carefully and in her best penmanship, and she'd mailed the letter off. While sitting at the table in her apartment now, she recollected most of the words she'd said.

Love is a pleasure of the heart, the most precious possession a man and a woman can share together. It is humbling and pleasing. Emotions grow to ripeness, stimulated every day in ways a person cannot imagine unless in the throes of it. Love is full and vibrant. And sometimes, it is difficult to know at what moment it began. It is the greatest of bonds and the whole of existence. To know love, just once in a person's life, is a joy beyond compare.

And also the bitterest of sweetnesses when a woman had to leave the man she loved . . .

But Truvy must. Because of one truth. No matter how much she loved Jake Brewster, she couldn't ignore one thing: She was good enough to make love to but not good enough to take to a town dance.

The Valentine's Day dance.

It was silly, she knew—wanting to go. Blame it on her birthday and the fragility of her heart. But she was hopelessly crushed he hadn't asked her to accompany him as his partner.

She wouldn't take Edwina up on her kind offer to go with her and Tom. Truvy didn't want Jake's not asking to mean anything; it had been *she* who had set up the rules of their . . . affair, not him—so it wasn't his fault.

Affair.

She didn't dare say the word. She barely could think it.

But she *was* conducting a scandalous love affair with a man who enjoyed their time together—and to be completely fair, she enjoyed it, too. Beyond that, there were no ties, no commitments, no proposals— good heavens. *Proposals.* Where had that come from?

A wedding proposal from Jake Brewster was as likely as the sky turning red. As red as the hearts symbolizing the day of Truvy's birth. In three days, Truvy Valentine would turn twenty-six . . . and find herself forever a bona fide old maid.

Truvy tidied up the dance studio, going through the room one last time. She made sure the recordings were neatly put away in their brown sleeves on the cabinet shelf. Not a trace of dust covered the black, wildflower-trumpeted Victrola or its cabinet stand. A coat of wax shined the floorboards. The wall of mirrors had been cleaned of smears and smudges.

Standing in the middle of the room, Truvy grew tearful and quickly put sentimental thoughts away before she became overwrought. Although she'd started off on the wrong foot—literally—she'd grown to like this room and the music and the dancing. Edwina would be closing Wolcott's Dancing Academy until another teacher could be found to take over the classes.

Yesterday, the bird watchers and Mrs. Plunkett had given Truvy a small farewell party after their last two-step lesson. They'd brought cake, bottles of soda pop, and charming little send-off gifts. Truvy had been touched by their thoughtfulness. The students from the Normal School had composed a poem for her and recited it to the beat of a Sousa march. The Barbell Club had had its last class before the Mr. Physique competition. Although she saw some of the men from time to time on the street, they hadn't exchanged many words. Oddly, they'd been looking at her as if trying to figure something out. But nobody spoke to her.

All that was left for Truvy to do was close the windows and curtains and lock the door one last time. She turned toward the long row but was caught short by the opening of the studio's front door.

Putting her attention on the sound, Truvy smiled. Weakly. Almost in a hopeless manner . . .

Jake filled the opening, tall and broad-shouldered. He was wearing a red plaid shirt and tan duckcloth trousers. He was without a coat, his cheeks flushed from the cold. A slant of midday sun cast its light on him as he entered. He had a heart-shaped box of candies tucked beneath an arm, and in his hand was a bouquet of the most beautiful red roses she'd ever seen.

"Happy birthday," he said in a low tone while walking toward her.

Today was the fourteenth of February.

"Jake . . ." Overwhelmed didn't begin to describe how she felt. "How lovely." The heady fragrance of roses overcame the studio. He'd taken her totally unaware. She hadn't been expecting him to buy her a present. In her mind, she'd told herself it was better for him *not* to. But now she was glad he had. Romantically and utterly glad.

She took the roses and brought them to her nose, inhaling deeply.

"Chocolates. With chocolate truffle centers," Jake said, giving her the heart-shaped candy box. She juggled the candy with the fanning bouquet of roses. A long white ribbon was wrapped around their stems.

Shifting his weight from one foot to the other, Jake removed his bowler and held the brim in his hands. Uncharacteristically, he twisted the brim in a slow circle as he spoke—a sign of nervousness. "Tru, I didn't want to ask you until today. I didn't want you to change your mind, and I had to take care of a few things."

Ask until today?

Her heartbeat surged; her throat constricted.

"Yes . . . ?" She barely formed the word.

He ran a strong hand through his hair, cleared his throat, then asked, "Would you do me the honor of attending the Valentine's Day dance with me tonight?"

The breath felt as if it were knocked out of her. So deflated were her feelings in that one instant—that single question—that she almost grew faint and weak at the knees. She'd been thinking about another question. Silly, oh silly her! Why had she even allowed her thoughts to run rampant like that? For even mere seconds?

The dance.

He wanted to take her to the Valentine's Day dance. Why had he waited so long to ask her?

"Oh . . . why . . . I hadn't planned on it. I'm packing this evening."

"I know."

They'd had this conversation last night. She'd told him that tonight she would spend the evening alone, packing. And getting ready for the morning train out of Harmony. Jake never stopped her. Never talked about changing her mind, so she had pressed ahead, knowing that by the next night, she would be back home. In Boise, in her room at St. Francis, reunited with her girls.

"This is short notice, Truvy—I'm really sorry about it. But I had to make sure something got here."

"The roses . . . they're lovely."

"You're even lovelier." He held his face over hers and kissed her softly on the mouth. "Happy birthday, Tru Valentine. Will you come with me?"

Heaven help her . . . how could she not?

"Yes, Jake. I'll go with you."

And it will be the last time I ever know bliss in your arms.

"I'll pick you up at seven o'clock. At your place. Right on the doorstep, for everyone to see that I'm there to collect my girl."

Her heart fluttered in her stomach. *My girl.*

"All right. I'm on my way out now. I'll be ready."

Jake left the studio and Truvy stood there a long time afterward, staring at her bouquet of roses and candy, thinking things that were too dangerous to think, wanting things she was too fearful to ask for— but determining that if she didn't speak her heart . . . she'd always regret not telling him.

Tonight, she'd tell Jake she was in love with him, that she expected no promise. No veils or doves. No rings or eternity. Just that she loved him, and she would always love him. And that he'd given her the happiest days of her life.

Truvy set her gifts on the Victrola table and went to close the windows.

The sun had begun to sink and cast its glare at the

panes. Reflections of light bounced onto the gymnasium windows, a few of which were open, too. A sharp orb of light from the sun made it impossible to see inside.

As she closed first one, then another window, she could hear voices on the other side of the alley. Gig and Milton. August and Lou and Walfred.

"We knew you'd do it, Bruiser," Milton Burditt said. "Soon as we saw the roses and the candy, we knew what you were about."

Snickers.

The set to Truvy's shoulders softened at the mention of the flowers and the candy. She held back, beside the window's edge, listening, not wanting to hear Jake's voice in return. But he was there.

The resonance in Jake's voice rose above the sounds of the clink and clatter of gymnasium equipment. "This has nothing to do with the bet."

A bet?

Dear God. A bet. They'd made another bet? About her?

"Really now, Bruiser," Gig broke in, "we knew you didn't want it to be said you had more of a chance escorting Walter Zurick's mule."

"And with a ribbon around its neck," Walfred said, then chuckled.

Guffaws.

"I told you, this has nothing to do with any damn bet. And so help me God, if you fellows say another word about it, I'll kick your butts out of my gym and you'll never be welcomed back again. I'm taking her because I want to take her. If you want to find out why, then come to the dance tonight and you'll see."

"I wouldn't miss it," Milton chimed.

August added, "Neither would I."

"Because this has *nothing*," Milton declared on the sly, "to do with that—"

Oomph!

Milton Burditt had obviously been punched by a man's fist.

Truvy pressed her back to the wall, hot tears seeping into her eyes. She blinked, trying to keep them at bay, but she was unsuccessful. Hot, plump drops came streaming down her cheeks.

How could she have been so gullible? She ached so badly inside, it was a physical pain in her ribs. Slicing and sharp. She couldn't deny it: Jake Brewster and his buddies made bets. Bets about dancing lessons and bets about taking a woman to a restaurant for dinner.

Why not make the biggest bet of all?

Get Truvy Valentine to fall in love with you.

Jake wore a new suit, its celluloid collars and cuffs still smelling like the cedar case at Treber's men's store. The tailored shirt was the best fine-weave cotton, so fine that it felt like silk. Hues of bottle-green with gold-thread trim made up the vest. The coat itself was black worsted and the trousers were the same, with pleats at the waistband pockets. He'd dusted his bowler, washed his hair and combed it dry, shaved twice, and put on a splash of his favorite shaving tonic.

The reflection in his mirror was one he barely recognized.

Hell, he'd never looked so refined. Like a regular swell. A gentleman's gent. Like somebody important.

Smoothing his lapels, Jake checked his breast pocket to make sure that little something he'd put in there was still there. A smile touched his mouth.

The clock in the office rang seven times. He was late. Damn, he'd spent too much time getting ready. But tonight was so important.

Jake left his room off the gymnasium, locking the building and walking swiftly to Truvy's apartment, the deep indigo sky overhead. Stars twinkled and a half-moon shone.

The evening was brisk, but it invigorated him. In fact, he'd never felt so good. It was as if the pump of his heart surged through him, but he hadn't even lifted an ounce of weight. The feeling was there naturally.

Rounding the corner, he took the steps to Truvy's, his hand loosely over the banister. Once at the door, his elation at the thought of Truvy greeting him was cut cold. Pinned on the door was a note addressed to him. He yanked the paper from the pin and held it to the moonlight.

Mr. Brewster—

   See Mr. Hess to collect your partner for this evening's dance.

                       Miss Valentine

The formality of the note didn't sit well with Jake. Truvy hadn't called him "Mr. Brewster" in too many weeks to count. What did she mean, collect his partner from Max Hess? Hess owned the livery below. Was Truvy down in it waiting for him?

Jake swiftly went down the stairs and entered the side door of the livery with its odors of hay and manure and damp mud. Truvy wouldn't be in here. Not in a party frock.

"Max?" Jake called. "Are you in here?"

Max Hess came out of the rear-walled office, wiping his hands on a blue bandana and stuffing the cloth into his denim pants pocket. "I wondered if you'd show."

"Of course I'd show. Where's Miss Valentine?"

"She's not here."

The low nicker of horses and clump of shod hooves softly sounded in the row of stalls.

"I didn't think so." Jake held the note out with Truvy's neat writing on it in slanted black ink. "She left me this on her door. What's going on?"

"I know what's going on," he said, shaking his head, "and I'm sorry to be the one to do this to you, Jake— but wait here."

Jake crumpled the note and tossed it into the cold forge. He didn't like the chill settling into his joints. Something wasn't right.

And he knew for sure the moment he saw Max back an animal out of the last stall and walk it toward him. A mule to be exact:

Walter Zurick's—with a red ribbon around its neck.

Truvy thought about not going to the dance after what she'd arranged with Max Hess. But the more she thought about it, the more she didn't want to cower and hide away in her apartment and . . . cry.

Far better to show up at the dance. Alone. And show the men from the gymnasium that she had outsmarted Mr. Brewster. What better way to save her integrity, her pride, than to come to the town's dance and act as if she was gay and happy? Not amused at all by their silly bet. Not having fallen for it.

Why, then, was she having difficulty smiling and putting on a brave front?

The members of that stupid Barbell Club were here, watching her with interest. Milton Burditt sported a black eye. The others looked uneasy, as if fearing Jake's reaction. To what?

She wanted to run and hide, and in the fifteen minutes she'd been there, fifteen of them had been spent convincing herself to stay.

This was Edwina and Tom's first night out together without Elizabeth, and Edwina looked radiant, so lovely on Tom's arm. They'd danced already, once. A band had been hired and played popular songs as well as traditional ballads and waltzes. Of course, every one reminded Truvy of Jake.

She wondered when he would find the mule. And what he would do as soon as he saw it. Would he come over to the schoolhouse and confront her? He wouldn't. Couldn't and save face. Because she'd make a fuss. A public one. She didn't care. She'd tell everyone how silly he was for believing she'd come with him . . . for believing that she—

Truvy had to turn away toward the rear of the large room and discreetly remove her hankie from her reticule. She touched its soft edge to each eye. It was mortifying. It was the worst. How could he have done this to her?

She didn't want to believe it.

Deep down, she *couldn't* believe it. Not after all she and Jake had shared. But she kept going back to the fact—he *did* make bets. He'd confessed before.

She faced away from the couples and the merrymaking long enough to regain her composure. Then she turned around and tried to look as if she belonged, even though her heart was breaking in two.

The schoolhouse's upper-grade classroom had been

cleared of desks and chairs, the three chalkboards covered with crepe paper. A radiator heater had the room hotter than an oven. Truvy fanned her cheeks, knowing they were a deep shade of red. She shouldn't have come; she shouldn't—

Don't think about that.

The decorations. Look at them. Heart-molded Japanese lanterns hung from the ceiling. Paper hearts had been strung like chains from each lighting fixture. The building ran on electricity, so the interior was bright and yellow. Tables had been set up with heart cookies and cakes and tea breads. Punch and seltzers and soda pops were served alongside.

The men from Jake's gymnasium were now crowding the refreshment table, giving her sidelong glances of confusion. Those of them who were married had brought their wives, and as far as Truvy could tell, not a one had spent more than a moment with his spouse. How awful. But she wouldn't waste thoughts on them or on what they were thinking. Instead, she'd keep her chin high and her smile plastered on until her cheekbones ached.

In the far corner, a floor-to-ceiling drapery covered a round table. On the guests' arrival, Minister Stoll had made a point to tell the party attendants not to lift the cloth. His edict aroused the curiosity of the crowd. Not Truvy's.

Perhaps she should go home. This was crazy. All around her, people were having a wonderful time. Most were couples. Many she'd met through Edwina. Matthew Gage and his bride, Meg. The woman was delightful and genuinely nice. She wore her hair short and curly to her shoulders, and her husband adored her; it was so clear by the way he rested his hand on the small of her back while they talked with Alex Cordova and his new bride, Camille. Truvy had thought Camille one of the most gracious ladies she'd ever met. It was amazing the statuesque blonde was the manager of the local baseball team; Truvy would have liked to spend more time with her. They shared a common enthusiasm for sports.

But Truvy wouldn't get the chance to know these women friends of Edwina's better. Because she was leaving. Right now. She shouldn't have come to the party. Shouldn't have dressed in her best blue dress to prove to Jake that she didn't care, when she cared more than her soul could bear.

Just as she made the decision to leave, she turned and saw Jake as he entered the room. He wore a suit that fit the mold of his body to sheer perfection. Nobody could fill it out the way he did. He was the tallest and most magnificent man she'd ever seen.

Everything she'd talked herself out of, his handsome face, his walk, his eyes, his demeanor—all touched her soul, and she was left with the actuality that he *was* everything she'd ever desired in a man. Dejection wilted her courage. If she could have made her feet move, she would have dashed past him, out of the building and into the night. But she couldn't get her legs to work.

She was held by an invisible thread, a pull toward this man that she was unable to break. He might have rendered her incapable of fleeing, but he would never know how deeply he'd wounded her.

Taking in a breath, she stared at him, refirmed the set of her chin, and threw her shoulders back. She had the same smile on her mouth that had been there since she'd arrived.

Jake stormed toward her, determination in his expression. She held on, fortitude keeping her outward appearance calm when her every nerve ending collided.

In several easy strides, he stood in front of her, his face mere inches from hers. "I'm thinking you know something about that mule," he said in a quiet tone without preamble, "and I'm here to tell you you're wrong about it."

Keeping her expression neutral, she batted her eyelashes at him. "Good evening, Mr. Brewster," she said, remarkably sedate. "I believe it's customary for a man to seek an introduction to a woman at a social event before he discusses mules with her."

He took her by the arm, gently guiding her to the corner of the room. It was all she could do to banish the shower of tingles that erupted over her skin where he touched her.

"I never made a bet about Walter Zurick's mule and you and this dance. You have to believe me, Truvy." He looked deeply into her eyes. "You must have overheard me and the men talking at the gym, but you misunderstood. They had one perception of tonight, and I had another."

Confusion danced in her pulse. He stood too close. All she could think about was the scent of his cologne, its enthralling masculine fragrance the same one that clung to her bedclothes, to her body after he'd spent the night with her. His wonderfully green eyes enveloped her in their depths. She wanted desperately to believe him . . . but she knew what she had heard—knew that he did make foolhardy bets with those men. It was . . .

"I know of only one way to prove it to you, Tru." The sincerity was all too convincing, and yet—

To her stunned surprise, he kissed her fully on the mouth. Right there in front of everyone. The hot moisture of his lips melted into hers as he undid her resolve, breath by breath. When she was dizzy and more confused than ever, he held her at arm's length and gave her an order. *An order!* "Stay here. Don't move."

Then he quit the schoolroom and left her alone.

By this time, Edwina and Tom had come toward her. Edwina took her hand, a tender smile in her eyes and on her mouth, as if she knew what Jake was doing, what this was all about. No wonder Edwina had tried to talk her out of leaving that mule for Jake.

"Edwina—I don't like this," Truvy said. "I think I should leave. People are staring at me."

"Wait a moment." Edwina squeezed her fingers. "Trust him, Truvy."

Jake reappeared in the doorway and he stepped aside, What, or rather, *who* came in his wake made Truvy clutch Edwina tightly.

"Aunt Beatrice! Aunt Gertrude!" Truvy exclaimed, then broke free of Edwina and went to her two aunts.

"Truvy, our dear!" The Aunts said, crushing her in a hug.

It was soothing to be in their arms. And so familiar. They smelled like vanilla and lavender, a mixture she'd always and forever associate with them. For long seconds, they held one another; then The Aunts pulled back.

"Let us look at you," Aunt Beatrice declared.

"Yes, let's!" Aunt Gertrude seconded.

Truvy gave them a loving gaze, taking in their appearances. They were still the same as the last time she'd seen them. Both were tall, with hair more on the red side than brunette, sharp blue eyes, and smiles that displayed very slightly gaping front teeth. They wore matching necklaces of glass beads and waists of hand-tatted lace with pulley belts and identical skirts.

"You never told me they were twins," Jake said, reaching her side.

"Didn't I?" she remarked, hearing herself reply but not really listening to her voice. All she could think was: *The Aunts are here.*

"Dears," Truvy said to the pair, "why did you come—what's happened? You're not ill, either one of you?"

"Good heavens, no." Aunt Gertrude laughed. "We're as strong as a pair of mules."

"Make that Mr. Zurick's mule," Aunt Beatrice added with a wink.

Truvy looked at them, then at Jake. Then back to The Aunts. "How did you know about the mule?"

Aunt Beatrice replied, "Jacob told us."

"Yes, Jacob told us," Aunt Gertrude echoed.

Truvy grew puzzled. "Why did he tell you that? Why *are* you here? I'm going back to Boise tomorrow and—"

"Perhaps not." Aunt Gertrude glanced at Jake.

"Perhaps not." Aunt Beatrice glanced at Truvy.

Jake stepped in and took Truvy's hand, then walked her to where the band played. She let him lead her away, her thoughts in a jumble, her gaze reaching over her shoulder once. The Aunts waved at her, smiling knowingly. They were in on this—whatever it was.

Jake asked the band to quit playing. The notes faded, and Jake raised his voice. "Attention, folks; I have an announcement to make."

All eyes rested on Truvy, and she tensed. She

looked at The Aunts for reassurance. They weren't distressed in the least. They clasped hands and had tears in their eyes.

Suddenly, the evening wasn't about bets and mules. Truvy knew it was something else. Something bigger ... and ... she wasn't sure. Didn't dare to think.

"As some of you may know," Jake said, hooking her arm through his, "this is Truvy Valentine's birthday."

Truvy swallowed hard, hoping her smile was nonchalant. *Oh dear Lord, please don't make a big to-do over my birthday. I couldn't bear it. Celebrating twenty-six with everyone in this room knowing my marital status.*

A sense of inadequacy swept over Truvy as he went on.

"There's a long-standing tradition in the Valentine family to marry on Valentine's Day."

Not that ... I don't need any reminders.

"How far did you say that went back, Aunt Beatrice?"

Aunt Beatrice? Jake called her Aunt Beatrice?

"Eighteen hundred and fifty-two."

Aunt Gertrude put in, "February the fourteenth of eighteen hundred and fifty-two, sister."

"Of course, sister."

Jake slipped his arm around Truvy's waist, and she looked up at him in astonishment, her pulse racing out of control.

"Since that's how the Valentines do things, and since I knew I had one chance to ask Miss Valentine to be my wife—or I'd have to wait one full year before we could get married—I'm using this evening to state my intentions." Turning Truvy toward him, he fumbled inside the breast pocket of his coat and withdrew something small and round, then held her left hand. She gazed at him with an effort not to tremble, but her knees quivered and she could hardly breathe. His hand was warm and callused. The richness of his voice wrapped around her heart when he said, "Truvy Valentine, I love you. Will you marry me?"

Her mind spun. All the doubts of late welded together in one swell of consuming yearning. How she wanted to marry him! And be his wife. That gentle and loving look in his eyes was honest and pure. True. He waited, as did everyone in the room. Watching. Wondering what she would say. There was only one answer. Now and forever.

"I . . . this is a surprise." Her throat was tight and her legs threatened to give out. "I thought you didn't"—she lowered her voice—"favor marriage."

Equally as softly, he answered, "That was until I met you." Then louder: "Will you, Truvy? Marry me?"

She saw every ounce of his love for her in his face, in his eyes, in the way he smiled at her. He meant it, truly and deeply. He was in love with her. Elation consumed her soul.

"I . . . yes, Jake, I'll marry you."

Relief relaxed his features. "I was hoping you'd say that." He slipped a ring on her finger. She looked at her engagement ring, a brilliant diamond and an endless gold circle. He pulled her to him for a kiss, and the room clapped and cheered. Blushing, Truvy spoke into the curve of his neck. "I love you, Jake."

"I love you, Truvy. A thousand times. I couldn't let you go," he said for her ears only. "I want to spend the rest of my life with you."

"Oh, Jake . . ."

The Aunts, militant marchers that they were, burst into a vaporous fit of tears.

Mrs. Plunkett could be heard blowing her nose into her handkerchief.

Jake bussed her cheek before turning Truvy toward the corner—and that mysterious curtain. "Okay, Reverend, you can pull the string now."

"I've been waiting with bated breath all afternoon to do this!" the minister said, then went to the table, found a corded pull, and grasped it. In one clean jerk, the curtain fell to reveal a wedding cake on the table. A grand affair, three-tiered, iced a snowy white, and decorated with red roses. On its top—the Valentine family wedding cake topper: two porcelain hearts, entwined.

The Aunts gleefully came forward. Aunt Beatrice said with her hands clasped in front of her, "We brought it with us."

Aunt Gertrude tittered. "Mr. Brewster said to send the wedding cake topper, but we knew as soon as we got his letter that we had to come with it."

"Oh, yes, sister—you're right. And with your mother's wedding dress, Truvy."

"My mother's . . ." Truvy barely breathed the words. "I didn't know she had one stored for me."

"We didn't tell you, dear."

"We wanted to surprise you when the time came."

"And we knew the time was coming as soon as you found Jacob uncouth but commendable. And you crossed out his nickname."

"I pointed that part of the letter out, sister."

"Correct, sister," Aunt Beatrice answered. "But it was I who noticed the part about his manners. And his joke about the woman on stilts."

"Quite."

Truvy listened to them, laughter bubbling up her throat. Suddenly, the structure of events for today and this evening fell into place. Jake had to have been planning this for a couple of weeks—The Aunts, the cake, the proposal.

"If we're to have a wedding tonight," the minister pointed out, "then I suggest we get on over to the church."

Edwina said, "Truvy, I'll help you change into your gown."

"It's at the hotel," Aunt Beatrice said. "That's where your young man has put us up. We got in just this morning and—"

"—we've been playing whist ever since. Jacob wouldn't let us go out lest you detected we were here. I wanted to play pinochle. In fact, we made Jacob play several hands with us this afternoon."

Truvy rested her cheek on the rough tweed of Jake's coat, loving him more than she'd ever thought possible. The picture of him playing cards with her aunts in a hotel room . . . just to surprise her . . .

Jake brought his mouth to her ear. "Why don't you go get that wedding dress on and I'll see you at the church? After we're married, we'll dance any dance you want. And we'll eat cake. And we'll dance some more. And then I will make you one bet."

The feel of his sensual lips against the curve of skin brought a shower of pleasure through her. "Yes . . . ?"

"I bet we don't go to sleep tonight."

❧Epilogue❧

Jake felt like an idiot.

Although nobody was on the pond at this hour of the morning, he was making an ass out of himself in front of his wife. Truvy had insisted they get up early from the Idanha Hotel and go ice skating on Pierce Lake. Boise's pond was deserted, except for some curious geese.

Slicing his way over the ice on blades strapped onto his shoes, Jake held his arms out for balance. He could go the distance with any boxer, lift weight beyond ordinary amounts—but couldn't ice skate. He didn't have the body or the coordination.

"I don't think this is going to work, Tru."

Truvy skated backward, clearing the way ahead of him. She laughed at his disclaimer. The tail of her blue scarf rippled in the breeze, and a knit cap covered her curls. "You aren't trying. Move your feet. Left and right. Push out with each leg and you'll slide longer."

Jake did as she told him and nearly tripped. "Forget it. I look stupid."

"Nobody's watching."

"You're watching."

"I'm your wife."

"I'm your husband."

That brought a wide smile to her mouth—a mouth he would never tire of kissing. And he'd told her she had a body he would never tire of making love to.

They'd married in Harmony three days earlier and had come to Boise to tell Truvy's students and employer that she'd no longer be teaching. Jake saw firsthand what she was giving up for him. The St. Francis Academy was no slouch outfit. It was a nice school, solidly built and well respected in the community.

He'd met the headmistress, Miss Lucretia Pond, who'd been surprised when Truvy brought him into her office with her. But she'd listened with an understanding and compassion for the situation Jake immediately respected.

Plans would be made to hire another economics teacher, but the fate of the sporting program at St. Francis would be undecided for now. There were few women who could talk politics *and* whack a tennis ball. Truvy had the market on that. She was one of a kind.

She had shown him her room, and together, they'd packed her things in trunks to be taken back to Harmony with them at the end of the week. She also introduced him to her students. He'd felt clumsy and awkward around all those young ladies. They'd swooned and gushed over him like fountains. They were sad to hear Truvy wouldn't be coming back, but they'd told her they couldn't be happier for her.

As for Jake, he'd never been more content in his life.

Truvy scissored her willowy legs, completely at ease on the ice. A soft pink touched her cheeks. She wore those tunic pants of hers that melded next to her body and revealed every luscious curve. "Push out, left and right. Left and right. Slow and steady."

He tried. Then tried harder. He hit a nub in the ice and fell, a sprawl of long, muscled legs. He swore.

His male pride hurt worse than his butt when she skated to him and knelt down on one knee. The seriousness on her face didn't foreshadow the playfulness to her question: "Are your cheeks cold, Jake?"

"Positively numb."

He laughed, then whipped out his arms and captured her in an embrace. She came down on top of him with a shriek. They lay there, horizontal on a bed of ice, on a cold February morning, a husband and wife. In love.

"I'm done," he said in defeat.

Propping her elbows on his chest, she pursed her lips. "You haven't gone around one time."

He grinned. "I'll go an extra round with you tonight."

She knocked him on his shoulder with a gloved fist. "You're horribly wicked."

"Maybe that's why you love me."

"Maybe."

Her eyes danced; the frosty air put color on her cheeks. She dipped her head and kissed him. He held onto her tighter, tracing her lips with the tip of his tongue. She murmured an "Mmmm" that he caught on his mouth.

"Your glasses are steaming up," she mumbled, gazing into his face.

"You steam my glasses up."

He'd been wearing the peepers since they'd been married and the world had taken on a whole new clarity. Except for when his wife got him hot and bothered and the lenses fogged up from their breathing.

"So when do we go back to the hotel?" he asked in a purposefully low and seductive tone.

"You are so terrible." She lifted her head, a lock of hair falling over her brow. Pushing at his chest, she stared at him. "You really mean it? No more skating?"

"No more. My butt's cold. I need to warm it up. In the bathtub. With some of that lemon verbena of yours."

"You'll smell like a woman."

"I'll smell like you."

She smiled. "All right. We'll go back."

"We'll read more of *Madame Bovary.*"

"Yes, I was quite certain that's what you had on your mind," she said, teasing him. Actually, they *had* been reading the book. Rather, Jake was reading it aloud to her. "But Jake . . ." She toyed with the end of her scarf, then met his gaze. "It's not the right time for me on that contraception table . . . and in fact . . . it's more a time for me to have a baby."

Jake cupped her soft cheek, and she nuzzled his hand. "Do you want to have a baby, Tru?"

"I wouldn't mind if it happened, Jake. Elizabeth is the sweetest thing."

"Could be a boy, you know."

"I know . . . and maybe—well, there's something I didn't tell you." She fingered a button on his coat.

"Twins run in my family. We could have two boys or two girls. Or a boy and a girl."

"I could handle that. You think I don't know how to change a diaper?"

"Do you?"

"Well, no—but I could do it if you showed me how."

She smiled. "Let's go back to the hotel."

He unbuckled his and Truvy's skates, and then they stood.

Walking off the pond, arm in arm, she said, "I've been thinking about something."

"What?"

"Now that we're married"—she bit her lower lip and gave him a quick glance—"it's not ungentlemanly of you to answer a certain question."

Jake held a pine bough out of her way so she wouldn't have to duck. As he stepped around it, he asked, "What do you want to know?"

She wrinkled her nose. "How do you get that fig leaf to stay on?"

The roar of Jake's laughter filled the clearing.

"Shushh!" she insisted, putting her wool-covered fingertip over his mouth. "This is serious. I've been pondering how that leaf could possibly stay on. I know how you're put together . . ."—she blushed a deep crimson—". . . down there. And no fig leaf is sticking to that."

Holding her closer to him as they walked, Jake gazed skyward and knew that life could never get better than this. "Well, the thing of it is, you have to have just the right leaf."

"Imported from Europe?"

"No, they're leaves from floral catalogs."

"Good heavens! Somebody could be decorating their arrangements with the same leaves you're putting next to your—"

"Yep." His smile broadened as they left the clearing and made their way to the Idanha Hotel. "As for getting them to stay on, you take them by the front and then you . . ."

Dear Readers:

I hope you enjoyed reading *Hearts* and fell in love with Jake and Truvy.

I had fun writing about a bodybuilder and gymnasium owner from 1902. Eugen Sandow was a real strongman around the turn of the last century. Modern bodybuilders press and lift much more than the two hundred and fifty pounds mentioned in *Hearts*. It seemed a minuscule amount to have Jake be known for lifting. But in the early 1900s, there weren't the vitamins, power drinks, and steroids of today's modern bodybuilders, who would scoff at a two-hundred-fifty-pound weight. I like to think of Jake Brewster as being all natural male and muscle.

The Mr. America competition was the forerunner for the Mr. Olympia and Mr. Universe competitions, for which Arnold Schwarzenegger is famous. I used to think bodybuilders were a bit mentally dense. But try reading Arnold's *New Encyclopedia of Modern Bodybuilding* and you'll discover what a truly intelligent and savvy businessman he is.

Frederic Remington did indeed study art at the Art Students League in New York around 1885. Bodybuilders really did pose for the budding artists. *Strongman On A Horse* was inspired by Remington's bronze *The Bronco Buster*. I'd like to think that Jake's statue in Harmony's town square was what gave the residents of Philly the idea to put a life-size image of Rocky Balboa on their courthouse steps.

Florenz Ziegfeld Sr. did indeed have an act at the World's Columbian Exposition in Chicago. In actuality, the featured "Strongest Man on Earth" was Eugen Sandow.

The "Fig Leaf Rag" wasn't published until 1908. I couldn't help myself—I had to use it. And as for that fig leaf . . . if you really want to know, write me and I'll tell you.

Hearts is my last book in the Brides for All Seasons series. I'm going to miss Harmony, Montana, and its residents. They've been a part of my life and yours for four books now. But it's time to move on to a new setting and new characters, which is very exciting for me.

I enjoy hearing from my readers. Drop me a note and be sure to include a self-addressed, stamped envelope. And when surfing the web, visit my site at:

http://www.stefannholm.com

Stef Ann Holm
P.O. Box 1206
Meridian, ID 83680-1206